ONE HOT SUMMER

ONE HOT SUMMER

Melissa Cutler

St. Martin's Paperbacks

This is a work of fiction. All of the characters, organizations, and events portrayed in this novel are either products of the author's imagination or are used fictitiously.

ONE HOT SUMMER

Copyright © 2016 by Melissa Cutler.
Excerpt from *One More Taste* Copyright © 2016 by Melissa Cutler.

For information address St. Martin's Press, 175 Fifth Avenue, New York, NY 10010.

ISBN: 978-1-250-07186-6

Our books may be purchased in bulk for promotional, educational, or business use. Please contact your local bookseller or the Macmillan Corporate and Premium Sales Department at 1-800-221-7945, ext. 5442, or by e-mail at MacmillanSpecialMarkets@macmillan.com.

Printed in the United States of America

St. Martin's Paperbacks edition / April 2016

St. Martin's Paperbacks are published by St. Martin's Press, 175 Fifth Avenue, New York, NY 10010.

10 9 8 7 6 5 4 3 2 1

This book is dedicated to working women everywhere, striving to balance work and love in these crazy, modern times. In particular, I want to thank one working woman. This story wouldn't have been possible without the funny, insightful knowledge shared to me by wedding planner Kelly Tharp All.

Chapter One

What caught Remedy Lane's attention first was a nine iron waving like a brandished sword from the driver's side of a golf cart careening up the path. When the nine iron's owner, a sour-faced, blue-haired golfer, saw Remedy, her eyes narrowed. She speared the club in Remedy's direction and bellowed, "A golf course is no place for an elephant!"

On the word *elephant,* Remedy tripped over an invisible crack and caught herself on a golf-scoring platform. Little yellow pencils rained onto the ground along with a mishmash of safety pins, Band-Aids, compacts of concealer and powder, and mesh pouches of pastel butter mints from her blazer's pockets.

The golf cart slammed on its brakes a few feet in front of her. The blue-haired driver and her balding, watery-eyed passenger scowled at Remedy as she regained her footing. "Did you mean an actual *elephant*? Down there on the course?"

"No, it's a piñata," the driver said. "Of course it's an actual elephant, and I want to know what you're going to do about it. We have a game to finish. It's shaping up to be my best of the week."

Remedy took her time restuffing the wedding emergency supplies into her pockets, stalling. Only one elephant had been permitted onto the grounds of Briscoe Ranch Resort that day—and she wasn't supposed to be anywhere near the golf course. According to the schedule Remedy had been given, the elephant's handlers were supposed to be grooming her for a photo shoot near the gazebo with the bride and groom of that afternoon's Kumar/Srivastva wedding.

The driver clanged the nine iron against the roof of her golf cart. "Don't just stand there like a dunce. What's your plan?"

Aruba. Remedy's plan should've been to find a job as a wedding planner in Aruba. What the heck had prompted her to relocate to a resort in the middle of nowhere? Worse than nowhere—Texas, which was tantamount to a dirty word in Los Angeles, like *wrinkle* or *Republican*. Actually, she was only too aware of why she'd chosen Briscoe Ranch Resort, which was why she had to make the job work.

She scanned the rolling hills that surrounded them. The resort's roof was visible in the distance, but no other employees were in sight.

"Hang on." Remedy trudged up the short grassy rise for a view of the course, feeling the golfers' judgy, impatient eyes on her back. The rise afforded a sweeping view of the rambling hillsides and lush landscape of Texas Hill Country that still had the power to awe Remedy, though it'd been more than two weeks since she'd moved to Texas. In the valley immediately below, the neatly manicured grass of the golf course flowed out in all directions, punctuated by the occasional sand traps, water hazards, golfers . . . and one very large elephant wearing a purple-and-gold headdress galloping over the grounds with unmistakable glee.

Swallowing a curse, Remedy did what any self-respecting

new hire would. She prayed that no one would blame the disaster on her as she brought her cell phone to her ear and called her boss. "Alex, it's Remedy. Tell me I'm hallucinating that the elephant we rented for the Kumar/Srivastva wedding is careening across the golf course at top speed."

Alex was silent for a beat, then, "Damn it, he brought Gwyneth again. I thought we had an understanding after last time."

Remedy watched the elephant pluck up a flagpole and run with it in her trunk as if she were Victory incarnate. Only two thoughts broke through Remedy's shock as she watched a pair of golfers dive into the brush at the edge of the course, out of the elephant's path. One: who would name an elephant *Gwyneth*? Because, seriously, that was a ridiculous name for an animal. And two, "This has happened before? Why is it the first I'm hearing about it?"

Alex sighed. "Hector said he was bringing Petunia for the wedding, not Gwyneth, which would've been great, because Petunia usually only eats flowers. But that Gwyneth, she's crazy about golf. Well, the seventh green, specifically."

After a head shake, Remedy checked the time on her phone. "The wedding photographer is slated to arrive in less than ten minutes, and the mother-of-the-bride specifically requested that the elephant be in the wedding photos. Something about getting her money's worth. Where's Hector and how did he not notice that his elephant's missing?"

"No idea," Alex said. "I'll send someone to find Hector. You stop Gwyneth before she reaches the seventh hole's water hazard. And whatever you do, don't panic."

"Wait, what?" She could either not panic or stop a thundering elephant, but not both. The two commands were mutually exclusive. "I can't do that. I'm a wedding planner, not an elephant whisperer." But Alex didn't answer. "Alex, are you there?"

Nothing but silence. He'd already hung up.

She shoved the phone back in her messenger bag, her mind racing and her hand unsteady. What the heck was she supposed to do now? "Shit."

A gasp sounded behind her. "Language!"

Remedy turned to see the golfer and her companion. Of course. Because why wouldn't they stay to watch the spectacle? That was one thing Remedy had learned in Hollywood. Everyone loved a spectacle. The bigger the train wreck, the better the entertainment value.

Remedy whirled to face the resort guests, a placating smile on her lips. "My apologies for my language. That was uncalled for, but I'm a little anxious because it looks like it's my job to, um, wrangle that elephant."

The driver shook her head. "Well, get on with it. The day's not getting any younger."

Remedy walked their way. "Yeah. There's just one thing." She patted the roof of the golf cart. "I'm going to need to borrow this for a few minutes."

"Beg your pardon?"

Leaving the golfers in her dust, Remedy careened down the concrete path at the cart's top speed. On her phone, she dialed the resort's catering kitchen. One of the line cooks answered, a man whose voice Remedy didn't yet recognize. "This is Remedy over in Special Events. I need someone to meet me at the seventh green, stat. This is an emergency. And bring all the bananas and apples you have."

"Huh?"

"No time to explain. Just bring me those bananas!" And Remedy had thought planning weddings in Hollywood had been a circus.

The golf cart's top speed was no match for Gwyneth's strides. Hoping to intercept the animal, Remedy cut across the fairway, waving spectators out of her path. She kept one eye on Gwyneth and the other on her phone as she activated the voice recognition search engine. "Look up 'how to stop an elephant.'"

The phone dinged, acknowledging the command; then moments later a computerized voice said, "I found 'how to stop a rampaging elephant.'"

Gwyneth was doing more frolicking than rampaging, but close enough. Remedy scrolled through the results, most of which were viral videos of vicious elephant attacks. Not cool. Maybe the cook with the bananas would show up soon. Or, better yet, Hector, the negligent keeper.

Without warning, the golf cart thumped off the grass and slammed to a hard stop. Remedy jerked forward, flailing to brace herself. As she caught her breath, she took a look around. She'd lodged the cart in a steep sand trap while Gwyneth galloped away.

Remedy banged her hands on the steering wheel. "Shit! Shit! Shit!"

The elephant ground to a halt and swung her attention to Remedy, ears pricked. Gwyneth dropped the flagpole and backtracked toward the golf cart.

Though her heart was racing, Remedy forced herself to smile. "Hiya, Gwyneth. Got your attention, did I? You like the curse words?"

Gwyneth's trunk rose. Her ears flapped.

Remedy slid to the passenger seat, her movements slow and deliberate. "Salty as a sailor, are you? Well, you're in luck because so am I. And I've got a lot more swearwords where those came from. How about this one: Damn it all to hell!"

Gwyneth's trunk lowered. Her head swung to face the water hazard and she raised a foot as though ready to run again.

Remedy sprung from the golf cart. "No, wait, don't do

that. You'll ruin your pretty headdress. Was *damn* not a dirty enough word? Okay, um . . . son of a bitch!"

Three steps into a trot, Gwyneth paused and took a second look at Remedy.

"Ass monkey!" Remedy said with gusto. Gwyneth seemed to like the term and trotted closer, but several of the gathering spectators laughed. Yeah, perhaps luring the elephant with foul language wasn't the most appropriate method.

From her bag Remedy withdrew a granola bar and unwrapped it. "The bananas aren't here yet, but how would you like a granola bar? It's organic and gluten-free. Mmm. I mean, bloody hell, it's gluten fucking free!"

Gwyneth snatched the bar right out of Remedy's palm. Remedy squeaked and stumbled back. That was one powerful trunk. Not a moment later, Gwyneth spit the granola bar onto the ground, then used her truck to sniff Remedy up and down as though on the hunt for a better goodie.

Remedy held still and tried not to cringe at the intimate inspection. "Yeah, I'm not crazy about that brand of granola bars, either. I'm definitely a gluten gal like you." She brought her fist up. "Gimme knuckles on that, sistah."

She'd meant it as a joke to help ease her own nerves, but Gwyneth curled the end of her trunk and bopped Remedy's fist.

"Okay, this is the weirdest job ever." She reached a tentative hand out and patted Gwyneth's trunk.

The chug of a maintenance truck engine sounded. A hundred feet or so away, it stopped. The young man in a navy blue maintenance shirt leapt from the driver's seat at the same time as his passenger, a short Mexican man who looked like he might be Hector. In the truck bed sat a bin full of bananas and apples.

"Oh, thank God," Remedy whispered.

Gwyneth spotted the treats, too, and lumbered in the other truck's direction, Remedy forgotten.

The passenger strode in the animal's direction, his arms spread wide. "Gwyneth, my baby. Why do you keep playing these games with me?"

Remedy staggered back to the stuck golf cart and sagged against it, catching her breath. Crisis averted, and not a moment too soon. She wasn't even going to contemplate the resort's liability if Gwyneth had accidentally hurt a guest or caused more than mild chaos.

Remedy was still resting against the cart, watching Gwyneth power eat the pile of fruit, when her phone rang. The caller ID showed the special events department secretary on the line. "Hey, Gloria, I just bumped knuckles with an elephant."

"Okay. I'm not going to ask. I called to let you know Emily's waiting for you in your office."

Remedy had to bite her tongue to keep another expletive from escaping her mouth. She'd rather wrangle elephants than meet with Emily Ford, the resort's surly executive catering chef, but there was no getting around it—today or any other day.

Ten minutes later, Remedy pasted a smile on her face and strode into her office. She might not be a famous actor like her parents were, but she'd long ago perfected a look of photo-ready red-carpet coolness. "Hello, Emily. What can I do for you?"

Emily was about the same age as Remedy's nearly thirty and, as far as Remedy had seen, never wore anything other than a white chef's jacket, black leggings, and bright green clogs, with her curly hair pulled into a tight ponytail and smiles limited to the sarcastic variety. By all accounts, she was a rock star of a chef. What she was *not* was easy to work with, which seemed to be a common fault among gifted artistic types, Remedy had learned from a very young age.

At Remedy's arrival, Emily shoved off the wall she'd been leaning against. "Two words: Baked Alaska."

Good grief. "We already discussed this. You can't serve Baked Alaska to firefighters. Just . . . no."

Remedy may have only had one real job prior to being hired as Briscoe Ranch Resort's special events manager, but even she knew that the first rule of being a new hire was not to piss off your coworkers, at least for the first week or two. But it looked like the honeymoon was officially over for Remedy and Emily.

Emily's narrowed eyes shifted their focus to the stack of files balancing on the edge of Remedy's desk. Her fingers twitched as though she was giving serious consideration to knocking the files onto the floor as a cat might. "You and I are going to have to agree to disagree on this, because I'm serving it."

Remedy slid the stack of files away from the edge of the desk. "How about a nice crème brûlée instead? You'd still get to torch the desserts, but in the kitchen, safely beneath the fire sprinklers. I'm sure the fire marshal would appreciate that."

The suggestion only earned Remedy a hard laugh from Emily as she stomped out of Remedy's office and through the maze of resort offices, shouting for Alex, Remedy hot on her heels. They found him standing in the center of the main ballroom, his trim black suit, black hair, and lanky, pale body perfectly at ease in command of the ornately appointed room as he directed a crew in the installation of an elaborate pillared *mandap* stage piece for the Kumar/Srivastva wedding that included elaborate flower arrangements and intricately embroidered purple and gold drapery. The Kumar/Srivastva wedding's awe-inspiring design was yet another reminder of why Remedy had taken this job over a resort in Aruba. No other locale the world over could transform a wedding into a work of art like Briscoe Ranch Resort. Runaway elephants notwithstanding.

Emily outpaced Remedy and strode across the room, paying no mind to the fact that Alex was mid-instruction to the installation crew. "Baked Alaska for dessert at the Firefighters' Charity Ball. That's a brilliant idea, right?"

"It's not brilliant," Remedy called before Alex could respond.

Alex strummed his fingers on his purple tie as his attention shifted between Remedy and Emily. His gaze glimmered and his lips hinted at a smile, as though he found their bickering delightful. "I heard you got to meet Gwyneth before Hector arrived. I also heard you commandeered a golf cart from a resort guest and crashed it into a sand trap."

Remedy took the long way around the dance floor, knowing better than to take her chances on the slickly polished wood. "That was not my fault. I was trying to stop a rampaging elephant." *More like* frolicking, *but whatever.*

As Alex chuckled, Remedy's right wedge snagged on a vacuum cord she didn't see until it was too late. She pitched forward, yelping, her arms flailing and her legs scrambling for balance as she knocked into the empty cake display table. The table toppled with an earsplitting crash, but Remedy stayed standing. As two workers bustled to right the table, she smoothed a palm over her skirt and composed her expression. *Easy there, Pink Panther.*

She turned to face Alex and Emily, her hands on her hips. Alex might be her boss, but Remedy outranked Emily. This was Remedy's call, and if Alex was as good a manager as he seemed to be he'd give her this chance to set a precedent with one of the key members of her special events team. "Like I was saying, serving Baked Alaska to firefighters isn't brilliant. Not only is it a cliché of the worst kind, but it's a recipe for disaster."

"A recipe for disaster? Who's the one with the awful clichés now?" Emily said with an eye roll.

"Forget about clichés," Remedy said. "I'm worried

about safety. I'm worried about getting approval from the fire marshal."

Alex huffed. "You should be worried about him, because Micah Garrity is a thorn in my side. But as far as safety goes, I'm thinking there's no safer time to serve flaming food than at a firefighter ball. We can almost guarantee that the resort won't burn down."

It was the *almost* guarantee that had Remedy worried. "It's not like the firefighters are arriving in their fire trucks, dressed for the ball in their uniforms, ready to fight fires should the opportunity present itself. We're talking tuxes and limos here. Have you ever seen a firefighter battling flames in a tuxedo?"

"No, but I'd pay to," Alex said.

Remedy actually had paid to see that once, complete with stage-effect flames, at an all-male revue while in Vegas with her girlfriends Cambelle and Maura, but that was beside the point.

Emily leaned against the nearest table, her gaze turning distant and dreamy. "It doesn't have to be food. For that picture you've painted me I'd be willing to set all kinds of things on fire."

Probably she was joking. *God, let her be joking.* Remedy decided to run with the hope. "Sure, that's a great idea. And while we're at it, how about I have decorative trees brought into the ballroom and arrange for some cats to be stuck in them."

Snorting, Emily squared up to Remedy and leveled a challenging glare at her. "Listen to you. You're so uptight, you're not going to last a week at this job."

Alex pursed his lips. "Play nice, Emily. I don't need you chasing off this one like you did the last two."

Seriously? Wow. All Remedy had been told when she interviewed for the job was that Mr. Briscoe's daughter—who'd previously managed the resort's special events—had stepped down from the family business in favor of opening her own wedding dress business and, as a result, the hotel's event staff had been reorganized. Alex had been promoted to Chief Visionary Officer of the special events department and Remedy was hired as the events manager.

The confirmation that Emily was, indeed, trying to sabotage Remedy's job didn't pack the same punch as when Remedy's mother had confessed that Remedy's father hadn't been her first husband, but it still gave Remedy that same off-kilter feeling.

Ignoring it, Remedy narrowed her eyes at Emily. "I've lasted two weeks so far, if you must know. And I plan to last a lot longer than that, no matter how difficult you try to make it for me." In truth, she planned to plant her feet at Briscoe Ranch Resort for a good long while—but only until she'd succeeded in building her reputation back up from the ashes so she could return to Los Angeles triumphant, but that was a plan she had no intention of sharing with her bosses or coworkers. "This Firefighters' Charity Ball next month is my first event for the resort, so I need us to work together on this. Please."

Emily's face was stony. "Then what *I* need is Baked Alaska. Screw the fire marshal. He's even more uptight than you are."

"Emily, Baked Alaska is a crazy idea," Remedy said.

Alex wedged himself between them, draped his arms across both women's shoulders, and met Remedy's gaze. "Well, you're in luck, then, because the first rule of wedding planning here at Briscoe Ranch Resort is that there's no such thing as brilliance without a little madness."

The man had a point. With a sigh of concession, Remedy angled her view around him to Emily. "A hundred firemen wearing tuxes isn't exciting enough for you all on its own?"

Emily's expression softened. "I'd like to see what those tux-wearing firemen look like in the glowing firelight of dozens of Baked Alaskas that are all sweeping into the room simultaneously as a dramatic finale to the exquisite four-course meal I've created for them."

Time to let Emily win this round, if only because it might pave the way to a peaceful truce. "I guess I'll have to see about renting some cats and trees, then. Just . . . please don't set the ballroom on fire."

Emily held up two fingers. "Chef's honor. And I'll tell you what—you can wield one of the torches that we use to light the desserts on fire."

That did sound like fun. Remedy offered her a broad grin. "Why didn't you say so in the first place?"

Chapter Two

"Of course I'm fine, Mom. You have to stop worrying. It's not like I'm in the middle of nowhere, scraping by in some shanty with an outhouse. The cottage I'm renting has indoor plumbing and air-conditioning."

Remedy smacked the side of the barely functional air-conditioning unit mounted in a living room window on the off-chance it might awaken the wheel-running hamsters she envisioned slacking off inside it. No luck. She stuck her face in the fridge and grabbed a water bottle, lingering there until the cooling fan kicked on.

Her mom sighed. "I can't help it. I'm an empty nester now."

Remedy was nearly thirty, but her mom was right. This was the first time the two of them had lived apart. Even in college, Remedy had lived at her childhood home and commuted. "Mom. Half the time we lived together you were off on location. So just think about this as my turn to be off on location. It's temporary."

"Got it. Temporary. I can handle that. I just wish I was there with you right now."

The thought of her mom sweeping into the sleepy town of Dulcet, Texas, and making concerned faces at Remedy's run-down cottage and the dark circles under her eyes made her wince. "I wish you were, too. But the show must go on, right? You and I are so lucky to have jobs we love that keep us busy, so you'll have to trust me when I tell you I'm okay. My job at the resort is stressful, but every new job is at first, so I'm dealing with it."

"Tenacity, it's one of my family's signature traits."

It was one of Remedy's dad's family's traits, too, but Remedy knew better than to bring him up. Since their divorce when Remedy was twelve, her parents had taken their acting abilities to a new level by each pretending the other didn't exist.

"You hang in there, baby. And if you need anything at all, just call me."

Remedy shouldered out the back door of the cottage and onto a small wooden deck that was little more than a platform for the steep staircase that dropped into a canyon that was thick with trees and underbrush. "Mom, you're on location in Budapest. If I need anything, what can you do to help?"

"I'm only here for a couple more weeks. Maybe I'll come be your personal assistant the way you were mine for so many years."

Please, God, no. "That's sweet, Mom, but this is something I need to do on my own."

"Okay, fine. At least tell me you got the champagne I sent."

Remedy eyed the stack of boxes on her kitchen table that had been waiting at her front door the day before. Her mom had sent two cases of champagne as a housewarming gift. Little had she known that Remedy's father had, too. "I did. Thank you. How'd you know I'd need a shot of decadence right about now?"

"I know my girl."

Loud, twangy guitar music and a diesel engine announced the passing of yet another band of rowdy locals along the two-lane road that cut too close to Remedy's cottage. She stood on tiptoes and caught a glimpse of a hulking black truck stuffed with guys in ball caps barreling down the road. The local boys were out in force today. Maybe today wasn't an ordinary Sunday but some kind of Texas holiday she hadn't had the pleasure of experiencing yet.

After wishing her mom good-bye and promising to call her again in a few days, Remedy followed the tug of fresh air and loped down the stairs into the canyon, eager for the shady promises of the trees. In moments, she was immersed in the woods. She followed a dusty, meandering trail through the trees toward the creek she'd discovered a few days earlier.

One of her resolutions in moving to Texas was to take advantage of every opportunity to live like the locals, and she'd heard enough country western music to know that enjoying life's simpler pleasures by sitting on a rock at a creek and dipping your toes in the water was pure country through and through. Besides, the grand city of Dulcet boasted a mere three blocks of downtown shops and eateries and, given that the next largest town was more than thirty minutes away, since she didn't feel much like driving or hanging out at the resort sitting creek-side would have to suffice as entertainment on this, her only day off that week.

Tall trees stretched over the trail, their branches shaggy with leaves and casting mottled shadows on the narrow trail. Remedy stuffed her phone in the back pocket of her jean shorts and marveled at the peace. If this had been the park nearest to Remedy's old apartment in Los Angeles, it'd be littered with trash and she'd be bracing for a homeless person to pop out from the dense tangles of underbrush.

After the weeks of stress and damage control that had accompanied her fall from grace in Hollywood, followed by weeks of even more stress and damage control at her new job at the resort, the heady scent of drying grass and live oaks was a balm for her battered spirit. As she strolled, she held her hand out so her fingers brushed the thickets of green that she passed—wildflowers perhaps, their blooms all but memories. This trail would be vivid with color in the spring, but the crisp heat of late June had baked the wilderness into a dull palette of greens and browns.

When she reached the creek, an egret startled and lit off on fast wings. Remedy slipped her feet from her shoes and climbed onto the rock that seemed to have been placed at the water's edge for just such a purpose. At the first touch of cool water on her skin, she released an exhalation she hadn't known she'd been holding on to. This was exactly what she needed today. Bracing her hands on the rock behind her, she closed her eyes and tipped her head back, smiling.

Another diesel engine rumbled by in the distance, reminding her how close the road was. As far as illusions went, the one she was fighting to hold on to—that she was out in the boonies, alone with nothing but her thoughts and nature—was a flimsy one. Squeezing her eyes closed, she flexed her toes out wide and concentrated on the cool water tickling the skin between them. A gusty breeze carried off the last of her misgivings. The street might only be a few hundred yards away, but this place was still a zillion times more beautiful and peaceful than L.A.

A man hollered from not too far away. Remedy's eyes flew open. The holler was followed by splashing, as if a fellow hiker was wrestling a fish. Then a white disposable foam cooler floated into view. Next into view was a pair of young, shirtless good ol' boys, sloshing through the creek in hot pursuit of the escapee.

The cuter of the two paused long enough to tip the brim of his black ball cap. "Afternoon, ma'am."

"Um, hi."

"Wind took our cooler clean off my tailgate." His light

blue eyes sparkled with mischief. She kept her gaze on them rather than give in to temptation to check out his ripped, smooth chest or thoroughly soaked red board shorts. He had to be at least five years younger than she and exactly the type of guy she'd pledged to her friends that she'd steer clear of while in Texas. He probably had a Skoal ring outline on his back pocket, like she'd seen so many times in Dulcet already.

Her girlfriends might have made her pledge a *suits, not boots* motto before she'd left L.A., but a little harmless flirting never hurt anyone. With an arch of her back, she pressed her lips into the beginning of a smile. "You can't let that happen. Without a cooler, what're you going to store your beer in?"

His broad smile in response revealed two deep dimples and a mouth of gleaming white teeth. "Exactly. Looks like you and I understand each other."

His friend crowded near him, holding the cooler and bumping the blue-eyed charmer's shoulder as he angled into Remedy's line of sight. "You're new to Ravel County."

This one was cute enough, too, with shaggy blond hair showing beneath a straw cowboy hat that made him seem more surfer than cowboy. He was as young as his friend and radiated a manic, yet harmless, puppy dog energy. She beamed at him. "That obvious?"

Blue Eyes rubbed his chin and squinted at her. "I bet you work at Briscoe Ranch."

"Lucky guess."

He waved it off. "Naw. Not really. More'n half the people here call Ty Briscoe their employer."

"You boys do, too?" A flutter of anxiety had her holding her breath. She'd kept her distance from Briscoe Ranch employee get-togethers because she was in management. It was one thing to have an occasional drink with her employees and quite another to let her hair down around them. And blatant flirting? That would be all kinds of wrong.

"No, ma'am," they said in chorus.

"Good answer." She ran her fingers through her hair and let her gaze dip below Blue Eyes' face. *Mm-mmm-mm*.

"Now it's settled," the shaggy blond said, his attention straying to her legs. "You've got to come have a beer with us. The rest of the guys probably have the party all set up by now."

Tempting. But she'd set off on her creek adventure to find peace and quiet, not play the part of the Daisy Duke–wearing prize for a bunch of country boys, even if they were lookers. She patted the rock. "I'm good right here, but thanks anyway."

Blue Eyes sloshed toward her, the shimmer in his gaze now a slow burn. "No way. You're new in town and we couldn't call ourselves gentlemen if we didn't introduce you around, help you get acquainted with Ravel County's finest."

She tipped her ear toward her shoulder and gave them a sidelong glance full of flirty interest. "You mean, you two aren't Ravel County's finest?"

They chuckled and puffed their chests out. Considering that she didn't plan to take the flirtation a hair past this harmless exchange, that comment had been a bit overboard, but she couldn't help herself. These boys were good-looking and sweet and, well, it'd been a while since she'd been objectified quite so deliciously.

Before she knew what was happening, Blue Eyes grabbed her by the hand and pulled her into the creek. She squealed at the cold water licking at the tattered hems of her shorts and gaped up at him, not so much mad as surprised. "Really?"

"Gall dang it, I'm sorry to accidentally get you all wet like that," he said without the slightest bit of remorse. "Now you've got no choice but to let me make it up to you with a beer or two." He set his hand on his chest over his heart. "I insist."

Well, Remedy. You wanted to learn how to fit in with the natives, and this is your chance. She didn't have anything waiting for her back at the cottage other than left-over macaroni and cheese she'd ferreted from the resort's kitchen the night before and a defunct air-conditioning unit. Peace and quiet be damned. The day was young and so was she.

She left them hanging for a long breath, then, "Okay, you win. A beer." She poked him in the chest. "But only because you owe me."

He held his hand out again. "Name's Chet Bowman."

She eyeballed his hand suspiciously. "You're not going to pull me underwater, right?"

"Wouldn't dream of it."

"I'll kick his ass if he does," Shaggy Blond said with earnest gusto.

Remedy shook Chet's hand. "Remedy Lane." She braced on the off-chance he recognized it. There weren't that many Remedys in the world and even fewer whose birth announcements had made it into the pages of *People* magazine. But all Chet did was beam, deepening those to-die-for dimples. "That's a right pretty name."

Shaggy Blond took her hand next. "Dusty Wilmington."

"Nice to meet you both. Let me grab my shoes and we'll get on with that beer you owe me."

Around the bend and down a ways from Remedy's rock, the creek curved near the road. Along the shoulder sat a row of trucks and cars, including the hulking black truck she'd seen from her back deck. The black truck's tailgate was down; sitting on top were a case of beer, a melting bag of ice, and two watermelons. Chet poured the ice in the cooler, then stacked beers on top. Dusty hoisted a watermelon onto his shoulder, then made a gallant attempt to lift the second. Remedy waved him off, then slid the watermelon off the tailgate and into her arms.

Loaded down with the party goods, they slogged along

a trail that followed the creek farther than Remedy had explored on her own. She was about to ask them how much farther they had to go when the scent of charcoal briquettes wafted through the air. They emerged from the trail onto a wide, sandy bank at the elbow junction of the creek and an expansive, slow-moving river.

Remedy froze, taking it all in. On the river, at least a dozen people floated in inner tubes of every size and color. Shade covers, beach chairs, and barbecues dotted the sand on both sides of the riverbank, and a rolling beat of a country song drifted through the air from speakers sitting on a folding table.

Dusty nudged her with his watermelon. "Welcome to summer in hill country, Bubba-style."

For the past two weeks, Remedy had been so busy moving in, ingratiating herself to Emily the chef, and chasing down runaway elephants that she'd barely taken a breath. This might not be a Southern California beach or the peace and quiet she craved, but it looked like all kinds of fun. She smiled at her two hosts. Bubba-style fun indeed. She could already see herself dragging one of those chairs to the water's edge and decompressing from her tough work-week with a beer in her hand.

"Chet, you're a genius. Thank you for insisting I join you."

He touched the brim of his ball cap. "The pleasure's all mine." He reached his arms out. "Let me take that watermelon from you."

Dusty and other strapping young men scrambled their way, their arms waving. "The police are here! Quick, everybody run for cover!" They jumped behind a wall of bushes. The music turned off and a madcap exit ensued.

Remedy's mouth dropped open. She gaped at Chet, hoping for answers, because why would running help if the police were on their way? Where would they go to escape and why would they need to? Were they doing something illegal? Instead of answering her questions, all Chet did was shove the watermelon back in her hands. "Here. You stall them. They wouldn't arrest a pretty thing like you."

"What are you talking about? Arrest?"

But Chet was already gone, along with the rest of the party attendees, leaving Remedy standing alone in the middle of the bank holding a damn watermelon, her face probably as red as one.

She knew she'd been the butt of a practical joke when out of the trees emerged yet another Texas good ol' boy, this one broader, taller, and a bit older than the rest. Beneath a dark cowboy hat he sported dark sunglasses and a smirk on his lips from which a toothpick balanced.

As he swaggered out from the shadow of the trees, she took note of a black gun strapped to his belt and a barbed-wire tattoo encircling his upper arm just below where the sleeve of his red cotton T-shirt stretched around his muscles. Yeah, this was no police officer. If this was a Bubba-style summer party, as Dusty called it, then this, right here, was the Alpha Bubba.

His gaze zeroed in on Remedy in an instant. The toothpick shifted to the corner of his mouth. His smirk twitched as though he was deliberating about smiling but decided against it.

"Nice melon."

Snickers and laughs coming from the bushes prompted her to look down at the watermelon in her arms, but her focus landed on the cleavage revealed by her tank top, which had apparently been tugged down by the watermelon.

Wait—did Alpha Bubba say melon *or* melons?

Remedy opened and closed her mouth a couple times before finding her voice. "Chet and Dusty . . ." She hooked a thumb over her shoulder.

"They put you up to this?"

"I helped them carry a watermelon." Damn, that came out sounding stupid, but Alpha Bubba had her all kinds of flustered.

It was impossible to see what his eyes were up to behind those dark glasses, but otherwise his expression remained that of bored amusement. "Got a name?" he drawled.

Though her heart was racing and she'd made herself out to be an idiot, she decided to own her dorkiness outright, because who the hell was this jerk to stand there and make her feel unwelcome and off-balance?

"Are you talking about the melon or me? Because I was thinking of calling this beauty Thelma." She shifted the melon higher on her hip and, though Alpha Bubba was as intimidating as any A-list movie director, she strode forward, plucked the hat from his head, and dropped it onto the watermelon. "That's better." She mimicked his drawl. "Thelma was getting a little tuckered out in this sun."

His light brown hair was sweaty and unruly . . . and way too dangerously sexy for a man who was taking advantage of Texas's open-carry gun law. His tongue poked against his cheek as his smirk turned into a grin. "You must think we're pretty quaint around here, don't you, California?"

"How did you know that's where I'm from?"

He lifted his hat from the watermelon and dropped it back on his head, then pulled it low over his forehead. " 'Cause that's where the crazies are, and a city girl like you would have to be crazy to let these fools talk you into partying with them."

"Hey now, Micah," Chet said, crashing through the bushes. "Nothing says we've got to share our beer with you if you're gonna be a dick."

Micah. It fit, even though he made a better Alpha Bubba—and she'd be better off referring to him as such, lest those smirking blue eyes and killer body made her liberal, feminist heart forget her *suits, not boots* pledge.

Chet dropped his hand onto Remedy's shoulder as the rest of the guys stomped back onto the riverbank. "I was just having a little fun with my new friend. You might call it an initiation into life in Dulcet."

"I can see that," Micah said dryly.

Behind Chet, Dusty cackled, his attention on Remedy. "You should've seen the look on your face when we yelled, 'Police!' and dove for cover." He dissolved into laughter and stumbled back to offer the gathering group of men high fives.

All right, fine. She was the butt of their joke. All that meant was that she'd called it right that she'd be an oddity on display at their little party. Whatever. Time to ditch the watermelon, grab a beer, and make the most of her decision to go along with Chet and Dusty's invitation. She shuffled to the nearest table and hoisted the heavy melon on top.

Feeling eyes on her, she glanced over her shoulder. Micah, continued his lazy perusal of her. As opposed to the harmlessness of the objectifying once-overs that Chet and Dusty had given her, Micah's almost-bored awareness of her threw her system into chaos. Must be all that alpha male testosterone oozing from his every pore. Or maybe it was that gun, the first real one she'd ever seen up close in person.

She forced herself to walk to him again, feigning red-carpet confidence.

At her approach, the toothpick slid across his lips, pushed along by the tongue she caught a flash of before his smirking smile returned. "What do you call the other one?"

She didn't follow. "Call what?"

He nodded to her chest. "Well, you said one of them's Thelma. Don't tell me the other one's Louise. That'd be downright unoriginal."

Remedy wasn't a blusher. She wasn't a prude or uptight in any way, but this man had gotten her tongue-tied and red faced for the second time in as many minutes. She didn't like it. Not one bit. And she didn't like him, either.

Behind her, a crash sounded. She craned her neck in time to watch the melon roll like a bowling ball along the table, picking up speed as it rolled and knocking over ketchup and mustard bottles before taking out a trio of red plastic cups. Plastic forks, knives, and spoons exploded from the cups into the sand. Remedy, along with three men, lunged, but none of them reached the table before the watermelon reached the edge. Its grocery store sticker caught on the plastic tablecloth and pulled as it went airborne. The melon landed on the ground with a crack as it split open. The tablecloth followed, landing on top of the crushed melon and leaving the picnic table completely bare.

Remedy closed her eyes, cringing. "Oops."

Micah knew trouble when he saw it, which was how he arrived at the conclusion that the woman standing before him dumbstruck and holding a watermelon while toe deep in Frio River sand was as harmless as a cupcake. He happened to have a fondness for cupcakes and a strong aversion to trouble, so Miss California and her melon—*and melons*—piqued his interest right away.

As the men gathered around her, helping to restore order to the picnic table, Chet elbowed Micah in the ribs. "She's a new Briscoe employee."

Well, hell. That didn't suit his purpose at all. And if he hadn't been so distracted by her cupcake-like qualities, he would've picked up on that on his own. "You know my policy on fraternizing with Briscoe's executives, so why'd you bring her here?"

Chet's eyeballs nearly fell out of his head watching her backside as she bent over the ground, picking up jagged pieces of watermelon. Micah had been doing the same out of the corner of his eye, but still, it got under his skin that Chet would be so crass.

"How do you know she's an executive?" Chet asked under his breath.

Oh, please. "You think she moved all the way from California to Ravel County, Texas, to work as a maid?"

"Okay, yeah, I see your point, but she was all alone when we found her and she's new to town. I didn't see the harm just this once."

"You didn't see the harm because she blinded you with that California tan and those itty-bitty shorts."

Chet shrugged. "There is that."

The woman tucked her chin over her shoulder, her attention going straight to Chet and Micah. Or, rather, straight to Micah. He knew that because her eyes sparked with indignation.

Micah moseyed forward, putting a little extra swagger into it and relishing the hint of incredulity his walk brought forth in her gaze. "I hear you're Briscoe Ranch Resort's newest executive. What do you do at the resort, specifically?"

Her answer would tell him everything he needed to know about how often they were likely to come into contact with each other. Maybe she was an accountant. That wouldn't be so bad.

"I'm the new special events manager."

A snort of laughter escaped through Micah's nose. *Of all the possible jobs . . .*

Her eyes narrowed. "Is that funny to you?"

This woman sure was wound tight. An afternoon of tubin' and drinkin' would probably do her a world of good, but she'd have to find another group of locals to enlighten her to the many glories of a Texas summer day, because if word got back to Ty Briscoe that Micah and his boys were getting overly friendly with the resort's new top dog, Micah would lose the leverage he'd fought for years to gain.

"Naw. Not in the least." It was his turn to extend his hand in greeting. "I didn't catch your name yet."

She wiped her palm on her shorts, then took his hand. "Remedy Lane."

That was one hell of a weird name, but somehow it fit her hipster princess vibe. She was monied, big-time, and trying desperately not to act like it. Her handshake was surprisingly firm, which wasn't at all princess- or cupcake-like. "Micah Garrity, Ravel County Fire Chief. Congratulations on your new job. I'm sure you'll make a lot of rich folks very, very happy."

Blinking back in surprise, she took her hand back and stuffed it in her pocket. He was surprised it fit, those shorts looked so snug. "You're the fire chief?"

"That I am." Much to the bane of the Briscoe family's existence. Speaking of which, it was high time for Remedy and Micah's crew to part ways. He brushed past her, beelining for the cooler of beers. "Chet, take Ms. Lane home. Our picnic is no place for a city girl."

Micah didn't need to look to know that Chet was winding up to challenge him on the directive. Since Remedy hadn't piped in with a sharp reply, Chet had probably signaled to her to stay quiet and let him handle Micah.

Sure enough, Chet fell in step behind him. "Come on, Chief. Just have a beer and relax. We saved you the best seat and everything. But you gotta understand, we promised her she could stay. Hell, it was my idea."

Micah shoved his hand to the bottom of the cooler where the coldest beers were and lifted one out, sluicing off the ice. "My decision stands."

With a snort and a shake of his head, Chet abandoned his cause. "Come on, Remedy. We'll have our own party, far away from this asshole."

In his peripheral vision, Micah watched Remedy take stock of Chet, as though she were seeing him for the first time and she wasn't crazy about what she saw. Maybe Chet's begging had turned her off, or maybe she'd just had enough of their hick ways. After a moment's pause, she peeled away from the arm Chet had roped around her shoulders and strutted toward Micah.

Micah stiffened and barely stifled a curse. He didn't need this in his life, some princessy resort executive mucking up his only day off that month, probably for the rest of the summer, if last weekend's slew of Independence Day fire emergencies were any indication and the forest service's fire season predictions rang true.

Remedy said nary a word as she flipped over the foam lid to the cooler and extracted a beer. She cracked it open and drilled Micah with a fiery gaze, one he met and held as she walked his way. He never was one to back down from a firefight.

"Chet," she said, standing nose to nose with Micah, her eyes still locked on his. "I think I will go home . . . and get my swimsuit. Looks like this party's just getting started, and I wouldn't dream of missing out."

"So that's how it's gonna be, hmm?" Micah said in a low growl for her ears only.

With a sly smile, she brought the beer to her lips. They were fine, strawberry pink lips that complemented her fine curves, her fine rack, and her particularly fine stubborn streak, which was definitely an attribute worthy of admiration. Ty Briscoe had hired her for one of the resort's top positions, which meant she also had a brain and ambition to go along with all those other fine qualities. Too bad Micah and Ms. Remedy Lane were on opposite sides of an immovable line, one she'd discover soon enough.

She hooked her arm around Chet's shoulders, then held her beer up like a trophy. "As I was saying. If Alpha Bubba here has a problem with me, then he can be the one to leave."

Wait, what? He couldn't have heard her right. "What'd you call me?"

Chet snickered. His hand snaked around her back and settled at her hip as his gaze met Micah's—a not-so-subtle staking of a claim.

Micah spit his toothpick into the sand, no longer

the slightest bit amused. "You're gonna regret this, California."

"Why? You planning to cause me trouble?"

She didn't wait for Micah's reply. With a flounce that belied her privileged pedigree, she put her back to Micah and headed away from the riverbank, Chet in tow like a lovesick moron. Micah found a fresh toothpick in his pocket and tucked it into the corner of his lips, his eyes tracking her movement as her last question echoed in his mind.

"Darlin', you have no idea," he said under his breath.

Sipping on his beer, he watched her calculated sashay until those too-tight jean shorts disappeared from view.

Chapter Three

Remedy dodged a palm tree coming at her on a forklift, her eyes on the droopy white tent being erected on the resort's west lawn. Well, maybe *erect* was overstating it at the moment.

"Get the tent some Viagra and let's move on," she said into her phone in the sweetest tone she could manage.

An outsider might have watched the spectacle today and wondered why a couple would come to Central Texas to stage a tropical wedding—after all, why pay for trees to be imported when they could have just held the wedding at a beach resort?—but the answer was simple. Couples came from all over the world for the Briscoe Ranch treatment. No request was too grand, and no detail was spared for a couple's happy day. In this case, the wheels for this wedding had been set in motion more than a year earlier by the legendary Carina Decker—the elder daughter of resort owner Ty Briscoe and the wedding planner who'd put the resort on the proverbial map for destination weddings.

Remedy had met Carina once, briefly, when she'd popped into Alex's office to congratulate Remedy on the job, but that was the extent of their contact. According to Litzy Evansburg, Remedy's main assistant assigned to her by the resort, Carina had surprised a lot of people the year before when she quit her job at the resort to follow her dream of owning a custom bridal gown boutique, which now claimed a corner of prime real estate in the resort's lobby.

Remedy was a big believer in people following their dreams—after all, Remedy had done just that—but Remedy had sensed from the minute she'd walked into her first interview at Briscoe Ranch that Carina's abrupt departure had left her family and the resort scrambling for footing. Hence the string of event planners who had come before Remedy and who had been unable to make the job stick. They must not have been as stubbornly determined as Remedy was. Their loss, her gain. Especially today, her first day running the show after Alex had passed the torch to her earlier that week.

She power walked across the palm tree–lined pavilion that surrounded the tent entrance, where guests would gather both after the ceremony to sip rum drinks as they watched a troupe of Polynesian fire dancers perform and again after the four-course meal for dancing under the stars to the music of a live band. Then again, the guests might be eating their meal on the pavilion as well if the tent vendor couldn't get the tent to rise for the occasion, so to speak.

Hands on her hips, she stood before the tent and willed its peaks to straighten so the impatiently waiting florist vendors and cake vendor could have access to the space. "Get up there, you stupid tent poles," she muttered.

"Maybe the poles need more foreplay."

She turned to see Alex, dressed to the nines in a three-piece suit, despite temperatures pushing triple digits. Perspiration beaded along his forehead near his hairline, but he wore a smile of amusement, held a giant convenience-store soda cup in his hand, and looked utterly relaxed. Must be nice to be the boss.

"If I thought foreplay would work, I'd be giving every-one here a show to remember," she said, forcing a self-deprecating smile to her lips.

"It would lighten the tension around here, that's for sure. How are you managing?"

It was tempting to list all the many details that had gone wrong so far that day, but she was hell-bent on maintain-ing an illusion of control in front of her boss and her event clients alike. As in Hollywood, in the wedding industry the rule was to never let them see you sweat. "Pretty good. With each event I'm getting better at executing Carina's visions."

"She was a one of a kind."

Would Remedy ever step out of Carina's shadow? "So you all keep saying."

He rattled the ice in his cup. "You're in Texas now. The word is *y'all*."

"I can't make my mouth do that. Like rolling my *r*'s in the word *burrito*. Not gonna happen."

While he tried and failed to roll his *r*'s in the word *bur-rito*, Remedy checked the time on her phone again. The tent vendor was supposed to be done almost an hour ago.

"Relax," Alex said. "Everything will work out."

"It better. At least we don't have to deal with elephants this weekend. The only live animals we have today are the butterflies that guests will release as the bride and groom leave the chapel after the ceremony. And those are already staged in the chapel vestibule, safely tucked in their spe-cial boxes."

Alex took a sip of soda. "And doves. Butterflies and doves."

A bubble of panic rose in Remedy's throat as she flipped through all four banquet event orders, better known as BEOs—aka the resort's end-all/be-all contracts signed by the bride and groom and outlining every last detail about their wedding and reception. No doves were listed.

Remedy would know about it, if it was happening, if only to steel herself.

"It won't be on there," Alex said. "Last-minute addition by the MOG. That's what I braved this god-awful heat to tell you."

MOG was wedding planner speak for mother-of-the-groom. Next to tequila shots, the MOG was often a wedding's biggest wild card because there was very little official business for her to do at a wedding to feel useful and even less prestige, despite that she was marrying off her precious baby boy. MOGs were notorious for pulling off attention-stealing stunts and being even more temperamental and needy than the worst Bridezillas.

"Mixing doves and butterflies creates a predator/prey situation. Have you ever seen doves eating butterflies at a wedding? Because I've seen it, and it's not pretty."

"The guests might be getting a lesson in Darwinism today, then, because it's too late for us to do anything about it," Alex said.

"How many doves are we talking about here?" *Please say two; please say two. . . .*

Alex's grim smile turned Remedy's bubble of panic into a tornado alarm. "Thirty."

Remedy shot out of her seat and paced the length of the room. "Nope. Nope, nope, nope."

"What? But you have a way with animals. You chased down a stampeding elephant last weekend!"

"Gwyneth was special!" Remedy snapped. With a deep inhalation, she fought to rechain her crazy. *Illusion of control . . . illusion of control,* she chanted in her mind.

With a gasp, Alex pressed a finger to his smiling lips. "Oh my God, are you afraid of doves?"

Hell, yes, she was afraid of those beady-eyed, razor-clawed terrors. "Of course I'm not."

Alex broke down in a chuckle. Remedy shot him a cutting glare.

"Relax, Remedy," he said. "There's nothing to be afraid of."

Since when had telling a person to "relax" ever been effective? And yet every single man on this planet seems to be born with that phrase preloaded into his DNA, ready to be released onto womankind at every opportunity. *Breathe, Remedy. And "take two" on that smile in three . . . two . . . one. . . .* "For your information, I'm not afraid of anything, least of all thirty feathered rats being set loose for no good reason. My only concern is for those poor, defenseless butterflies."

"The dove handler isn't worried about his birds eating the butterflies. He said he'll make sure to feed them first and he'll take care of releasing them, then corralling them back into their cages once the guests are tucked away in the reception tent. You won't even have to go near them. You can station yourself safe and sound under the tent eaves during their release and then beat it inside before they've cleared the chapel. Easy as pie."

Easy as pie. Right. Then again, Alex had obviously never had to contend with twenty attack doves that decided that instead of flying off into the sunset it'd be more fun to dive-bomb the poor first-time wedding planner before descending into the reception room to roost on the wedding cake.

Litzy, Remedy's assistant, popped her head around the tent's corner, her black hair shimmering in the sunlight in a bob cut with severe bangs that gave the illusion she was even younger than her twenty-four years. "The fire marshal's here for his inspection."

Alex clapped his hands. "Hallelujah. The day has finally arrived when handling the fire marshal is your job, Remedy. Good luck with that."

In a flash, he was fast-walking back toward the resort, probably to get out of sight before the fire marshal saw him.

Remedy had a *gee, thanks* on the tip of her tongue when a surge of panic nearly shot her out of her shoes as she realized what Litzy's presence meant. "Litzy, what are you doing out here? You're supposed to be tending to the bridal party in the prep suite. You're supposed to stick to the bride like glue."

"The bride's fine. She's happily sipping champagne and getting her hair done."

Wrong answer. A niggle of panic tickled Remedy's throat at the idea of having another assistant she couldn't trust. After the Zannity scandal, enough was enough. She draped her arm across the jacket of Litzy's fresh-from-the-rack gray pantsuit and walked her away from Alex. "Litzy, we've talked about this. You need to get back to the prep suite immediately. I don't want to see you again until the ceremony. Got it?"

"But Alex always—"

Litzy's laid-back approach might have flown with the equally laid-back Alex, but if the day had truly arrived in which Remedy was in charge then her directive to "stick to the bride like glue" left no room for interpretation.

"Alex hired me to be the resort's wedding planner, so we're doing things my way now," Remedy said. "Is that going to be a problem?" Yes, she hated to be *that* kind of boss, but she wasn't about to let another assistant sabotage her career.

"No. It won't happen again."

"Excellent. Thank you."

They'd cleared the reception pavilion when a metal cage holding a mess of white feathers was thrust into her face. "You the boss around here?"

Suddenly she wanted to give that title back to Alex. "Yes. Remedy Lane. And you must be the dove man?"

"Skeeter Cowles, at your service." Skeeter was a slight man, with arm and legs that looked as limber as Gumby's and wearing overalls that were at least two sizes too big and a cream-colored cowboy hat that was even more ill fitting. He leaned in, as though confessing a secret. "Actually, they're not doves. They're pigeons. But that's just between you and me."

Remedy nearly choked on her spit. "The groom's family ordered doves."

"Doves can't be trained. My homing pigeons can, though. They look like doves and they sound like doves, but they're superior in every way. When I release them, they'll fly around a little bit for show so the wedding guests can ooh and ahh, and then they meet me at my truck when I blow my special whistle."

"They're whistle trained?" Litzy asked.

"That's the beauty of pigeons. You can't reason with a dove, but these babies are as trained as dogs. I just set their cages open in the back of my truck, blow my whistle, and they come on home to Daddy."

The birds' bodies were plump, their feathers a pretty cream color. Not at all mangy or pigeon-like.

Skeeter knocked on the top of the cage, much to the obvious displeasure of its occupants, who set feathers flying with the flapping of their wings. "Say, I have an idea. How 'bout I give y'all a live demo right now?"

"Oh, Skeeter. That's . . . wow . . . But I'd rather save the doves—"

His expression turned sympathetic. "Ma'am, these here are pigeons," he said gently, as though she were daft.

"Right, but we're calling them doves today, aren't we? Let's save them for the wedding ceremony. We don't want to tire them out."

"Hogwash. We've got plenty of time for me to show you 'bout their whistle training." And before she could protest further, he flipped the doors of all four cages open.

"Duck!" Remedy called to Litzy as she dropped to the ground, her arms shielding her head.

"No, ma'am, they ain't ducks neither!" Skeeter called over the din of thirty birds taking flight. "They're homing pigeons, see? You sure have a lot to learn."

Remedy couldn't think of a darn thing to say in reply. She didn't hear any wings flapping and so chanced a look past her arm. The pigeons were on the lawn about twenty feet away, pecking the grass.

Clearing her throat, Remedy stood and smoothed out her skirt in a valiant attempt to regain her air of authority. Between Gwyneth and Skeeter's pigeons, Remedy was starting to feel more like a zoologist than an event planner. Sounds like it was time to talk to Alex about adopting a "no live animal" policy.

"The pigeons don't seem very interested in flying," she said.

Skeeter bumped his cowboy hat up so he could scratch his head. "Hmph. Not sure what happened. But I'll get 'em to fly."

The last thing Remedy needed was an overalls-clad man chasing pigeons on the wedding lawn, but her protests went unheeded. Shouting and flapping his arms, Skeeter chased them down. Looking as bored as lazy cats, the pigeons hopped and flapped their way on top of the reception tent.

"Skeeter, please. I think it's time to show us that whistle trick."

"Yes, ma'am." He shoved a grimy metal whistle between his lips and blew, producing a shrill note that made both Remedy and Litzy wince.

The pigeons turned their heads in unison toward the sound. Cooing, they took to the air, flying high over Skeeter, Remedy, and Litzy like a flapping, feather-shedding, cream-colored cloud. Remedy covered her hair with her arms and closed her eyes in a prayer that they didn't bomb her as they passed. When she opened her eyes again, it was to see the birds flying over the wide expanse of lawn and up the hill to the chapel—right over a young woman clad in a flowing white wedding gown.

"Oh my God, is that the bride?" Remedy said on a gasp. She grabbed Litzy's arm. "What is she doing here? I thought you said she was getting her hair done."

Litzy wrung her hands. "She is. I mean, she was. I don't know what she's doing out here. Oh my God. Why couldn't she just stay put?"

"Those doves had better not bomb her!"

Skeeter pulled a handkerchief from his pocket to wipe a splotch of bird poop off his cheek. "Bless your heart, ma'am, but them there are pigeons, not doves. Guess that's a tricky fact to keep in your head."

Remedy didn't have time for this. Not Skeeter's lectures on bird species or a wandering bride.

She had to clench her teeth to keep her voice modulated and quiet. "Skeeter, it's time for you to get those birds under control. Now."

"Don't worry, ma'am. I'll get 'em where they belong before the guests arrive. You have my word."

Remedy wasn't sure how foolproof Skeeter's word was, but she didn't have much choice. When she turned back toward the tent, Litzy was still standing there. "What's the deal, Litzy? Why are you here?" Her voice was shrill, but she couldn't help it. Not a single damn thing was going her way.

"I was watching the pigeons, ma'am."

Oh boy. "Get that bride back in her prep suite before she sees the trouble with the tent or the pigeons or any of this craziness. We're trying to put on a wedding, not a circus, damn it. And a wedding is no place for a bride!"

"I'm hoping that just came out wrong," said a drawling male voice behind her.

Remedy closed her eyes. The last hour had been pure insanity, but she'd done a pretty good job keeping her cool right up until she'd seen Litzy gawking at the birds instead of doing her job. *Deep breath, Rem.*

She pasted a serene smile on her face, transforming herself into a picture of cool calmness, then turned to face whichever vendor or resort employee had witnessed her mini-meltdown.

She wasn't prepared for the sight of the Alpha Bubba himself. Her serene façade vanished in an explosion of shock. "Garrity."

"Ms. Lane." Amusement danced in his eyes as the tip of his tongue appeared, pressing against that ever-present toothpick at the corner of his mouth. Was he fighting a smile? Was this all some kind of joke to him? And, furthermore, what was he doing in the middle of her job site cracking wise about the way she conducted herself and smirking down at her like he owned the world and she was but a plaything?

Too late to wish she'd worn platform heels so she could meet him eye-to-eye. She snapped her spine straight, all bravado and contained panic. "What are you doing here?"

He nodded toward the tent, which was now— thankfully—perfectly erect. "I'm here to inspect your setup. I told that poor assistant of yours that you just reamed out to let you know I'd arrived."

"Inspecting the event setup is the fire marshal's job."

He shifted his weight to his heels and hooked his thumbs on his belt, a clipboard tucked under his arm. "Which is why I'm here."

"But you're the fire chief."

He rocked on his boot heels. "I'm sure in California, what with all your sophistication and rivers of money, even the smallest community can afford to spread the public servant jobs around to a lot of men—"

"Or women."

"I was gettin' to that, but thanks all the same for making me sound like a sexist asshole."

God, she wanted to rip that toothpick out from between

those smirking lips and snap it in two. "I'm sure you didn't need my help to achieve that."

As if hearing her thoughts, he produced a second toothpick from his pocket and held it out to her. "Toothpick?"

It was her turn to sneer. "Disgusting."

The triumph in his eyes made her wish she'd taken the damned toothpick. It would've given her something to grit her teeth around.

"As I was saying, as opposed to California, out here in the sticks the fire budget isn't large enough to support a separate chief and marshal. The good folks of Ravel County voted to combine the jobs years ago. So as long as you're working at this resort, you're going to have to deal with me. Every week, every event. You think you can handle that?"

No. "Of course I can. You're not my first fire marshal."

"Let's not start comparing the notches on our respective bedposts, darlin'."

Oh, this man. "Moving on." From her clipboard she pulled a diagram of the tent's interior layout and handed it over. "Follow me."

She strode through the main entrance of the tent as if it hadn't been on the verge of collapsing only minutes earlier, her heels clicking on the wood flooring in time with her pounding pulse. Three steps in, her messenger bag snagged on something. She lurched forward, then snapped backward, staggering. A rolling cart loaded down with centerpiece arrangements of hurricane vases and bright, exotic flowers and greens careened past her, the florist scrambling after it. It banged into a rack of chairs, sending birds-of-paradise flying like javelins.

Remedy scurried after them and up the fallen stems. "Sorry about that," she said to the florist. "Maybe lock the brakes next time?"

The florist muttered in Spanish, shaking her head as she took the birds-of-paradise from Remedy.

Remedy pasted that cool smile on her lips again and glanced in Micah's direction. That annoying almost smile was back on his face, accompanied by a twinkling in his eyes as he whipped out a measuring tape and walked to the florist's cart.

Was he actually going to measure the distance between the top of the candle and the top of the vase? Sure, she'd watched fire marshal deputies do that occasionally before weddings in Los Angeles, but they were always overeager newbies, not seasoned professionals like Micah, who probably did hundreds of fire inspections every year at the resort. He had to know already that the resort was in compliance. *Weren't they?*

Those centerpieces had been constructed weeks ago, and not under Remedy's supervision. Swallowing hard, she hustled to his side. "Look, I know size matters, but isn't this a little extreme?"

The measuring tape retracted with a snap. "Size *does* matter, Ms. Lane. And I'm glad you're savvy enough to recognize that. But if you think my adherence to the law is too extreme, then that's only because you have no idea what foolish fire risks this resort has attempted to get away with in the past, the special events planners included."

He pulled the measuring tape out again and zeroed in on a second vase. She thrust a printout of the wedding's floor plan in front of his face, impeding his progress. "As you can see, we're in one hundred percent compliance with Texas state regulations on tent occupancy codes, number of exits, and exit clearance space."

He stepped left, away from the printout, and jammed the measuring tape into another vase. "That's a nice story, but you're over the occupancy code by sixteen people. And that's not counting the servers, the band, and your crew. The two extra tables probably also mean some of the aisles are too narrow, which is also against code."

Impossible. She shook the paper. "You barely glanced at the layout."

He raised an eyebrow. "You think this is my first rodeo?"

No. No, she didn't. But as she looked at the layout, doing some fast math about the square footage and the number of guests set to arrive, it was becoming embarrassingly obvious that it was hers. What had Alex and Carina been thinking, renting a tent that was too small for the wedding party? And why hadn't Remedy thought to double-check that?

"I'll nix the extra tables." That shouldn't be a problem. The bride and groom hadn't elected to assign seating, and there was no chance of every single guest showing up.

"See that you do." Micah retracted the measuring tape again. "You're going to need shorter candles, too. These are off by two inches. If you use Maria Valleros as the florist in the future, you'll have to watch her about that. She's almost as notorious a code violator as Ty Briscoe himself."

Damn it. "Done. Fine." There had to be thirty candles and vases in the storage room next to Remedy's office that her assistants could swap out in time for the wedding.

She turned away before he could catch a glimpse of the heat rising on her neck like a neon sign announcing her mortification. If there had ever been a man she'd wanted to not look like a fool in front of, it was Micah Garrity.

"Funny, isn't it, how raking in buckets of money makes people feel above the law?"

Throughout her life Remedy had found that to be unequivocally true, but she refused to give Micah the satisfaction of her agreement. "What is it with you and money? It's not like it killed your dog or stole your Bible or something."

"You don't know that."

With the wedding only a few hours from starting and the addition of the code violations she had to correct, she didn't have the time or patience to stand around and dicker with him. With her professional mask back in place, she spun on her heel to face him again. "Are we done here? It looks like I've got a lot of work to do, so I'd like to get on with it."

He nodded at a far corner of the tent, to a cluster of brawny men clad in traditional Polynesian tribal attire standing near a side exit. "First, let's talk about what they're doing here."

Oh, for heaven's sake. "They're Polynesian dancers. This is a tropical island–themed wedding and they're the entertainment. What's the problem now?"

"And how do you explain those torches they're holding?"

She caught her hands squirming and forced them to still against her clipboard. "Those aren't torches. They're batons."

This time, there was no "almost" about it. Micah's eyes glowed with genuine amusement. He rolled those full lips over each other like he was formulating the perfect cutting remark to put her in her place. Then he turned to the dancers. "Hey, Tito, are you and your crew planning to set those batons on fire tonight?"

"Hey, Chief. Good to see you, man. Yeah, you bet we are."

Damn it, damn it, damn it.

"Inside or out?" Micah asked Tito, walking his way.

"Out."

"They'll be performing on a stage outside during the cocktail reception after the ceremony. Perfectly safe," Remedy said.

Micah turned to face her again. What she wouldn't give to wipe that smug grin off his face. "Do you know what I'm going to ask next, Ms. Lane?"

Forget wiping off that grin, she'd pay good money to get her hands around his neck. She hated that he made her squirm. She hated that he had all the power in their interaction. Hated that he was getting off on it, too. She dropped her voice an octave, her words coming out as a rumbling hiss. "You want to see the stage."

"Well, since you offered so sweetly."

She took off marching toward the exit on to the pavilion. Micah snagged her sleeve and ground their progress to a halt just inside the tent opening. "Hey, California, I know you think I'm asshole number one right now, but—"

The sincerity in his tone caught her off-guard again. Was this another ploy to keep her off-balance? "Got that right," she muttered, jerking her arm out of his grip.

His cheek twitched. "But you and I both know why the rules are in place. We both know what's at stake. I don't take pleasure in shutting you down or traipsing with you all over hell and creation to prove you're breaking the law. That's not the part of my job I enjoy."

"I'm not sure about that. That swagger of yours and that smirk you've been wearing since you got here seem pretty self-satisfied."

His gaze rolled to the heavens, as though he was praying for patience. "I saw that stage you're walking me to when I arrived. I can already tell you that it's too close to the surrounding structures to accommodate fire dancers. It'll need to be moved."

"Like hell it does."

His hands went to his hips. "Please tell me that Alex explained to you that the stage can't be so close to the main building. Please tell me he explained to you that Briscoe Ranch Resort is more than fifty years old and made entirely of wood. The original structure in the main building is nearly seventy-five years old. Even the nails in the original building are wooden. This place is a pile of tinder waiting to explode."

No, Alex most certainly did not tell her that. Any of it. Not about Maria the florist or the too-small tent he'd okayed or, apparently, the very valid reasons Micah Garrity was in contention with the resort.

"Dramatic much?" said a droll voice behind them. Alex. Remedy ground her molars together, tamping down her anger at him. If there was such a thing as a time and a place to confront her new boss, this certainly wasn't it.

Remedy could practically feel the waves of irritation radiating from Micah's body as he faced Alex. "I'll never understand how you can be so flippant about fire safety, knowing what Xavier's family has been through."

Remedy's ears perked up. Xavier was Alex's husband. Alex's office was wallpapered with photographs of the two of them, along with their sweet twin toddlers, and Remedy had heard innumerable stories about their family, but never once had Alex broached the subject of a fire disaster or something that Xavier's family had gone through.

"I'm not as militant—no, *obsessed*—as you are, but that doesn't mean I'm flippant about fire safety," Alex said, standing taller. "But there's a balance, Micah, and I'm willing to work with you to find it, like I always am. Just don't bring Xavier into this."

A vein in Micah's neck had become visible. "Don't bring Xavier into this? Are you bullshitting me? Here's a better question: Do you have any idea how long it took me to make peace with the fact that he married a Briscoe Ranch executive?"

Assuming a bored frown, Alex lifted an eyebrow, droll, his voice flat. "Was it equal to the horror I experienced when I found out my boyfriend was your best friend?"

Remedy had to be hearing this wrong. She angled into Micah's line of sight. "Hold on. You're best friends with Alex's husband? How—"

"Stay out of this, California."

"I don't think I will," she countered. There was no staying out of it because Alex had embarrassed her in front of Micah and caused her tons more work because of all the code violations today, work that she and her staff would have to scramble to complete, and yet here he and Micah were snipping at each other as though there was a whole lot more to the story of their animosity beyond a professional disagreement—and she was supposed to mind her own business?

But Micah didn't seem to hear her as he stepped around her to get nearer to Alex. "I was in his life first, and I'm a godparent to your children—who live only a few miles down the valley and would be directly in harm's way if a wildfire swept through the county land toward your house—and I'm the one with the law on my side. So I'll bring Xavier into this if I want to. In fact, I might bring it up with him tomorrow morning at the range. I'm sick of this dance you and I keep doing every wedding at the resort. I'm sick of training your new employees for you."

Alex fumed silently, his face flushed as red as Micah's.

Micah pushed the tent diagram into Remedy's hands. "Move the stage another twenty feet away from the surrounding structures and you'll be in business tonight. I'll be back this evening to check that you followed through on the changes I ordered, so don't let Alex put any clever ideas in your head."

Then he was off across the lawn, no swagger in his angry stride in the direction of a massive white diesel truck with a red stripe along the side containing the words *Ravel County Fire Chief* in block white lettering.

"Alex, is all that true? Is Micah Garrity your twins' godfather?"

Alex didn't reply. At the continued silence, Remedy tore her attention from Micah to catch a glimpse of Alex disappearing through an employee entrance to the resort.

Chapter Four

A scream sliced through the air as Micah mounted the porch steps of his best friend's house. So much for his worry about waking the sleeping rulers of the Xavier and Alex Rowe household. Apparently, the rulers—or tyrants, as they seemed to be since they turned one and a half— were already awake and terrorizing their poor dad. If Xavier's voice mail from earlier was any indication, they'd been at it for the whole day and most of the previous night.

Before Micah could raise his hand to ring the doorbell, the door flew open.

Xavier, wrangling a whimpering, struggling Isaac. Behind him, in a high chair at the dining room table, sat Ivy, screaming her fool head off. The twins must not have gotten the memo that they weren't supposed to turn into little demons until their second birthday, a whopping five months away.

Xavier's brown eyes were bloodshot and his hair was frizzing out, looking weeks overdue for a cut. His dark skin was sheened in sweat and he had a bit of a funky smell going on. Or maybe it was the sweatpants and filthy T-shirt he was wearing.

Micah held up the paper bag he'd brought. "Trade ya."

Xavier's shoulders dipped. "That's the sweetest sound I've ever heard, and I don't care if it's dog poop in that bag."

"Blueberry lemon muffins, actually." He pulled Isaac from Xavier's arms, though the little guy wasn't eager to let go of his daddy. It took some wrangling to release Isaac's grip on Xavier's shirt. "You look like hell, by the way. Smell like it, too."

"Gee, thanks. You always were good with the compliments." He opened the bag and followed Micah toward the dining room table. "Are these muffins from your secret admirer?"

Isaac turned his body in toward Micah and cried into Micah's neck. Micah jiggled Isaac's sweet belly and gave him raspberries on the cheek until Isaac stopped crying and smiled. "Yup. But I figured you could use them more than me today."

Once or twice a week since before Christmas, Micah had opened his front door to find sweet treats wrapped lovingly in layers of paper plates and foil, then tucked in nondescript paper lunch bags. Often muffins or croissants, sometimes, when he got lucky, huge, sticky, decadent cinnamon rolls. The treats never included a note or any identifying information. He supposed he could play detective and ferret out the person's identity, but that hardly seemed like a way to pay back the mystery person's generosity. Clearly, they didn't want to be discovered. Plus, he kind of figured it was Mrs. Mayfield, an elderly widow who lived in the house behind his, because he'd saved her cat from a tree last year and because tasty aromas often wafted from her kitchen windows.

Xavier bit into a muffin and started to sit down on the chair facing Ivy, but Micah gave him a friendly shove. "I've got both these yahoos. You go eat and take a few minutes to catch your breath. Shower or something. Did I mention that you stink?"

Micah had been around Isaac and Ivy since they were

born via a surrogate, and with his experience with them and with his three siblings' kids he felt totally qualified to handle both toddlers at once. Especially when one was conveniently contained in a high chair, even if she was screaming loud enough for all the angels in heaven to hear.

"Like I said, you're always generous with the compliments." But even as Xavier grouched, he relinquished the seat, wolfing down another bite of muffin as he shuffled to the kitchen and opened a beer.

Ivy's eyes were squeezed so tightly closed as she wailed that there was no way she'd even registered ol' Uncle Micah's presence.

"Are they still teething? Is that the reason for all this drama?" Micah asked. He had vivid memories of the torture his firstborn niece, Savannah, inflicted on her parents when she was teething. That was one of the few aspects of parenthood he wasn't looking forward to.

Xavier splashed water on his face in the kitchen sink. "Let me tell you about teething. It's a downward spiral into hell. The pain wakes them up in the middle of the night, and then the next day they're even crankier because now they're sleep deprived and in pain from the teething, and so then they won't nap because they're too tired to nap, and then they won't eat because their mouths ache. So then they're hungry, tired, and in pain. The perfect storm. And then it starts all over again the next night."

"Sounds miserable." Micah tucked Isaac into place against his chest with his left arm, bouncing his leg to keep the little guy moving as he stroked Ivy's cheek, trying to get her attention. Failing to distract Ivy from her misery, he scooped up a baby spoonful of white mush. "What is this stuff?"

"Mushed bananas and rice cereal."

Nasty. "Hey, baby girl. It's Uncle Micah."

She stopped screaming long enough to level at him the most pathetic, dejected expression he'd ever seen.

"How about some of this banana mush your daddy fixed you?"

After a bit of lip trembling, she burst out crying again. Micah figured, *What the hell,* and shoved the spoon into her open mouth. He used her upper teeth to scrape the mush off the spoon, figuring even if she spit most of it out maybe some of it would sneak into her gullet.

In the kitchen, Xavier removed the wrapper from the second muffin. "Alex texted me this afternoon," he called over Ivy's cries. "He said you two got into it."

How annoying that Alex would burden Xavier even more by venting to him about their disagreements at the resort when Xavier was already at his wit's end with their kids. "We get into it most weekends." *Because he refused to comply with the fire code for every goddamn wedding he planned and he always had.* "Nothing to go bothering you about." Isaac made a play for the spoon, but Micah evaded his outstretched hand. "Isaac eat yet?"

"Not yet."

Micah set Isaac up in the matching high chair next to his sister as Xavier approached, eyeing Micah skeptically. "You mean, that's not why you're here tonight? To complain to me about Alex?"

Micah fed Isaac a banana mush bite. Unlike his sister, he ate eagerly. "Hadn't crossed my mind. In the voice mail you left me, I could hear both kids crying in the background and you sounded stressed. And I'm overrun with baked goods from my secret pastry pipeline these days, so I figured I'd stop by and drop off some sustenance."

Xavier poked him in the shoulder. "Don't you dare do that swooping-in-to-save-me bullshit. I hate it when you do that."

"I know you do. With good reason." Xavier got his knickers in a twist whenever he decided the hero complex he'd diagnosed Micah with was kicking in. Apparently, Micah had a way of overstepping, but he was working on it. And, honestly, it was a hard habit to break, after everything Micah and Xavier had been through together.

Micah couldn't shake the instinct to protect his friend. He'd spent the better part of his childhood fending off bullies from bothering Xavier, his next-door neighbor at the time, about being gay or being black in a town that tolerated neither. And then, when they were eleven, when the Knolls Canyon Fire struck, Micah had been the one to pull Xavier into Micah's mom's minivan as the two families fled together.

Or maybe that protective instinct had taken permanent hold of Micah after the fire, when Xavier's family decided to start over in a new town, at a new school, where Micah was powerless to be Xavier's protector against school bullies anymore. Or perhaps it had taken root after Xavier enlisted as a volunteer firefighter under Micah's command, counting on Micah's judgment as chief to help keep him safe. After a lifetime of looking out for Xavier, Micah was still having trouble shaking the feeling of being responsible for his well-being.

"I'm not swooping in to save you and I'm not here to complain about Alex. Just dropping off muffins and saying hello to my two favorite toddlers. Stop being so suspicious."

"Sorry. I'm just tired."

Micah jammed another spoonful of mush through Ivy's parted lips. Thankfully, her wails had subsided into halfhearted whimpers. "No apology necessary. I'd be cranky if these hooligans had kept me up all night, too."

Xavier sprinkled Cheerios onto the trays of both high chairs, then dropped into a chair at the table. "I guess I should just be grateful that you and Alex haven't strangled each other, but maybe you could take it a step further and stop getting to the point where you both wish you could strangle each other?"

"Not likely." He scraped the last of the mush from the bowl and fed it to Isaac, since Ivy was already macking on the dry cereal. "Someday, you'll be too old to eat this nasty slime your daddies have you chowing on. And then your Uncle Micah can take you for out for burgers, and pie, and teach you how to fish."

"I already called dibs on teaching them to fish."

Micah leaned in to kiss Ivy's forehead, the only clean and dry skin on her face. "I don't care what your daddy says. You, your brother, and I have a fishing date in two years," he whispered into her ear.

Ivy pushed her mushy, slimy index finger into Micah's nose and kicked her legs out with gusto, which Micah interpreted as the little gal's way of sealing the deal.

Together, Micah and Xavier cleaned the kids up and pulled them from the high chairs and into their arms. Micah was tempted to make one more offer to watch the kids while Xavier showered, but he couldn't decide if that would be interpreted as swooping in for the rescue or not and so decided against it.

He rubbed Ivy's belly and cuddled her close. "Okay, Rowe family. I've got to hit the road. I have a stop to make before I turn in for the night." An unwanted bolt of energy zipped through him at the thought of the person he'd be encountering on that stop. Remedy Lane. Maybe they'd even get into a sparring match again as they had that afternoon.

"I know that tone of yours," Xavier said. "You're going to check up on tonight's wedding at the resort."

He was really that obvious? "Look, I know what you're thinking. But reminding the Briscoes and their employees that they're not above the law is a full-time job, especially with the string of new event planners that have come and gone over the past year. It's like they've never even heard of the fire code."

"Be nice to Alex, would you? For me. I don't need a cranky man walking through that door after the day I've had."

All Micah could do was sigh. "Understood. Just know that he's not making it easy on me. Him or the latest wedding planner he hired. She's a helluva lot easier on the eyes than Alex—no offense—but she's almost as obnoxious and law flaunting as he is."

Obnoxious, law flaunting—and Micah couldn't get her out of his head. Anticipation of their next run-in, their next battle, sent another surge of electricity through his body. He was tempted to say her name aloud, to feel it on his tongue. He sucked his cheeks in, fighting a smile.

Maybe Xavier sensed Micah's shift in mood, because he watched Micah with interest as he said, "Alex likes her a lot. He says she's bright and ambitious. He thinks this one will stick, unlike the last two."

Stick? Unlikely. And there was no use in pretending otherwise, no matter how alluring she was. "I wouldn't be too sure, the way she treats me and the folks of Dulcet like a bunch of clueless backwoods rednecks."

"You are a backwoods redneck."

"And proud of it. All I'm sayin' is that there's no way an upper-crust executive from California like her will be happy here long term. However charmed she may be by small-town life in Dulcet, she'll still be out of here the first chance she gets. Mark my word."

Xavier's interested gaze turned reticent. "You know who she is, right?"

"Yup. Remedy Lane. Displaced California princess and already a major pain in my ass. Why?"

A flash of headlights flickered against the dining room wall, followed by the rumble of a car parking in the driveway.

With Isaac hitched on his hip, Xavier brushed past Micah, his eyes toggling between the car and his phone.

"What's Alex doing home so early? Doesn't look like I missed any texts from him. Hopefully everything's all right." He spun to face Micah, his finger already wagging. "Play nice."

"Don't I always?"

Xavier rolled his eyes as he tried to tame his hair in a mirror near the door. "Before you say something snarky or goading, think, 'Xavier was home alone all day with two teething toddlers.' Think, 'I'll take mercy on Xavier, because he hasn't gotten a solid eight hours of uninterrupted sleep in the past nineteen months.'"

"Since the twins were born? Really?" *Geez.* Add that to the list of things he wasn't looking forward to with parenthood.

Xavier had the door open for Alex before he mounted the porch stairs. "Everything okay at work?"

After a kiss to Xavier, Alex took Isaac in his arms and handed Xavier his briefcase. "Yep. All is well. I let Remedy take the reins today, so I figured I'd get out of her way."

"I like this whole *getting home before midnight* perk of having a competent wedding planner working for you," Xavier said, helping him out of his sports coat so he didn't have to set Isaac down.

Alex adjusted Isaac in his arms, then directed a phony smile at Micah. "I see there's no escaping you."

Behind him, Xavier shot Micah a warning glare and mouthed either *teething* or *sleeping,* Micah wasn't sure which. Not that it mattered, determined as he was to abide by Xavier's plea that he play nice.

In the spirit of that agreement, Micah blurted out the first nice, neutral topic that popped into his head. "I was just making plans with Isaac and Ivy to take them fishing in a couple years."

Alex stepped right up to Micah and gave Ivy a succession of quick kisses on the cheek until she giggled. "I think Xavier already has dibs on that."

Ivy reached out, straining for Alex to hold her, too. "So I heard. Here, Ivy wants her papa."

Alex set Isaac down and held on while the little guy got his balance. As Isaac toddled toward some toys in the corner, Micah handed Ivy over.

"You didn't stop back by the resort to make sure we moved the stage and got rid of those extra tables," Alex said to Micah, every word dripping with poison. "Are you feeling under the weather or something, to miss a chance at harassing me?"

What was it with Alex that he wouldn't stop needling Micah? It was getting damned old trying to be the bigger person all the time. "I knew you were good for it. But, despite that, I'm on my way to the resort right now to check up on the wedding anyway, because I don't want your latest ingénue doubting my follow-through."

"Is that really necessary?"

Yes. Yes it was. But Micah bit back his retort.

Xavier flitted between them, looking stressed. "Enough, you two. Please."

All this playing nice was torture. Absolute torture. Time to skedaddle before his big mouth got the better of him. "Okay, everyone, Uncle Micah's out of here, for real this time. Sorry to intrude on your night, Alex."

He didn't bother offering his hand to Alex to shake, having learned years ago that kind of gesture was too overt an acknowledgement of any kind of mutual respect between them.

"Bye. Thanks for the help tonight. And the muffins. See you tomorrow at the range," Xavier said.

A note of defeat had entered back into Xavier's tone. That and the way he'd bent over backward trying to keep peace between Micah and Alex put Micah in a fighting mood again. It was really friggin' tough, ignoring his instinct to try to fix Xavier's unhappiness. Not that Xavier would dare admit to being unhappy with his life or his marriage, not when he'd grown up believing that neither of his dreams of having a husband or children would come true, given Texas's fraught history with gay rights.

But anyone could see how Alex's demanding job kept their family in a perpetual state of stress. He put his career first, working long hours including evenings and weekends for Ty Briscoe, who was, by all accounts, a demanding, workaholic boss. For the life of their relationship, Xavier had spent a lot of time alone, and, now that they had kids, he was parenting alone, which was particularly hard for Micah to watch. There was nothing more he could do for his friend tonight, though.

Micah was at his truck, digging his keys out of his pocket, when the squeak of the front door caught his attention. Alex, with Ivy still in his arms.

Alex closed the front door behind him and walked to the porch rail. "Hey, just a sec. About something you said in there."

Micah drew a patience-mustering inhalation. "What's that?"

Swallowing hard, Alex shifted Ivy higher in his arms. "It's not an intrusion to me. You, being here."

Well, butter Micah's butt and call him a biscuit. Was Alex actually putting himself out there with a gesture of kindness? Could he be trying to bury the hatchet?

"Okay. Good to know."

"You're like family to Xavier," Alex continued, "which means you're like family to me. Maybe not my favorite family member, but, hey, we don't get to pick our families, right?"

So close to kindness. So maddeningly close. "Right. That we don't. 'Night, Alex. Go easy on Xavier. The twins gave him hell today."

On Micah's drive through the web of pitch-black, twisty, two-lane roads leading across town and through the backcountry hills to the resort, his annoyance at Alex and

Xavier's situation gave way to thoughts of Remedy Lane again. What the hell was he doing, going out of his way tonight to spar with her? He hadn't crashed a Briscoe wedding reception in more than a year, probably longer. True, it wasn't a bad idea to make sure she understood that he followed through with his threats and all that logic—but that wasn't why he was headed to the resort. Not if he was being honest with himself.

She got his blood pumping.

For that reason alone, he should have flipped a U-turn and headed home. Nothing could come of his attraction. Nothing. Because fraternizing with a resort executive would stink of corruption, of selling out. It would set a horrible example for the men under his command.

He was still wondering why he lacked the mental fortitude to turn his truck around and reject Remedy's pull on him as he eased to a stop in the guest parking lot near the resort's chapel. From his truck bed he pulled a supply bin onto the tailgate. Being that his current shirt was covered with banana mush, dried tears, and snot, he pulled out a spare collared uniform shirt with the fire department logo silk-screened on the chest and made a quick change.

After a moment's debate, he pushed his shirtsleeve up to show off the barbed-wire tattoo that circled his upper arm, then completed the look with a black Stetson and a toothpick in his mouth. Pure redneck, just because he knew it'd crawl under Remedy's skin. He would've added a proverbial cherry on top of the look by strapping on a hip holster and Taurus pistol if he'd been in civilian clothes, but guns and official fire department business didn't mix. That was one rule he was in no danger of fudging.

He'd shoved the last of the shirt hem into his pants when he noticed that one of his favorite people in the world was seated on a bench on the hilltop next to the chapel, gazing dreamily at the resort and the wedding in the distance. June Briscoe, better known as Granny June—the paradoxically ancient-yet-ageless matriarch of the Briscoe family and Ty Briscoe's mother. She was an itty-bitty thing, all moxie and wrinkles, who delighted in perpetuating the rumor that she was off her rocker and senile. Micah knew better.

A long time ago, he'd learned that the secret to having any kind of clout at the resort meant going along with whatever crazy notion the Briscoe matriarch cooked up, but somewhere along the line the two of them had bonded in a genuine, irrevocable way.

The truth was, even though the chapel parking lot was out of the way, Micah had taken to parking there because he loved catching Granny June in her quiet moments, when her crazy antics gave way to the reflective, wise soul she kept close to the vest. She reminded him of his own grandma, his dad's mother, who'd died not long before the Knolls Canyon Fire. Granny June reminded him of what his mother should have been like, the conversations he should have been able to have with her, if only the fire hadn't ruined everything. Astonishing, how that one event had come to define so much about Micah's life.

He'd only taken a few steps in Granny June's direction when she noticed him climbing the rise to the bench on which she sat.

"My prayers are answered!" she declared, hoisting her half-full lowball glass. The ice clinked as she beamed at him.

A grin broke out on his face. "Which prayers are those?"

"That a beefcake hunk of burning love would come to sweep me off my feet tonight."

He kissed her cheek and waited as she cleared room on the bench for him by moving a second, full lowball glass and a blue candle in a glass jar.

"Oh, please. You best be savin' your sweet talk for the charity ball next month," he said.

"Honey, I've got so much sugar in me, I'll be sweet-talkin' you from beyond the grave."

It was only a joke, but the idea of Granny June's eventual death punched a hole in his heart. She had to be at least eighty, but, God willing, she'd be raisin' hell around the resort for another couple decades.

"You threatening to haunt me? Because I'm not sure that's how Tyson would want to spend his eternity by your side."

She patted the bronze plaque affixed to the bench's seat back. Beneath her hand Micah spotted the word *Briscoe*. "My Tyson knows he'll always be the only man for me."

When her hand moved, Micah read the plaque.

In memory of Tyson Briscoe, 1919—1990
My One and Only Valentine

"I don't think I ever knew this bench was dedicated to him."

"It was his favorite spot. I come by here after every wedding at the resort to light a candle in his memory and have a drink with him, since he and I were the first folks to get married at the chapel here. Did you know we built that chapel with our bare hands, dragged the wood from the forest yonder and cut it into lumber ourselves? Those were the days."

Speaking of punching a hole in his heart . . .

Hearing about the enduring love that she and her husband shared cut him right to the core, thinking about the heartache she must have suffered when Tyson had passed. "He sounds like a tough cookie."

She raised her glass heavenward. "He was a badass. Not too many men like him around these days. The world's gone soft."

"I didn't mean to steal his seat."

"Pshaw, son." She winked at him. "You're one of the few who would've given Tyson a run for his money."

He stretched his arm out on the bench behind her. "Are you flirting with me again at your husband's memorial bench?"

"He don't mind. He knows my heart only belongs to him."

Granny June and Tyson's enduring love was legendary in Central Texas and the envy of everyone who knew their story, Micah included. He curled his arm around her shoulder in a loose hug. "May we all be so lucky as to find a love like you and Tyson found."

"No luck about it. True love is part of the grand design. And don't you worry. Love is coming to you soon." She touched a hand to his chest over his heart. "I can feel it in your aura."

Micah didn't put much stock in fate, but one of his favorite things about Granny June was how she walked the line between being a faithful Christian and a modern-day mystic with a love for auras and jinxes and all other manners of witchy magic.

"If only my aura could make predictions about something other than my love life, I'd be in business. Maybe you could look at it real close and see if it has any messages about this fire season we're in."

"It's already shaping up to be a hell of a bad fire season. Don't need no aura reading to know that. How's your family doin'? Your brother Junior still fixing cars?"

"Yes, ma'am. Business is booming at his garage," Micah said.

"Praise be. And your dad? I always liked him."

"He's good. Keeping busy at church and babysitting my sister Michelle's kids now that she's working. Got a teaching job at a preschool."

"Like your mama always did for work," Granny June said, her tone softening.

"Yes." Exactly like his mother had done, a point that hadn't been lost on anyone in the family or their church. As far as Micah knew, no one had had the guts to ask Michelle about why she'd have any desire to go down that path.

Granny June kicked her drink back, tossed the ice on the lawn, and produced a smartphone from her pocket. "Picture time. Come on and get in here, nice and close. Nothin' quite as fun as making the ladies on Facebook jealous that I was having a drink with a hot number like you."

Micah shook off a sudden cloud of melancholy and indulged her, even posing with his lips puckered against her cheek for a shot. When they were done, she stood. "You'd best get on with your night. I know your girl is waiting."

"My girl? What girl?"

Instead of answering, Granny June gestured with her empty glass to a tricked-out golf cart parked behind the bench. "I'll get you down to that wedding reception in no time."

She couldn't possibly expect him to get in her golf cart with her. No way. Granny June was, without a doubt, the worst driver in Texas. Her driver's license had been yanked by the state authorities after her last fender bender, but that didn't stop her from careering all over the resort and terrorizing hotel guests in her golf cart that had been tricked out in white and maroon, complete with a Texas A&M flag flying from the rear.

"Thank you, but it's such a pleasant night. I'm looking forward to the walk."

She hoisted herself into the driver's seat. "Don't argue with an old lady. Now get that fine tush in here so I can put the pedal to the metal."

Disappointing Granny June wasn't on his agenda that night. So, stifling a cringe, he blew out the candle she'd left lit on the bench, then ducked under the golf cart's maroon roof and took a seat.

"Hang on!" she called, which was good advice, seeing as how there weren't any seat belts or doors—or a roll bar, for that matter.

Tires churning over grass and mud, they went flying

down the hill, *Dukes of Hazzard*–style. Swerving around meandering guests and landscape features alike, she honked and hollered and, indeed, kept the pedal to the metal, speeding toward the glowing lights and faint strains of music of the wedding reception in the distance. It was tempting to close his eyes and pray, but then he wouldn't have been able to warn her of unseen dangers or grab the wheel from her if necessary.

By the time she slammed on the brakes not a foot from the low brick wall surrounding the reception patio, Micah's throat ached from calling out warnings to people trapped in her headlights and his head was spinning. He took a moment to catch his breath, then stretched out of the cart, refraining from the urge to drop to his belly and kiss the ground. "I mean it sincerely when I say thank you for not killing us both."

Her eyes twinkled. "I've got too much pride to end my days in a golf-cart accident. When I go, I'm going out with style."

He ducked his head back under the golf-cart roof and grinned at her. "And not for a long, long time, please." He clutched his heart. "I couldn't bear to live without you, darlin'."

"You'd best save your smooth talkin' and flirtin' for your true love."

"You still haven't told me who she is. The girl you mentioned."

With a chuckle, Granny June raised her cane and pointed across the reception patio. Strings of twinkle lights zigzagged in the air above the dance floor where the die-hard wedding guests were boogying down to a disco tune from the band—on the stage that had, indeed, been relocated according to Micah's specifications. Remedy Lane stood at the edge of the festivities surrounded by an eager gang of tuxedo-clad groomsmen who were falling all over themselves trying to reel her in. Even in the shadows and mood lighting he could read her polite-yet-distant expression clear enough.

The longer Micah watched, the more idiotic the groomsmen looked, like Dusty and Chet had when Remedy crashed their Sunday barbecue at the river. What was it about her that had the men in town twisting themselves in knots to get her attention?

Then it hit him what Granny June was playing at. He folded his arms over his chest. "Are you trying to play matchmaker with me?"

Granny's eyes twinkled. "The only matchmaker I know is the Good Lord himself." She nudged Micah's thigh with her cane. "I'm just giving you a push."

He gave her his best rakish grin. "Oh, so now you're calling yourself the hand of God?"

"Maybe I am, honey. Maybe I am. It's been far too long since you've had yourself any fun."

Since Micah's last steady relationship had run its course a couple years before, he hadn't actively sought out anything more than the occasional romantic fling. Work and his other civic duties kept him busy enough and happy enough. Totally drama-free—a term that in no way described Ms. Remedy Lane. "And here I thought my life was already a barrel of fun."

"Get on with you now. Time for me to get some beauty rest."

He walked around to the driver's side and kissed her cheek. "Thanks for the ride, sweet stuff."

By every indication, the wedding reception was getting long in the tooth. The near wall of the tent had been peeled open, revealing a cavern of mostly empty round tables—the correct number of them now, he noted—as everyone had shifted outside for dancing under the stars now that the stifling heat of the day had given way to a muggy but temperate night. Little plates of cake slices littered the outdoor tables, uneaten, though the bartender was still jumping with orders. It looked like the photographer had already left, the food servers were done, and the tables inside the tent had been cleared of everything except a smattering of glasses.

He focused his attention on Remedy again. She was still dressed as she had been earlier that day, in a simple short-sleeved black dress topped with a tasteful blue scarf that coordinated with the wedding colors. She was pretty—there was no denying that—but there was nothing fancy or outstanding about the outfit or her long, wavy hair that had been pulled back with a black headband. He bet she'd dressed that way to blend into the background, like the Dulcet Theater backstage crew did. None of which explained how she'd drawn such a moony-eyed crowd of men around her—or why Micah hadn't been able to stop thinking about her all week.

One of the particularly dopey-looking groomsmen tugged on Remedy's scarf, pulling her off-balance. He caught her in his arms and, though she squirmed away without forfeiting the pleasant smile she wore, a spark of impatience flared in her eyes.

Micah had seen enough. He strode her way, suddenly and acutely aware of his appearance. Deodorant still working? Check. Hair not sticking out funny around his hat? Check. Shirt tucked in? Check. He huffed out a laugh. Who was the idiot falling all over himself now?

When she noticed him, her shoulders stiffened and that pleasant smile flattened. She squared up to him and folded her arms over her chest. Her eyes shone with challenge, highlighting to him just how artificial her previous expressions with the groomsmen had been. This, the real Remedy, was who got his blood pumping. This was the woman who'd consumed his thoughts all week.

She shouldered past the groomsmen. Her hips cocked as she swaggered his way. He tore his attention from her body and locked gazes with her, his pulse pounding. A fire kicked to life inside him. *Time for some fun. . . .*

"How is it that you have the power to wrap every man you see around your little finger?" he said.

"Except you," she tossed out with a shrug.

"I'm impervious to your feminine wiles." He nodded to the groomsmen who still stood in a cluster where she'd left them, as though they couldn't accept that they'd been dismissed. "Unlike those half-wits."

"That wasn't my feminine wiles you were witnessing with those guys. That was my finely honed skill of wrangling drunk people."

"That's something you've devoted a lot of time to practicing, like at one of those California party colleges? I wouldn't go bragging about that if I were you."

"Not college. Weddings. Drunk wrangling is a big part of my job. Huge."

So much for the romance of weddings. "You're kidding."

"Every week, every wedding."

Now that he was considering it, she had a point. Near about every wedding Micah had attended produced an overabundance of drunkards by the end of the night. "My condolences, though the drunk wrangling doesn't explain why every single groomsman at this reception was hitting on you."

With a wry smile, she ran her hands down her dress. "Look at me. I'm unobtainable and dressed like a virgin librarian. All those guys you saw want to be the one man with the macho power to corrupt my innocence and introduce me to the world's many wicked pleasures."

He laughed at the deprecating self-descriptor. Yeah, her getup was drab as hell, but still, a virgin librarian she was not. "It's a good thing they didn't see you prancing around in that bikini last weekend at the river or they'd realize they're the ones in danger of being corrupted by your wicked ways."

An image rolled through his mind about the way her water-slick, tanned curves had writhed and bounced as Chet and Dusty had dragged her into the river shallows and tried to teach her how to two-step. Shifting, his body turning restless, he locked his jaw and set his focus on the stars lifting up from the dark silhouettes of the hilltops. He could not have this woman. He had rules against that kind of fraternization for a reason. He should have followed his gut and made that U-turn to home instead of returning to the resort tonight.

Her voice cut through his self-flagellation. "Are you making a crack about my virtue?" She set her hands on her hips and thrust her chest out. "Because my virtue happens to love this season's Dolce & Gabbana swimwear collection, thank you very much."

That was the most ridiculous sentence he'd heard uttered outside of his TV set. He pinched the bridge of his nose against smiling, but a snort of laughter still managed to escape. Man, was she out of place in Ravel County. "For your information, California, I was making a crack about the groomsmen's narcissism, not you." He flicked a glance in her direction, valiantly fighting the urge—and failing—to rake his gaze over her body. "But don't get me started about how those itty-bitty pieces of fabric you were wearing at the river threatened to corrupt *my* virtue."

He braced himself for a witty retort or scathing commentary on the irredeemable nature of his virtue, but she didn't take the softball pitch he'd tossed her.

From the corner of his eye he watched her shoulders lift as she inhaled deeply. On a purr of an exhale, she smiled, triumphant. "Mmm. Chief Garrity, I love knowing how much that bothered you."

The huskiness in her voice stripped him of all control. Done fighting the urge to drink his fill of her, he tore his gaze from the horizon, but all he caught was her trademark sashay as she left him in her dust and walked into the tent.

Whistling under his breath, he spun away from the re-ception and started back toward his truck. Time for him to get the hell out of California's orbit before he lost his careful control and fell into rank with the groomsmen trailing behind her like a pack of fools.

Chapter Five

Thursday evening, Remedy dropped into a chair in Alex's office, which shared a wall with her own on the south side of the resort's main building. She hadn't yet forgiven him for hanging her out to dry with Micah the previous weekend, but she decided that rather than confront Alex about fire code compliances that were now her responsibility anyway, she'd take away the lesson about paying more attention to those kinds of details in the weddings she executed and never again give Micah Garrity a reason to make her feel two inches tall.

"Tell me this weekend's weddings are going to be easier than the rehearsal I just attended. No, scratch that, the rehearsal I just refereed."

Alex looked at her over a pair of thick-rimmed reading glasses. "Bride troubles?"

"No. MOB troubles. All of a sudden she's in a panic that her daughter's wedding isn't going to be special enough for her precious baby girl."

"Well, bless her heart," Alex said, his words dripping with a perfect blend of condescension and dismissal.

So far, that was Remedy's favorite Texas saying. She could listen to it said in a wry drawl all day long. Would she ever be Texas enough to get away with tossing out *bless your heart* grenades the way Alex and Litzy and Skeeter did? One could dream, though Remedy had the sinking feeling that she'd forever be an outsider in Dulcet.

"Sometimes I want to sit the brides and their mothers down," she said. "I'd tell them, 'I'm sorry to break this to you, but I've thrown forty other weddings that were identical to yours, and that's just this year alone. This is as special as it gets.' "

"I wish. Especially with this family. You've already gotten a taste of their unique brand of dysfunction. Last summer, they held a wedding here for their eldest daughter and it was a scene. Not the worst we've had, but close. Oh, and they're drinkers, too. Every last one of them. For tomorrow's wedding we've ordered four times the usual order of tequila."

Remedy groaned. Tequila shots were a wedding planner's worst nightmare. Sometime between Jimmy Buffet's "Margaritaville" and Pee-wee Herman's table dance, it seeped into the collective American consciousness that tequila shots equaled an insta-party. Combine that with an inhibition-lowering event like a wedding and throw in a bunch of people who weren't big drinkers in their everyday lives and even the most wealthy, conservative demographic could devolve into a tequila-fueled, hedonistic hot mess.

"Dysfunctional family drama *and* rowdy tequila drinkers? Fantastic." She flipped through Alex and Carina's meticulous notes on that weekend's BEOs. "Are we ready with everything we can control?"

"Definitely. Including extra security that will be on hand until three a.m. both weekend mornings," Alex said.

"Judging by the room reservation block to wedding guest ratio, it looks like almost all the guests are staying at the resort. At least we won't have to worry about drunk drivers."

"That's a very good thing." Alex stifled a yawn. "I suggest we all go home and get a good night's sleep, because it's going to be a hell of a weekend. Besides, Xavier's starting to expect me for dinner every night, now that we found ourselves a wedding planner worth her snuff."

The compliment caught her off-guard, so much so that she didn't register the moment as the perfect window to ask about Micah Garrity being best friends with Xavier. "Thank you, darlin', and bless your heart," she said in her best southern drawl.

Alex snorted through his nose. "Nice try, but your accent still needs work. And, FYI, saying 'bless your heart' when someone compliments you is actually insulting."

"Really? Darn it! I thought I was getting the hang of all this Texas lingo. I'm trying to blend in. Do as the natives do and all that."

With a shake of his head, he stood, stuffing his phone in his pocket in preparation to leave. "Remember when E.T. tried to disguise himself in lady clothes?"

She winced. "I'm that bad?"

"Maybe stop trying so hard to fit in. Embrace your otherness. Part of the reason we hired you is the fresh perspective you offer the resort."

Remedy's otherness was something she'd long ago made her peace with. She'd been an outsider, a downright alien, most of her life, even in Los Angeles. Yes, sometimes it was isolating and sometimes the loneliness seized hold of her in vulnerable moments, late at night or when her job got her down, but there was nothing to be done about it—even if, just once, it would be a refreshing change of pace to fit in somewhere.

After bidding Alex good night, she walked through the maze of hallways to the employee exit. Stepping outside, she groaned at the wave of sticky heat that hit her. Chet and Dusty had mentioned at the river that it was shaping up to be a hot, dry summer, but she didn't even think it'd be possible to light a match at the moment, given all the moisture in the air.

She cut a path through the soup-like humidity to the nearest golf cart and took off to the employee parking lot at the southwest edge of the resort. Lifting her chin to the hot wind would have to suffice until she got home. *Please let the air conditioner be working tonight.*

As she drove, she ran a mental check of the food in her fridge. Unless the grocery fairies had visited while she was at work, she was out of luck. She hoped something in town would be open besides the grocery store.

She rounded a line of hedges hiding the parking lot from resort guests' view, and the moment her car came into sight she slammed on the cart's brakes. "Mother-fucker."

The roof of her car was covered with Skeeter's runaway pigeons.

Honking, she gunned the engine on the golf cart. "Get off my car, you beady-eyed bastards!"

The vermin were nonplussed.

Waving her arms, honking more, she pressed the gas pedal all the way to the floor. "Stupid vermin! You're sup-posed to be homing pigeons, so go home and leave me alone!"

The front edge of the golf cart bounced off the bumper of her car with a decisive crunch of glass and metal. The pigeons didn't stir, but if one were to look close they'd probably see actual, literal smoke coming out of Remedy's ears. Too angry to curse, she smacked the steering wheel, then craned her neck out of the side of the cart and growled. Two birds looked her way, bored.

"You've got to be kidding me."

What the hell was it going to take to get those rodents off her car? She grabbed her purse and leapt from her seat, swinging her purse over her head and shouting. The pigeons did take notice of that. She lined a nice fat one up in her sights and swung, but as her purse curved in its direction the whole flock fluttered off her roof and congregated in the nearest tree.

"That's right!" she hollered, pointing at them. "You'd better fly away, you weasely-ass monkeys! You're a hundred times worse than Gwyneth."

At the sound of a gasp, Remedy's eyes went wide. *Oh, God.* She wasn't alone. On the far side of the lot, an older woman in a housekeeping uniform gaped at her. And who could blame her? Remedy looked downright bonkers. Remedy slapped a smile on her lips, smoothed her skirt, and waved. "Just working through some anger management issues. Have a great weekend!"

Without waiting for the other woman to respond, Remedy pivoted on her heel and marched to the golf cart. No matter how many times she turned the key or how vigorously she pleaded with it, the engine wouldn't catch. Maybe it needed to sit and rest overnight. That sometimes worked, didn't it? It wasn't blocking any other cars, so what was the harm? She'd try starting it up again the next morning before contacting Maintenance. After her run-in with Gwyneth and the sand trap, the last thing Remedy needed was another ruined golf cart during her first month on the job.

She didn't bother to count the number of bird poop splotches on her car's roof as she unlocked the door. Between the pigeons, the backcountry roads she traversed every day, and the afternoon thunderstorms, her car would never be clean again anyway. That was one luxury she hadn't realized about living in Los Angeles—when she got her car washed, it had stayed clean for a while.

With the housekeeping employee looking on in stunned silence, Remedy attempted to back her car out without hitting the golf cart. She tapped it a few times with her front bumper, but only a little. Not that an extra scratch or dent would be noticeable, given either vehicle's current state.

She waved again at her spectator as she pulled past her, then gave a subtle raising of her middle finger to her new feathered enemies who were still watching her from above, and didn't release her first full breath until she was out of the lot and on the road to downtown Dulcet.

Dulcet had already rolled up its carpets by the time Remedy turned onto the main drag. In search of a restaurant that was still open, she cruised slowly past brick churches, a grocery store, several salons, a library, a post office that shared a building with the city offices, and a lot of shops that seemed to support the wedding industry at the resort. She counted at least three jewelers and a handful of bridal shops, though two of them had banners strung up in the windows advertising "going out of business" sales.

She let her attention linger on the firehouse, a tall, boxy brick building dominated by two huge roll-up garage doors. It looked as though the firefighters' residences were behind the garage, in the back of the building, judging by the lights glowing through the windows along the side. In a driveway between the firehouse and the residential cottage next door sat a hulking shiny white truck tricked out with plenty of bells and whistles and with *Ravel County Fire Chief* painted on the side within a fire engine red stripe. Micah Garrity's truck.

A rush of awareness flooded through her. They didn't grow them like that in Los Angeles. Big and tough. Virile in a way that even the stuntmen in her parents' movies couldn't pull off. Every move he made and every word he said was infused with a full-throttle confidence that commanded attention. And while that made him infuriating and domineering in exactly the way she hated men to be, she'd still given his oh-so-ripped body a thorough perusal every chance she'd gotten.

She wasn't the only one sneaking glances, though. There had been no mistaking the heat in his gaze when he'd watched her that first day they met at the river or last Saturday night at the wedding reception. She had no interest in letting an alpha male take over her life, but there was no denying their mutual attraction—an attraction she planned to keep fighting tooth and nail.

She chuckled through a grimace at that realization. It'd been a while since a man had gotten under her skin, and Micah Garrity had done it while chewing on toothpicks and smirking at her from beneath the brim of his cowboy hat. *Go figure.*

She indulged in one last look at his truck, then wrenched her gaze away. "Oh, Remedy. You're hopeless. Absolutely hopeless."

She kept cruising until the downtown area faded into a residential neighborhood. All right, then, she had two dinner options besides the grocery store: the ice-cream shop and Petey's Diner. On the sign next to the carefully carved letters of the diner's name was a painting of a stout white dog with a black circle around one eye smiling out at the street. The dog looked vaguely familiar, but she couldn't place where she'd seen that before.

She parked her car on the street out front and stepped into the heat again, becoming instantly sticky with perspiration. Dodging a massive crack in the sidewalk filled with muddy water that rippled in the breeze, she hustled through the diner door.

The moment she pushed the diner door open, the meaning of the diner's name and the dog painted outside dawned on her. Every square inch of wall was covered with memorabilia from the *Little Rascals*. Petey, she now recalled, was the Little Rascals' dog. She spun a slow circle, taking in the walls of framed magazines and newspaper articles, movie posters and autographed head shots. So much old Hollywood that the diner felt like a sliver of home.

Home. As though Burbank and the Hollywood scene had ever felt like home when she'd lived there. Maybe it had felt like home, after all, but in the thick of the L.A. drama she hadn't recognized its place in her heart. Maybe when she went back someday it'd feel different. Familiar.

Maybe.

But she had no plans of going anywhere anytime soon. Head down, nose to the grindstone, she was going to keep pouring 100 percent of herself into her job at Briscoe Ranch.

The man behind the diner's main counter was freckled, with black hair and a cowlick worthy of Alfalfa. He cast a bored gaze at Remedy as he stacked red plastic food baskets beneath the kitchen pass-through window. "Welcome to Petey's. Sit where you want. I'll send Barbara over."

A few families and groups of teens were scattered at tables throughout the restaurant. Remedy slid into a chair at a table along the wall, the better to people watch. She plucked a menu from the stack stuffed into the napkin holder, but her attention was caught by the television mounted behind the counter, where a commercial for her dad's new movie was playing. It was an action flick about a kidnapped daughter and had a bland, generic title Remedy couldn't remember.

Her mother liked to grouch that the new flurry of action roles for male actors in their fifties and sixties were pandering to the men of the world's midlife crisis fantasies, but Dad just laughed her off. The movies paid well and Dad was having a blast.

Long after the commercial ended, about the time that Remedy concluded that this Barbara waitress was imaginary, the diner door jingled, opening. The threshold was filled from floor to ceiling with Micah Garrity's silhouette. Remedy's heart did a little skip—like she was a smitten schoolgirl. *Pathetic*.

He wore a dark ball cap pulled low over his eyes and a snug-fitting navy blue T-shirt, the stretched cotton molding over his muscles. From beneath his dark jeans a pair of black boots jutted out. No sir, they definitely did not grow them like that in Los Angeles. He was a pure Texas male to his core.

The man behind the bar broke out in a huge smile. "Chief, hey! Welcome. Let me get Barbara to show you to our best table."

He tipped the brim of his ball cap. "Much obliged, Petey, but I can find it myself."

Then he ambled to the counter—which was the only word to describe the slow shift of his hips as he moved—and stuck his hand out for Alfalfa, er, Petey, to shake. Remedy might have hummed, just a little, in the back of her throat, at the fine view Micah gave her by leaning over the counter.

When he turned in Remedy's direction, she sank behind her menu. Despite her efforts, she felt his eyes on her as he walked to a table across the room from where she sat. He took a chair facing her, and when she dared raise her head to look at him straight on she watched a smile touch his lips as he used his tongue to shift a toothpick from one corner of his mouth to the other. Stupid toothpick, always drawing her attention to his mouth like that.

She raised her menu to block him out again.

"You're still holding your menu. Barbara hasn't taken your order yet?" That deep drawl, on top of everything else about his look tonight, was too much. How was this guy even real?

Remedy summoned her courage and lowered her menu to the table. "I was starting to believe Barbara is a figment of Petey's imagination."

Micah absentmindedly picked up his butter knife, then tapped the edge against the table. "Good guess. But I'm thinking that she probably took one look at your ID badge and headed in the opposite direction. A lot of folks around here aren't big fans of Briscoe Ranch."

Remedy's hand went to her chest, her fingers closing

around the ID badge clipped to her shirt collar and that she'd been unaware of until he'd mentioned it. She tore it off and stuffed it in her purse.

So Barbara was real and she wasn't a fan of Briscoe Ranch, which didn't make any sense but matched the muted hostility Remedy had felt from other Dulcet citizens—and from Micah—since the moment she'd arrived in town.

Before she could think better of the idea, she pushed out of her chair, grabbed her purse, and stomped to Micah's table. He didn't bother sitting up straighter and his bemused expression never wavered.

She dropped her purse on the table, then sat in the chair across from his. "I don't get it."

"Get what?"

"Why the people of Dulcet wouldn't be fans of Briscoe Ranch. The resort brings in tons of revenue and tourists all year long. Not to mention how many townspeople it employs. You'd think they'd be grateful for the extra business the resort brings in."

With a flicker of his eyebrows, he took his toothpick out and tossed it on the table, then tipped his chair back onto two legs. "Here's a tip. Don't ever launch into corporate justification that begins with 'you'd think they'd be grateful.' "

"But—"

He slammed the chair legs back to the floor. "You want to survive in this town or not?"

She locked eyes with him. "I do. Badly."

His hard glare softened, but he didn't look away, so she didn't, either. Such long lashes he had. She'd noticed that at the wedding reception the previous weekend. Long lashes framing dark, soulful eyes set in a perfect, rugged face. If only he wasn't such a righteous alpha jerk—the thorn in her side, the perfect descriptor that Alex used.

"All right," Micah said. "I'll answer your question. The

shops in town that cater to the tourists are doing well, for the most part, but all those tourists you mentioned have transformed our main street into a series of trinket shops and tourist diners, which has divided the town into those who are drinking the resort's Kool-Aid and those who aren't so impressed with having their home invaded by a steady stream of entitled snobs." He busied himself lining it up perfectly with the fork and spoon. "And then there's the faction of people who will never forget that Briscoe Ranch was indirectly responsible for the worst fire this part of Texas has ever seen."

Something about the twitch of his facial muscles and the way his eyes turned distant gave her the sinking suspicion that Micah fell into that third faction. "When was that?"

"Twenty-four years ago."

"That was a long time ago."

"Not so long, not to the people who were affected."

A jingle of keys distracted them both. They turned toward the sound.

The key jingling was coming from the key ring hooked to the belt loop of a thin brunette of about fifty, give or take, wearing a long-sleeved black T-shirt with Petey the dog silk-screened on the front and with the sleeves pushed up to her elbows. She stopped at their table. "What can I get you, Chief? We've got your favorite tonight. Cherry pie."

"Good evening, Barbara. I'll take a slice of that and a glass of milk, thanks."

A grown man ordering milk like he was wholesome incarnate. *Unbelievable.*

Remedy opened her mouth to order, but Barbara had already turned away.

"Hey, Barbara. Just a sec," Micah said. "My pie can wait until you take Ms. Lane's order. She's liable to blow a gasket if she doesn't get taken care of like the special snowflake she is. California princesses don't like to be kept waiting, or so the rumor goes."

Remedy raised her hands and wrung an invisible neck.

In response, he had the audacity to wink at her, his cheek muscle tugging as though he was fighting a grin.

This man was driving her crazy. She should get up and walk away. She should go to the grocery store and buy some ready-to-eat food and be done with Barbara's lousy service and Micah's teasing and this town that didn't want her.

"I'll get to her after I serve your pie," Barbara said, turning toward the kitchen again.

"Barbara, please. Will you get the lady a chicken salad first? If she expires out of hunger, then I'd have to be the one to revive her, and I'm not keen on getting so close to such a prickly creature."

Did he really order for her? Exhibit A of why she didn't mess with alpha men. "You haven't seen prickly yet."

Heat and amusement warred in his eyes. "Something to look forward to," he crooned in that drawl, low enough that Barbara couldn't hear.

"Why did you order for me?"

"I was trying to save you."

Oh, please. She shot her hand into the air, wiggling her fingers. "I've got to get Barbara back here. If you're going to criticize my diet, then I'm going to make it a double cheeseburger, because my new favorite hobby is ticking you off."

"How's that, in any way, logical? You need me, and I'm not just talking about tonight."

He was right. She did need him—in a professional capacity. And she was going to keep on needing him on her side if she hoped to keep her job. A fire marshal with a vendetta could make a wedding planner's life a living hell—Remedy had seen it happen a time or two—but having him flaunt his power over her like that made her see red. Mister Big Shot was about to learn that he might be king of Ravel County, but not every citizen there was his royal subject.

"You think there's no way for me to do my job without your support? Challenge accepted," she muttered from behind gritted teeth.

Then Barbara was back, her pad of paper and a pen in hand. "You need something else, ma'am?"

Ma'am? Ouch. "Barbara, would you please cancel that chicken salad. I'll have a Double Spanky Burger, extra bacon."

Micah made a choking sound in his throat. And was that a discreet shake of his head?

Barbara gave Remedy a long, quizzical look, then grinned. "If you say so."

What was with these people, judging her for ordering a burger instead of a salad? "It's like I'm back home in Hollywood, where salad eating is practically a religion."

"I didn't think people actually lived in Hollywood."

They didn't. "I meant the real Hollywood. Burbank. Where most of the actual moviemaking takes place."

"No kidding, huh? I had no idea."

A lot of people didn't. "Ergo why I simply say I grew up in Hollywood."

And that was all she was willing to say about her youth and Hollywood. One of the things she liked best about Dulcet was that she felt normal for the first time. She was simply Remedy, not Virginia Hartley and Preston Lane's daughter or the wedding planner who wrecked Zannity's impending nuptials. A lot of good Remedy's newfound anonymity would do her if she started blabbing about her Hollywood roots.

He frowned. "Back to your earlier statement. I wasn't trying to goad you into accepting a challenge. I was stating a fact. You need me, even if you're too foolhardy to admit it. It's not going to be long before you come to grips with what every other event planner at Briscoe Ranch Resort has learned either the hard way or the easy way, Alex Rowe included. Carina Briscoe, too. Not a single special event in a public venue takes place in this town that doesn't get my seal of approval first."

Remedy's throat tightened. She'd thought their feud was personal, fun even, but he really did hold her future at Briscoe Ranch Resort in his hands. "Are you threatening me?"

He opened and closed his mouth, then straightened. His lips quirked into a grimace. With a scrape of his chair legs over the linoleum floor, he stood. "Barbara? Hold on a sec." He waited until the waitress had turned back to face them. "My apologies to the cooks and to you, but Ms. Lane and I need to cancel both our orders." He held a twenty-dollar bill out to Barbara. "Bless her heart, but Ms. Lane forgot she's got somewhere else she needs to be."

"No, I don't. Not until I've eaten a delicious, greasy Double Spanky Burger with extra bacon."

Barbara looked from Micah to Remedy, then back to Micah. She tucked the twenty in her apron and nodded. "If you say so, Chief. Let me know if there's anything else I can do for y'all before you go."

After Barbara left, Remedy kicked Micah's boot with her pump. "What the frack? Did you feel a sudden need to demonstrate your power in this town? Proof that I need you or else I don't eat? You've got about three seconds to explain before I go postal."

He pushed his chair in and handed her purse to her. "I wasn't criticizing your diet."

"Whatever you say, Alpha Bubba."

"Alpha Bubba?" He shook his head. "You know what? Never mind. I don't want to know. Let's get out of here."

"Excuse me?"

He rolled his head on his neck, oozing exasperation. Then he braced his knuckles on the table and loomed over her, his voice lowering to a harsh whisper. "I'm going to get you some food before you go postal, but the only food fit to eat on Petey's menu is the pie and the chicken salad. All I was trying to do was save you from experiencing the worst cheeseburger in Texas."

"The worst?"

"It's legendary. Or, rather, infamous."

She followed a vein from his wrist over his muscled forearm to his elbow, then skipped up the rest of his body to look him in the eye. "What game are you playing at?"

"I know where to find the best cheeseburger you'll ever eat, guaranteed, and since I cut your dinner short here, it's the least I can do to steer you toward burger nirvana. No game, promise."

"From threats to promises? My little ol' head's spinning."

He grabbed her hand and pulled her out of her seat. "We're leaving now. My sense of charity can only weather so much snippiness."

Did everyone in this backward town do everything Micah commanded? They must, because he sure was unaccustomed to being told no. Even she was having trouble with the word, seeing as how she let him drag her from the diner, through the parking lot. When they passed her car, she planted her feet firmly on the blacktop. Wherever he planned to take her, she had enough street smarts to know she should drive herself.

"Now what's wrong with you?" he said.

"You were taking me to your truck."

"How did you expect me to take you for burgers?"

She pulled her arm from his grip. "I'll follow you in my car."

His features softened. "I'm not going to kidnap you."

She dug through her purse until her fingers touched on her car keys. "Good to know."

The harsh edge of irritation disappeared from his voice. "Remedy, I'd never harm you."

Was that the first time he'd called her by her first name?

It must have been, because the word on his lips sent a shiver over her skin.

No, she didn't believe he would harm her, and she could tell how much the idea that she might think he would genuinely bothered him, but a precedent needed to be set about her not jumping to comply with his every command. "Says the wolf."

He sighed. "Okay, I get it. I've got two sisters, so I get it. Wait for me in your car while I go across the street and get my truck."

"Why are you taking me to dinner? We can't breathe in each other's airspace without ticking the other one off."

She braced herself for a snarky comeback, but his earnest expression held fast. "I've got a new plan for dealing with you. I'm going to show you why this county and the people matter. Why I'm such a hard-ass about the fire codes at the resort and why I'm willing to keep being a hard-ass indefinitely to make sure that this land and the people who call it home are safe."

Micah Garrity, the great protector of Ravel County. "That's a relief to know."

"What is?"

"For a crazy moment there, I thought you were calling for a truce between us."

He swaggered a step closer and looked down at her from beneath those impossibly perfect lashes. "Why would I do that? We're only getting warmed up as enemies."

Indeed they were. "Let me get this straight. You're taking me on this harebrained burger quest to prove that you're right and honorable and just and I should bow down prostrate at your boots just like the rest of this town?"

"Pretty much," he said.

"At the risk of repeating myself, challenge accepted."

There it was. Her favorite look of his. That straining attempt to keep the smile that touched his eyes from showing on his lips. *And, God, those lips . . .*

"Why is your car all banged up? Did you get in an accident?" he said.

"It's a long story that involves pigeons and a golf cart."

His earnestness broke, replaced by a cocky half smile that might curl a lesser woman's toes. "Sounds embarrassing."

"For the pigeons? Very." And maybe a little for her. Just a smidge. "I changed my mind. I'll drive with you." *What the hay.* She wanted to spar with him more, and riding in his truck would present all kinds of opportunities. Not that she'd ever succumb to the charms of a gun-carrying, toothpick-chewing good ol' boy no matter how long his eyelashes were or how fast that cocky smile got her heart beating.

"God, help me," he muttered, then took her hand again and led her across the street in the direction of his truck.

Chapter Six

He was certifiably crazy for doing this. True, Remedy had been about to eat a disgusting excuse for a cheeseburger, but so what? It wasn't like the soy filler that Petey's used in their ground beef or the mysterious origin of those plastic orange squares that Petey claimed were cheese would kill her. At least, Micah hadn't heard of any "deaths by soy" in the county.

What did he care if Remedy were to choke down a Petey's burger and learn her lesson the hard way? The better question was why he was going out of his way on a work night to play county tour guide for a stuck-up Briscoe Ranch short-timing executive. But he knew why. It was like he'd told her outside Petey's. Once she understood exactly how precious a place this county—hell, this *state*— was to the people who called it home, then maybe tempting disaster with Polynesian fire dancers during one of the state's driest summers on record wouldn't seem so appealing. Nobody wanted to be the cause of a catastrophic fire. The trick was getting rich snobs—or, rather, the people doing the rich snobs' bidding—to believe that the world beyond their stuck-in-the-air noses mattered. That's what tonight was really about. Opening Remedy's eyes to reality.

He glanced over at her, sitting in his passenger seat like it was her throne, the breeze ruffling the hem of her skirt and blowing her hair all over. She looked good in the Texas wind. She looked good in his truck, too, with her fingers strumming her bare knee in time with the country rock blaring on the speakers. The only way she could look prettier was if she had that spark of indignation in her eyes that she got when he provoked her.

And, boy howdy, he did love to provoke her. How had she put it? Ticking him off was her new favorite hobby? Yeah, that train ran both ways. His gaze settled on her legs again. He was seized by the wild urge to swing by his house, grab a pile of blankets, and take her out into the backcountry to strip her down beneath the stars and find out what those long, tanned legs looked like in the moonlight. There were certain parts of his anatomy that wanted to see her come undone in a real bad way.

He wrenched his attention back to the road beyond his headlights.

Nope. You are not taking her to out tonight because she's pretty. That cannot be the reason. There were plenty of attractive women all over the county who would appreciate being doted on and taken out to dinner by him, which circled him back around to the question about why he was spending his evening with the one he couldn't have.

Part of his job as fire marshal. Opening her eyes to reality.

Right.

It was a perfectly logical reason and he should feel quite satisfied with his maturity and logic.

"Why do the guys singing these country songs go on and on about girls gyrating and shimmying all the time? And what kind of sexist pig coined the term *moneymaker*? Like we're all strippers in training or something? Before I moved here, I had this image in my head that the men in

Texas would be walking around with wallets loaded with cash, waiting for a girl with ass-shaking skills to shimmy by so they could throw money at her. I figured that's why the women of Texas carry such big purses. To hold all that cash. Imagine my disappointment that I haven't had a single dollar thrown my way since I moved here. I'm not sure what that says about the quality of my moneymaker. Maybe I'm not shaking it hard enough."

Ah, hell, who was he kidding? Remedy had been right to call him a wolf. He felt pretty damn wolflike at the moment. One hundred percent carnivore. And that had nothing to do with his job or protecting Ravel County. One look, one word, from her made him simultaneously want to smile like an infatuated fool and throw up his hands in frustration.

"Don't kill the messenger here," he said, "but I think that term is referring to the idea that girls who can shake their moneymakers stand a good chance of landing a rich sugar daddy to marry."

"That's disgusting."

Yes, it really was. "In your business, I bet you see that all the time. I guarantee that every richie rich wedding you've planned features a bride who knows how to work her moneymaker and a husband whose bank account is loaded."

She shifted in her seat to study him. "Are you saying that millionaires aren't capable of pledging deep, abiding love to each other in marriage?" It would have been a sentimental question if her words hadn't been dripping with sarcasm.

He turned off the highway and onto Old Route 47, a dark, two-lane byway that cut the corner of the two main highways at the edge of Ravel County lined with nothing but tired ranches and Hog Heaven, their final destination.

"I don't doubt that there's a little room left in their gold-plated hearts for deep, abiding love," he said. "But I'm pretty sure the love part doesn't happen until the requisite ass shaking and money throwing have occurred."

She tapped her chin, a sly smile spreading on her lips that made it hard for him to keep his eyes on the road. "What do they call someone who's prejudiced against wealth?"

She was talking about him, of course—and she wasn't far off. "No idea."

"Someone who hates technology is a Luddite. A man who's prejudiced against women is a misogynist. And a person who hates people is a misanthrope." She smoothed her hand over his shirtsleeve, following the curve of his triceps and sending a shot of electricity right to his core. "So what do they call people like you?" she mused.

"A realist?"

She snapped her fingers. "I know! A liberal Democrat."

Like hell he was. "You'd better watch your mouth, California."

She threw her head back and laughed at her own joke. "I think I love Texas." Then, in a paltry imitation of a twangy accent, she added, "Y'all are so easy to tease."

Micah spun the volume dial on his sound system, cranking the music up. Any more teasing from her and he was liable to pull over to the side of the road and wipe that grin off her face with a kiss.

He strangled the steering wheel with his grip. *A kiss? Really, man?* Not cool. And definitely not professional. He'd never been so grateful to see Hog Heaven's neon lights in the distance.

He cleared his throat. "We're here. Burger nirvana, better known as Hog Heaven."

The roadside bar wasn't much to look at. A low-ceilinged one-story building with wood siding and a neon pig wearing a halo sticking up from an ancient wood shingle roof. Smokers spilled out around the front door in packs. The country rock blared from the windows and doors, loud and raw as though from a live band. The gravel parking lot was jammed with cars and trucks and motorcycles to the point that most new arrivals looked to be parking on the street. Just another night in hill country.

Remedy ducked her head and peered up at the neon pig as they passed it in search of a parking spot. "Oh my God, that name. Hog Heaven. I love it. But it doesn't explain why you're bringing me to a roadside diner that specializes in pork to eat hamburgers."

He pulled to a stop past the last parked vehicle on the side of the road. "Because they put ground, raw bacon right into their burger meat." And it was the best damn thing Micah had probably ever eaten in his entire life.

The bar was just as crowded inside as the parking situation suggested. The dark, smoky air did indeed smell like hog heaven, a result of the wall-to-wall crowd and the briskets and chickens and pork they smoked every day, along with the burgers they were cranking out from the open kitchen to the left of the bar. He'd been right about there being a live band playing, too.

Remedy's eyes lit up as she gave the place a once-over. "There's sawdust. Cool. And a dance floor. I hope you brought some small bills, because I'm seeing a lot of moneymakers being shaken out there."

"You gonna shake yours tonight? I've heard you could use a little practice." *Damn it all to hell.* What had made him say something so stupid, because what if she took him up on that challenge?

She arched an eyebrow at him. "Depends on if I see any sugar daddies who could handle the likes of women such as myself." Then she smacked her own ass, her eyes skimming the crowd as though she was assessing the crop of sugar daddies in the room.

He caught himself admiring the way her purple skirt hugged her moneymaker just right, and turned away, scowling. "I thought we were here for the burgers, not so you could snag yourself a man."

She angled into his line of sight again, a triumphant smile playing on her lips. "I swear on the wig of Dolly Parton that I'll never tire of the way you frown when you're annoyed at me. Your eyes practically glow red. It's my favorite look of yours."

The only person he was annoyed at presently was himself. "I see a table opening up on the far side. Let's snag it." He grabbed her hand, tugging her behind him as he wove through the crowd.

"This place doesn't look like it specializes in burgers. Most people are eating plates of roast beef."

"That's brisket." At the small round table near the dance floor he pulled out a chair and ushered her onto it.

"Maybe we should try the brisket instead of burgers."

He braced a hand on the table and curled down over her, getting close to her ear so she could hear him over the music. "Let me give you a phrase to practice sayin' while I go put our order in at the food window. Here it is: 'You were right. I was wrong.'" He clapped a hand on her shoulder. "You work on that while I'm gone."

She twisted in her chair to face him, her knees straddling his leg. "And inflate your ego even more? I don't think so."

"I'm trying to be helpful. You're gonna be sayin' that a lot to me this summer, so you might as well get used to it tonight."

"How about this line instead? 'Kiss my moneymaker, Micah Garrity.'"

He leaned in even closer, ready with a zinger about how he'd never agree to be her sugar daddy when his focus snagged on her lips.

Hellfire.

The seconds ticked away while he tried to remember what snarky comeback had been on the tip of his tongue.

The trouble was, thinking about his tongue got him thinking about her tongue. This burger quest had been a mistake of epic proportions.

He peeled away from her.

There he went again, straddling the line between wanting to throw his arms up and walk away and pulling her right up against him and kissing her senseless. Absolutely infuriating that he was having so much trouble keeping his desire in check.

"That's two staring contests you've lost to me tonight," she said, preening. "Guess I'll just call you Bubba now, because there's a new alpha around these parts and her name is Remedy Lane. Kiss that, Chief!"

No doubt about it, if he survived this night without throwing Remedy over his shoulder and dragging her off to his house, caveman-style, it was going to be some kind of miracle.

Thank goodness there was a line at the food window, because Remedy needed the time to get a grip. What had gotten into her tonight? One minute she was reveling in her ability to irritate Micah, and the next she was flat out flirting with him. And not just flirting but also touching him too much, wondering what his lips would feel like against hers. She wanted him in a major way. And that just wouldn't do.

From this point forward, she'd be distant and polite. She'd chow down her burger in a most unsexy way, insist on paying him back for her meal, and demand to be returned to her car. In fact, she didn't even have to sit and make small talk with him while they waited for their food to arrive. She could dance. She wanted to fit in in Texas, and that would never happen by sitting at a sticky bar table watching the world happen all around her.

As if in answer to her dilemma, the final notes of a guitar-heavy dance tune faded and the band called everyone onto the dance floor to learn a line dance called the Cowboy Charleston. She'd never heard of it, but the way the crowd turned electric at the announcement piqued Remedy's interest. So she figured, *When in Rome . . .*

She slipped off her chair and joined a line of women at the back of the dance floor. A quick survey of footwear confirmed her duck-out-of-water status. She was the only woman not wearing cowboy boots. She hoped her open-toed three-inch Valentinos wouldn't prevent her from boogying down to the Cowboy Charleston—or get her feet maimed by a boot-wearing dancer with two left feet.

Note to self: Buy some boots, stat. She could only guess what her friends in L.A. would have to say about that.

A perky young waitress wearing a white cowboy hat hustled to the front of the dance floor and ran through a quick tutorial on the steps. Remedy could only see the waitress's hat bobbing above the crowd and couldn't hear a thing except the ladies in front of her gabbing about Miranda Lambert's latest hit, but when the music started she concentrated on following the legs of the women around her, getting into the rhythm. For the most part, she turned at the right time, managed not to kick anybody or get kicked herself, and even shook her moneymaker when the choreography demanded.

On a turn, Micah caught her eye. He was sitting at their table and the only word she could think to describe the way he was watching her was *hungry*. That was some trick the bar's warmly lit atmosphere was playing on her eyes. He was probably glowering. He probably hated that she was enjoying herself independent of his company. She smiled brighter, shook her ass harder, and put on a show.

When the song ended, the band segued seamlessly into another dance-ready song, though most people were free-styling instead of line dancing anymore. After darting a glance at her table to see if the food had yet arrived, which it hadn't, she stayed on the floor. She glommed onto a group of friendly-looking women about her age and managed to enjoy herself despite Micah's unwavering gaze for another couple songs.

In no time the waitress in the white cowboy hat was back, this time to teach them the Darlin' Mambo. As the first notes of the song reverberated through the room, a hand curved on her waist and the scent of maleness hit her nose. Micah.

"Enjoying yourself?" he rumbled into her ear.

"I am."

"I haven't seen any sugar daddies throwing dollar bills at you yet."

She turned to face him, to watch those lips curving in amusement. He did not release his hand from her waist or back up to give her space.

"Imagine my disappointment," she said. Could he hear the flustered quality of her words? Could he guess at how his nearness was affecting her, despite her valiant effort to ignore her reaction?

He nodded toward their table. "The food's here. And these burgers are too good to eat cold."

She forced herself to break away from him and leave him to trail her to their table, where two towering burgers and two frosty pints of beer sat waiting. "It's about time. I'm starving."

It was a good thing that the band was so loud, because Remedy's reaction to her first bite of her burger was downright orgasmic. The bun was warm and squishy, the lettuce, pickles, and onions crisp. Salt and smoke and spice exploded in her mouth. She raised her left hand heavenward in a hallelujah act of praise as she chewed and swallowed. This place was, indeed, burger nirvana.

Micah folded his arms over his chest and leaned his chair back. "I'm ready."

She was too impatient for her next bite to talk. "For what?"

"Go on. Say it."

She closed her eyes to block him out so she could concentrate on the flavor tsunami happening in her mouth, making him wait for her answer until she'd taken her time enjoying that second perfect bite. "You were right. This is the best burger I've ever eaten. But—"

"No buts. It's the best burger, period."

This was true, but she wasn't about to miss an opportunity to harass him. "But how can I be sure it's the best, period? I'll never know if it's better than Petey's because I was kidnapped before I had a chance to make a comparison."

She silently congratulated herself at coming up with such an inspired word as *kidnapped* on the spur of the moment like that.

Sure enough, he choked around his bite of food. "Kidnapped?"

"That's my story and I'm sticking to it."

Keeping one bemused eye on her, he gulped his beer. "No comment."

That was a lazy way out of their back-and-forth, but Remedy didn't mind. The silence made it easier to keep chowing down. Not that slowing down was a realistic option. Frankly, she was afraid to set the burger on her plate lest the entire messy creation fall apart.

As a rousing, banjo-heavy two-step played out before them, Micah polished off the last of his food, though Remedy followed him shortly. That had to be some kind of speed-eating record.

"You're a fast eater like me," he said.

"Some things are too damn good to go slow." She didn't realize the flirty innuendo until the words were out of her mouth. Her face flushed hot.

Micah drank some beer, then cleared his throat. "Now that the beast has been fed—"

"Did you just call me a beast?"

"You keep calling me Alpha Bubba, whatever that means, so I figure it's open season on nicknames. Would you rather I call you a virgin librarian?"

Not so much. She'd rather be a beast any day of the week. "As you were saying, now that the beast has been fed . . ."

He shifted his body toward hers, his knee rubbing up against hers. "I've got a question."

The urge to set her hand on his knee was a strong one. Instead, she gripped her beer and let the chilled glass cool her overheated thoughts. "Let me guess. You want to know how my parents chose the name Remedy? Everybody asks me that."

"No. You grew up in the real Hollywood, if I recall, so a crazy Californian name makes perfect sense."

"Is it about my life growing up in Hollywood?" she said.

"Not unless there's anything noteworthy about growing up there that you're inclined to mention."

Her whole upbringing and parentage were considered noteworthy to most people, but Micah had a deep mistrust of rich people and she had no interest in introducing her privileged childhood and celebrity status into the conversation now that she and Micah were finally getting along. "Nope."

"Okay then. Here's my question. Why wedding planning?"

Her parents asked her that all the time, and her answer was always the same. "Why not?"

He scratched the back of his neck, then adjusted his ball cap. "I've gotten the feeling that you're not some gushy romantic type, so your job doesn't make a lot of sense. You're stubborn and you like to get your own way, as you've demonstrated abundantly to me, but planning a wedding puts you at the mercy of whoever hired you. Which has me curious. Why wedding planning?"

He was right. Where he was concerned, she'd been absolutely stubborn. But the role she played in her job was different with the brides and grooms who hired her. "You're right. I'm not a hopeless romantic, and I'm definitely stubborn. I fell into wedding planning from corporate event planning because weddings are even more of a challenge. The bride and groom, their parents, all those complex family dynamics, and working with a budget and with hotels and vendors. The list of challenges goes on and on.

"Every wedding is a gauntlet of negotiations and complicated problem solving. And when I do it right, when I solve the puzzle and all the pieces click into place, I've masterminded the most memorable day of a couple's lives. It's extraordinary work."

He nodded. "You make it sound extraordinary. You also make yourself sound like a megalomaniac, masterminding the most important day of someone's life," he said with a smile and a wink, which she returned.

"That's it. You've discovered my secret. I'm drunk on my own power."

"I knew it." He produced a toothpick from God-knows-where and positioned it between his lips. "Your turn. Ask me a question."

"All right. What's up with you and toothpicks?"

His wolfish smile carried all the way up to his eyes. "I like having something for my tongue to play with."

Clearly, it was a canned reply, meant to ruffle feathers— and it certainly did tonight. A coil of desire tightened inside her, hot and low-down. She fought to keep her cool demeanor, though her pulse raced. She bet all the ladies giggled and blushed when he let that line roll out in that lazy drawl of his, but Remedy decided to take his words as a challenge. If he was going to flirt with her, then she could beat him at that game, too.

She took a sip of beer, then licked her bottom lip, nice

and slow. "Have you considered getting your lip pierced so your tongue has a more permanent plaything?"

With a slow blink, the playful spark in his gaze turned dark, covetous, the same heavy-lidded gaze as he'd looked at her with while she danced. He lifted his beer to his lips. She watched the roll of his Adam's apple with his swallow, trying not to squirm in discomfort though the silence that stretched between them was thick with implication.

She wasn't supposed to be flirting with her nemesis. She wasn't supposed to be thinking about his lips or that gorgeous, hard body. She wasn't supposed to be wondering what it would be like to be his tongue's permanent plaything, but the lid was off that Pandora's box and there was no replacing it now.

She tore her gaze from him and let out a long, slow exhale. A familiar face near the door caught her attention. The shock of it made her gasp.

She pressed her hands to the table and whipped her attention back to Micah. "I can't believe she's here. Do you know who that is?"

He craned his neck to follow Remedy's line of sight. "Of course. Ty Briscoe's daughter and her husband. Carina and James Decker. Most people consider them royalty round here."

Carina was dressed casually in dark jeans and a flowing white cotton top. Her blond hair was pulled back with a red headband. Her husband, whom Remedy only knew by name, ran the stables at the resort. By the look of him tonight, he fit his cowboy reputation from head to toe. Not in the way all strapping Texas men like Micah exuded a cowboy essence, but in a bona fide horse-wrangling, bow-legged, sun-kissed tan kind of way.

"You seem distressed that they're here," Micah said. "Are you having problems with Carina or something? Because I got on with her as good as could be expected when she was the resort's wedding planner. Everyone seemed to like her all right."

Remedy was distressed, though she couldn't put her finger on why. She picked up the damp cocktail napkin. "I've only met her once, my first day on the job. But Carina is a legend at the resort, the patron saint of wedding planning who's responsible for putting Briscoe Ranch Resort on the map."

"I thought Granny June held that title."

Remedy was still getting used to the force of nature that was Granny June, who attended every single wedding held at the resort and had a penchant for inserting herself right in the middle of wedding prep so she could snap photos for the resort's Facebook page. "Maybe they share it."

"Can you share a sainthood?" Micah asked.

"You're missing the point."

Micah focused all his attention on Remedy. His hand fell on hers, stilling her progress in ripping the napkin to shreds. "Enlighten me."

With one eye tracking Carina and her husband, Remedy tried to explain. "Alex, along with Emily Ford, the special event caterer at the resort, takes every opportunity to remind me that I could never live up to the bar Carina set."

Micah had the gentlemanliness to cringe. "Do they really say that outright?"

"Alex only in so many words, but Emily, yes."

"Ouch."

As though on cue, Emily appeared by Carina and James's side dressed in a red-and-white floral sundress, her curly hair loose and flowing down to her shoulders.

Remedy's heart sank. "Shit. This is so bad. Emily can't see me here with you."

"Why not?"

"Word at the resort is that she's driven the last two event planners away because none of us can replace the sainted Carina. I've spent the past month trying to ingratiate myself to her and Alex, but Emily won't even give me a chance to prove myself. We finally bonded over our mutual annoyance of you and I was starting to gain some ground in her eyes."

Micah's fingers curled down over Remedy's hand. His thumb stroked her skin in soothing circles. "Glad I could help, I think."

Carina, James, and Emily stood near the entrance and craned their necks looking for seats. It was only a matter of seconds before they spotted the empty table that had just cleared out next to Remedy and Micah, so Remedy did the first thing that came to mind. She shot out of her seat and tugged on Micah's arm. "They're headed this way. Come on."

He allowed himself to be dragged across the dance floor. They wove through the dancers until they were safely in the shadowy corner on the far side of the dance floor, between the emergency exit and the DJ stage.

Remedy took hold of Micah's arms and positioned him so that his back was to the bar, using him as a shield. She rocked up to her tiptoes to look over his shoulder at the unwanted bar patrons, who had assumed seats at the very table she'd predicted. Unless all three of them left or all went to the restroom at the same time, there would be no way for Micah and Remedy to get to the exit without the risk of being seen.

"So this is the big plan?" he said. "We hide here until they leave so you can keep up the illusion with your co-workers that you can't stand me?"

"I can't stand you. You're absolutely insufferable."

His hand brushed down her side before settling at the curve of her waist. "Right. Let's stick to that story. Back to your plan. What do we do now?"

She used his arm to steady herself and rocked up on her tiptoes to peek over his shoulder at Carina, James, and

Emily again. "I have no idea. My mind's all fuzzy. I can't think straight."

"Why's your head all fuzzy? You only had one beer, unless you've been sneaking tequila shots while I wasn't looking."

"Why indeed." She darted a glance at him but chickened out from meeting his gaze because he was looking at her like that again, like he had been at their table after her plaything comment. Hungry. Interested. "I meant because of the burger. I'm still coming down from that high."

He pressed his lips together, his eyes on the emergency exit sign. "Right."

"That was a great burger."

"Told you. But you had a great point that I should've let you eat a bite of a Petey's burger first so you'd realize exactly how grateful you should be that I saved you."

"Micah Garrity, the hero of Ravel County."

"That's me." The arm around her waist tightened a bit. His face grazed her hair.

Remedy wobbled. She took hold of Micah's shirt to steady herself on her tiptoes and a whiff of his scent tempted her nose. She'd first noticed in his truck that he smelled fantastic, like summer itself. As though he'd spent his day walking through fields of freshly mowed grass under the crisp summer sun. She wanted to bury her nose in his neck and take a long, slow sniff.

It wouldn't do. It wouldn't do at all. "You smell like bacon and ketchup," she said.

His hand slipped down to the small of her back. "Funny. I was thinking your shampoo makes your hair smell like a new car."

Then she did refocus her gaze on his face. "I smell like a new car? I think I'd rather smell like bacon and ketchup."

Clearly, he was fighting hard against a laugh, his lips

quirking and his cheeks sucking in. "Everybody loves that new-car smell."

His words struck her funny bone. She cringed through a snort of laughter at what a ridiculous corner they'd painted themselves into. Not only physically, in trying to dodge Remedy's coworkers, but with each other. Work nemeses who were predestined to be enemies but were out together at a bar, on a dance floor, flirting shamelessly. Smelling each other's hair and skin as they clutched in the dark.

"This is terrible. What are we going to do to get out of here?" Remedy said.

Micah tipped his head to the side, considering. "Well, I am a fire marshal. I guess I could run an unscheduled test of the emergency exit."

That reminded her of the question she'd meant to ask him before, until she'd gotten sidetracked by his toothpick and thoughts of his tongue. It wasn't like they had anything better to do while they bided their time while hiding. "Why firefighting?"

"Pardon?"

"You asked me why wedding planning, so now I'm asking you. Why firefighting?"

He blinked down at her. "You're asking me that here? Now?"

"You have any place better to be?"

With lips flattened into a tight line, he twisted to glance at Emily and the Deckers, then returned his attention to Remedy, all hint of amusement or playfulness gone. He ducked his head, bringing his mouth close to her ear. She was learning that was a habit of his; Every time he had something serious to say he got close and said it directly into Remedy's ear. "I've known I wanted to be a firefighter since I was eleven, when the Knolls Canyon Fire burned my whole neighborhood down. Leveled it in a matter of minutes. My siblings, my parents, and I piled into our minivan along with my best friend's family, who lived next door. We escaped with nothing but the clothes on our backs."

She loosened her grip on his shirt and smoothed her hand over her chest, over his heart. "Oh my God. That was the fire you mentioned earlier. The one that happened twenty-four years ago that Briscoe Ranch was indirectly responsible for?" At his nod, she added, "I had no idea."

No wonder he came down so hard on the resort about fire regulations. So many puzzle pieces fell into place.

His eyebrows flickered up. "No one who grew up in Central Texas will ever forget that fire. In my town alone, four people lost their lives that night. More than thirty people altogether in the county. And before you ask, yes, they caught who did it. Two rich teenage punks who were in town staying at Briscoe Ranch. The night of the wedding they were in town for, they stole a maintenance truck, drove out in the backcountry to smoke and drink. They brought sparklers that had been used in the wedding they'd attended that night."

"Wedding sparklers started the fire? I don't know what to say."

She wasn't sure what she'd been expecting him to say when she'd asked the question about why he chose to be a firefighter, but it sure wasn't anything that serious. She'd merely assumed he'd been drawn to the job because he'd been born with a hero complex. But now everything was clicking into place in her mind. His mistrust of Briscoe Ranch employees, his dislike of the wealthy. Why he and Alex butted heads at every turn. "That's what you meant last weekend when you asked Alex how he could be so flippant about fire safety after everything Xavier's family had been through. They were in that fire."

"I figured Alex had filled you in that day after I left."

"No. You're not his favorite subject and I was too chicken to ask."

He leaned so close that his lips brushed her earlobe.

"Xavier was the best friend I mentioned, the one who lived next door, who my family escaped the fire with."

Remedy blinked back. "What a small world that you were best friends as a kid with Alex's husband."

"That's the way it is in rural towns. We're still best friends, actually. Until Xavier quit to raise their kids, he was my top volunteer firefighter. We still go shooting every Sunday morning, and I'm one of Isaac's and Ivy's godparents."

Remedy pressed a hand to her forehead, overwhelmed by the amount of new information coming at her, least of which was the surreal nature of hearing the names of her boss's babies on Micah's lips. "Shooting? Like, with guns?"

His grin returned. "You're adorable, California."

"But you and Alex can't stand each other. He says you're a thorn in his side, but yet you're his kids' godfather?"

"One of the two godfathers, along with Alex's brother," Micah said. "And Alex is just as big a thorn in my side as I am in his, trust me. He's not my favorite person in the world, but we have a prickly truce in effect for the sake of Xavier and the twins. Like all worthwhile things in life, it's complicated."

She liked that idea. All the worthwhile things in life were complicated. She'd certainly found that to be true in her own life. She glanced past him, at Emily, Carina, and James. "I'm sorry about all this."

"What's that you're saying?" Micah cupped his ear, his voice mocking. "You're sorry about flouting my authority at every turn? I'm glad to hear that."

She gave his chest a gentle push. "Not that. I'm pretty proud of all the flouting I've done. I meant hiding in a corner like a couple of teenagers who don't want to get caught by their parents."

"If that analogy were accurate, we'd be necking right now."

Chill bumps skittered over her skin. Necking with the

town hero in a dark bar was a plan that sounded better and better by the second. As she contemplated the idea, Emily stood and headed toward the bathroom.

Remedy patted Micah's chest. "Emily's going to the restroom. This is our chance."

"You're not worried about Carina and Decker seeing us?"

"I've only met Carina once, so maybe she won't recognize me. It's dark in here."

"She'll recognize me," Micah said.

"Maybe she'll think you're here with some hot blond firefighter groupie."

He laughed outright. "Right. Because there are so many firefighter groupies in Dulcet." He took her hand. "Ready?"

Remedy drew a breath. "Ready."

"I'll lead." He started off around the edge of the dance floor.

"Of course you will, Alpha Bubba."

He swung his gaze over his shoulder and shot her a devilish grin that made her heart skip a beat. "There's only one Bubba in my family, and that's my dad."

"So you're Junior Bubba?" she called over the music.

"Junior's my older brother. What's wrong with calling me Micah?" He stopped just shy of the start of the dance floor and pulled her close. "Or, better yet, Chief Garrity."

She forced out a laugh. "Oh, you'd just love for me to call you that, wouldn't you?"

A slow smile spread on his lips. "I kinda would."

It was her turn to take the lead. Tugging him by the hand, she started moving again. "Come on. Before they see us."

They were nearly to the front door when a female voice called, "Micah! And Remedy Lane, is that you, too?"

Damn it. Resigned to their fate, they stopped walking. Micah squeezed Remedy's hand in a show of support. "I guess you're more memorable than you thought."

Remedy pasted a smile on her face and turned to Carina

and James, who stood tall and quiet behind his wife, his hands stuffed in his pockets.

After an exchange of pleasantries with Carina, Micah released Remedy's hand and offered it to James to shake. "Decker, nice to see you, man. Have you met Remedy yet?"

"Not before tonight, but I've heard plenty of rave reviews about the job you're doing at the resort," he said, shaking Remedy's hand. "If you're ever over by the stables, swing through and say hello."

Carina waved her hand in a circle that encompassed Remedy and Micah. "What's happening here, Micah? Since when do you socialize with resort employees?"

"This isn't social," Remedy said, perhaps a smidge too exuberantly.

"It's more a teacher/pupil interaction," Micah said.

Remedy nearly choked on her spit. "What?"

"Carina, it seems that you and Alex failed to teach your ingénue here about the perils of ordering burgers at Petey's Diner."

Carina's eyes bugged out. "You ordered a cheeseburger at Petey's?"

"It's not like this town comes with an instruction manual," Remedy muttered.

Micah draped an arm loosely across Remedy's shoulders, like they were old pals. "So, you see, I rescued her from burger hell and took it upon myself to enlighten her about this fine dining establishment. And that's the end of the story."

"Yep. The end," Remedy said, ducking away from Micah's arm.

"I see." Carina's gaze flitted between Micah and Remedy as though she wasn't buying that explanation for a second.

At that moment, Emily strode out of the restroom. Remedy startled, which Micah must have noticed, because he nodded toward the door. "If you'll excuse us, Carina and

Decker, we've got to dash. As you can see, Ms. Lane needs her beauty sleep."

The nerve. "Gee, thanks."

James, or Decker, as Micah called him, chuckled, shaking his head. "Have a good night, you two."

Micah sped his pace and burst through the front door with a nod to the bouncer. The moment he and Remedy were outside, he took hold of her hand again and hauled her along behind him at a faster clip than she would've preferred in the direction of his truck.

She tried to wriggle out of his grasp, but his grip held strong. "So I need my beauty sleep? That's rude."

He afforded her the barest of glances. "You didn't want me to give them the impression that there was something illicit happening between us, did you?"

With the same baffling impatience, he dragged her around to the passenger side of his truck. "Well, no, I—"

And then his hands were on her hips, crowding her against the truck door. His eyes were dark with a fierce hunger and the promise of untold pleasures. Something illicit *was* about to happen between them—and she couldn't wait.

He brushed his thumb against her lips, as though waiting for permission to proceed.

"Yes," she breathed, tipping her head back.

His thumb stroked her cheek. "Yes, what?"

He was so powerfully built, so intensely male, that her mind cleared of everything except pure, raw lust. "Yes, kiss me."

Their lips came together in a shock of sensation that snapped her body rigid. She rose up onto her tiptoes, every cell of her taut and straining, reaching for more, harder. Wrapping her hand around his neck, the other threading into his hair, she pulled him to her and got her tongue involved, daring him to give up the last shreds of his control and go wild with her.

Instead, he ended the kiss with a grunting exhalation. Breathing hard, he rested his forehead against the truck door above her shoulder. "You are trouble, California." His voice was little more than a hoarse growl. "And I don't like trouble."

His breath on her perspiring skin made her shiver.

He was right. Everything about what they were doing had the potential to be a whole lot of trouble. Already they were sneaking around to avoid her coworkers, and that was before they'd kissed. This town was too small for an affair with the fire chief to go unnoticed.

She splayed her hands over his chest. He was so fine, so exactly what she loved about men, the perfect blend of hard angles and muscled curves. So what the two of them together spelled trouble? Yes, she might be sabotaging her career for a second time, but as she pressed herself against Micah, his taste lingering on her lips and her body thrumming with need, the potential self-destruction seemed worth the risk.

"What's a town hero without a little trouble to keep him in business?" she said.

Her question seemed to jolt him out of his thoughts. He pulled his face back and sought her gaze, then took her cheeks in his hands. Could he feel the pounding of her pulse in his fingertips the way she felt his heart thudding fast against her palms?

Then his lips descended over hers again, harder than before. He pinned her body against the truck and took her mouth in a deep, wet, absolutely dirty kiss that went on and on until she was dizzy and lost and loving it. His hand dragged down her body, curving over her breast, her waist, and around to clutch her ass. She melted into him like liquid, offering her complete surrender to his touch and to his mouth—to his masterful command of her body.

This time when he broke the kiss, she was the one panting. He kept his face near hers, breathing into her. She fluttered her eyes open and found him looking at her.

That fierce hunger remained in his eyes. "My bed or yours?"

His gruff voice made her whole body ripple with anticipation. Goddamn, she wanted this tonight. She wanted him. Worse than she'd wanted a man in a long time. If he screwed anything like he kissed, then she was in for the time of her life.

"You're the Alpha Bubba. Surprise me."

Chapter Seven

"Buttons open," Micah bit out.

He kept one eye on the dark road and the other on Remedy's purple skirt, on the way it bunched high on her thighs, showing off those legs that he couldn't wait to get his mouth on. Anticipation pounded beneath his skin, flooding his muscles and flesh and organs with a need that threatened to unravel him.

The air in the truck cab was thick with intention as she followed his command, making a show of releasing each button on her shirt. She hitched a knee up on the seat, twisting to face him, and spread her shirt open. He hissed through gritted teeth at the sight of her breasts rounding over the tops of two beige, lacy bra cups, her flesh moving with each labored breath through her parted lips.

Smooth talking wasn't his forte and would've taken far more brainpower than he currently possessed, but if he could've found the words he would've told her how sexy she was, how beautiful. He would've told her how his desire for her had built to a crescendo through the night, with every fractured conversation and touch of their hands or bodies, until he could think of nothing else but kissing her, nothing else but pleasuring her slow and sweet and all night long. He would've told her it'd been a long, long time since a woman had made him so crazy with lust that he felt like a teenager again—impatient, invincible, and absolutely reckless.

At least his conscience had shut up about that whole fraternizing with Briscoe executives rule. Remedy Lane was one regret who'd already proved to be worth it.

He couldn't get the correct angle to touch her breasts, but her legs were more than enough to feed his hunger to touch her until they arrived at his place. He wrapped his hand around her knee, his fingers brushing the sensitive skin on the back of her thigh.

With a hum of pleasure, she widened her knees and slouched, shifting his hand higher, to the hot, silken skin of her inner thigh.

His heart was beating out of his chest. He blinked straight ahead, forcing his focus back to the road. All this foreplay would be for nothing if he got them in an accident. Lucky for him, the streets were empty.

She squirmed and fluttered her hand over his wrist. "A little higher."

If that's what the lady needed. He reached, caressing her flesh as he moved, until the sides of his fingers bumped the damp fabric between her thighs. *Fuck*. Ten minutes. They'd be at his house in ten. Naked and on his bed in ten and a half.

He rotated the pads of his fingers over the fabric, over the plump and pliant flesh below it. Then she rocked her hips, working in counter-rhythm to his fingers, using him for her pleasure. With a ragged breath, she threw her head back against the seat and lifted her chin, her eyes closed. Moving, feeling. Her arms flew out. One gripped the door handle and the other found his shoulder. It was the hottest damn thing he'd ever seen.

He stopped his ministrations and hooked a finger inside

the crotch of her underwear. With a flick, he snapped the elastic against her skin. "Take 'em off."

Even as he growled the command, he was berating himself to slow the hell down and ease off the heavy petting until he could lay Remedy back and do her right. Too late now, though, because Remedy was definitely on board with the road lovin' plan. Her hair cascaded around her face as she wriggled out of the lacy material and looped a leg hole over his rearview mirror.

Bold move. Sassy. Like her.

He couldn't resist the temptation to touch the underwear, to find that wet spot. When he did, he rubbed the material between his fingers, choking back a groan of approval. "So fucking hot."

She took hold of his wrist and moved his hand between her thighs. "I was thinking the same about you."

"Darlin', you ain't seen nothing yet." He dipped a finger between her folds. At his first touch of the hot, wet flesh between her folds, he accidentally jerked the steering wheel and swerved onto the shoulder. Like he'd thought before, it was a damn good thing the roads were empty tonight.

His finger found the swollen pearl of her clit and swirled over it until she released a strangled cry. He kept at the movement, working a relentless little circle over the bundle of nerves. Her hand flew back to his shoulder, balling his shirt in her fist as her body sought its pleasure with his hand.

He slowed his movement because he didn't want her to come like this, here in his truck. Not really. Because he wouldn't be able to watch her succumb and she wouldn't get to move or scream as she needed to, seeing as how he'd just made the turn onto Main Street and there were a few folks out and about. But there was nothing saying he couldn't get her right to the edge.

He barely registered the last few blocks home or pulling to a stop in his driveway.

The second he threw the truck in park, she pressed his seat-belt release, then climbed over to straddle his lap. She had the button and zipper of his jeans undone in seconds flat. His cock surged against his briefs, eliciting a grunt of relief at the release of pressure. She rubbed him over the cotton, and even that dulled touch had him gritting his teeth at the assault to his senses.

He slipped his hands around to cup her backside beneath her panties as her lips and teeth found his neck. Then her hand breached the elastic band of his briefs. Her fingers found the blunt tip of his cock.

He threw his head against his seat and rolled his neck, fighting for composure. A light in a window of the firehouse caught his attention. Tonight Dusty was manning the fire station. He would've heard Micah's diesel engine pulling into the drive, and for all Micah knew, he'd come to the window to call out a hello and check in with Micah, as he often did. There were decent odds he'd already gotten an eyeful of Remedy's partially naked body. No good. Time to move this party inside.

Micah swabbed a hand over his face, getting a grip. "Let's go inside. I want you naked, but not in my driveway."

She gave him a dreamy blink of her eyes. "That's probably a better idea."

He made a clumsy attempt at rebuttoning Remedy's shirt before she took over the task. "Why are we parked next door to the firehouse?" she asked.

"This is where I live. The house is owned by the city." He dropped his mouth over hers with a kiss that turned sloppy fast.

Locked together, they poured out of the driver's side and onto the driveway. Micah didn't bother refastening his pants as they shuffled, kissing and touching, to his front door. He couldn't get enough of her, any of her, not her mouth or the way she smelled, the feel of her hair, the taste of her skin, and the sound of her voice. The whole Remedy package made him drunk with lust. In a haze, he pushed the front door open and the tripped inside, right over a paper bag on the doorstep that he hadn't seen.

More baked goods? That made twice this week, which was rare.

"What was that?" Remedy asked.

He tossed the bag on his entryway table, then kicked the door shut. "I'll tell you later."

He gathered her close, but she pressed a hand to his chest.

"Are you sure you want to do this?" she asked, her voice breathy and strained.

"What kind of question is that?" Was she having second thoughts, because she sure wasn't acting like it and he didn't think he'd read her signals wrong.

"You were reluctant before, when we were kissing outside the bar," she said. "I wanted to make sure I wasn't taking advantage of you. Consent and all that."

The ridiculous comment tickled his funny bone, evoking a chuckle. Wasn't it supposed to be the other way around, with the obligation falling to the guy to check in with a lady's consent? Then again, they did things pretty backward in California.

She gave his chest another gentle shove. "I'm serious. Are you sure about this? You and me together, you were right, it's going to be complicated."

Damn. She was serious. And she was correct. He had been reluctant at the bar. Probably he should still be, because the list of reasons why sleeping with Remedy was a terrible idea was a long one. But he didn't give a damn about one single reason on that list.

He answered her by pulling his boots off and chucking them aside. He shoved his briefs and jeans down and off. His cock sprung up, steel hard and getting harder under Remedy's hungry gaze. He didn't give much thought to his body except to keep it at the peak of fitness for his job, but times like this, standing naked in front of a beautiful woman, his demanding workout schedule didn't seem such a burden.

She let her fingers bump from his chest down the ridges of his abdominals. "You should never wear a shirt. Ever."

He snorted out a chuckle. Guess she liked his answer. Since she'd checked in with him, it seemed only right to bounce her question back at her, even though the flush on her skin, the fervency of her kisses, and the way her fingers were dipping ever nearer to his goods spoke plainly that she wanted him as desperately as he wanted her.

"What about you? Do I have your consent to proceed?" What strange words. Formal. As though they were about to enter a legally binding partnership instead of have a one-night stand.

Only one night? He hoped not, but the question fled his mind when she backed up, struck a seductive pose, and made short work of unbuttoning her top.

She spread the shirt open and plumped her breasts in her hands, giving him a show. "You have my enthusiastic consent."

Her bra was sheerer than it'd appeared in the dim light of his truck. Stiff pink nipples squished against the material and, frankly, looked like they needed rescuing from their tight confines. Micah was just the man for the job. Fingers twitching with eagerness, he stepped toward her, but she matched his movement and skittered a few steps back while crooking her finger, teasing him to come and get her.

He didn't notice that she'd bumped against the coat tree near the door until it teetered. Micah lunged past Remedy, reaching for it, but he was too late. Top-heavy with a pile of coats and jackets, the tree toppled sideways and smacked into the coffee table, knocking his fern off the edge of the table. It shattered with an explosion of terra-cotta and potting soil.

Remedy hovered over the mess, aghast, her hands gripping her hair, but there was no way in hell Micah was going to let a minor mishap interfere with the night he had planned for her.

"Oh my God. I'm sorry. I didn't—"

It was Micah's chance to do what he'd been dying to all night. He threw her over his shoulder in a fireman carry and hauled her straight to his bedroom.

Micah laid Remedy on his bed with a tenderness wholly opposite from the brute force he'd used to sweep her off her feet. The shaft of gray-blue moonlight from behind the gauzy curtain over the window illuminated his muscled arms and shoulders and cut a spotlight over his torso, shading and highlighting hard pecs and ripples of abdominal muscles that she was desperate to explore with her lips.

In the shadowy darkness, with the only sounds the subtle whir of the air conditioner and their heavy breathing, Remedy felt transported out of time, out of Dulcet. On his bed, with his powerful body curving over her, the world narrowed to heat and flesh and the irrepressible chemistry that drew them together like magnets.

The mattress dipped again as he brought his other knee onto the bed. She spread her legs, inviting him forward with a nudge of her feet to his sides. He dipped his head and kissed her. Clutching his back, she dragged him down on top of her. His skin was hot to the touch. Muscle and bone moving and flexing, powerful.

His body curved over hers. The openmouthed deep, wet kisses he gave her obliterated every coherent thought. All that existed was Micah and kissing and the white-hot ball of need building inside of her with every stroke of his tongue against hers. So much kissing. She was starved for the taste of his mouth, the spicy scent of his skin.

His hands roved over her body, touching her everywhere, as though mapping her physical form, pausing at her breasts. He broke their kiss and dropped his mouth over her nipple, suckling in a complicated rhythm of movements with his tongue and lips until she had no choice but to cry out with the bliss of it.

She snaked a hand between them and stroked his erection. Grunting, he moved to her other nipple and continued the same expert care. She stroked him, pulling skin over steel faster and faster until his hips got in on the action, moving in time with her.

Without notice, he rolled off her body and lay on his side against her. His hand found her pussy again. She arched, urging him onward. As in the truck, his touch was exploratory at first. She showed him with moans and whimpers where she wanted him to go. When the blunt tip of his finger hit the sweet spot on the side of her clit, her body was wracked with a shudder of ecstasy.

"Found it," he crooned, rotating his finger over the spot, over and over, absolutely relentless. Then his lips dropped over her tight left nipple and sucked.

Yes. "Harder," she whimpered.

"My mouth or finger?"

"Both," she bit out. The impossible ache of need turned molten. She felt the build of release with every scratch of his finger and relinquished her grip on his cock to roll her head back and submit to the all-consuming sensation.

She gave a strangled moan of protest when his lips left her nipple and traveled over her belly, even though she knew where he was headed. Even though she knew how fantastic it was going to feel.

Then he was between her thighs again. His chin and lips grazed the strip of hair on her mound. She gripped the sheet in both hands, hanging on to the buildup, the desperate anticipation.

He breathed a slow, hot stream of air onto her body's center.

"Micah." The word trembled out of her on an unsteady breath.

His fingers opened her and even that slight touch sent ripples of pleasure through her body. This was going to be good. It was going to be everything.

The flat of his tongue licked up the length of her tender flesh. She groaned at the torture of it. Normally, she liked it slow down there. She liked every fold and wrinkle of skin tended to by her partner's tongue, but tonight she was all about her clit and surrendering to the raw, wild pleasure of their explosive lust. Thank goodness Micah felt the same way. It took a little searching, but his tongue found the same hot spot as his finger had. She rewarded him with a cry and raked her fingers through his hair.

It wasn't long before she felt the building pressure again. "I'm close. Oh damn, so close."

His tongue stopped. She peeled her eyes open to find him looking up the length of her body. His chin and lips glistened with her wetness and his nostrils flared. Untamed, powerful. All hers.

"Come now or come while I fuck you? Or both? Tell me what you want." His voice was rough and thick, his breathing labored.

She loved that he asked. Loved the lack of assumptions about her body and her needs. She'd experienced a lot of first times with lovers and so understood how rare his approach was.

The pressure of her need for release verged on painful, but the prospect of having him inside her, of finding her pleasure while they moved together, was too alluring to resist. Straightening her leg, she skimmed the length of his body with her toes. "While you fuck me."

There was that wolfish smile again.

He pushed up and sat back on his heels, then stretched his legs off the bed. She squeezed her legs together as she watched him walk, drinking her fill of his flexed muscles and hard planes, of the jut of his thick, long cock.

Condom on, lube from a bottle in his nightstand. Such a classy move, like his asking was. He knew women's bodies. He cared about the details in a way few of her other lovers had, and the easy, confident way he commanded every aspect of her pleasure left her with nothing to worry over. No need for her to educate him or stroke his ego. She was free to relax into the way he made her feel and the way she wanted to make him feel—the way they felt together.

Then he was back on the bed, near her knees. He took hold of her ankles and propped her feet on his collarbone, which pushed her knees higher and tipped her hips up. He shoved a pillow under her butt.

"Ready?"

"Like you wouldn't believe."

He pressed his torso toward her, arching her back and pinning her lower body in place as he lined his cock up with her entrance. "Bet ya I do."

His lubed-up fingers found her clit again. He stroked in a tight circle, sending shocks of sensation coursing through her. "Is this position working for you?"

Despite her hazy grip on reality, the corners of her lips kicked up in a smile. *Such a gentleman.* "Yes."

He dipped two fingers inside and winced, groaning. "Damn, that's so fucking good."

"Take me, Micah."

With their eyes locked on each other, he did just that, sinking into her with a maddening slowness. The languid, easy coupling didn't last long before the raw, desperate desire that had been building between them all night gave way to a hard, fast fuck. She could see it in his face, the moment he let go of his control and gave in to his basest feelings, in his scowl, his bared teeth, in the way his eyes went distant and dark.

Her legs fell from his shoulders, spreading. He pitched forward, locking their bodies together again and surging deeper into her. She wrapped her legs around his waist and moved with him in a frenzied spiral to the end. She cried out with that first burst of release and clutched him tighter with her legs and arms as waves of pleasure rocked her body. He buried his face in her neck and his body jerked. His staccato breath cooled her perspiring skin as he joined her in rapture.

It took her a while for the haze to clear, and when it did she was lying side by side with Micah in his bed, their arms and shoulders touching. His eyes were closed and his chest heaved with labored breaths.

Holy shit. She'd slept with Ravel County's slow-drawling, toothpick-chewing, gun-toting, diesel truck–driving, fire-fighting Alpha Bubba. And it had been great. Damn great. *Wow.* That was going to take some time to sink in.

He rolled his head to the side. "What are you smiling about?"

"I think I need a post-sex cheeseburger."

He let out a belly laugh that would have shaken the heavens. It was a wonderful sound, rich and warm. "I've created a monster."

"We should probably talk about our jobs."

"Do we have to?"

Yes, they did. There was so much they needed to say, so many details to work out, because this couldn't be their only time. She wanted endless summer nights like this one. She wanted to ride their affair until it crashed and burned. Or until she left for Los Angeles again. It was bound to be complicated given their careers, but their raw, wicked connection would make up for that in spades.

She mustered her courage, then laid it out there for him. "Once wasn't enough for me."

He rolled to his side and tucked his hand under his pillow. Even in the dim moonlight, she saw his eyes glimmered with sincerity. "You read my mind, but that's about the only thing I know for sure right now. I keep circling back to what happened at Hog Heaven when your coworkers showed up. I keep thinking about how we need to keep this totally separate from our jobs."

She raked her fingers across his chest. "Our little secret."

"I like the way that sounds."

"To be clear, I'm not going to stop fighting to give my clients every last detail of their dream weddings just because you and I are . . ." She almost said *romantically involved*. But this wasn't romance, and she sincerely doubted the two of them had much in common beyond their physical compatibility. Their worlds were too disparate. "Because we slept together."

"Understood. I'm not going to bend the law for you or for the resort, even knowing how crazy sexy you look in my bed."

Her neck flushed hot. That was one way of putting it. "You're going to hate the weddings I have coming up this weekend."

She expected a groan or even a swearword, but he tucked a strand of her hair behind her ear. "Is it wrong that I'm looking forward to battling it out with you?"

He bent his face toward hers, but as their lips brushed, a radio on the bedside table buzzed, then chirped to life. "Chief, it's Dusty. We've got a Signal Two with a possible vehicle fire, in the southbound lane Route 275 just inside the Ravel County limits. Riverfield and San Angelo were also called in."

Micah cursed under his breath. "Speaking of my job." He swiped the radio up. "Roger that, Dusty. I'm on my way. Call Chet?"

"He's en route," Dusty said. "See you in a minute."

Micah stuffed his legs into a pair of slacks. "This is the part of the job I don't like."

Remedy grabbed a T-shirt from his closet and pulled it over her head. "Why? What's a Signal Two?"

He yanked a navy blue polo shirt from a hanger. "Major vehicle accident with possible injuries. Which is also a part of the job I don't like, but I was talking about having to run out on you like this. I'm really sorry."

How could she care about their night being cut short when somebody might be hurt in a car accident? "If someone's hurt or there's a fire, then that's where you need to be. Nothing to be sorry about."

"Grab that radio please." He wedged his feet into a pair of lace-up boots. "You'll stay until morning?"

Radio in hand, Remedy followed him out of the bedroom, toward the front door. "Can't. Saturday's my busy day. I've got to be at the resort early."

He rummaged through his discarded jeans for his wallet. "I'm driving my truck to the crash, but wait here and I'll take you to your car when I'm back."

She picked up his keys from the entryway table. "The diner's only a block away. An easy walk."

"Don't go doing something dangerous like walking in the dark alone."

His protectiveness was sweet, even if she was already charting her midnight walk to the diner. But she didn't plan to burn up any more of his response time debating it with him. She handed him his radio and keys. "Roger that, Chief."

He stuffed the radio in a pocket, angled in for a kiss that was awkward enough to remind Remedy that they were still strangers, even after all they'd done. "Lock the door behind me, okay?"

"Don't worry so much. I can take care of myself."

With a cringe, he glanced from her to his poor upside-down fern.

She shoved him out the door. "Oh, shut up."

"Woman, I didn't say nothin'!" he called as he jogged across the driveway to the firehouse and out of sight.

Not more than a minute later, the paramedic truck roared out of the firehouse garage, its sirens wailing and lights flashing, with Micah following close behind in his truck. Remedy opened the window and propped a hip on the sill to listen to the siren and watch Micah's taillights until they disappeared around a corner. What a noble and scary life, to be the one to run toward danger and injury no matter the hour, to be the one with the skills and mental fortitude to drop everything and save lives and restore order to the world's chaos.

When silence descended on the house again, she closed the window and turned to deal with the mess she'd made. She shook potting soil out of Micah's jackets and righted the coat tree, then found a broom and dustpan in a kitchen closet. The poor fern's pot was ruined, so she repotted it in a mixing bowl the best she could, pressing potting soil around the base and cooing and apologizing to the wounded plant for being so impossibly out of balance with her surroundings.

It wasn't until she'd tripped over Micah's cowboy boots while donning her work clothes that the reality of her situation seized hold of her again. She was half-naked in an Alpha Bubba's house after he'd seduced her with bar food at a sawdust-covered roadside joint called Hog Heaven. Growing up, she'd been cultured to be a champagne and caviar girl. Sports cars, not diesel trucks.

"Suits, not boots," she whispered on a groan. What a narrow-minded snob she'd been.

She walked the boots to Micah's bedroom and lined them up in front of the closet next to a half-dozen other pairs. Like the rest of his house, his bedroom was tidy and awash in blues and reds, from the paint on the walls to the plaid bed linens. Patriotic, masculine—perfectly Micah.

She tugged the sheets flat, then flipped the quilt into place on the bed.

"Ho-ly shit," she said, drawing out the words in slo-mo

before descending into laughter. Only the underside of the quilt was done in plaid. Spanning the entire top was a massive red fabric map of Texas.

She smoothed her hand over the gold felt star that had been sewn over Dulcet's approximate location. "Oh, Micah. You proud, proud redneck." The teasing on this—it was going to be merciless. She couldn't wait.

Whistling and light of step, not only with the giddiness over the Texas quilt but also her top-rate Big O, she finished dressing. On the table nearest to the door sat the paper bag they'd tripped over on their way into the house. She grabbed it, curious. Before she had the bag open, she smelled cinnamon and sugar.

"Score," she said with a laugh. Inside she found two fat cinnamon rolls, their tops thick with glossy white icing. Forget about a post-sex burger; she'd take a cinnamon roll after a roll in Micah's bed any day of the week. What a wild and wonderful night all the way around. She wasn't even going to try to guess why he'd had sweets sitting in an unmarked bag by his front door.

A cinnamon roll in hand, she strode down the quiet street, feeling satisfied and full of joy. No one bothered her on her walk and the only sign of life she saw was a flock of homing pigeons roosting on her car roof.

Chapter Eight

The photographer was thirty minutes late to the chapel, and Remedy couldn't get him on the phone. Her Big O afterglow had given way to sleep-deprived nerves that weren't coping well with the task of wrangling seven bridesmaids and seven groomsmen, along with the bride's and groom's families and stepfamilies—all of whom had arrived at the chapel waiting for pre-wedding photographs at varying levels of intoxication. She was jumpy enough as it was anticipating a showdown with Emily and Alex over her hookup with Micah. There was no way Carina hadn't told Emily that she'd seen them at Hog Heaven. Remedy had girlfriends; she knew how the gossip superhighway worked.

Well, Emily and Alex were just going to have to deal, because Remedy had no plans to take sides in the ongoing war between the resort and the fire department. Actually, now that she was considering it, being caught in the middle made a kind of poetic sense, as it seemed to be her lot in life to forever be a floater between worlds.

Remedy's ringtone sounded. "Finally," she muttered, slipping out of the chapel for privacy so the families didn't have to hear her bitch out the photographer for his tardiness.

When she saw the readout of who was calling, frustration flooded through her all over again. Not the photographer, but her mother. She really had to stop texting her mom in the morning before work, because nine times out of ten her mom returned her call at the worst possible moment. It was uncanny.

"Hi, Mom."

"Got your text. What's new?"

Deep breath, nice and calm. No need to take her frustration about the photographer out on anyone else. "Missing you, as always."

"I'm missing you, too, sweetie. So much. But I bet that's not why you called this morning. There's something else going on with you. Something personal."

Though her mom had been pulling semi-clairvoyant stuff like that all Remedy's life, Virginia retained the ability to amaze her. Her mom's sensitive intuition probably had a lot to do with why she was such a flawless actress. What would it be like to be so innately talented? A shimmer of envy made itself known until Remedy beat it back, as she always did.

Yes, she had called her mom to fill her in on the latest developments of her personal life. Not her first choice, but there was no one else to talk to about Micah. Any of the fledgling friendships she was forming in Texas were with her coworkers, and if she'd told her friends in Los Angeles they would've been horrified that she'd gone and done exactly what they'd warned her against. *Maybe they're not such great friends, after all.*

After a scan of her surroundings to make sure she couldn't be overheard, she sat at the bench on the edge of the chapel's hill. "I kissed someone last night."

She'd done a lot more than that, but, hello, boundaries.

Mom gasped. "Remy, you've only been in Texas for a month. How is that possible?"

Remedy started to answer, but her mom cut her off.

"Wait! That was a horrible question. Of course the gentlemen in Texas are falling all over themselves to get your attention. You're irresistible."

"Thanks, Mom. This man is pretty irresistible, too." Her cheeks heated. God, had she really said something so corny? Even if it was true.

"Tell me everything," Mom said, sounding like an overeager celebrity news journalist. Remedy opened her mouth to answer, but her mom cut her off again. "No, wait! Let me pop a bottle of champagne. This calls for a celebration. Helen! We need champagne, please. And make it snappy."

Remedy drew a long, silent breath. Helen was there. *Okay. Fine.*

Helen West had been Remedy's mom's hairstylist forever, on set and off, and the two had become the best of friends. Remedy had distinct childhood memories of playing with Helen's daughter, Cambelle, who was Remedy's age, and of their challenging each other to hoist her mom's Oscar trophies over their heads. Cambelle and Remedy had managed to stay semi-close acquaintances over the years, even after Cambelle had decided she wanted to break into show business herself when they were in high school.

Helen transformed herself into the quintessential stage mom, and not long after Remedy's parents' divorce, when Remedy's mom had been lost and drifting, she'd followed Helen's lead by attempting to convince Remedy to take up acting, too. When it became clear that no amount of cajoling or impassioned monologues on the subject would sway Remedy, her mom abandoned the cause and threw her support and influence behind Cambelle's nonstarter of a showbiz career, much to Remedy's relief at the time. Since then, Cambelle had landed unmemorable roles in several dour indie movies but was still looking for her big break, much to Helen's and Remedy's mom's frustration.

Judging by the sounds of glee over the phone, Helen was as happy with the news of Remedy's love life as her mom was. Which meant it was only a matter of time before Cambelle—the author of the battle cry *suits, not boots*—heard the latest about Remedy's love life. So much for keeping her friends at home in the dark.

Cringing through a smile, Remedy looked heavenward, waiting patiently as Mom narrated Helen's pouring of the champagne. "There. I've got my champagne. Tell me everything about this boy you kissed."

"Not a boy. A man, Mom." A fine, strapping man with a slow Texas drawl and a way with his tongue.

Mom turned predictably giddy at that correction. "Oh my, that sounds juicy. Tell me more about this *man* you kissed."

Remedy didn't know where to start, which didn't matter, because Mom wasn't ready to cede the floor yet. "Wait! I have one more question first. He doesn't chew tobacco, does he?"

"Mom, please."

"You're in Texas. It's an honest question."

"Not all men in Texas chew tobacco." Good thing, too, because that would've been a deal breaker.

"Does he own a gun?" Helen called in the background.

"Tell Helen yes, he owns a gun. Probably a lot of guns." And he'd looked damn fine with one strapped to his hip that first day, if Remedy was being honest with herself.

Mom gasped. "Is he a Republican?"

Probably. No, definitely. "I have no idea."

"What did she say?" Helen asked.

"She doesn't know." Mom tsked, unappeased. "You're going to need to ask him that before you kiss him again. Or, for God's sake, before you even *think* of sleeping with him. I can't have my baby falling in love with a conservative."

"Mom. Come on. Would you stop lobbing Texas stereotypes at me? You grew up in Oklahoma, for crying out loud."

"Which is how I know what the men out there are like."

"You're being ridiculous and prejudiced."

"No, I'm being a mom. My heart would break if you gave me a brood of gun-toting, tobacco-chewing Republican grandbabies."

The description conjured the image of a roomful of toddlers holding toy guns and dressed in Ronald Reagan onesies. *Speaking of ridiculous.* "Like Grandpa Hartley was?"

The line was silent, then, "My dad was an exception to the rule, may he rest in peace. Was this man at least a gentleman to you?"

As if being a Republican gun owner made him some kind of barbarian by default. Except for Grandpa Hartley, of course. "He was a perfect gentleman." And by *perfect gentlemen* she meant the kind of man who fingered her to a near climax in his truck before hauling her over his shoulder to his bedroom and screwing her to a soul-altering orgasm. "Do you want to hear the story or do you and Helen have more questions?"

"I'm shutting up now. Continue."

Remedy rolled her shoulders. "Thank you. He's a firefighter. Actually, he's the Ravel County fire chief."

"He's a firefighter," Mom whispered, presumably to Helen, before humming her approval. "You get your taste in men from me, you know. Rugged. The most interesting man in the world types. I bet your man looks like Tom Selleck."

There was nothing to do but chuckle at her mom. As her father was fond of reminding Remedy, Mom was a wild child at heart and she always would be. But unlike her dad, who saw that quality as a personality defect, Remedy embraced her mom's eternal youthfulness.

"He looks absolutely nothing like Tom Selleck." *Thank goodness.*

"No firefighter mustache?"

"No, but he rocks a wicked five o'clock shadow."

Her mom sighed at that, weary. "These days, they all do, my dear. It's the new 'in' look. Lumberjack Chic. Beard abrasion is the worst. Did I ever tell you about rash on my lips inflicted on me by Robert De Niro? He and I were in that political thriller a few years ago, and he was quite the kisser, but—"

"Mom, can you never, *ever* again tell me about beard rashes you've gotten? Please?"

"Fine. Back to your firefighter. How did this night of kissing come about?"

How indeed. But that was a story for another time. "I have to get back to work. Big wedding tonight. But you and I will talk more tomorrow, okay?"

"At least tell me his name."

"Micah." As though summoned by the sound of his name, Micah's truck came into view on the resort's main entrance road. A thrill shot through Remedy and she couldn't stop a goofy smile from spreading on her lips.

"When are you going to see Micah the fire chief again?" Mom asked.

"At work? In about two minutes. Outside of work, I don't know. It's complicated."

Micah's words echoed in her mind. *Like all worthwhile things in life, it's complicated.*

Mom gave a dreamy sigh. "Complicated can be so much fun. All right, all right. I'll let you go. Good luck tonight. You just keep putting on world-class weddings and you'll be back to work in Los Angeles in no time."

That was the plan. "Gotta go, Mom. I love you."

Remedy turned to scan the resort for another sign of Micah's truck but jumped at the sight of Alex and Emily, grinning like fools.

"Congratulations," Emily said. "You and Micah, hmm?"

Congratulations? So much for the third degree she'd been expecting. "Micah and I were just grabbing dinner together last night. As friends."

"And kissing. As friends, right?"

Remedy cringed. "You weren't supposed to hear that."

Looking annoyed, Alex folded his arms over his chest. "I was afraid this might happen."

"Why? Does Micah go around seducing every new resort executive with cheeseburgers? Is that his big move?"

"Micah? No way. He has a policy against any firefighters fraternizing with the resort's staff. But at last week's wedding you two couldn't tear your eyes off each other."

"That's because we were arguing over Polynesian fire dancers. Nothing's happening with us." That was her story and she was sticking to it.

"Are you sure?" Emily asked. "Because it would be really good for the resort if it were. Maybe you can help him take that stick out of his ass. You know, butter him up. Keep him happy."

Again, that was not the reaction Remedy had expected. "Um . . ."

She chanced another look at Micah's truck and found him walking through the grass in their direction. "You guys better wipe those grins off your faces. He's almost here. Do *not* ruin this for me."

"Wouldn't dream of it," Emily said, though her Cheshire-cat grin did not inspire trust.

Alex threw his hands up. "I'm staying out it. I'll be in my office if you need me."

He marched up the hill toward the resort's main building.

Micah was dressed in a navy blue crewneck T-shirt embroidered with the RCFD logo identical to the one he'd donned last night when the radio call came in. He'd tucked the shirt into khaki slacks, belted at the waist—and not with one of the audacious belt buckles her mom might have expected from a gun-toting Republican. New to the ensemble were dusty black boots and a black cowboy hat. His barbed-wire tattoo cuffed his upper arm. No firearm and no toothpick, but just enough bad-boy attitude to command Remedy's full attention.

When he reached the bench he nodded first at Emily, then at Remedy. "Ms. Ford, Ms. Lane, good afternoon."

The man was all business, exactly as he and Remedy had agreed to be at work. "Chief Garrity, good to see you."

Emily started giggling.

"Don't you have some salmon to bake or something?" Remedy said.

"There's always time for awkward morning-after talk."

Terrific. Thanks, Emily.

Micah's lips twitched. He raised an eyebrow at Remedy.

Remedy gave him a small shake of her head. "She meant the morning after two friends enjoyed burgers at Hog Heaven. Right, Emily?"

If anything, Emily laughed harder. "I'll give you two lovebirds some privacy, but first"—she pulled a paper from her arm and handed it to Micah—"I happen to have a safety permit here for the Firefighters' Charity Ball that I'm going to need you to sign off on. I'll be serving Baked Alaska for dessert, delivered table-side."

Remedy rolled her eyes so hard at Emily's not-so-subtle transition that it was a wonder she didn't tear something in her eye sockets.

Micah frowned down at the document. "As in *delivered table-side while on fire*? You're pushing your luck with that plan."

"Surely there's some wiggle room for us to negotiate," Emily said. "After all, I'm doing you both a favor by keeping your affair a secret from Ty Briscoe. I can only imagine how he'd use that information to manipulate the situation."

What the frack, Emily? "Not so hard to imagine. It's probably a lot like how you're trying to manipulate the situation," Remedy said.

Emily shrugged, her palms up, the picture of sweet innocence. "What can I say? The culinary world is cutthroat. And for women? It's Darwinism all the way. Survival of the fittest."

Micah was not amused. "The safety of the people at the ball and in this hotel isn't negotiable—ever."

"You're blowing this out of proportion," Emily said. "It's an ice-cream dessert. The flames won't be active for more than thirty seconds, a minute tops. It'll be perfectly safe."

Micah glowered at Emily. "You do realize that this hotel is made almost entirely of wood, right? Old wood."

Emily yawned. "So you've mentioned."

With a sigh, Micah skimmed the permit. "This does look within the scope of the county's fire safety regulations, but I'll need a diagram of the layout first. Too many tables too close together could spell disaster if your staff's pushing trays loaded down with flaming desserts through the room. I won't risk it."

Emily handed him another sheet of paper. "I've got the diagram right here."

She must have lifted that right off the file on Remedy's desk. Emily wasn't using the principles of Darwinism; her tactics were Machiavellian all the way.

"I'll take this with me to the ballroom for today's inspection and give it some thought," Micah told Emily.

Emily seemed satisfied with that. "Deal, and you won't be sorry. My Baked Alaska is the best you'll ever taste. Guaranteed."

"Now that I do believe," Micah said.

"Smooth," Emily said.

"I have my moments."

Emily clapped Remedy's shoulder. "I think this is the

start of a beautiful relationship with the three of us." With that, she bounded down the hill toward the resort.

"This wasn't a calculated business decision!" Remedy hollered to her retreating form.

When Remedy looked at Micah again, his cheek muscle twitched, then a smile broke out on his face. He raised an eyebrow. "A calculated business decision?"

"Emily shouldn't have cornered you like that. It doesn't matter if she tells Ty Briscoe that you and I slept together, because there are no rules against it. Emily's just trying to get under our skin. There was a reason I didn't want her seeing us at Hog Heaven. I told you she's been trying to sabotage my job."

"You called it."

"Are small towns always like this?" Remedy said. "With everybody in everybody's business? I thought that was a cliché."

"Nope. No cliché. Welcome to Dulcet." His expression softened, turned intimate. "How are you this morning?"

"Awkward morning-after talk aside, I'm doing great." Except for the fact that she kinda wanted to drag him behind the chapel and see if he was as good a kisser as she recalled. If only she weren't in the throes of the wedding from hell with a missing photographer crisis to deal with. "But we should get busy. This wedding tonight has a lot of moving parts and I need to stay on my A game."

"Understood. But I'm not leaving here today without getting your number, something I was remiss in not doing last night."

"I think I can manage that."

He reached out and stroked her arm, his eyes all heat and intimacy, then wrangled his expression back into a neutral business face. Clearing his throat, he brandished a ballpoint pen that he'd pulled from his shirt pocket and made a show of clicking the end. "Let's start with the ballroom, shall we? You have the diagram of the layout for me?"

"Right here." She handed him a paper from her bag. While he looked it over, she dashed off her cell phone number on a sticky note and stuck it to the diagram.

He peeled it off and slipped it into his pocket, a private smile on his lips that was gone as fast as it'd appeared.

They took a golf cart around to the back of the resort where the grand ballroom's direct entrance was. The curved outer wall of the ballroom was entirely made of windows that looked across the resort's vast spread of land, which included the golf course and the lake beyond it. "The layout for tonight's wedding is standard," Remedy said as she drove. "The exits are easy to get to and the room is a hundred people under capacity, you'll be happy to know. The only fire element at all is the candles in the centerpieces, and I learned my lesson from last weekend. You'll see that they're in votive holders that are tall enough to contain the flames according to fire marshal regulations."

They were nearly to the ballroom's entrance when Remedy caught a swath of white in a tree. Those darned homing pigeons again. Remedy let out a curse that Gwyneth the elephant would've approved of.

"What's wrong?" Micah said.

"They're stalking me."

"Who?"

She swerved right, planning to hide the golf cart behind a tall hedge while she called Skeeter to come get his damned vermin already. "The pigeons."

"Those look like doves."

"I know, but they're really pigeons in disguise, and they're plotting against me." She pulled her phone from her bag as she navigated.

"I don't think their brains are large enough to plot against you."

"Doesn't matter. The beady-eyed bastards," she muttered.

"Remedy!" He jerked the wheel from her, but it was too

late. The golf cart slammed into a low cinder block and stucco wall protecting a knot of irrigation pipes and valves. Micah and Remedy pitched off their seats into the dashboard. Remedy's head knocked against the steering wheel, but none of that compared to the feeling of mortification that was sinking like a stone in her belly.

Micah's hands roved over her back, her arm, her hair, testing, searching like a doctor might. "You okay? Does it hurt anywhere?"

"I'm fine. I just—" She sat back in her seat and lowered her head to the steering wheel. "Not another golf cart accident."

His assessing hands stilled. "Exactly how many golf carts have you destroyed?" Amusement crowded out his tone of concern.

"*Destroyed* might be an exaggeration." At his raised eyebrow, she smoothed the fabric of her skirt and lifted her chin as though she had nothing to be ashamed of. *Yeah, right.* "Only three."

"Ever consider upgrading to an ATV?" Micah said. "Something sturdy and used to being roughed up. Something Remedy proof. Might save the resort a lot of money."

She gave his shoulder a shove. "What happened to Mister Big Town Hero, worried about everyone's safety?"

He had the audacity to chuckle. "Seems to me, this town needs more protecting from you than the other way around."

"Chivalry is dead."

"I am being chivalrous. I'll have you know that, out of respect for you, I'm refraining from wiping that cute-as-hell grimace off your face by laying a big, fat kiss on you because you're at work and we're about to be surrounded by your coworkers."

Remedy twisted to look behind them. Sure enough, maintenance and landscape workers were rushing their way.

With his clipboard out and ready, all business again, Micah slid out of the cart and dusted imaginary debris off his pants. Then he walked around to the driver's side and helped Remedy out.

Her body didn't feel sore, which was the first thing that'd gone her way all day.

"You sure you're all right?" Micah said.

"Fit as a fiddle."

"Good." He handed Remedy the ballroom diagram as well as Emily's safety permit, his signature of approval on both. "Diagrams look fine. I'm going to trust that you're not going to try to sneak Tito's fire dancers into the building or anything stupid like that from now on."

That was an unnecessary dig. Then again, he was backing off on his inspection, so who was she to complain? In fact, maybe a little sugaring up was in order. "I would never, because this place is a pile of tinder waiting to explode into flames."

He winked at her. "I'm glad we're seeing eye-to-eye on that."

"Yeah, well, I've heard the town's Alpha Bubba is not a man to be crossed."

He touched her shoulder, letting his hand linger there a shade too long to be professional. "Glad we're starting to see eye-to-eye on that, too." He eyed the growing crowd of resort employees working around the golf cart and inspecting the irrigation lines, then tipped his hat to her. "My work here is done."

She indulged in her desire to study the way his backside moved while he walked all the way back to his truck across the grounds, figuring she deserved the visual holiday given that she was just in a minor accident. He was nearly to the parking lot when Remedy's cell phone chimed with a text from a number she didn't recognize.

Is Sunday your day off?

Micah. At the top of Chapel Hill, he turned her way.

Though acres of lawn and garden paths separated them, she held his gaze as she typed her answer. *Yes.*

Pick you up at six for dinner?

Her heart did one of those flip-flop flutters. An actual bona fide date with Mister Big Town Hero Alpha Bubba. *Burgers again?*

I might change it up. Alpha's prerogative.

She shook her head at him, though she couldn't get the smile to wipe off her face. *As long as I get the same dessert as last night . . .*

It was hard to tell from so far away, but he looked to be grinning as big as she was.

Chapter Nine

Sunday morning, Micah stifled a yawn as he pulled into the dirt parking lot beneath the carved wooden sign announcing the Ravel County Rifle Range in bright red letters, a hill country landmark that had grown to popularity long before Micah's dad had brought him there to teach him how to use the birding shotgun he'd been given for his eighth birthday.

Xavier's car was already in the lot. Micah backed his truck into the spot next to it, then sat blinking into the sun, finishing the last of his coffee and trying to wake up.

Probably he had no business shooting a gun at all that morning, seeing as how he'd been up all night chasing down three small fires across the county. A brush fire outside Dulcet city limits that seemed to be the result of a lit cigarette being thrown from a car, a trash-can fire thanks to improper disposal of a firework leftover from Independence Day, and a house fire started by a bottle rocket that crashed through a living room window and ignited the upholstery. Good times.

Given the meager rainfalls the previous winter and the higher than average temperatures forecasted for the rest of the summer, the county land commissioner was hinting that a countywide burn ban was coming through the courts that would include fireworks, sparklers, and bottle rockets until at least October and even stricter bans in the backcountry on edgers, lawn mowers, and other heavy equipment that had the potential to spark a blaze.

Micah was all for that. Fire season had already ravaged sections of West Texas, and even though hill country wasn't directly affected yet, the risk remained high. Ever since fireworks had gone on sale during the weeks before Independence Day, his fire response radio had been chirping nonstop with reports of blazes across the state. It was like people couldn't celebrate their country without trying to burn it down.

After a night like he'd had, Micah wasn't prepared for the sight of Ty Briscoe stepping out of the driver's seat in the parking spot closest to the entrance. He was a scrappy, bald bulldog of a man who hadn't seemed to age a day since Micah had known him. The king of Ravel County—more like the bane of Micah's existence.

Ty looked right at Micah, as though he'd been anticipating Micah's arrival. He pulled a long black gun bag from the backseat of his truck, set it on the ground, crossed his arms over his chest, and leaned back, waiting. *Just terrific.* Micah's only way into the shooting range was going to be through his mortal enemy. *So be it.*

Stalling, he floated a fresh toothpick between his lips and dialed Xavier's cell phone number. He picked up on the second ring.

"Don't tell me you're not coming," Xavier said in lieu of a greeting.

"Naw, I'm here in the parking lot. Just one question: Why are we up so dang early on our morning off? I'm tired. Long night."

Xavier snickered. "Join the club. And we're here so early because it'll probably be pushing a hundred degrees on the range by mid-morning. Stop whining and get your ass in here. My Remington and I are ready to show you up."

Micah looked again at Ty Briscoe, who was now polishing an invisible smudge off a long black sniper rifle, a wad of chew under his lip and an arsenal of deadly weapons in a bag at his feet.

Micah supposed the rifle was to intimidate him. That was a cute theory.

Micah ambled out of his truck, nice and slow, then took his time strapping a holster around his waist. He snapped a full cartridge into his Taurus, loaded the chamber, and slid it to rest against his right hip. Grabbing his gun bag from the truck bed, he double-checked that his expression was full of bored confidence, then infused his walk to Ty with a loose-limbed swagger. Full Alpha Bubba mode, as Remedy probably would've called it.

Ty spit on the ground between them. "You look like hell, boy."

Every man was a *boy* or *son* to Ty Briscoe. Didn't matter that Micah stood a half head taller than him and had the law on his side, because Briscoe honestly believed he was above said law—which, to Micah's way of thinking, made him one of the most dangerous men in Texas.

"Look at you, slumming at a public range. Aren't you afraid our working-class values will pollute your delusions of grandeur?"

Briscoe pushed off his truck and squared up to face Micah. "Knew I'd find you here. I need a word."

My ass. "A word? Aw, come on. I know you didn't come here to chat me up and I hope you're not here trying to bribe me. I'd like to think you've figured out by now that you can't own me or my department like you do the rest of the county. Which only leaves one option. You're here to threaten me. Go on, then. Spit it out. I don't have time to wade through your bullshit."

A hard smile spread on Briscoe's lips. "You giving my new event planner hell yet?"

It was a turn of the conversation Micah hadn't seen coming. Micah's instincts sounded an alarm. Whatever Ty had cookin', if it involved Remedy there'd be hell to pay. "No more'n I usually give 'em."

"Not what I heard, which is the reason for our little chat this morning. Remedy Lane's connections are going to bring in a steady stream of high-end clientele that'll do wonders for the city of Dulcet. In fact, with that in mind, the city council just accepted my generous donation for a beautification plan to bring the city up to the same five-star quality as my resort. I've devoted a lot of time and money in this project and I won't have you interfering with my"—he rolled his tongue over his teeth—"let's call it an investment in Remedy Lane and what she represents."

Her connections? "You're going to have to spell out your threat more clearly, because I'm not following. How do you figure that me making sure your resort guests are safe is, in any way, interfering with your schemes?"

"What I'm saying is that, from now on, you are going to leave Remedy Lane alone, son. Professionally . . . and personally. She's too valuable an asset—to me and to this town—for you to go dicking around with her and send her running back to California in a fit of female histrionics with a broken heart."

Briscoe knew. Had Carina told him? Micah hadn't thought they'd had a close father/daughter relationship. Looked like he'd been wrong. Unless Emily had recanted on her word.

Forcing a grin to his lips, Micah hooked his thumb on his holster belt and chewed his toothpick. "And if I don't give a shit what you think?"

"Then I'll go before that same county council I just bought with that beautification money to present my vision for making Ravel County safer. It seems they don't realize that you're spread as thin as a one-man band, acting as both the fire marshal and the fire chief. It's time to hand some of those instruments off to others, ease your burden. I'll propose the appointment of a separate fire marshal position that'll answer to the county commissioners' office. Let you focus on fighting fires instead of enforcing minor ordinances and antiquated penal codes."

Well, goddamn. Micah's blood was boiling in an instant. He had to forcibly keep his smile glued on and his teeth from snapping the toothpick in half. He should have seen this coming, long before Remedy waltzed into the picture. Since Micah couldn't be bought, of course Briscoe would make a play to wrest Micah's authority from him and assign it to someone more amenable to bribery. Now that Micah was considering it, the only shock he should feel was that it hadn't happened sooner.

"I'm sure you've got a perfect candidate for fire marshal in your back pocket," Micah said. "But, just so you know, until that day arrives, expect that the vise grip I've had your balls in for the past ten years is gonna get real uncomfortable, real fast."

With a bark of a laugh, Briscoe grabbed his crotch. "That's funny, because my balls are feeling just fine. I'll tell you what, though; if you ever want to get that good vise grip on them that you're salivating to do, then you'll have to buy me dinner first. Maybe at Hog Heaven?"

"Clever."

"What'll it be, son? Do we have an understanding? You leave my employee alone and I'll let you continue with business as usual."

Micah had underestimated Briscoe's ruthlessness, but his eyes were wide open now. With all the scheming Briscoe had done to protect his so-called investment in Remedy—bribing the city council, coming here this morning to confront Micah—then it was only a matter of time before he went to Remedy directly and backed her into a corner. If he hadn't already.

The thought of that, of the many ways Briscoe could manipulate Remedy, got Micah's blood boiling all over again.

Briscoe picked up his gun bag, all but dismissing Micah.

Micah didn't think. Channeling his anger, he surged forward and clapped his hand on the back of Briscoe's neck, gripping it hard as he got in his face. "One more thing, *boy*. If you threaten her. In any way. Then you will discover the limit of my restraint. You think you're meaner than me, but that's only because you've never come after my family or friends before."

Ty jerked his body back in an attempt to escape Micah's grip. When that failed, Ty screwed his mouth up and spit tobacco juice on Micah's boot.

That nasty son of a bitch. Micah shoved him by the neck against his truck, then wiped his boot on Briscoe's gun bag. "Good talking with you," Micah said, picking up his own gun bag. "Enjoy your time at the range this morning."

On legs shaky with adrenaline, Micah strode through the range's lobby and past the check-in desk with a nod to Joe, the weekend manager.

"I put you and Xavier on Range Four!" Joe called.

"Don't put Ty Briscoe anywhere near us or I'll be tempted to use him for target practice," Micah said, keeping moving.

Xavier was seated at the shaded prep table on Range Four, dressed in shorts and a T-shirt and fiddling with his beloved Remington .22, one of the last gifts his father had given him before passing away several years ago. He nodded at Micah. "What's wrong with you? Still pissed about those fires last night? I heard about them on the news."

"Yeah, those sucked."

"Doesn't explain why you're trying to choke the handle of your gun bag to death."

Micah set the bag on the table. "I ran into Ty Briscoe in the parking lot just now. He was waiting for me."

"Why would he do that?"

Micah paced to the range's wall, too agitated to sit. "To talk about Remedy Lane."

"Word on the street is that you and she are an item." Xavier waggled his eyebrows and all Micah could think was, *Here we go. . . .* God sure had an ironic sense of humor, because Micah had given Xavier hell for complicating all their lives when he'd started dating Briscoe Ranch's wedding planner and yet here Micah was, doing the same.

"By word on the street, you mean Alex filled you in on the latest Briscoe Ranch gossip?"

"You have your pillow talk and we have ours."

Micah was still coming down off his adrenaline crash from his confrontation with Ty Briscoe and really needed to bounce the confrontation off Xavier, but that story would make a lot more sense to Xavier if he knew what was going on romantically between Micah and Remedy. "Remedy and I went out to dinner on Friday night."

Xavier set his rifle on the table and tipped back in his chair. "I already knew that, and don't get me started on what a lame idea it was to take a date to Hog Heaven."

"It was spontaneous. It wasn't supposed to be a date."

Xavier cupped a hand behind his ear. "Why is that now? Because you have a strict policy against socializing with resort employees?"

The deadly calm of Xavier's tone reminded Micah of the way his mama used to act when she picked him up from the principal's office at school when he got in trouble for fighting. She'd be absolutely stone-cold collected until they got home and she ripped into him. Just as Xavier was probably winding up to do.

"Not so strict anymore, is it?" Micah scraped a chair

back from the table and dropped into it. "All right, let me have it. I can take it."

"Whatever do you mean?" Xavier said, all sarcastic sweetness.

"How about you start with, 'You hypocritical asshole,' " Micah suggested.

"I'm not going to call you an asshole."

"I gave you hell for dating Alex."

Xavier frowned. "You gave me even more hell when I told you I was proposing to him."

The edge of pain in Xavier's voice made Micah wince. "Yes, I did. And I'm sorry. I didn't understand how complicated it can be."

"How complicated *what* can be?"

Micah wasn't going to say *love,* because it was way too soon to even contemplate that profound emotion. He almost said *relationships,* but that wasn't accurate, either. Not yet. "Chemistry."

"Tell me more about this chemistry between you and Remedy."

Micah swabbed a hand over his face, searching for the right words. "It's like this. That night at Hog Heaven, I knew that I shouldn't be there with her like that. It went against everything I stand for. But when I looked at her . . . when she looked at me . . . it was—"

"It was chemistry."

"Exactly. One minute I was telling myself to back off because of who she is and who I am and the next minute I was kissing her. And then the next minute after that I was tossing her over my shoulder like a caveman and carrying her to my bed. Afterward, we agreed that we wouldn't let it affect our jobs. We both get what it means that we're on opposite sides of an immovable wall. We didn't make any promises to each other, but that lasted about two minutes. We have a date tonight."

Xavier lifted his rifle again and popped open the chamber. "So now you know. Some people are worth breaking the rules for."

Now he knew. "I guess I had to learn that for myself. Except now she's caught in the middle between Ty Briscoe and me. You should've heard him threatening me if I interfere with her job at the resort or drive her away to California. I hate that dating her gives that asshole ammo to use against both of us. It's a big mess already."

"But it's worth it," Xavier said. "This'll be fun for me, too. I hope you get to meet her parents." He loaded a cartridge, then paused, tipping his head. "Is it bad form to ask for their autographs the first time you meet them?"

"Why would I do that?"

Xavier looked at him like he was nuts. "Remedy's parents."

"Yeah, okay. Why would you want her parents' autographs?" Xavier's weird question about autographs reminded him of Briscoe's mention of Remedy's connections, but Micah still wasn't connecting the dots.

"You mean, you still don't know who she is?" Xavier loaded a second round into the chamber, then cocked it. "Oh, honey. Bless your heart."

Micah smacked Xavier's shoulder. "Did you just 'oh, honey' me while cocking a rifle?"

Xavier pinned him with a wry gaze. "Being a gay man in Texas is complicated."

"So it has always seemed. What makes you such a Remedy Lane expert that you know more about her than I do?"

"I'm a Remedy Lane expert because I've watched her grow up, like everyone in the country—or world, really—who's clued into celebrity news."

Micah was absolutely lost. "Come again?"

"Remedy Lane is Hollywood royalty. Her parents are Virginia Hartley and Preston Lane. The actors."

Micah knew who they were. Everybody knew who they

were. Micah's vision went fuzzy, as did his mind. He pushed out of his chair and started pacing again. Preston Lane's *Indigo Run* was one of the first movies Micah's dad had taken him to see in a theater and Virginia Hartley was one of those award show darlings who could sneeze and win an Oscar for it. "You're shitting me, right?"

"You're the one shitting me that your girlfriend never told you she was famous. Man, didn't you two talk about your families at all?"

They'd talked. Some. "She said she grew up in Hollywood, but she didn't mention something as fundamental as being the daughter of two of the biggest movie stars of all time. I didn't even know they had a kid together. They're not married, right?"

"Not for a long time. Their divorce was a huge deal in the late nineties."

"I just—This is some kind of joke, isn't it? You're pulling one over on me."

"If you don't believe me, look her up online."

Right. Online. Because Remedy was a celebrity. He could probably type her name into a search engine and her image would pop right up alongside a picture of her famous-as-hell parents. With unsteady hands, he pulled out his phone and typed in her name.

In less than a second, her pretty face filled the screen. He scrolled down to her description. "Remedy Rose Lane, the only daughter of Virginia Hartley and Preston Lane, the stars of over two hundred movies combined."

Xavier didn't bother leaning over to look. "That's her."

Stunned silent and numb as hell, Micah clicked on the images tab of the search engine and scrolled through a veritable photo album of Remedy's life. Right before his eyes, she evolved from a spunky kid to a willowy teen to the beautiful woman he'd slept with two nights ago. A lot of the shots looked like they'd been snapped by paparazzi, especially those taken around the time of her parents' divorce, while others boasted the polished glow of a professional photographer. There were shots of her on red carpets of big celebrity events and attending fashion week in Paris, and shots of her jet-setting all over the globe. No wonder that sashaying strut came so naturally to her.

Ty Briscoe's words came back to him about her connections bringing a lot of high-end clientele to the resort. No kidding.

Then he thought of Remedy's answer to Micah's question about if there was anything noteworthy about her childhood in Hollywood that she wanted to tell him. Right then and there she could have come clean about who she really was. But she'd made a conscious choice to leave him in the dark. Call it a hang-up, but after what Micah's mom did to their family he'd lost all tolerance for lies of omission.

"With a life like that, what is Remedy even doing in Texas?" Micah said, more to himself than anything. That question, and the fact that he didn't know the answer—that he hadn't even thought to ask what had brought her to Briscoe Ranch—was a stunning reminder of how little time he and Remedy had spent getting to know each other.

"I know the answer to that."

Of course Xavier did. He was a Remedy Lane expert.

Xavier tapped the edge of Micah's phone. "Start a new search. Type in *Zannity. Z-a-n-n-i-t-y*."

"What's a zannity?" Micah asked as he typed the letters in.

"Not a what. A who. Two whos, actually. Zannity was the nickname for the celebrity power couple Serenity Lee and Zander Brogue."

"Never heard of them."

Xavier flashed him a droll frown, unimpressed by Micah's celebrity ignorance. "Sometimes I wonder if you live under a rock. Their breakup was all over the news."

There wasn't a more boring topic in the world to Micah than celebrity gossip—until now.

He clicked on the first article listed in the search results and skimmed it. Reading about the woman he'd made love to getting raked over the coals by the news media for the Zannity wedding ending in disaster did odd things to his defensive shields. Made him wish he had Ty Briscoe by the throat again. Made him want to drag her behind his shields and protect her from every last person who'd tried to do her harm.

"I kind of want to knock some heads together," Micah said. "That Zannity situation was nothing but a pile of cow dung."

"Exactly. When Serenity caught Zander cheating on her on their wedding day with one of Remedy's assistants and called it off, he and the assistant blamed Remedy for pushing them by causing them undue stress about the wedding due to her incompetence. It was a huge scandal. She resigned from the high-end wedding-planning company she worked for and left Hollywood. Nobody knew where she went. Probably still don't, or we'd have some bottom-dwelling paparazzi sniffing around the town. Or maybe everyone has just moved on to the next scandal. She's old news now."

That story had gotten more bananas by the second. "That whole mess is inconceivable to me."

"Number one, that's showbiz, baby. Survival of the fittest—and the thinnest, but that's beside the point. And number two, you can't use the word *inconceivable*. It's been retired."

"You can't retire a word," Micah said.

"It's like in sports, how a great player's number is retired when they leave the sport. *Inconceivable* has been retired. It can only be used in one context from here to eternity, so if you're not quoting *The Princess Bride* then pick a different word."

Micah shook his head. Sometimes Xavier baffled him

with all his pop culture jibber-jabber. "How is it that you and I are such good friends?"

"Alex asks me the same thing when your name comes up."

"I'm sure he does."

Xavier handed Micah a pair of headphones, then secured his own in place and pressed his eye to the Remington's sight. "Firing!"

Micah barely got his headphones in place before Xavier emptied his rifle's magazine into the target at the far end of the range, his every shot within centimeters of each other right at the heart of the torso silhouette.

Remedy was rich and famous. She'd spent her life traveling around the world and having her every whim catered to by staffs of dozens. And Micah had plied her with a bacon cheeseburger and beer at a backwoods bar with sawdust on the floor. What was she doing in Nowhere, Texas? Yes, Xavier had answered that already, but Micah couldn't get the question out of his head. Sure, she'd been the subject of a scandal, but how bad could it have been? New celebrity scandals broke every day and folks in that industry seemed to have short memories of people's screwups.

No wonder Ty Briscoe was falling all over himself to protect his investment in her. He was probably already counting his future profits from all the celebrity weddings he expected her to bring in. Was Remedy aware of Ty's motivation? Was she in on it? Had she already tapped her celebrity contacts for weddings in Dulcet?

The more questions like those that Micah considered, the more pissed off he got that she hadn't been honest about herself, pissed off that nobody had told him the truth. Not her, not Xavier or Alex. Nobody. Worse, all those jokes she'd made about people in Texas and Micah being a Bubba and that fake twang she assumed sometimes took on a stench of condescension. How dare a rich princess sashay into his hometown and treat them all like darling little zoo animals?

His grandparents' kitchen table flashed through his mind, the place he'd found the note from his mother and realized she'd abandoned them. He shook the image away. "Why didn't you tell me this sooner? About Remedy?"

"Hey, chill out. You tell me all the time that you don't like gossip."

"It's not gossip. It's the truth about a woman I slept with, a truth that she and everybody else kept from me."

Xavier threw up his hand. "Don't rope me into this. I didn't know she mattered to you. Last time you and I talked, you still thought she was a major pain in your ass."

Micah hadn't realized until he'd been confronted with her deception how deeply she was starting to matter to him. How he'd unwittingly made plans for the two of them. He'd gotten notions in his head about her, about the possibility that the two of them together might be the start of something big. Stupid, trusting, romantic fool.

Micah picked up his bag of untouched guns. "I'm outta here, man. Between this whole Remedy thing and Ty Briscoe, I can't concentrate on hitting paper targets. It's time for me to get some answers."

Xavier touched Micah's arm. "Hey, maybe you'd be better off waiting until you cool down. Give it some thought instead of confronting her with your guns blazing. No pun intended."

Shaking his head, Micah pulled away. "I'm too pissed off to go home and stew. I slept with her and that means something to me, damn it. But she lied about who she was. She *lied*. And I deserve to know why."

Chapter Ten

At the sound of someone pounding on her front door, Remedy startled and splashed champagne from her glass onto the kitchen counter. It was the good stuff, from one of the cases sent to her with love from her mom along with two dozen chocolate-covered strawberries. *Bless her heart*, and Remedy meant that sincerely, not in the sarcastic Texas way.

The pounding had sounded angry, so she picked up the baseball bat she'd stationed by the door as she looked through the peephole.

Micah was pacing from the front bumper of his truck and back to her door like a caged lion. Remedy had no idea what he could be angry about. The sight of the gun holstered to his hip made her heart race even more than his pissed-off scowl. Would she ever get used to the presence of guns, a variety of weapon she'd been brought up to fear above all others?

"Hi, Micah. You look upset," she called through the door.

"We need to talk." His voice was tight with barely harnessed emotion.

She set the bat down and put her hand on the doorknob

but couldn't find the courage to unlock it, even though she knew in her heart that Micah would never harm her. "What's with the gun?"

Arms wide, he looked down his body, then shook his head, as though he'd forgotten he had the weapon on him. With a curse, he stormed back to his truck, then returned a moment later, the gun and holster gone. If anything, he looked even more peeved than before.

"I forgot I was wearing that."

She opened the door. "You were at the range this morning with Xavier?"

He held his phone out, the screen displaying a photograph of her and her mother on the red carpet at the Oscars two years earlier. "Yes, and when I told Xavier that you and I had a date planned tonight he asked me to get your parents' autographs for him. I had no idea what he was talking about."

Her heart sank. So much for being taken at face value without being under the shadow of her parents. It'd been nice while it lasted. "I'm sorry you were put in that position."

He stuffed his phone in his pocket. "Remember when I asked you if there was anything about your childhood in Hollywood that was noteworthy? At Hog Heaven. You remember that?"

Yes, she did, and she remembered the choice she'd made not to divulge her past to him. "At the time, we were still enemies. I barely knew you." Why was she bothering to explain? He'd already judged her and wasn't ready to listen to her point of view. He'd come for the express purpose of ripping her a new one.

"You've had plenty of opportunities to enlighten me. If you and I are going to date, if we're going to sleep together, then I deserve better than lies of omission."

Red fireworks burst in her brain. How dare he. "Why is that, Micah? Because you bought me a beer and burger?

Does that make me beholden to you? Or was it because I let you under my skirt? Now you own me, is that it?"

"Around here, sex like that means something. But I shouldn't have expected a Hollywood princess like you to understand our hick ways."

Shit. This fight was going to suck. She was going to need more champagne to handle this one. After opening the door wider in invitation, she returned to the kitchen. He closed the door behind him and followed.

She took a sip of champagne and let the flute linger at her lips, stalling, stalling. . . . "I didn't take sleeping with you lightly, but that still doesn't mean I owe you full disclosure of the details of my past—details that I had a reason for keeping to myself."

"Look at you, sipping French champagne and eating chocolate-covered strawberries. Am I going to open your refrigerator and find caviar?"

He would because she had a lifelong weakness for the stuff. "Possessing caviar is not a personality defect. Nor is having wealthy parents."

"How'd you choke down that beer the other night, huh?"

She'd called it right. He wasn't there to listen, just to vent at her. Well, he could go ahead and get it all out of his system. She topped off her champagne flute.

"Did you call your friends back in Hollywood the next day, tell them about how you went slumming with a local Bubba?" he said with a huff. "It all makes sense now. But you know what? I am a redneck and proud of it. I love this community and everything it stands for. And I have dedicated my life to protecting it from entitled rich folks. And yet here you are."

Everything he'd listed about himself was a quality that made him who he was, and she *liked* who he was. She liked him a lot—except for the assumptions he was making about her and her values based on nothing but conjecture and his own prejudice against wealth.

"Yes, here I am."

His accusations of her were so outlandish that it was easy to divorce herself from emotion and view their fight from a safe distance. His chest was all puffed out and a vein in his forehead was visible. His neck had truly turned red. Anger made him handsome in a dangerous way she found appealing on a very basic level. Not to mention that he smelled as though he'd come from an action movie set. He smelled like a stuntman. She'd always had a thing for stuntmen.

"You're probably worth even more money than all the Briscoes combined, aren't you? You could probably buy that resort out from under them if you got it in your mind to. You could buy this whole town."

The whole town? Either of her parents could, but probably not her. She bit her lip and kept her mouth shut.

He braced his hands on the counter and leaned toward her, piercing her with a furious glare. When he spoke, his voice was low, his tight control returned. "Please don't tell me you and Ty Briscoe have some sort of backroom deal to exploit our town."

Oh, for Pete's sake. On impulse, she puckered up, stretched across the counter, and kissed him on the lips.

He reeled back, wiping his mouth. "Why did you do that?"

She had no good answer for him. "To shut you up."

He shook his head, so angry that his lips pulled back to show his teeth. "You had no right."

"Probably not," she said. "But I refuse to defend myself against your baseless accusations and I refuse to feel guilty about who I am. You're drawing conclusions about me based on nothing but your own prejudices and what you read about me online. Which is really boring, you know that? I would've thought you'd have been more original than to make the same assumptions about me that people have been making my whole life."

"You're accusing me of being *boring?*"

That's the part of her rebuttal he latched on to? Fine, then. "You're being boring and assumptive and bitter. And you know what I've learned to say to people like that?" She smacked the counter with her open palm. "I say, bring it on, because I've been judged unfairly my whole life. When you grow up under a microscope like I did, you either develop a really thick skin or let it crush you. And I didn't let it crush me. I've lost count of the number of celebrities' kids I grew up with who became either addicts or vapid, morally corrupt losers dependent on their famous name to skate through life. That's not me. I won't let it be."

He threw up his hands. "Are you looking for a blue ribbon for not ending up in rehab? You think that makes you special?"

"What I think is that I'm not going to let a prejudiced, angry man tell me who I am and what I stand for. I don't have some shady backroom deal with Ty Briscoe and I'm not here to exploit Dulcet. I'm here for a chance to start over with my life. Where I came from doesn't define me. What defines me is that I work my ass off and I'm a good person."

He sucked in his cheeks. His eyes narrowed as though it was taking the effort of his life to hold back from blowing his top. Without another word, he stormed down the hall and through the front door, slamming it closed.

Allowing herself a moment of pure, melodramatic venting, she raised her fists to the heavens and growled. Loudly. Then she topped off her flute all the way to the brim of the glass and chugged it down with the speed of a frat boy during pledge week. "That glass alone was probably fifty bucks' worth of champagne!" she hollered at the door. "How's that for wasteful and entitled?"

Then she bit off a whole strawberry from its stem.

"I'm not going to apologize for who I am!" It wasn't her fault that her bank account rattled his alpha insecurities.

She wasn't going to make herself appear less than she was for a man's ego.

She bit into another strawberry, barely chewing before she swallowed it down and grabbed another one. Nothing wrong with a little indulgence after a fight like that.

A knock on the door stopped her mid-chew.

Apprehensively, she walked to the door. Micah again, his hands on his hips and his eyes rolled up to look at the roof eaves.

She flung the door open. "Back for round two so soon?"

He stepped forward and took her shoulders in his hands as his mouth descended over hers, hard and demanding. She froze, processing the turn of events, then wrapped her arms around his neck. His fingers plunged into her hair. His tongue caressed hers. She could feel the passion and the frustration pouring out of him as he gave himself over to her, so she poured her passion and frustration right back into him.

How dare he show up at her door unannounced and ruin her morning with unfair judgments and accusations? How dare he drive her so mad with lust for him?

He opened his eyes and held her gaze. His eyes were stormy still, but the fury was gone. "Let's get out of here."

Stubbornness prevented her from blindly agreeing to his command. "What makes you think I'd go anywhere with you?"

He didn't answer but brushed past her and strode to the kitchen.

"You don't have central air, do you? It's sweltering in here," he said, nodding at her wall unit. "That thing even on?"

Remedy bristled. He didn't get to stomp around like an angry bear, criticizing her and her house, disregarding her wishes. "It's a bit temperamental, but it works." Sometimes.

He grabbed the champagne bottle, then another from

the box on the floor, and put them in a plastic grocery bag along with the rest of the strawberries.

"What's going on here? Why did you come back? I thought we were done," she said.

He swallowed hard. "It's like you said the other night. Who am I without a little trouble to keep me in business?" He grabbed a lap blanket from the back of her sofa, then another from her reading chair, and handed them to her.

"That doesn't explain how you went from being furious at me to wanting to picnic."

He held out his hand to her. "Because you're driving me crazy, that's how."

She only hesitated for a moment before taking it. "You're driving me crazy, too."

Micah drove them out of town like a bullet. He needed the balm of dirt roads and empty space to clear his head. Maybe they'd find a little solace out in the sticks, where he could simply be a country boy and she could be the girl he was sweet on. They could shed who they were and enjoy the heat of the day under the shade of a pecan tree along a riverbank.

As the miles of road faded behind them, his righteous indignation peeled away until he realized that he wasn't entirely sure why he'd gotten so blasted mad at Remedy. She was right that it was unfair to judge her background the way he had, except that every experience he'd had in life told him that it *did* matter. Who you were, who your parents were, and the values you grew up with mattered. A lot. But that didn't make it fair or just. Actually, she'd been right about a lot of points she hurled at him, including him not having a right to an opinion about her life.

He glanced her way. She'd been as quiet as he was on the drive, for the most part keeping her face turned into the wind from her open window.

The hell of it was, he wanted a right to an opinion about

her life. He wanted her. It was a stupid choice, because he'd known from the day he'd met her that there was no way she was going to stay in Texas. Even if Ty Briscoe didn't drive her away with his conniving ways, Micah gave her another month, two tops, of lying low before she grew weary of small-town country living and packed her bags, heading back where she belonged.

His heart gave a squeeze. Would she give him the courtesy of telling him she was going? Was that a risk he was willing to take?

He stretched his arm across the seat back, and when she didn't protest he let his fingers brush lightly through her hair. Though he kept his focus on the road ahead, he watched in his peripheral vision as she shifted to study him. He let her look her fill until they'd left the final paved road and bumped their way along the dirt path to his favorite backwoods spot.

He had so many questions for her, he wasn't sure where to start. Maybe at the beginning. "What was it like growing up with famous parents?"

Her sigh seemed to well up from the bottom of her soul. As the silence stretched, he started to doubt she'd answer him.

"Not as strange as people expect, because I didn't know any other life," she said finally. "I traveled a lot with one or both of my parents, going wherever their movies were filming or premiering, wherever their press junkets took them. I always went along. Until they divorced when I was twelve. And then . . ." She thought for a moment. "Actually, it wasn't that different after the divorce. They were still off filming and promoting movies on opposite sides of the earth, and I still tagged along with them as much as I could. My mom always said that our home wasn't a place but each other. I like that."

Bitter memory welled up inside him. Home wasn't a place but your loved ones. It was true, but he hadn't figured that out until after the fire. After his mother had left the family and disappeared. He and Remedy had both lived displaced lives. He would've never thought they'd have that fundamental part of themselves in common. "I learned that, too, from the fire, that what really matters in life is family and faith and community. Nothing brings that into clearer focus than loss. When the fire destroyed our house, we lost everything. Photo albums, clothes, toys, electronics, neighbors, friends, people we thought we could count on who weren't there for us in our time of need."

He swallowed back the resentment that had crept into his tone. At that moment, he understood why Remedy hadn't disclosed certain details of her past to him. There were some things that you just couldn't verbalize, some people you didn't want to waste one more iota of your energy on.

She turned and hitched her knee up on the seat to regard him. "You're a good man, Micah."

After all the nastiness he'd hurled at her during their fight, for her to come back with a compliment was incredible. She was incredible. He wouldn't forget that again. "What did you do about schooling since you traveled with your parents so much?"

"Most years I had private tutors, and sometimes I attended private school in L.A. It was a great life, a great childhood. It really wasn't until high school that I realized what an oddity I was."

He pulled the truck to a stop right on the edge of the road where the start of a thin trail cut through the wild grass. "You're not an oddity."

"Yes, I am. And most of the time that was okay with me, because it had to be. I never fit in with my parents' friends' kids and I never fit in with normal kids. I mean, I had friends, some really good friends, even, but it's not the same."

He'd heard that same sentiment before, from her and

from Xavier. "You sound like Xavier when he talks about growing up, being gay and black in a mostly white town. He had it rough in school. Still makes me spitting mad to think about everything he went through."

She touched Micah's leg. "You're one of those people who gather misfits around you like moss on a stone because of how stable and solid you are."

It'd never felt that way with Xavier. Just the opposite, actually. "Maybe it's the other way around. Ever think about that? Maybe instead of misfits being drawn to me, I'm drawn to them. I think I must crave a little bit of unconventionality in my life."

After a beat of hesitation, she leaned across the seat and kissed his cheek, soft and sweet.

He covered her hand with his. It was right of him to bring her here, to make this effort to reconcile. "Stay where you are. I'll come around."

Once he'd helped her down, he grabbed the bag with the champagne and piled the blankets in her arms. "Follow me."

He led her along the dirt trail through the tall dried grass that was so familiar to him, he could've traversed it blindfolded with nary a misstep. Only a few birds were braving the summer heat, but as he and Remedy passed into the thicket of trees that edged the creek they spotted more wildlife. An armadillo nosed through the fallen leaves, jittery lizards were doing push-ups on the rocks, and dragonflies and butterflies and other winged creatures darted all around them.

The trail led them straight to his special pecan tree at the edge of Barley Creek, the tree with his initials carved in the trunk. As ever, it provided a wide umbrella of shade that made the crisp heat bearable, an oasis for just the two of them in the middle of summer. "We have arrived."

He took the blankets from her and spread them out one on top of the other for cushion against the hard ground, right to the edge of the riverbank's drop-off. Then he stuck the unopened bottle of champagne right into the water and lodged it in place between two twisted roots so it could cool.

Remedy's head was on a swivel, drinking it all in.

"Pretty, isn't it?"

"So pretty. Even more beautiful than the creek by my house."

He nodded to the *MG* in the tree trunk. "This is my tree, since I was a boy. This is where I came to be alone with my thoughts and catch the occasional tadpole or two."

She traced the *M* of his initials. "It wasn't affected by the Knolls Canyon Fire?"

"No. Isn't that a miracle? The fire crews set up a fire-break about five miles from here and were able to contain the blaze before it ruined this place. Wish I knew which fire crews made that happen, so I could thank them."

Her attention roved over the trees and past the opposite bank of the creek. "Did the resort make restitutions for the fire?"

He released the deep breath her question dredged up. "In some ways. The Briscoes or their lawyers never acknowledged their role in the fire, but they did shovel out heaps of money to the forest service to improve fire roads and build wilderness fire response outposts."

She rubbed her arms. "I don't know how I'd ever make peace with it if sparklers from a wedding I planned were the cause of so much destruction and pain."

Victory achieved. For the first time in all his years as a firefighter he'd managed to impress upon a Briscoe Ranch executive how much was at stake when fire safety measures weren't heeded and why the resort should be an ally with Micah instead of treating him like the enemy. But Remedy's understanding of the stakes said far more about her compassion and selflessness than it did about Micah's efforts. All it said about him was that he'd made some pretty terrible assumptions about her based on nothing but his own prejudices.

He brushed a hand over her back. "Let's sit, drink this champagne before it gets warm."

He'd forgotten to pack glasses, so when she'd settled on the blankets he handed her the open champagne bottle, then settled across from her, the strawberries between them.

They passed the bottle between them. The champagne wasn't that cold, but it was tasty. He couldn't remember the last time he'd had champagne. Probably at a wedding. He got invited to most weddings around town but was rarely able to indulge in more than a sip or two of alcohol, since he was usually on call for work.

"The firefighter ball is in three weeks," she said. "Are you going?"

She sounded hopeful. He took that as a good sign that she was on the road to forgiving him. "Me and all my crew. Wouldn't miss it. Are you working the ball?"

She bit into a strawberry. The juice stained her lips pink and dripped down the side of her hand. She licked it off. "Not only working it. I'm planning it. It's my first solo event for the resort."

"Are you nervous about that?"

She polished off the rest of the strawberry, tossed the stem in the creek, then took her time licking the tips of her fingers. Micah's body stirred to life at the sight. He couldn't decide if she was consciously flirting or if it was part of the whole chemistry thing they had going on, but either way, he approved.

"I'm a little nervous," she said. "Everything's ready and there's no way to predict what's going to go wrong, so there's no sense getting too anxious yet. Better to reserve my energy for when the problems actually start popping up, which they always do."

"Bet you're not even going to have time to dance with me."

"I might be able to work that out."

He handed her another strawberry. This time, if any strawberry juice found its way onto her hand he wanted to be the one to lick it off. Meanwhile, he pulled her foot onto his lap and removed her sandal. He loved women's feet. Not in a kinky fetish kind of way, but because they embodied some of the things he loved most about women. Women's feet were soft and slender and graceful, with tiny toes and brightly colored polish, and they were sensitive and responsive to skilled caresses.

Remedy's toenails were polished a quiet pink that brought out the pink tones of her skin. Her heel was rough with calluses, probably because she spent the majority of her job on her feet. He massaged down her arch, then brushed a thumb over her heel. "You need more comfortable shoes for work."

She reclined back, propping herself up on her arms. "Comfortable shoes don't match my outfits."

He rubbed his way back up her arch and watched her squirm in response. "Are you ticklish?"

"A little."

He started a methodical massage of her foot, beginning with her toes. "I will file that nugget of information away to hold against you some other time. But not today."

When her foot had been thoroughly tended to and the worry lines on her face had disappeared, he removed her other sandal and started the process all over again.

She sank into her arms, her chin tipped back and her face basking in a patch of sunlight in the mottled shade. "Is this your way of apologizing?"

He slid both his thumbs up her arch. "Depends. Is it working?"

"Maybe."

"Okay, then, how about this. The next phase of my grand plan. Scoot to the edge of the riverbank and put your feet in the water."

She shifted to her knees and leaned over the edge of the bank, eyeing the creek suspiciously.

"I promise that there aren't any foot-eating monsters down there."

"You said there are tadpoles in the creek."

Good grief. "There were also tadpoles in the Frio River, and I've witnessed you splashing around in that."

"That was before I knew about the tadpoles."

"You really are a princess." He took off his shoes and socks. His feet looked like pterodactyl talons compared to her pretty little feet. "I'll show you how it's done."

He got his butt right up to the edge of the blankets, then dropped his feet into the water. The cool temperature gave his skin a bite, probably because the air was so warm in contrast. "See? No foot-eating tadpoles."

She scooted close to him and dipped a toe in. "That's cold."

"That's a good thing on such a hot summer day."

She eased her foot the rest of the way in, then the other. "If something wiggly starts to nibble at my toes, I'm done."

"Deal."

He fished the second bottle of champagne out of the water, popped it open, and handed it to her. They were quiet for a while, together, each alone with their thoughts.

Micah got to thinking again about what different worlds they were from. Remedy was acting like this was her first time lying creek-side, her toes in the water, something Micah had done on a near-daily or weekly basis for his entire life. "During our fight, you said that where you're from doesn't define you, and even though I was off-base with almost everything I said, I've still got to disagree about that one point. I think where we came from has a huge impact on who we turn out to be, for better or worse."

She drank from the bottle, her expression turning distant. "I've fought for my whole life not to let my parents' fame or their larger-than-life personalities and career successes define me, but it did anyway. How could it not? They raised me in their own incredible insulated bubble of a world, so of course that made me who I am. But you know what? It was such a relief coming here to Texas where nobody seems to realize or care who my parents are. In Dulcet, I'm just Remedy the new Briscoe Ranch executive. Not Remedy the daughter of Virginia Hartley and Preston Lane."

She was too vivacious a personality to ever be "just Remedy," even though he understood the point she was trying to make. "You might not believe there are many parallels to our lives, but it's not so different in a small town. Everybody knows everything about you and your family, and they've been making assumptions and drawing conclusions about everybody else. My dad's a deacon at his church and sits on the town council, so living up to his reputation hasn't been easy. And even though he did a great job raising me and my brother and sisters, there will always be townsfolk who bring up stupid choices I made as a teenager."

"What happened to your mom?" Remedy asked gently.

He gave her a weak smile. "A story for another time."

"Got it." She tangled her toes with his in the water. "So back to how you described small towns, think about that, except imagine that happening to you everywhere you go, even on vacation. There's no escaping the recognition, or the unsolicited opinions about my life. New York, Chicago, Los Angeles, it doesn't make any difference where I go. When your birth announcement photo makes the cover of *People* magazine, the whole world thinks they've watched you grow up."

"*People* magazine? Seriously?"

"You didn't find that one in your research?" she said.

He reached into his back pocket and found his phone. "This I've got to see."

It took two attempts to get the wording right for the Internet search engine to find the cover shot, but there it was, Virginia Hartley and baby Remedy on the cover of a magazine. "Well, I'll be damned."

"Told you. Try living that one down, especially with such a unique name like Remedy. Everybody knows who I am."

"I didn't."

"Now you do."

Yes, he did. But it didn't feel like he was spending the morning with the rich and famous Remedy Lane. This was Remedy the burger-hungry, golf cart–crashing, klutzy wedding planner who had a fire for life that he was fast becoming addicted to. This was the woman he'd made love to in his bed, whose body trembled like mad when she came, and the woman who presently had the most alluring strawberry stains on her lips.

When she noticed him watching her, he turned his attention back to his phone. "Your mom looks like you. The eyes and the shape of your cheeks."

"I love that I look like her. She's one of the most beautiful women in the world and she's such a great mom. She's a free spirit, but she's always been there for me, no matter what."

Must be nice. "You two are close?"

"We are. Not as much as when I was younger, but we still talk a few times a week."

The love in her eyes as she was talking about her family hit him right in the heart. Family was his everything, and he could see it was Remedy's everything, too. "Your parents still live in Los Angeles?"

"Yes. My mom in Burbank and my dad in Malibu."

"Do you miss home, Los Angeles?"

She was a long time in answering. "Yes. Some parts. Others, not so much."

"From everything I read this morning, you were all but forced out of Hollywood because of that Zannity scandal."

She swirled her feet in the water, causing enough waves to splash water up the sides of Micah's calves. "You can't believe what you see online. There is very little ethical concern for reporting the truth in celebrity gossip news."

"I may be a quaint country boy, but even I knew that."

She pinned him with a weary smile. "You aren't a quaint, simpleton country boy, no matter how badly you want me to believe that."

"Touché." He drank deeply of the champagne, gathering his gumption for the next question he was going to ask. "How long do you give yourself in Texas before you go back to L.A.?"

"What makes you think I want to go back?" But he could tell in her wry smile and the sharp glint in her eyes that she did want that. "Briscoe Ranch Resort is one of the most acclaimed destination wedding locations in the world. I've only been here six weeks and I can already see why."

Yes, it was, but that didn't mean squat. "Look at the facts. You were the victim of a scandal, so you got the hell out of Dodge to bide your time in the middle of Nowhere, Texas, until everything blew over. Tell me I'm wrong."

She didn't. Hunching forward, she rubbed her arms, her gaze turning distant. Micah sensed the disquiet his question had stirred up in her and was sorry all over again for causing her more distress. "I don't understand the accusation in your tone. Is it because you think I belong here in Dulcet? Because I don't. Any more than I ever fit in in Los Angeles. Neither is my home, so picking one over the other isn't a moral judgment. It doesn't matter where I go, my whole life I've felt like a foreigner or some freak alien on a covert mission to Earth. Everyone is slightly foreign and everything is off just enough that I can't catch my bearings. It doesn't matter what I do or how I act, I can't figure out how to fit in. But I have something to prove to everyone who wrote me off in L.A., so that's what I'm going to do. That's the plan."

"Asking again. How long will you be here in Texas?"

She shrugged one shoulder. "A few months, a few years. I'll know when it's time."

Her words hung in the breeze. Was that what his mom had done? Waited for years until her instincts told her to go, like some sadistic internal alarm clock? Or had the fire made the decision for her in an instant? He forced the questions out of his mind. "Even in Los Angeles, even after high school, you never felt like you fit in there, ever? Because in all those pictures I saw online you looked absolutely in your element," he said.

"I was never part of that world, the Hollywood scene. I didn't belong. It was so much easier to work for them, to plan their parties and be a sober observer to their extravagance."

The image of that struck his sense of irony. "And all the while you were richer than any of them, I bet."

"Some of them, not all."

"Oh, please. With who your parents are? I bet you outrank every person at those richie rich weddings you plan. Every single one of them."

"You're missing the point."

A knot of frustration lodged in his gut. "You're missing mine, too."

"What's your point, then?"

He ate a strawberry, trying to figure out how to articulate the complex jumble of thoughts pinging around his head about her. "I guess my point is, What does it matter if you fit in or not? Or prove people were wrong about you? Why bother? You're above them all. You have enough power and money to never have to worry about what anyone thinks about you."

He watched a welling of sadness overtake her. "It's isolating, okay? It gets really damn lonely sometimes."

He reached for her hand as he registered the longing in her words, the pain etched into her face. He hated that he'd brought that about. During their fight she'd been full of fire, but this look could only be described as defeat. "You've been hurt. Deeply."

She swallowed hard, then stalled, her mouth open, as though picking her words carefully. "It's hard to have friends or boyfriends when you're never sure who's using you for your trust fund or your family, which guys are angling for an invite to A-list parties or hoping you'll give their screenplay to your parents." She shook her head. "There's been so many stupid boys. You have no idea."

No, he hadn't had any idea that having fame and money could cause a person so much pain. No idea at all. "I hate that I was just like all those assholes who judged you for your money."

She touched his face, offering him a tentative smile. "You're coming around, though. Don't you see? That's what's been so nice about Dulcet. I still don't fit in, but at least people are taking me at face value. I'm judged on my own merits for a change. I'm out of my parents' shadows finally."

Protectiveness flared inside him. She wasn't out of their shadows, because Ty Briscoe was fully planning to exploit her connections. She deserved to know, even though now wasn't the time to alert her to Ty's motives. Micah had distressed her enough as it was. But the hard truth was that she was correct about how isolating her wealth and family name was.

He was starting to see how it'd be impossible to trust that people weren't using her. Even if she ended up leaving Texas when the clouds of scandal parted, that didn't change her fate of being someone other. Anywhere else she went next, it would be the same. She was right; that sounded damn lonely. He would've kept his background a secret, too, if he'd been in her shoes.

"You need to know something about your job and Ty Briscoe. He's using you, Remedy. He met me at the range this morning to talk about you. He thinks you're going to be bringing in a whole lot of celebrity clients."

She was quiet. "That's not a surprise, even though I haven't brought in a single celebrity wedding to the resort—and I don't have any plans to. I'm so over navigating the media circus and security details and flagrant narcissism of celebrity weddings. No thank you."

"Even still, be careful. Ty Briscoe is a dangerous man with no scruples."

She fiddled with a button on his shirt. "Sounds like he should've been a movie producer."

"I'm being serious."

"I am, too. Listen, I've grown up learning how to deal with men like him. I've got this."

She sounded so self-assured, he believed her. "Okay. But for the record, the overdeveloped hero complex that Xavier keeps telling me I'm cursed with is not keen on leaving you to handle Ty Briscoe yourself."

"I can't wait to meet Xavier. It's good to know you have a friend to keep your ego in check."

"He treats that like his number-one job."

"This is getting so complicated. You, me. Our jobs," she said.

He stroked her hair. "We knew that when we started down this road. Do you regret it? Do you want to stop?"

"God, no." She brought his hand to her lips for a kiss. "But this is your home, your life, and your livelihood. Are you sure you're okay with all of these complications?"

"It's your life and livelihood, too."

"It's not the same."

A corner of his lips kicked up into a melancholy grin. "Because you've got a trust fund cushion?"

"To some extent, yes. But mostly because this isn't my home."

"Yet," he couldn't help but add. "And for your information, I've got a nice nest egg cushion built up, too, so maybe we don't need to think so hard about having our safety nets in place, anticipating the demises of our careers at the hands of Ty Briscoe."

"Maybe we'll just keep driving each other crazy and enjoying the ride."

"You've got yourself a deal." She snuggled in closer. They might not be meant to be, but Micah couldn't wait to ride this train as far as it went. He did need to make one point crystal clear, though. "I might have judged you unfairly, but I'm not using you for your fame or fortune. I want to make sure we're solid about that."

She squeezed his hand. "I know you're not. You hate rich people on principle."

"Not all rich people."

She pinned him with a withering look. "Who's a liar now?"

"I guess the most honest answer is that I'd never met a wealthy person I liked before you." Which was the truth. "Enough talk. Lie back with me."

He tugged on her shoulder until she reclined back with him, settling into the crook of his arm as though she were born for it. He wished he hadn't gotten that emergency call the other night. He could've fallen asleep in his bed with her like this so easy. He combed his fingers through Remedy's hair and swirled his feet in the cool water, letting his mind wander to the sound track of the wind in the trees, the hum of cicadas, and the babble of the creek.

A hot breeze puffed over them, reminding Micah of an oven. Or Remedy's house. "I have one more pressing question for you, if you don't mind."

She stiffened. "What now?"

He stroked his hand along her side, trying to soothe her worries. "If you have a trust fund, then why haven't you sprung for a new air-conditioning unit?"

Her body melted back against his, but this time she was grinning. "That's a fair question. I've been too busy with work. Plus my current air conditioner has personality. I'm having fun with it. I named it Luke. As in *Cool Hand Luke*."

"That might be funny except your Luke isn't all that cool."

"I'll tell him you said that." She poked one of his shirt's buttons through the buttonhole, then started on the next one and then the next until she'd opened enough space for her to stick her hand through the opening and touch his skin.

Guess he wasn't the only one in the mood for some lazy Sunday lovin' out in the boondocks. He wasn't sure he deserved this second chance, but he planned to make the most of it.

Though it was tempting to help her get the rest of the buttons undone, they weren't in any kind of a hurry. Instead, he cupped her cheek and captured her lips in a gentle kiss. "I know you don't feel like you fit in anywhere in a permanent way, but for today I'd say you belong exactly where you are—under this tree by the creek. With me."

Her eyes fluttered open to gaze at him with a look of wonder. She shifted up to her knees, then slid her leg across his body and straddled him. "It's my turn to ask you one last pressing question," she said, unfastening the remaining buttons of his shirt.

"All right."

She splayed his shirt open and ran her hands over his chest. The tips of her hair tickled his skin. "What's up with the Texas quilt in your bedroom?"

The question was so out of left field that he snorted out a laugh. "You liked that?"

She gave him her best *oh, please* look. "You went down on me while I was lying in the middle of an image of Texas like I was a sacrifice to the redneck gods."

He tugged a lock of her hair. "Who says you weren't?"

She gave his chest a playful shove.

"It was a gift from my older brother right before he got married. He called it his getting lucky quilt. Said he didn't need it anymore now that he was getting hitched."

"Okay, that is disgusting. Ew. Ew. Ew." She poked Micah's ribs in time with each word.

He squirmed, ticklish, then slid his hands up her legs, under her dress, his hand exploring her soft curves all the way up to the sexy-as-hell flare of her hips. "It's not like I didn't wash it after he gave it to me."

"Micah, there's not enough hot water in the world to wash the nasty out of that . . . that . . . quilt of depravity."

Digging his legs against the riverbank for leverage, he held her in place against him and sat. Her position on his lap gave his mouth perfect access to her chest, so he dropped his lips to her skin and kissed a path along the edge of her dress.

"I've got news for you, darlin'. The quilt stays. It's a family heirloom," he said against her skin between kisses.

"Next time we do it in your bed, I'm going to shout out, 'For the glory of Texas!' as I come."

He dropped his forehead to her chest and chuckled at the image that evoked. "Careful now. That's a slippery slope. Only a matter of time before I'm taking you to get a cute little Texas tramp stamp tattoo for me to admire when I'm riding you. I'm sure all your Hollywood friends would love that."

Her fingers toyed with the hair at the nape of his neck, sending shivers down his spine. "When is that happening, by the way?"

He hoped she meant him riding her, but he couldn't pass up the opportunity to tease her. "The tattoo? Say the word."

Smiling ruefully, she grabbed the champagne bottle and brought it to her lips. Suddenly there was nothing he wanted in the whole wide world more than to find out what champagne tasted like on her skin.

He drew her lower lip into his mouth. The taste of tart sugar and strawberries flooded his senses. A guttural rumble of pleasure vibrated through his chest. He released her lip and took her whole on the mouth, finding her tongue with his. Her tongue was cool and tasted less of champagne and more of Remedy, absolutely addictive.

Bracing her back with his hand, he shifted to his side and lowered her to the blanket.

He took a moment to worship her legs right and proper with his lips and hands. It'd been too dark on Friday night to take in many visual details of her body, but he remembered that California tan from the riverbank party the first time they met. He hadn't been able to take his eyes off her that day. The way she moved, the way she laughed. And now here she was, her legs around him, her heavy-lidded eyes watching him love on her, those champagne-strawberry lips parted in pleasure.

Rocking up to his knees, he took the bottle in hand again and poured a splash of champagne on her bent knee. She shivered and inhaled sharply at the cold. Micah chased the droplets up her thigh with his tongue and lingered there at the junction of her hip and leg to tease the edge of her panties with his teeth.

Her fingers splayed against the blanket. Her back arched as he put his hands on her hips and slid her dress up her body, past those pale pink panties trimmed in black lace, past the creamy stretch of her stomach until he saw a hint of a pink-and-black bra.

He kissed his way back down to her belly and scratched his chin against her mound, letting her clit know he'd be tending to it before too long. But first that stomach deserved his devotion. He set the bottom of the bottle against her flesh. She startled at the feel of cold glass; then her breathing turned shallow as he dragged the glass in loops along her waist from one hip bone to the other, then up her middle between her ribs to the base of her bra.

"Brace yourself," he murmured before drizzling champagne into her belly button.

She sucked in a sharp breath and gripped the blanket in both fists.

He buried his face in her middle and licked off every drop of champagne. He couldn't get enough of that blend of sweet wine and even sweeter skin. The more he tasted her, the more insatiable his hunger got.

He drizzled champagne over her panties, turning them transparent, the hair below becoming a rich brown now that it was wet. He pressed his lips to the wet fabric, reveling in her scent and the blended flavor of champagne and her arousal—a combination he'd never experienced before. He'd had no idea what he'd been missing.

He'd occasionally dabbled in food play at the request of his partners, but they usually stuck to the usual suspects of chocolate syrup and whipped cream. Nothing like the pleasure of having Remedy Lane laid out on a blanket under his favorite tree, her tanned, toned body drizzled with what was probably a very expensive bottle of alcohol.

He peeled the panties down her legs and tossed them on the blanket, then gave her a series of long, slow licks that made her whimper again, which was fast becoming his favorite sound in the world. Time for a new flavor addition to the party. What went best with champagne? Strawberries and chocolate, of course.

He nibbled the end off a berry, then traced her opening and along each fold and wrinkle, painting her flesh a deep pink. With each stroke of his strawberry paintbrush, she writhed. The blanket twisted in her grip and pulled from the ground. He loved that he could drive her wild, loved imagining how hard she was working not to grab his face and ride it like a cowgirl.

Time to reap the rewards of his efforts. He brought his mouth to her pussy and followed the same path as the strawberries, lapping up the heady blend of flavors. He would never think of strawberries or champagne again without his mind going back to this summer day with Remedy. Time to sink his fingers into her wet, tight body and take her all the way home.

He wet two fingers and pushed them inside her, so gently and sweetly that her flesh melted around him and her hips strained for more. The decisive thrust he gave her next wrested a whimper from her throat. He closed his eyes and gave himself over to the feast, massaging her G-spot with every thrust and licking her swollen clit with a building rhythm of soft and firm, slow and fast.

When she shattered, her cry echoed off the trees and sent birds flying. Her feet pedaled against the bank and her hips rose off the ground. He hooked his arms around her legs and locked his mouth against her, riding the wave of her release until she collapsed back, spent and panting.

For the first time since he'd gotten his mouth on her body, Micah became aware of his own arousal. His dick was hard as stone and pressing uncomfortably against the seam of his jeans. He sat back on his heels and unsnapped his fly. As he palmed himself over his underwear, his attention shifted to Remedy. Her legs were splayed on either side of him, her panties were soaking wet, and her chest heaved with the effort of breathing.

He dipped his hand inside his briefs and gave himself a rub. The first touch of his fingers against the base of his head made him see stars. Goddamn, Remedy revved his engine like no one else.

"Go ahead and say it," Remedy breathed, her eyes on the clouds.

"Say what?"

She barely mustered a lopsided smile, she was so relaxed. "Make a corny joke about me being the picnic."

"I considered it, but I'm still stuck on thinking about you as an offering on my redneck altar."

"But I've been waiting patiently for a picnic joke."

Though her tension had been sated, he was too consumed with driving need to make a joke. He released his erection and reached out to take her hand. "Do you have any idea how sexy you look right now? You're so damn hot that I'm not going to be able to sleep tonight, thinking about what you let me do to you today."

Remedy raised her hand and watched the mottled shadows dance over her skin. "They teach you how to do all this in alpha school?"

"What, food play?"

She molded his hand to her breast. "How to make mind-blowing love to a city girl out in the sticks."

He brushed his thumb over her breast until he could feel her nipple harden. "I'm not going to claim I've never made love out in the backcountry, but being here with you isn't like anything I've ever done before."

She arched, pressing her breast more firmly into his hand. "I'm your first celebrity lay?"

"How'd you know I didn't mean my first Briscoe Ranch Resort executive lay? Because you're that, too."

"For the record, you're not like anyone I've ever been with, either."

No surprise there. "Let me guess. . . ." He brought his hand up to enumerate on his fingers. "First Texan, first firefighter—"

She nudged his ribs with her foot. "First Alpha Bubba lay."

"I was gettin' to that part."

"Then I think it's time for the part I was gettin' to." She sat up. Drops of champagne and strawberry juice slid down her body like liquid jewels. "My turn."

If anyone were to stumble upon Remedy and Micah, they'd get quite an eyeful. He'd never considered himself an exhibitionist, but the thought sent a thrill through him. Out here in the Texas wilderness on a blanket with her he felt wild and free—and he loved every second of it.

She knelt before him and he had a moment's debate whether this was the direction he wanted to take their afternoon in. He'd wanted this picnic to be all about her pleasure, but the way she pressed lingering kisses to his stomach, her chin nudging his cock, destroyed his resistance.

She pulled the elastic band of his briefs down, freeing him. That act alone, the air hitting his bare flesh, was enough to rock him where he stood. He rolled his head back, his eyes closed, and concentrated on the feel of her hand stroking him.

At the first touch of her tongue, his breath left his body with a primordial grunt. He let his face fall forward and looked down the length of his body only to find that she was looking up at him. The way the sunlight and shadows hit her face, he could see the complicated hues of her eyes. Flecks of amber and black danced in the blue. Thick black lines rimmed her irises. Her eyes were so full of passion he almost forgot his name.

In that moment, staring into her eyes, he realized that she was, perhaps, this woman who'd crash-landed into his little town, one of the most complicated and fascinating souls he'd ever met. Making love to her was just as complicated and fascinating. Touching her, kissing and loving on her, charged him up with an undeniable electricity, even as the heavy sense of their connection smoothed out his rough edges.

This affair was going to change him. *She* was going to change him. He braced himself for a chaser of doom or fear to spoil the pure pleasure of it all, but it didn't come. She sank her mouth over his erection, taking him deep, and he was lost, body and soul.

Chapter Eleven

Wednesday was Remedy's favorite day of the workweek, a day of calm before the storms that rolled through her life every weekend. Thursday brides and their mothers would start lighting up her phone nonstop, anxious about last-minute details, and Fridays were burdened with a ticking-clock pressure and a to-do list that only seemed to get longer as the day wore on. But Wednesdays were Remedy's chance to have brainstorming conversations with future brides about their dream receptions, catch up on industry blogs, and peruse vendor catalogs at her leisure.

After a long morning meeting with Emily and Alex regarding that weekend's weddings—including two big productions with three-hundred-plus guests and two small events with simple ceremonies in the resort's wedding gazebos and reception dinners held in semiprivate rooms within the resort's main restaurant—Remedy was grabbing a breath of fresh air when Litzy sprinted by her in the opposite direction while pushing a rolling cart piled high with white tablecloths.

Remedy grabbed her sleeve as she passed. "Not so fast."

Litzy ground to a halt, though her body practically vibrated with impatience. "Sorry. I'll slow down."

"Rule number one in event planning: We never run, because we set the tone. No matter how dire the emergency, we're calm and in control. You never know if any resort guests or members of a bridal party are watching."

Litzy was a good employee—not great, but she was slowly getting the hang of Remedy's way of doing things—but they'd been over Remedy's rules before and apparently this particular one hadn't sunk in yet.

"Yes. Got it." Litzy seemed to be only half-listening. Her attention darted between Remedy and the end of the building. Remedy followed her gaze and saw the back bumper of a gray minivan.

Alarm bells sounding in her mind. Remedy was trying her best to trust Litzy—she truly was, because there was no logical reason to expect a repeat of the Zannity disaster—but it was obvious that Litzy was trying to hide something. Why was she pushing a rolling cart of white table linens out of the building? There were no special events at the resort that day. And what was up with that minivan? Remedy intended to find out.

"Good," Remedy answered. "Now go forth and be cool. Nice and easy."

Litzy shot another furtive glance toward the minivan. "Nice and easy. Got it."

She walked with forced slow steps toward the end of the building. Remedy waited, watching until Litzy had disappeared from view. Remedy stealth walked to the edge of the building and peeked around the corner. Litzy and a Latina woman who looked about Remedy's age were unloading the tablecloths into the back of the minivan.

"Litzy, what's going on?" Remedy said in her calmest, most collected tone.

Litzy and her accomplice jumped and whirled around in a fruitless attempt to shield their nefarious activity behind their backs.

Litzy gestured to the other woman, whose expression

redefined the term *poker face*. "We were just . . . moving some tablecloths."

"I can see that. Moving them where, precisely?"

"The resort won't need these until Friday's wedding," the other woman said.

So they weren't stealing, per se, but merely borrowing the linens for a day. Relief swept through Remedy. That she could handle. As long as Litzy wasn't sleeping with any of the grooms from the resort's upcoming weddings, Remedy could handle anything.

Remedy offered the other woman her hand. "I'm Remedy, the new special events manager. And you are?"

She eyed Remedy's hand, unimpressed. "Skye Martinez from Housekeeping. Maybe you've heard of my mother, Yessica, who is the head of housekeeping at Briscoe Ranch. As was her mother before her. Or maybe you know my father, Beto, who runs the maintenance department here and has been with the Briscoes for thirty years."

In other words, her family's legacy at the resort was almost equal to that of the Briscoe family itself. Skye was no dummy, which was exactly why she'd name-dropped her parents. It was a tactic Remedy had often used to great effect in Los Angeles when the need arose.

For the record, Remedy was no dummy, either, and she would rather aid and abet an unsanctioned tablecloth loan than start a war between the event staff and the housekeeping staff during her first month on the job, so she smiled brightly at Skye. "Then it's especially nice to meet you. I'll just be on my way and let you two get back to whatever perfectly lawful activity you're currently engaging in."

"We're not stealing," Skye said.

Remedy eyed the minivan, her eyebrow raised in question.

Skye lifted her chin higher. "We're borrowing these for the evening. We'll have them back before dawn. Please, if you could just keep that to yourself."

"I was planning on it," Remedy said. "Is this a common practice that I'm not aware of? Does Alex know?"

Skye's stony expression cracked. "He wouldn't understand."

Litzy clutched Remedy's arm. "Please don't tell him. He'd freak out. We'll never do this again; it's just—"

"I swear, I'm not going to tell anybody. Just have them back before anyone notices." Remedy tipped her head toward the minivan. "Out of curiosity, though, what are you using them for? A family party?"

Litzy squirmed. "A wedding. In town."

Good thing Remedy hadn't taken a drink from her water bottle, because she would've spewed it everywhere. "Uh, can you say 'conflict of interest'?"

Skye shook her head. "It's for Albert Dorcchi's wedding. He grew up in Dulcet and left to join the army. He came home this week to tell his family that he's shipping out on deployment to the Middle East and to propose to his girlfriend Tabby."

"She's not a cat. *Tabby*'s short for *Tabitha*," Litzy blurted out.

Skye set a hand on Litzy's arm. "Anyway, Albert and Tabby decided to get married before he leaves. They were prepared to go to a justice of the peace, but his mother wants a wedding. So the whole town is coming together today to give them one. Believe me that these tablecloths are for a noble cause."

"You had me at *deployment*," Remedy said. Her dad had always devoted most of his charitable work to organizations that aided veterans, which meant she'd grown up visiting VA rehab centers with him, helping build houses for wounded vets, and sitting at VIP tables at charity balls next to the veterans who were attending as guests of honor. There were fewer causes nearer or dearer to her than those supporting soldiers.

Litzy just about melted, she was so relieved. "Oh, thank you, Remedy."

"The wedding's tonight?"

Skye nodded. "Yes. At Great Redeemer Church. The reception will be in the fellowship hall. Like I said, we'll have the linens returned before anyone else notices they're gone."

Remedy ran through her mental list of wedding musts. "Do Tabby and Albert have centerpieces? Flowers?"

Skye and Litzy exchanged befuddled looks. "We're not sure. We only volunteered to take care of the tablecloths and punch."

Hmm. Remedy would have to get details about the reception décor herself. White tablecloths alone did not a once-in-a-lifetime memory make. "What do you mean by *punch*?"

"For the reception," Litzy said. "You know, a classic wedding punch."

"I've never heard of that. I thought champagne was the classic wedding drink." That and tequila shots, naturally.

"I don't think champagne is in their budget." Skye enumerated on her fingers. "All you need for wedding punch is a quart of orange sherbet, lemon-lime soda, and pineapple juice."

That sounded disgusting.

"Will you do it, Remedy? Will you keep our secret?" Litzy said. "Do it for the army. Do it for love."

Oh boy. "I'll like to do more than keep your secret, if you could use the extra hands. Let's get these linens in the minivan and get them over to the church."

"You're coming with us?" Skye asked delicately.

"I'll follow you over, in case I need to run back here and grab something else for the wedding. If I'm going to be an accessory to your crime, then we might as well see if Albert and Tabby need anything else from the resort."

"You're serious about this?" Litzy said.

"I really am. I can't think of anything I'd rather do today than give Albert and Tabby the best day of their lives."

Great Redeemer was an imposing brick building set behind a long green lawn. The parking lot was already crowded with cars and trucks when Remedy pulled in behind Skye's minivan. A wall of smoke and yummy smells of barbecued meat wafted over her when she stepped out of her car.

Behind an impressive line of grills on the far end of the lot was an even more formidable line of strapping Texas men, Micah in the middle of them, his signature ball cap pulled low over his forehead, a tight charcoal gray T-shirt stretched over his hard body, and a pair of tongs in his hand.

Remedy's heart did a little jump. Before she'd moved to Texas, when she'd thought of the state her mind never took her to runaway trained elephants or communities pitching in to throw a last-minute wedding. It never took her to shady creeks or never-ending kisses on a champagne-soaked picnic blanket. It never led her to the likes of Micah Garrity.

He'd looked mighty fine on Sunday evening when he'd picked her up for dinner at an upscale bistro on the outskirts of San Antonio, dressed in a sports coat and with his hair slicked back and styled. But she preferred him like he was today—a down-home country boy manning a grill, a local hero right in the middle of the action in the town he'd sworn his life to protect.

After dinner on Sunday, they'd fallen into her bed with the familiarity of longtime lovers. He hadn't slept over, though. He might have if she'd asked him to, but he'd seemed restless to check in with the fire station. Which was fine. They both led busy lives, and neither was quite certain how to navigate the terrain of their relationship given the demanding nature of their jobs.

Today, he didn't notice her right away, so Remedy pitched in with Skye and Litzy to unload the tablecloths and carry them inside by hand.

Remedy was headed back to the minivan for a second load when Micah ambled her way. "Well, well, well. If it isn't California. What are you doing here?"

"I'm helping, same as you. After all, true love must prevail." She didn't register the sarcasm she'd let slip into that phrase until it was too late.

Micah pressed his lips together, amused. "Is that a fact?"

"Oh, yes. That's the number-one rule of life. True love must prevail." Damn it, it'd come out sarcastic again.

"Why do I get the impression you think of that sentiment as more of a corporate motto and not a rule of life?" he said.

"Why can't it be one and the same? When you're a wedding planner, true love is your business."

He regarded her for a long minute, though she couldn't fathom what he was thinking; then he hooked his thumb over his shoulder, gesturing to the line of barbecue grills. "As much as I'd love to stand around and talk about true love, I'd better scoot. I've got meat to tend to."

A half-dozen dirty replies popped into her head. "We are at a church, so I'm going to just let that one go."

The desire smoldering in his expression took her right back to Sunday night and the look in his eyes when he'd raised his head from between her thighs to croon filthy compliments to her. A rowdy, reckless lust seized hold of her.

"Hey, Chief!" Chet called from behind one of the grills. "Need a second opinion on this brisket."

Remedy tipped her chin in Chet's direction. "Duty calls. You'd better go tend to your meat."

Micah's attention didn't waver from Remedy. His jaw tightened and his attention dropped to her lips. Then his eyes shifted, taking in the bustling activities all around them in the parking lot. "There are way too many people around right now."

She knew exactly what he meant. Probably they shouldn't even be flirting like this, talking low and making *fuck me* eyes at each other in front of his firefighting crew and Litzy and Skye and a town's worth of people who would probably love a fresh piece of gossip about their fire chief and the new wedding planner in town.

"You and me again. Soon," she said.

He smeared a hand over his chin as though fighting for composure. "Oh, it's on," he said in a husky whisper. "Tonight. Here, your place, my place, the resort. First time I catch you alone, it's on. Mark my words."

He looked her up and down; then, with a head shake and a growl, he turned on his boot heel and returned to the line of grills with a loose-limbed swagger that she couldn't take her eyes off of. Hot damn, she loved the way that man moved. He walked like he made love, all alpha confidence and muscled, masculine grace.

"Promise?" she called after him.

She caught notes of a low, deep chuckle as he tucked his chin over his shoulder and sent her one last heated look that curled her toes.

An elbow nudged her ribs. "You're watching him."

Shaking herself out of the spell she'd fallen into, she turned to find Litzy grinning at her.

"What? No. I don't know who you're talking about," Remedy said. "I was just wondering who I should talk to about centerpieces and smelling all that grilled meat cooking. Makes me wish I could stay for the reception."

"I'm sure you could. Albert and Tabby invited the whole town—including Chief Garrity," Litzy added along with a shoulder shimmy.

Remedy fought a cringe. "Can you pretend not to know about that?"

"Don't worry. Every woman with a pulse in Dulcet has

a crush on him, so you're in good company. Oh, and I checked with Tabby. She said you'll want to talk to Barbara Kline about centerpieces. Bright red hair, pink jogging suit. She's inside. You can't miss her."

Could it be the same Barbara who'd ignored Remedy at Petey's Diner? She was about to find out. Inside the fellowship hall Remedy saw some faces she recognized from the resort, but none with names she knew. A handful of women, including Skye, were adorning the tables with the tablecloths already, and one even had a centerpiece in place. Remedy buzzed the table, admiring the ingenuity of the centerpiece, a mason jar tied with a raffia bow and filled with wildflowers. A box along the wall was stuffed with similar arrangements. Sweet, simple, and perfect for a spontaneous summer wedding.

It was, indeed, the same Barbara from Petey's whom Remedy found wearing a pink jogging suit. She was standing near the buffet table laying out trivets and serving spoons.

"Barbara? I don't know if you remember me, but I'm a friend of Litzy's named Remedy. I'm wondering if there's anything I can help with."

Barbara set her hands on her hips and seemed to look right through Remedy. "Of course I know you. You're that wedding planner. We've got everything pretty near done, but thanks."

And dismissed.

But Remedy was nothing if not persistent. "What about wedding favors?"

Barbara's sigh of impatience was audible. "We're going to worry about those tonight. The food's all taken care of, I've got Jimmy running the dance music, Bob's daughter taking the pictures, the Randolph girls out buying sheet cakes, and I can't remember who's donating a cake cutter, but someone is. This isn't some fancy schmancy wedding like your type are used to."

Geez, she sounded like Micah. "No, it was an offer to donate them, if that would please Albert and Tabby."

Barbara's peeved expression softened. "Well, that's . . . That'd be nice."

Remedy had a huge order of pastel butter mints sitting in her office, neatly packaged in mesh pouches. That would do for tonight. "What about champagne?"

"That's too much money, even for you. We got Albert and Tabby a bottle, and the rest of us can toast with the drink we have in our hands at the time."

Champagne for a whole church of people would be pricey but not outrageous, and Remedy had two cases of it at her house. She'd swing by and get those first, then go to the grocery store to load up on more bottles, then stop at the resort for the mints and to borrow some champagne flutes from the catering kitchen supply room.

A sliver of dread snaked through her. She was certain that Ty Briscoe wouldn't approve of this. Neither would Alex or Emily or any of the other bigwigs at the resort. But if Ty was truly planning to use Remedy, as Micah believed, then he wasn't going to fire her for this minor infraction.

With only a few hours until the wedding, it was time to get to work. After a quick stop at her house, she drove her car right up to the resort's employee exit near where Skye had parked her minivan. She loaded boxes of champagne flutes onto a dolly on top of the box of butter mints, then crept back down the hall, out the door, and onto the final exterior walkway to her car, her heart pounding the whole time. Just because she didn't think she'd get fired didn't mean she wanted to get caught, either.

"Remedy!"

Shit. Remedy gritted her teeth. "Hi, Emily."

Emily was dressed in a worn chef's jacket, black leggings, and army green clogs. Her hair had been gathered under a red-and-green bandanna, though sweaty tendrils of curly hair had escaped around the edges. "I need a new oven."

"I know." As it had been explained to Remedy by Alex, Emily's favorite lineup of ovens were failing holdovers from a bygone era, but Emily hadn't found a suitable replacement in all the ones the hotel had attempted to install. "What happened this time?"

"Those wedding bell cookies that my pastry chef was baking for Friday's wedding are coming out uneven. Again. That stupid oven never works right when I need it most and Alex is such a cheap ass that he won't buy me a new one until next quarter. So now my pastry chef is pissed and I've got to waste my night helping her bake a whole new batch instead of perfecting the menu for the firefighter ball."

"Do you have a new oven in mind this time?"

"That's not the point. The point is you need to talk to Alex."

Not likely anytime soon, given Emily's track record and Alex's annoyance about it, but she wasn't going to stand around and debate it while standing with a stack of pilfered champagne flutes and butter mints. "Will do, next time I see him."

Then genius struck. After a moment's pause to debate the wisdom of her idea, Remedy said, "Instead of tossing those wedding bell cookies out, could I have them? I'm attending a wedding in town tonight."

"You are? For real?"

"Yes. I was invited."

"By Micah," Emily said.

"No, Skye Martinez." *Sort of.*

"And you want to give them the burnt cookies?"

Remedy feigned a casual shrug. "If you don't mind."

"The only thing I would mind is if you told anyone they came from my kitchen. I will not have my professional name associated with imperfection."

"Noted." On a wild hair, Remedy added, "You should come with me to the wedding tonight. Let your pastry chef make the cookies. The groom's family invited the whole town. I'll be there and so will Litzy and Skye. We could hang out."

Emily adjusted her bandanna, not quite meeting Remedy's eyes. "Oh. No, that's okay. I never know what to do with myself at things like that. Parties, you know? All those flashbacks of high school. So awkward. I'd probably end up in the church's kitchen trying to help, and that's stupid because, like I said, I've got a fresh batch of cookies to bake here before I can go home for the night."

Remedy hadn't known Emily was capable of rambling or insecurities. She gave in to the urge to hug Emily, she looked so discomfited by the idea of relaxing at the reception as a guest.

Emily stiffened in her embrace. "What are you doing?"

"Sorry." Speaking of awkward. What had gotten into Remedy? She and Emily weren't on hugging terms. "I'll just grab those cookies and get out of your hair."

By the time Remedy returned to the church there were some seriously mouthwatering smells coming out of the grills in the parking lot. The men manning them, Micah not among them, filled the air with gregarious laughs and loud stories, which probably had something to do with the nearby trash bag that was stuffed with empty beer bottles and cans.

Chet raised his tongs in greeting but kept his distance until Remedy hauled the dolly out of her backseat and popped the trunk. Then he was beside her, scooting her out of his way and stacking the boxes. He insisted on pushing the loaded dolly through the fellowship hall to the kitchen.

Micah had his back to them at the kitchen sink, elbow deep in dishwater and scrubbing a pan. When he glanced in Chet and Remedy's direction, he did a double take, then nodded discreetly at her.

"Thank you, Chet. How's the barbecue coming along?"

"It's going to be the best meat you've ever had."

She waited until Chet had left again before whispering, "Doubtful," just loud enough for Micah to hear.

He took a long look at her lips before shaking his head and getting back to tackling the dishes.

Barbara buzzed across the room with speedy purpose, but Remedy managed to snag her attention. This time, Barbara looked right at her and offered a tentative smile. "You're back."

"Yes, with party favors. Cookies and mints." She opened a plastic bin filled to the brim with sugar cookies in the shape of wedding bells, their edges turned a slight toasty shade.

"My goodness, thank you. I'll get someone to set those cookies on a tray and put the mints around on the tables."

Remedy held a flap of the box open so Barbara could see the champagne bottles within. "Oh, and, um, I was handed these boxes in the parking lot by someone who asked me to keep her identity anonymous. She said she wanted to help Albert and Tabby."

Barbara gasped. "Oh my, that's incredibly generous. I can't believe how this whole town is coming together. Delinda, look!"

An elderly woman hobbled over and hooked arms with Barbara. "Gracious."

"And, um, after she handed me the champagne to give to you, I realized you'd probably need champagne flutes, so I scrounged some up," Remedy said.

Her mouth agape, Barbara lifted one of the flutes out and admired it. "You have all these glasses at your house?"

"Well, I'd rather not say where they came from, if it's all the same to you. I'll just need to have them back where they belong by tomorrow morning."

Barbara squeezed Remedy's hand. "Thank you. And

please tell that anonymous donor thank you, too. Whoever she is, she's a mighty generous woman."

The way Barbara said it let Remedy know she wasn't pulling any wool over anybody's eyes about who had donated the supplies, but it would guarantee the focus remained on the bride and groom and not shift any spotlight to Remedy.

"The flutes will need a rinsing, but I'll take care of that after I find room in the refrigerator for the champagne," Remedy said.

While she was on her knees transferring bottles to chill, a pair of stockinged legs shuffled to her side. Delinda, the woman Barbara had called over.

"I'm Tabby's grandma, Delinda. Ain't nobody done something so nice for us before as everybody in Dulcet is doing today. Thank you." Delinda's voice hitched twice as she spoke.

Remedy slid the last bottle into the refrigerator and stood.

Delinda threw her arms around Remedy's shoulders and wept. It wasn't the first time the mother- or grandmother-of-the-bride had shed tears on Remedy's shoulder, though it usually wasn't out of gratitude but because of some element of family drama or the memory of a loved one who'd passed and wouldn't get to witness the wedding.

Remedy walked Delinda into the hall and pulled a chair out for each of them. Remedy held her hand and listened to tales of the hard road her daughter had chosen, her early death, and Delinda's choice to raise Tabby on her own. She talked about how grateful she was for Albert and Albert's family because she didn't think she had much more time left, but she could die at peace because Tabby wouldn't be alone, especially since Delinda had moved to an assisted-living facility.

Around them, wedding prep continued at a frenetic

pace. Every so often, Remedy caught sight of Micah out of the corner of her eye, but she kept her attention fixed on the woman before her. If there was one thing she'd learned from years of putting on weddings, it was that they dredged up all manners of vulnerabilities for the people involved—family secrets, old hurts, memories long suppressed, and a sentimentality that the grind of everyday life suppressed. Because of that, listening was often the most important aspect of Remedy's job. Not that it was easy to slow down and take the time to sit when she was being pulled in a million different directions, but that was why she had assistants.

Speaking of assistants, the next time Litzy appeared Remedy waved her over. "Would you make sure the bride has everything she needs in the prep room and bring her some champagne, like you do at Briscoe Ranch? You're so good at that."

"I'm on the job."

But before Litzy had crossed the room, the bride herself appeared in the fellowship hall, an older woman trailing behind her and fussing over her dress.

Tabby was a freckled, fair-skinned redhead who was young enough that she didn't quite seem to belong in the slightly wrinkled lacy long-sleeved wedding gown that almost fit her, though not quite.

She spotted Delinda and walked with heavy steps to their table and sank into a chair on a sob. "Tabby, baby. Why the tears?" Delinda said.

"I miss him already."

The women in the room flocked around her, cooing and offering words of support.

"What am I going to do with myself when Albert leaves? How am I going to bear being in the apartment every night alone?"

"Oh, honey, we'll make sure you're not alone," Barbara said.

Litzy took her hand. "You could come work with us at the resort. Evenings, weekends, that's when we're busiest."

Tabby dabbed at her tears with a tissue. "It'd be fun to work with you. And at least I wouldn't be home."

Litzy had no business offering Tabby a job, but it wasn't a bad idea. Remedy needed more help, and she'd already checked with Alex to make sure there was room in the budget for another wedding assistant or two.

Remedy touched Tabby's shoulder. "If you came to work at the resort, would it be difficult for you to be around so many happy couples, since Albert won't be here?"

Pain shadowed Tabby's face. She drew a shaky breath. Remedy felt like a heel for reminding her of the painful times ahead, but Tabby would be better off realizing now that being a wedding assistant might be too emotionally difficult than once she was on the job.

"I think I'd be okay," Tabby said with a sniff, reaching for another tissue from the box. "It might help me stay strong to focus on what matters most and remind me of what'll be waiting for me at the end of Albert's deployment."

Remedy squeezed Tabby's hand. "Your true love will be waiting for you."

"Yes. My beautiful husband, my true love." Her eyes welled with tears.

It was enough to put some cracks in the shield of cynicism guarding Remedy's heart. It was enough to almost make her believe in true love as more than hocus-pocus—more than a corporate motto or a celebrity's publicity stunt. Remedy had always thought deep, abiding love was a relic of a bygone era. But what if it wasn't? What if it'd been hiding out in modest church fellowship halls and small towns in Texas all along?

Chapter Twelve

The reception was in full swing by the time Micah finished serving the brisket, tidying the kitchen, and having his ear bent by a continuous stream of townsfolk who wanted his attention. He stepped into the fellowship hall with a plate of food and a beer, his eyes scanning the crowd for a head of blond hair and a California tan, along with one of the prettiest faces he'd ever laid eyes on.

He had yet to get Remedy alone all night. His hope of sitting next to her during the ceremony was dashed when he was flanked by members of his fire crew who were giving off weird, aggressive vibes, though he couldn't imagine why they'd be tense and out of sorts, and they hadn't been interested in explaining to him the cause. After the ceremony, he'd been the one to disappear on kitchen duty. The next time he'd located her, she'd been busy assisting with wedding photos by fluffing the bride's gown and suggesting camera angles.

But now the eating was done, the cake had been cut, and all that was left was the socializing and dancing. He wasn't going to let anything or anyone stop him from getting close to the woman he'd had his eye on all day.

He found Remedy near the punch bowl, cradling a

punch cup in her hands and talking to Litzy Evansburg and
Skye Martinez. Remedy definitely looked out of her element, but he had to give her credit. She'd borrowed from
the hotel, surely at the risk of her job, and she'd worked
tirelessly all afternoon and evening—and all without taking over the wedding planning in an overbearing way or
looking down her nose at the humble event or its working-
class crowd.

Micah had taken a step in her direction when Chet
passed him, thumping his shoulder against Micah's, a cold,
distant look in his eye as though he didn't recognize
Micah. What the hell was going on with these guys?

"Chet!" Micah called, walking after him. "The brisket
was a huge hit. Good call on adding brown sugar to the
barbecue sauce."

Chet held up his hands in a shrug and backed away.

"Hey, what's up with you, man? You pissed at me about
something?"

Chet's expression turned even harder. "Nope."

So then, that was a yes. Well, that was just tough shit,
because Micah didn't feel like dealing with Chet's or anyone else's immature drama that night. If none of them were
man enough to spit out what was bothering them, then
Micah wasn't going to beg for answers.

He turned his attention to Remedy again. Though Skye
and Litzy were busy in an animated conversation, Remedy frowned into her cup of punch. She had a faraway look
on her face. Wistful. Good thing he knew just the way to
cheer her up.

Micah snagged two flutes of champagne from the drink
table. As he walked to Remedy, he got busy brainstorming places he could steal her away to and have his way with
her. A Sunday schoolroom? The church library near the
main office? Then again, he could get her in his truck and
take her someplace private. Like his house, only a few

blocks away. Didn't matter to him as long as he got his hands and mouth on that hot body of hers, pronto.

When she saw him coming she smiled, but it didn't quite touch her eyes, as though she couldn't get past whatever deep thoughts she'd been engrossed in.

"Great barbecue, Chief," Skye said when he joined them.

Several years back, Micah had entertained the idea of asking Skye out, because she was a looker with a fiery personality, but her family had a lot of clout and a long history at Briscoe Ranch, so he'd shied away. As attractive as Skye was, the fact that he'd so easily decided against getting involved with her romantically because of his fraternization rule told him all he needed to know about their compatibility, especially given how Remedy had wrapped him around her little finger the moment he laid eyes on her.

"Thank you. It was a team effort. How's your dad doing these days?" To Remedy, he added, "Skye's dad suffered a minor heart attack a year or so ago. Chet and I were the first on the scene."

"You got him to the hospital in time to save him. Thanks to you, he's made a full recovery," Skye said.

Remedy bit her lip against a smile. "Chief Garrity is pretty good at saving the day."

He squared up to her, painting a look of indignation on his face. "Only pretty good?"

Shaking her hair away from her face, she held his gaze, her eyes glittering with wicked playfulness.

Skye cleared her throat. She linked arms with Litzy. "Excuse us. We've got to . . . uh, go over there."

Litzy's face scrunched with confusion, but she allowed Skye to drag her away, which was right kind of Skye. Thank goodness for her womanly intuition to sense how badly Micah wanted to get Remedy all to himself.

He set the extra glass of champagne on the table behind her, then clinked his champagne flute against her paper cup. "You're a tough one to get alone tonight. And I can't even blame a bunch of delusional groomsmen who want to corrupt you."

She opened her arms. "Thank goodness a red top and black skinny jeans don't exude any virgin librarian vibes."

"But they do give off an onslaught of sexy-as-hell wedding planner vibes." The urge to wrap his arms around her and lay a big old kiss on her was a strong one. But there were still too many eager eyes around them for any public displays of affection, not if they didn't want the whole town to talk. "What were you thinking about before I got over here? You looked lost."

Her expression shifted to the dance floor where Albert and Tabby were cutting a rug amid a circle of friends. "I was thinking about how I'm going to talk to Alex about giving active-duty soldiers and local Ravel County couples a discount on weddings at the resort. And maybe I can set up some low-budget wedding packages. I don't think it would've helped Albert and Tabby, but it's a start in the right direction. The resort has a lot of resources to help the town, but it's not taking the opportunity, as far as I can tell."

"I agree, one hundred percent, but why do I get the feeling that wasn't what was actually bothering you? What's really on your mind?"

That melancholy smile returned. She set her punch cup down and held her index fingers against the sides of her head, rotating them like antennae. "I am an alien on a foreign planet tonight. I'm not fitting in well, despite my best efforts."

He grabbed her closest antenna and brought it down so he could hold her hand, threading their fingers together. He'd be damned if he just stood there and let her feel alone. "I'm sorry you're feeling out of place again."

"That's okay. I'm used to it."

She didn't sound used to it. She sounded weary. It had to be draining to never feel like you belonged. Suddenly he wasn't in a hurry to get physical. It was nice to stand next to her and hold her hand and talk, help her feel more like she belonged in Dulcet. "You didn't look like you were enjoying the punch."

She shrugged. "It's interesting, but too sweet for my taste."

"Haven't you ever had wedding punch before?"

Grimacing, she shook her head. "Can I confess something to you?"

"Of course."

"You're going to snicker," she said.

"The suspense is killing me."

She drew a deep breath, then lifted the extra champagne flute he'd brought and drank. "That's good and cold."

"Out with it. What am I going to snicker about?"

Her mouth contorted, as though she was either building up the courage to say something more or trying to find the right words. "I've never been to a wedding reception at a church hall before. It's . . . nice. Sweet."

She had to be joking. Even so, he tamped the urge to snicker, as she'd predicted he'd be apt to do. "Are you serious? But you're a wedding planner."

She sipped more champagne, and he could tell she was winding up for a big speech as she was apt to give. "The big, expensive weddings I plan, they're seldom about the bride and groom's love for each other, or about family in any real sense of the word. They're about showing off. You know what I ask every bride before I start working with her? 'Why are we doing this? What's the goal of this wedding?' They never say love. Never. It's either so their parents can show off, or it's to show up their friends, or about sibling rivalry. Sometimes it's about revenge on an ex or a publicity stunt to help the bride's or groom's career."

"That's genuinely sad," he said, meaning it. Not just about all those couples with screwed-up values but also for their friends and the people who worked at the weddings. For Remedy.

She continued, "This wedding tonight might have been for Albert's mother's benefit, but it really is about true love. You can see it written in every detail of the wedding and on Albert's and Tabby's faces. This is what love looks like. It's . . . wonderful. It really is."

"I've been noticing how jaded you are for a wedding planner. There've been a few times I've wondered at what point in your career you'd gotten that cynical."

"Early. Weddings aren't all they're cracked up to be."

A bark of laughter escaped him, but he couldn't help it. That was the last thing he would've expected her to say. "The wedding planner is anti-marriage?"

"Not anti-marriage. Just anti–big weddings. If I ever get married, it will be exactly the kind of wedding Albert's mom didn't want for him," Remedy said.

"You want to be married by a justice of the peace at the courthouse?" What a depressing thought.

"Yup. Fast, simple, and stress-free."

"That's the most unromantic thing I've ever heard," he said.

"Yeah, well, big weddings aren't all that romantic, either. And before you clutch your pearls at that," she said, drawing an imaginary strand of pearls on his chest, "you should know I'm not the only planner who feels that way. You can ask any one of us and we'll all say the same thing—at least, those of us who want to get married. Most wedding planners are divorced."

This conversation was getting crazier and more depressing by the moment. "You're kidding."

"Dead serious. I'm a romantic fool compared to my colleagues. There's something about planning wedding after wedding that sucks all the magic out of it."

He rubbed his chin, considering. It wasn't a surprise that she was jaded about weddings—he'd sensed that when they'd talked in the parking lot that afternoon with her true love corporate motto—but it still rubbed him wrong. "Not here tonight. You were right about all the love in the air. I feel it, too. Albert and Tabby are the real deal."

Remedy held up her champagne flute. "To the happy couple."

He clinked his glass against hers. Acting on a hunch, he said, "The champagne was a big hit."

"Yeah, it seemed to be."

"The label on the champagne bottles looked suspiciously familiar." He took another sip. "Tastes familiar, too."

Her baby blue eyes met his. "Albert's father mentioned in his speech that it came from an anonymous donor," she said.

Uh-huh. "That's one bighearted donor. Probably a hopeless romantic."

She nudged his ribs with her elbow, a bona fide genuine smile playing on her lips now. "Albert and Tabby deserve the best for their special day."

The first strains of a disco-era golden oldie started from the speakers. The makeshift dance floor in the center of the room was only half-full, mostly the newly-weds and their pals. But Micah wasn't going to let that intimidate him. He wiggled their joined hands. "Let's dance."

"What happened to 'It's on. Tonight. Mark my words' now that you've got me alone? Shouldn't we be sneaking off together?"

"The night is young and I've got the sudden urge to show a certain sexy alien that she might fit in with the earthling town she crash-landed in better than she thinks."

Her smile brightened.

He led the way to the dance floor. "A word of warning: I'm a terrible dancer."

"Then why do you want to dance?"

"Because the good people of Dulcet love to see their

very important fire chief make a fool out of himself and I love to make them happy. You're wearing closed-toe shoes, so at least your feet aren't in too much danger."

Her laughter did a funny thing to his heart.

Unlike Remedy with her slinky, practiced moves, Micah tried to find the rhythm in the song, but he was a hopeless mess. Even his step-tap was off-beat and throwing his elbows around didn't seem to improve his style at all. He got a lot of hoots and hollers from the crowd because everyone knew how terrible he was, but that was fine. Indeed, maybe he was a trendsetter, because after he and Remedy took to the floor a flood of people crowded onto the dance floor and joined in. Probably because Micah made them look good.

Ignoring the teasing, he focused his attention on Remedy's sexy moves and even sexier body. But even she couldn't stop chuckling. "You really are awful!" she called over the music.

"Told ya. Be grateful I didn't try to dance at Hog Heaven last Friday."

There were a lot of Briscoe Ranch employees at the reception. He doubted Remedy even realized that she was dancing among so many landscapers and maintenance workers, stable help, and housekeeping staff—and they kept sneaking glances at Remedy like she really was an alien among them. Resort executives didn't mingle with regular townsfolk, and they definitely didn't dance at hometown weddings.

But Remedy wasn't any ordinary executive. She was so much more than her pedigree. Micah's pride and life experiences had kept him from acknowledging it, but he couldn't deny it any longer. He wanted her. Not only her body, and not only when on the occasional date, but all of her, all the time. She had no idea how long it'd be before she moved home to Hollywood, but until that happened he was going to make the most of the time they had. When she packed up and left he wanted her to feel what she was giving up.

He stopped moving. "Hey."

"Hey what?"

So help him, he just couldn't keep away from her for one second longer. He cupped her neck as his other arm slid around her waist.

"There are still too many people around," she said, even as she crushed her breasts to his chest and melted into him. Her hand stroked up his arm, touched his cheek.

Their eyes locked together. It was the damnedest thing, but every time they got this close he could actually feel the electricity surging between them, racing across his skin, vibrating through his muscles, lodging deep in his bones. Before he'd met her, he'd thought the idea of getting lost in someone's eyes was corny and stupid, a mockery of the way the real world worked, but he could lose himself so easily in Remedy it was no joke.

"I want to date you, Remedy. Officially. Exclusively."

"Is that the champagne talking?"

He shook his head. "This is all me."

The delight that sparked in her eyes sent another ripple of electricity through him. "Then I'd say you should kiss me. Officially."

Hell, yeah, he should. He lowered his lips to hers, drawing hers open with his tongue, taking her deep and sweet and hot, with all of Dulcet as their witnesses.

Chapter Thirteen

"This is no ordinary Bible." Granny June's palm smoothed the glass case covering the sepia-toned-paged book displayed in the vestibule of the Briscoe Ranch Chapel. Colored light from the stained-glass windows turned the papery skin of her hands red and gold and green. "This was a wedding gift from Tyson's parents, passed down through six generations of Briscoes. Every Briscoe birth and Briscoe wedding is recorded in this Bible. It is the keeper of our family's history."

Remedy had been in the middle of a whirlwind day of planning for the firefighter ball and a multitude of weddings when Granny June had appeared at her office door, determined to lure her away from her desk for a tour of the resort grounds. With the day Remedy was having, she should have refused, but one of her favorite parts of working at Briscoe Ranch was its history and the grounding sense of the Briscoe family's legacy present in every building and garden. No one encapsulated that family history better than Granny June, and there was something about the twinkle in her eye that rendered Remedy helpless to rebuff the invitation.

So here they were in the quiet majesty of the chapel,

the last stop on a tour that had taken Remedy through the original wing of the hotel, along a windy garden path past the original stable and groundskeeper house where Carina and her husband now lived, and up to the Briscoe homestead tucked out of sight in a far corner of the land at the edge of the vast wilderness beyond, with sweeping views of canyons and hilltops and an endless sea of trees.

The chapel had always seemed to have a mystical quality to it, Remedy had thought from her first day on the job, but she was learning from Granny June that it was far more historically important to the Briscoes than she could've imagined. She'd already known Granny's late husband was interred in a plot behind the chapel, but she'd had no idea that Tyson Briscoe had built the chapel himself, including the altar and the cross that hung behind it. And she'd never noticed all the Briscoe family artifacts that graced every wall and corner of the chapel's interior, the family Bible included.

Standing behind Granny June, she leaned over her shoulder and read the description etched into the bronze plaque affixed to the Bible's glass case. *The Briscoe family Bible, from 1876; Open to Ruth 1:16–17, a reading from Tyson and June Briscoe's wedding, the first of such ceremonies held at this chapel, December 1954.*

"We didn't have reason to host any more weddings here for another ten years, after we'd transformed the original homestead into a hotel, but in all those fifty-two years no couple who's ever married here in the month of December has ever gotten divorced. Folks around Ravel County started calling it the Mistletoe Effect. Well, the truth is I suggested that name for the phenomenon in an interview I did with *The Dallas Morning News* sometime in the eighties. And the name stuck. It's what the resort is best known for now."

No wonder the chapel had a mystical quality about it. The whole resort, really. Even if the popularity of the

Mistletoe Effect proved that there were a lot of couples out there who were as jaded about the power of true love as Remedy was, since they looked to a bunch of superstitious malarkey to help them stay married.

One of the stipulations of Remedy taking the event planner job at the resort was that she'd be working without a break between Thanksgiving and Christmas Eve, with at least one wedding taking place every day of the week during that time. Remedy agreed, partly because she had no idea if she'd still be around then to worry about it.

Granny flitted away from the Bible to another display in the vestibule's opposite corner. "This way. I've got one last thing to show you and it's priceless. Tyson's and my wedding album."

"The actual album? Here where all the resort guests can flip through it?"

"The very one." She flipped the album to the first page, a black-and-white formal shot of a beautiful young woman with Granny June's spitfire eyes and sly smile, that same pointed chin and regal posture, standing in embrace with a much taller, strapping man whose face was eerily similar to Ty Briscoe's. "After he died, I couldn't bear to have the album in our home. I felt haunted by it, and by his memory. So filled with grief that I was lost to the world."

Granny's eyes had gone watery. "And then one night Tyson came to me in a dream, and he told me that I needed to celebrate his memory with all the world, not hide him away on a shelf. The day I moved the album here along with our family Bible was the day I found peace. He and I accomplished so much together. This resort, the weddings we host, it's everything to me and my family. Always has been. And now, when I'm in this chapel, I can feel Tyson's spirit all around me. It's the most magical sensation. This is the place I feel most at home now on the property. Here, with him."

Another piece of Remedy's cynicism fell away as she

flipped through the wedding album. "You two have the deepest love I've ever heard of. I've never seen its equal."

Granny June dabbed at the corner of her eyes with a handkerchief, then patted Remedy's hand. "Someday you will find a deep, abiding love of your own. And when you do, you'll understand the magic."

She had Remedy hook, line, and sinker. Magic, the mistletoe phenomenon, a land steeped in history . . . Briscoe Ranch Resort was one of a kind.

They were strolling out of the chapel when Remedy's ringtone sounded with a call from Micah. It'd been a week since he'd kissed her at Albert and Tabby's wedding. In the days since then, they'd both been busy with their jobs, so sheet-scorching, sleepless nights together had become their new norm. As today was a workday, a phone call, rather than a text, was unusual.

A tingle of unease tickled her throat. He'd talked a lot about the increased risk of fire in the backcountry that week and had prepped her for the possibility that he and his crew might get called away to help should one such emergency arise. She'd never had a boyfriend who regularly risked his life, and she wasn't a fan of the fear it evoked. Not one bit.

"It's Micah. Do you mind if I answer it?"

Granny June's lips pursed in that same sly smile Remedy had glimpsed in her wedding day portrait. "He's a fine young man."

"Very much so."

"Don't keep him waiting."

"Hi. Is everything okay?" Remedy asked him.

"I'm declaring war," he said.

The declaration was said with a hint of lightness, and Remedy knew immediately that today was not the day he ran off to face the ravages of a fire head-on. "War with who?"

"Not a who, a what. Your damned pigeon groupies.

They must have followed you to my place, because I opened my front door and there they were demolishing the sweets from my pastry pipeline."

Skeeter had better get his pigeons soon, because this was getting out of control. "Oh, no! The secret admirer pastries? What a waste!"

"Right? And when I shooed them off they took a dump all over my truck before flying off in the direction of the resort. Returning home to you, I'm sure."

"I'm so sorry. I'll call their owner again and see when he can come try to coax them into their cages again."

Micah snorted. "I've got a better idea. You ever been pigeon hunting?"

"We can't kill the pigeons."

Granny June nudged her. "Oh, yes, we can, especially after they ate those muffins today. Tell 'em to come over and we'll go pigeon hunting any time he wants. I've got a .22 in my golf cart and I'm a crack shot."

Terrifying, that nugget of information. Remedy couldn't decide who the bigger danger to the resort at large would be if the two of them went pigeon hunting in a golf cart: her or Granny June.

"I heard that," Micah said. "Are you with my other favorite lady?"

"Yes. Granny June was giving me a tour of the resort."

"You'll have to tell me all about it tonight. Meanwhile, you tell her that I know all about last year's opossum incident and if I see her handling a .22 I'm going to confiscate it as a matter of public safety."

Atta boy. To Granny June, she said, "Dare I ask about the opossum incident?"

Granny waved her off. "My son blew that all out of proportion. And if he thought confiscating that Remington was gonna make me lie down and play dead, then that just means the boy don't know his own mother very well. Same with your man here. Tell him I thought he knew me better'n that."

Micah clicked his tongue. "Someday I'll convince the good men at the Ravel County Rifle Range to stop selling to her, if it's the last thing I do for this town."

The call-waiting chime sounded on Remedy's phone. "I'm getting another call, Micah. I'll see you tonight."

"Count on it, California."

The call was from Ty Briscoe's secretary, who insisted Remedy come to Ty Briscoe's office immediately, though she wouldn't say why. Granny June offered to drive her in her golf cart, but the thought of Granny packing a .22 somewhere on her rig, given what a crazy driver she was, was enough to make Remedy swear off ever driving with her again.

Located at the end of a hall of administrative offices behind the main check-in desk, Ty's corner office over-looked the golf course and the lake. Remedy had only been in it twice. For her final interview and on her first day of the job, when she swung through to thank him in person for the opportunity. Other than that, he had remained largely invisible but an ever-present specter in her life—one that she kept her eye out for with dreaded anticipation every day.

Was he as ruthless as Micah had characterized him? Or as much of a killjoy as Granny June had made him out to be? Or perhaps Remedy had been worried over nothing and he was the devoted, loving father figure that Carina saw him as.

Ty's secretary waved Remedy into his office. He stood at the wall of windows with two women, slim blondes who were impeccably dressed in white skinny jeans and breezy, bohemian blouses—cookie cutters of each other. Mother and daughter. Women whom Remedy would know anywhere.

Remedy's lungs seized up until she shook herself out of the trace. "Cambelle? Helen? Is that really you?"

At the sound of Remedy's voice, all three people turned in her direction.

Cambelle's hands shot into the air and she squealed, "Surprise!" Then she lowered her left hand and struck a pose to show off the massive diamond ring on her ring finger. "I'm engaged! And I'm here so you can plan my wedding!"

Wait, what?

Helen rushed past her daughter, her tasteful French-manicured fingers reaching for Remedy. "Oh, sweetheart, you look as fresh and beautiful as a poppy in a sunny field. No. A daffodil. That's what you are." She hugged Remedy tightly and petted her hair. "A tall, bright daffodil reaching for the sun on a temperate summer day, moving in the breeze, and—"

Sounded like Helen still fancied herself a budding author. "Helen, it's great to see you. And I see congratulations are in order." She gestured to Cambelle. "But how? I mean, you weren't serious about any of the guys you were dating when I left L.A. and my mom hasn't mentioned that you were seeing anyone. When did this happen? Who is this guy?"

Cambelle braced her hands on Remedy's shoulders. "Wynd Fisher happened. He swept me off my feet. We're so in love. I asked your mom to keep it a secret so I could tell you myself."

Remedy's mouth opened and closed. She darted a glance at a mirror on the side wall to make sure she still projected the look of a seasoned professional. "Wynd Fisher, the music producer?" The sixty-five-year-old pot-bellied, frizzy-haired music mogul worth billions? Maybe she and Cambelle had grown further apart than Remedy realized, because this was the woman who'd come up with the rallying cry *suits, not boots* to make a point about the caliber of men who were worthy of them.

Then again, a billion dollars was a lot of caliber.

Cambelle clapped with her fingertips. "That's him.

That's my Wynd. TMZ is calling us WestWynd. Isn't that perfect?"

Don't think of the two of them kissing . . . don't think about the two of them having— "Oh my. Wow. That's . . . wow. You've dated him how long?"

"Four weeks. That's enough time to know," Helen said. "It's magic. There's no other way to describe it. He's magic to my Cambelle's muse. The fire to her flame."

"He's all that and more." Cambelle swooned.

"And you want me to plan your wedding?" Remedy said.

"Of course they do." Ty's voice made Remedy jump. She'd forgotten all about him.

"I know we can trust you," Cambelle said to Remedy. "You understand what it's like to live in the public eye. Constant vigilance is what it takes. The only photographs of this wedding that we want in magazines are the ones we sell to them."

"Of course. We'll hire the best security in the world to keep this wedding on the down low," Ty said.

"We'd never thought of Cambelle getting married somewhere as—well, no offense, Ty—coarse as Texas, but your mom can be very persuasive," Helen said.

And that, right there, told Remedy everything she needed to know. Her stomach twisted into a knot. "Yes, she can."

"Let's sit down," Ty said. "Tell us how we here at Briscoe Ranch Resort can give you both the wedding of your dreams."

As they found their seats, Remedy ignored her growing anger over her mom's motives for springing this on her and tried to recall her usual questions for new clients. She blurted the first one that came to mind. "Have you given any thought to a specific color palette or theme?"

"We want understated elegance," Helen said.

"And fireworks," Cambelle added.

Helen raised her arm in a sweeping gesture. "Think pots of blue orchids lining a marble tub in Paris, the Eiffel Tower outside the window. Think timeless, as Cambelle and Wynd's marriage will be."

"Lots of fireworks," Cambelle said, bouncing in her chair. Her eyes went wide. "Do you think you could find exotic parrots with feathers that match our color scheme to have on display?"

"We're going for understated elegance," her mom scolded.

Ty nodded, clearly on board with all this insanity. "Parrots are elegant."

"Actually, uh, live animals aren't the most reliable option at weddings. So many things could go wrong," Remedy said.

Cambelle pouted—an actual, honest-to-god toddler pout. "I want parrots."

"Then parrots you shall have. Parrots and fireworks and anything else that will make this the best day of your life."

Forget his reputation as a villain or a killjoy or a doting father—Ty Briscoe was a shark of a salesman. No wonder he was so successful.

Cambelle gave a swish of her hand. "Oh! I have a new idea. A theme. I was thinking on the drive from the airport about this. Mom, what do you think about Redneck Chic?"

Um . . . what?

Helen clapped. "Isn't that a riot? Cambelle's got such an artist's eye, always has."

"I want horses and red Solo cups and hay bales and parrots and fireworks."

"Done, done, done, done, and done," Ty said. "And did you know we have a specially designated barn just for weddings?"

They did? That was news to Remedy.

"I think your guest list will be too extensive to hold the reception there, that will need to be in our grand ballroom, but the barn would be perfect for photographs or perhaps the rehearsal dinner," Ty said.

Helen slapped her knees. "What a hoot! Oh, Cambelle, this is meant to be. Wynd's going to love it as much as he loves you."

"What is the wedding date you're aiming for?" Remedy asked.

Cambelle squirmed anxiously, but Helen patted her knee. "That's the catch."

Remedy scooted to the edge of her chair. That stress knot in her stomach turned to lead.

"It's no catch," Ty assured her. "No catch at all. Our girl Remedy here has everything under control."

Remedy unclenched her teeth. "What's the catch, Helen?"

Cambelle burst out, "We have to get married on the last Saturday in August."

"Next year?" Remedy squeaked.

"Next month."

"Six weeks," Ty said. "Plenty of time." He winked at Helen for good measure.

Helen reached across and clasped Ty's hand. "Excellent. Of course, Wynd told us to tell you he'll be paying you a premium for the trouble."

If Remedy squinted hard, she could probably see actual dollar signs in Ty Briscoe's eyes. She stood and slid along the front of Ty's desk, facing Helen and Cambelle and trying to gain some sense of control over the spiraling conversation. "And . . . and . . . how many guests, approximately?"

"Five hundred."

A five-hundred-guest wedding and reception with beefed-up security and live animals and fireworks. In six weeks. With Remedy already executing more than twenty weddings in the interim, as well as the Firefighters' Charity Ball in two weeks.

Oh boy.

Three hours later, Cambelle and Helen preceded Ty and Remedy out of the resort's special event barn, ready to be whisked away to the resort's day spa for complimentary treatments at Ty's invitation in advance of their late-evening flight on a private jet to New York to be reunited with their beloved Wynd.

Ty lingered just inside the barn door. "Nice work, Remedy. I knew you were a gamble worth taking. With your parents' help, Briscoe Ranch is on target to be the next hot celebrity wedding locale."

Remedy stopped in her tracks. *Her parents' help? Oh, hell, no.* Her mom might have persuaded Cambelle and Wynd to hold their wedding at the resort, but that sort of thing couldn't keep happening. How could Remedy forge her own path in the industry if her parents didn't give her a chance?

"All due respect, but you hired me, not my parents."

"On your parents' recommendation."

"Excuse me?"

He pulled a red handkerchief from his pocket and dabbed at the sweat on his forehead, though his eyes remained cold and sharp. "Before I made my final decision to hire you, your parents called me personally. I assumed you knew that."

No, she most certainly did not. "They called you . . . together?"

"Separately. One after the other. But they both said the same thing. That given their influence in the industry, I'd be a fool not to hire you. They were right."

The number-one rule of wedding planning was not to let 'em see you sweat. That went for brides—and bosses.

She'd deal with her parents later, but before Ty left she had one last point to hammer home. "My point was let's not forget that my parents aren't the ones who will be planning this wedding. I will. And all of Wynd's and Cambelle's celebrity friends who attend will be seeing my genius, not my parents'. When word of mouth starts to spread around Hollywood about Briscoe Ranch"—and about her skills as a wedding planner—"which it will, immediately, it will be because I made it happen, along with you and the resort's many exceptional qualities. Let's keep the credit where the credit's due."

Ty's smile was as unexpected as it was disarming. "You're a lot like me, you know. Ambitious. I had opportunities handed to me, just like you, and I realized right away that it's not about who opens the door for you but about how driven you are when you walk through it."

She hoped to God that the two of them were nothing alike. "Yes, sir."

"How about I deliver the Wests to the spa and leave you to get a head start on planning this wedding?" Ty said.

"Thank you. There's no time to lose."

He flashed her one last smile. "Not for the ambitious."

The moment the door shut behind him, Remedy dropped to a hay bale, overwhelmed and in disbelief at the surreal turn her day had taken. She wasn't sure what had her more off-balance. The tight time frame? That her Hollywood past had descended into her present life? That twenty-nine-year-old Cambelle was marrying her sixty-five-year-old producer? That having the wedding at Briscoe Ranch had been Remedy's mom's idea?

No. Remedy knew the answer. It was the revelation that Ty Briscoe had hired her not because of her credentials or vision but because her parents had gone behind her back to ensure it. As though they didn't believe in her ability to forge her own career separate from them.

She would never forget the look on her mother's face

when she told her she was let go from her job in Los Angeles because of the Zannity scandal. She would never, ever get over her father's palpable disappointment in her in that moment. Disappointment that was apparently so dire that her parents had actually, for once in their lives, overcome their mutual distaste of each other to conspire together.

And yet, if they hadn't intervened, would she not have gotten this job that she was genuinely enjoying? Maybe Ty was right and it didn't matter who opened the doors of opportunity for you, but there was opening doors and then there was coddling a grown, intelligent, ambitious woman who had expressly asked her parents to stay out of her business. Maybe she should be thanking them.

Maybe.

She dialed her mother's number. As it rang, she felt seventeen again, with the part of her that was desperate for freedom warring with the self-doubting part of her that feared herself incapable and wondered if independence was worth the risk of her parents' disappointment.

"Sweetie! What a nice surprise. And me without champagne!"

"It's not that kind of call." Her pulse beat in her throat. She hated confrontations with her parents. Hated them more than anything in the world. Her parents were her home, her people. Nothing made her feel more drifting and lost and alien than being at odds with them.

"What's wrong, dear?"

She swallowed hard. "I saw Cambelle and Helen today. Cambelle and Wynd Fisher are getting married here, at Briscoe Ranch."

Her mother gave a whoop of triumph. "Isn't that wonderful? You should see them together, Remedy. He's crazy about that girl. I was bursting, having to keep that secret from you for so long."

Remedy shook her head. "He's only crazy about her

because he's a senior citizen and about to marry a woman thirty-six years younger than him."

"Don't be such a sourpuss. They're great together. You'll see."

"Mom, Helen said it was your idea to have the wedding at Briscoe Ranch. Is that true?"

"Of course, dear. It was the least I could do for my darling daughter."

"I wish . . ." Tears pricked Remedy's eyes. *Damn it.* She stood and paced to the nearest window. "You should have come to me first to make sure it was okay with me. You need to let me handle my life. You—"

"You're not happy?" It was a question that seemed borne from genuine confusion.

Remedy's instinct to avoid conflict by lying was a strong one. But her parents had crossed the line and it had to stop. Right now. "No, I'm not."

"That doesn't make any sense. Cambelle and Helen are like family. And Wynd is a close friend of your father's. There was no question that you were going to do them this favor."

Did her mom even realize she was fabricating the truth? "According to Helen, there was a question. She said they'd needed some convincing because Cambelle didn't want to get married in Texas."

"And, you know," Mom continued, as though Remedy hadn't spoken, "this wedding is a bit of a favor to you."

Remedy spun away from the window and flattened her back against the wall. So then, her mom really didn't have faith in her to fix her own problems. Well, that cleared up a lot. But Remedy wanted to hear her admit it aloud. "A favor to me how?"

Mom huffed, indignant, as though this was common knowledge that didn't need spelling out. "Remedy, please. This is your shot to get back in the media's good graces. This is what you were waiting for to redeem your reputation so

you can come home. You should be grateful for this opportunity instead of picking it apart to find the flaws."

Micah was right. Telling someone that they should be
grateful was the apex of obnoxiousness. "It wasn't your
place to fix this for me. It's manipulative."

"Oh, honey, don't be that way. We were devastated
when you became persona non grata in our circles. No par-
ent should ever have to hear the kind of slander we were
subjected to about you. It broke our hearts. We're only trying to help."

"Since when do you refer to you and Dad as 'we'? You
hate each other."

"We don't hate each other. We have a child together, for
God's sake. We still talk, especially when you need us."

Remedy couldn't wrap her brain around that one, not
after years of listening to them each complain about the
other's lack of communication, from her dad missing Remedy's school events and blaming her mom for not telling
him about them to her mom bitching about her dad's
failure to inform her of travel plans he'd invited Remedy
along on. "I'll plan Cambelle and Wynd's wedding, but
after this, no more help from you. Or Dad. When I make
my triumphant return to Hollywood, it's going to be on my
terms, because *I* revitalized my career, not you."

That had been her goal all along, but it didn't explain
why the words sounded hollow to her heart all of a sudden. She was falling in love with the quirky town of
Dulcet and its even quirkier resort. She wasn't ready to
end things with Micah. Was she really that person who'd
walk away from a good job, a good town, and a good man
to mollify her ego and show up all the people who'd
spurned her? That plot belonged in one of her mother's
movies, not Remedy's life.

"Don't be mad at us, sweetheart. We're trying to help
you bust out of there."

There was that *we* again. *Bizarre.* "I'm not in prison, Mom."

"I miss you. Don't you want to come home? By the time the dust settles and Wynn realizes what an asset you could be to his company in Los Angeles, planning all their big events, I'll be done filming. We can be a family again for the holidays."

Remedy bit her tongue against asking who she was including in the *we* this time or from pointing out that she and her parents hadn't been together as a family since she was twelve and that Remedy's holidays ever since had been a complicated dance of divided time between her parents' households.

The holidays were the busiest time of the year at Briscoe Ranch Resort, as well as the most beautiful, she'd heard, with the whole resort transformed into a winter wonderland. Remedy couldn't wait to be a part of that and to see Granny June's Mistletoe Effect in action. Already Remedy was busy planning weddings for nearly every day of the month of December for so many sweet, optimistic, love-struck couples. She'd have to pass that off to a new planner or to Alex. How could she leave Granny June, Alex, Emily, and the rest of her coworkers in the lurch like that? How could she leave Micah like that?

"I've got to go, Mom. I've got a lot of work to do."

Regardless of the choice she made or if Cambelle and Wynd's wedding marked the beginning of Remedy's end at Briscoe Ranch, there was one inescapable truth. Hollywood was about to invade Dulcet, Texas, and there was no way, no how, this town—or Remedy—was ready for it.

Chapter Fourteen

Every year, Micah sprung for tux rentals for his crew to wear at the firefighter ball. It was his thing, and the day of the tux fittings was always a great chance for them to take a pause from the stress and danger of the fire season to get together and let loose. The tux rental rep made a house call to the firehouse, and they all chipped in for pizza. But this year, the tension Micah had first sensed at Albert and Tabby's wedding was thick and uncomfortable.

Micah had all kinds of theories, most of them revolving around the possibility that his crew had somehow gotten wind of Ty Briscoe's threat to separate the fire marshal job from the fire station, but that seemed improbable, given that Briscoe hadn't yet acted on his threat in any measurable way.

It was a safety issue now, because if they got a call for a fire they'd need to work like a well-oiled machine, not a dysfunctional family. By the time the tux rental rep had taken all the measurements and left, the chilly silence in the room had Micah ready to burst. He shut the door and faced the dozen men in the room. "All right. That's enough. Time to clear the air. What's going on with you guys? Why are you pissed at me?"

Nobody spoke. Dusty and Chet exchanged a look.

"Dusty, start talking."

All he did was shoot another look at Chet.

Chet stepped forward. "You're a hypocrite is what the problem is."

"What are you talking about?"

"Remedy Lane. You threatened us all within an inch of our lives to stay away from her. You kept insisting that Briscoe Ranch Resort executives were off-limits, so that's what we've been doing all these years, but I suppose you wanted to keep them all for yourself, because there you were at Albert's wedding, kissing Remedy. And almost every morning since then she's doing the walk of shame out of your house."

Micah's stomach dropped. So that was it. This was about Remedy. Of course. He should've predicted his guys' hostility. More than that, he should've been the one initiating this conversation the minute he'd learned that word had gotten out that he'd kissed Remedy. First things first, though. "Don't let me be hearing that term again, and not just with Remedy. You don't get to shame someone for doing something you'd do in a heartbeat, just because she's a woman."

"Way to deflect the issue, asshole," Dusty said.

Chet squared up to Micah, a smirk on his face. "Like I said, I suppose you wanted to keep her for yourself."

Dusty piped in. "That's low-down, Chief. Not that I wouldn't have done the same thing, but that's low-down that you didn't even give us a shot at winning her."

"She's not some prize to be squabbled over."

Chet swaggered forward. "So that's how little she means to you, boss? Better not let her hear you talk about her that way. For the record, if she'd been mine I would've treated her like a prize. Like a goddamn treasure. But I guess we'll never know, because you didn't give me a chance with her."

This was spiraling out of control way too fast. Time to

dial it back. "That's not what I meant. She's not a prize, because she's a person who makes up her own mind."

"Seems to me like you helped her make up her mind. Once you laid claim, there ain't another man in this county who'd dare cross you on it. Must be nice to be the top dog."

The idea that Remedy was so weak-willed as to be so easily influenced about who to date or that he had the power to claim a woman as wildly independent as her was laughable, but he kept a stony expression firmly on his face. "I didn't know this was going to happen between me and Remedy."

He let their scoffs die down, then added, "I didn't. Truly. I'm fully aware that I broke my own rule about fraternizing with resort executives. It wasn't my intent to keep you all from having a chance with her. Or keep you from socializing with any other Briscoe employees, either."

"But that's exactly what happened," Chet said.

Other than the whole "laying of claims" objectification of Remedy and the assumption of her lack of agency in her romantic affairs, they were right about him forbidding them from pursuing her only to go and pursue her himself.

"You're right. You're all right. It was hypocritical of me and I should've come talk to y'all straightaway when I realized things were happening between her and me. I can't turn back time and I don't know how to make this right with you, because what's done is done."

"You've got to break it off with her."

That wasn't going to happen. "Next suggestion?"

"What about that slippery slope you're so fond of preaching about? About us getting complacent, about us crossing lines and bending rules about public safety if we let ourselves succumb to the charms of the Briscoe Ranch people?"

For the first time, Micah considered Ty Briscoe's threat of shifting fire marshal duties to a different department.

What if that was for the best? Micah and his team could concentrate on fighting fires instead of enforcing the law and worrying about conflicts of interest with the resort staff. The only trouble was, whoever Briscoe handpicked to be the new fire marshal would be little more than his bought-and-paid-for puppet, which would put the entire county—the entire hill country region—in grave danger. Micah couldn't let that happen any more than he could let his crew be divided by his lack of leadership since Remedy had crashed into his life.

He felt like asshole number one when he said, "I know what this looks like, but the safety of the people of Dulcet and the guests at the resort is still my top priority. I'm determined to keep the boundaries between my personal life and professional life as firm as possible."

Chet gave a hard laugh. "Yeah, while you're banging Ty Briscoe's top employee. Do you really expect us to believe you're not going to be skipping an inspection here or there, or making special allowances for your new bed warmer?"

A sudden burst of anger gripped Micah's chest. Calling him on his mistake was one thing, but nobody was going to get away with disrespecting his woman. He dropped his voice low so there would be no room for misunderstanding of Micah's intent. "Do yourself a favor and never talk about any woman that way again—especially Remedy."

Chet surged forward, like he was ready to thump chests with Micah or some other macho bullshit, but one of the guys pulled him back. Lucky for Chet, because pounding through Micah's blood was that old familiar need to protect his family and friends no matter how tough the fight or how mean he had to get. Micah held his ground and let his savage streak show on his face, in the flare of his nostrils and the hard set of his jaw.

Dusty planted himself between Chet and Micah, his

arms out as buffers. "Back down, Chet. You too, Chief. I'm not going to let this family lose its shit over some girl. She ain't worth it."

Dusty was right. Not about Remedy being not worth it, because she was and then some, but he was right about Chet and the rest of Micah's fire crew being his family, too, rather than an enemy threat to the people he loved. He drew a measured breath, tamping his anger down.

"Look, guys. All I can give you is my word that I'm going to keep that hard edge between my private life and my personal life. And y'all deserve for me to trust you to do the same in your personal lives, too. No more rules about who you can and can't socialize with when you're off work. And what I need from you in return is that you give Remedy the same respect and protection we give all the other girlfriends and wives of the crew."

"To be clear," Dusty said in a neutral tone. "You've told Remedy that the county commissioner finally went through with the burn ban until November? She knows the resort can't do any kind of pyrotechnic or fireworks display?"

Guilt pierced through his conscience. "The subject hasn't come up yet."

Dusty's eyes turned dull with disappointment. Chet snickered. "Right. Okay, Chief. No special treatment. We get it."

"I would like to think that my record for keeping our town safe is enough to keep your trust. I'd like to think you know me well enough to understand that my responsibility to the people of this town is solid enough to withstand my dating life."

"We'll see, Chief. We'll see."

They would see, because Micah was determined to handle all the complicated facets of his life tugging at his

attention—his relationship with Remedy, his job, Ty Briscoe's threats. Now he could add to that list repairing the
trust he'd broken with his team.

On the day of the Firefighters' Charity Ball, Remedy rose
in the dark after only a few hours of restless sleep. Micah
pulled her into his arms for a groggy kiss. The gesture was
grounding and gave her hope the two of them would find
their way back into sync after the relationship funk they'd
fallen into during the past couple weeks.

With him being in the middle of fire season and her being in the middle of the summer wedding season and
with Cambelle and Wynd's wedding date fast approaching, Remedy and Micah didn't do a whole lot of talking in
the late-night hours they carved out to see each other, the
only available time they had. No more Sundays off,
Remedy was pushing herself seven days a week. Micah,
it seemed, was doing the same.

Sometimes her instincts picked up the vibe that he was
keeping something from her, but she didn't need to have a
psychology degree to figure out that she was probably just
projecting, since she still hadn't found the words to tell him
about the Cambelle and Wynd wedding beyond the bare-
bones explanation that she'd had a five-hundred-guest rush
wedding dropped in her lap.

She scratched her nails along the thick stubble covering his cheek. "I can't wait to see you in a tux."

His eyes fluttered open, then closed again. "I can't wait
to attend a Remedy Lane signature event, this time as a
guest."

She slipped out of his embrace and out of bed. "Go back
to sleep for now. I'll see you this afternoon when you come
for your inspection."

His eyes snapped wide open. "Hey, about that. I'm
bringing Chet with me for the inspection and we're going

to be thorough. My guys are grumbling about me giving you special treatment."

Perhaps that was the reason he'd been so stressed out and distant.

"I'm on board with you going by the book, always. I don't want you to go lax on my events because we're dating."

Frowning, he sat up. "I haven't been lax. I would never compromise people's safety."

"I know that, and I didn't mean to suggest otherwise. I was trying to say that I support you with whatever you have to do for your job."

"Then you should probably also know that there's a burn ban in effect, countywide, along with most other counties in Texas. No more fire or fireworks or live explosives at the resort for the rest of the fire season."

No fireworks? Cambelle and Helen weren't going to like that one bit. Her expression must have revealed her panic, because Micah said, "That going to be a problem?"

"No. Of course not. It's just that this wedding I'm planning, the rush one for next month, it's got my stomach tied in knots."

"Why did you take on this rush wedding job if it's so stressful? Don't you have a policy about *x* number of planning months minimum or something? If you don't, you should."

Her attention shifted to the clock. She was set to meet Litzy and Tabby at seven thirty to start prepping for the ball. Tabby had been a revelation. She'd helped Litzy focus in a way that Remedy had been unable to. In a matter of weeks, the two of them had become a dream team of assistants—something Remedy had previously wondered if she'd ever find, given the betrayal by her last assistant in Los Angeles—but they didn't do her any good if Remedy wasn't there to give them guidance that morning with the millions of tasks that needed to be accomplished before the ball. But this conversation with Micah was long overdue. She needed to tell him now about who the rush wedding was for or it would be a lie of omission, a serious breach of trust between them.

She could feel her heart beating fast against her ribs and in her throat. "I do have a policy like that, but this wedding is for two family friends."

Those serious dark eyes shuttered. "You haven't mentioned that you know the couple who're getting married."

"I know. And I don't know why I didn't." How did that lie pop out like that? Was she really so afraid of Micah's reaction? "Actually, that's not true. I didn't tell you because I was afraid you wouldn't take it well. You hate wealth and these friends are . . . kind of snobby and really famous. It'll be a huge wedding that will get a lot of media attention."

Hunching, he propped his elbows on his knees and tapped his thumbs against each other. "It sounds like the kind of wedding you've been wanting to plan that will put your good name back on the map." He spoke slowly, as though selecting every word carefully.

She walked to his side of the bed and perched on the edge, her arm around his waist. "That's exactly what it is."

He angled his face away from her. His tapping thumbs stilled.

"I'm not planning on leaving Dulcet anytime soon. I'm not ready and, besides, one high-profile wedding alone does not reinvent a career."

She braced herself for him to get angry or jealous or for his prejudice against wealth to rear its ugly head, but instead he angled his lips over hers and kissed her. His hands roved over her backside and bunched her sleep shirt higher.

Her attention shifted to the clock again. "I want to stay here with you, but I have to go."

"Yeah. I know you do. But I don't have to like it."

Did he think she'd meant leaving Dulcet for Los Angeles? Because that was true, too. *Wasn't it?*

That question haunted her while she showered and dressed for work and while she stood in the silent kitchen and ate an apple cinnamon muffin, the latest treat left for them by Micah's secret admirer.

"Hey," he called when she was near the front door.

She turned and found him standing in the doorway to his bedroom, clad in black boxer briefs and a deep scowl that turned his eyes hard. "You know I'll support you in whatever your goals are—I'd be a shitty boyfriend if I didn't—but consider yourself warned that my goal is to make it mighty tough on you to choose Los Angeles over me."

Her throat constricted. "Micah, it's not as simple as an either-or choice."

"Like hell it's not."

It was the seed of an argument that could have no winners but would make losers of them both. She walked to him and planted a kiss on his unyielding lips. "I'll see you this afternoon."

Chapter Fifteen

The Dalmatians arrived in the ballroom two hours ahead of schedule. The two dogs had been Remedy's bright idea, as part of a whimsical Polaroid photo opportunity she'd created for the ball guests, but that had been before she'd found herself placating a runaway elephant or being stalked by thirty vagabond homing pigeons.

She'd vowed to never again incorporate live animals into the events she planned, but as long as these dogs stayed with their trainers, leashed to the fire hydrant props in front of the old-fashioned firehouse facade she'd commissioned from a Dallas theater company set building crew, all would be well. She'd take a pair of trained dogs over pigeons or elephants any day of the week.

At an hour until showtime, Remedy completed a final walk-through of her masterpiece, which had turned out even better than she'd imagined. Inspired by Emily's insistence on serving Baked Alaska, Remedy had decided to take as many firefighter clichés as she could and turn them on their heads to create a whimsical theme that was both familiar and fresh. Dozens of delicate paper and wood prop trees clustered around the edges of the massive ballroom, their branches draped with tiny white strands of light. But rather than doing something corny such as having cats in the trees, as she'd joked to Emily and Alex, she'd commissioned an artist in San Antonio to create strands of origami butterflies hanging from the branches, with the number of butterflies representing the combined population of all the Texas counties represented by firefighters at the ball—the number of citizens whose safety rested in the hands of this humble group of first responders.

On each round table she'd clustered framed copies of historical photographs of Texas firefighters and firehouses, then sprinkled the tables with vintage candies, from little boxes of Red Hots and cellophane-wrapped sarsaparilla drops, to taffy and butterscotch nips. At each place setting, Litzy and Tabby had set out clusters of peppermint sticks and cinnamon sticks bundled with raffia.

And, of course, in the back of the room, near one of two cash bars, was Remedy's brainchild, the old-fashioned firehouse photo set, where guests would be able to dress up in vintage costumes, including old-time firefighter gear, and pose for Polaroid photographs with the Dalmatians. Event staff members were on hand to snap the photos, then mount them in distressed vintage-style frames as the ball's party favors.

"It didn't have the full effect when I was here this afternoon for my inspection. But with the lighting and those Dalmatians and that firehouse you created, I'm blown away. I can't close my mouth."

Remedy turned at the sound of Micah's voice, but she was the one blown away at the sight of him looking debonair in a perfectly fitted tuxedo, complete with a black bow tie and fancy black cowboy hat. "Micah, look at you."

"Forget about me; look at this room. Everywhere I turn, I see new little touches that blow my mind." He gathered her in his arms and kissed her. "You blow my mind. I've never been to anything like this before. It's a whole new level from the charity balls in years past."

She smoothed her hand over his jacket collar. "That was the idea."

"You're brilliant, you know."

She felt brilliant and on top of her game. This was her first signature event at Briscoe Ranch and everything was perfect, including the man who was presently wrapping her in his strong, sexy arms. "Thank you, and I was just now thinking that you look pretty brilliant in that tuxedo."

"I'm serious, Remedy. Ty Briscoe's not going to let you go without a fight. I think he and I are going to join forces on that goal."

He just had to go there, didn't he? Right on cue, her stomach twisted into a knot. She squirmed out of his embrace. "Could we not talk about that tonight and enjoy ourselves without worrying about the future?"

"You can't have it both ways. You can't be making all those private plans of yours to leave and drop that bomb on me this morning about that celebrity wedding next month, then tell me not to think about it."

He was right, as usual. "Micah, I—"

A loud whoop of joy sounded behind Remedy and silenced the workers in the room.

Granny June strode their way, dressed head-to-toe in purple sequins and waving a darkly stained wooden cane. "Whoo, boy, if it isn't the most handsome man I've ever laid eyes on."

Micah brushed past Remedy. "What are you doing here? I was supposed to come pick you up in a couple hours or so, so you could make a grand entrance after everyone else had arrived."

Her eyes twinkled with mischief. "Oh, we're still on for that, don't you worry. But I saw those Dalmatians arrive and wanted to come see what the fuss was about. I do love me some dogs." She clapped her hands. "Say, here's a thought, Micah. Let's snap the first photo of the night together, now that those sweet doggies have arrived. Any time I post pets to my Facebook page, the people on there go crazy. Those are my most popular posts, besides all the pictures I snap of you. The ladies on Facebook just adore a hunky young man. Just imagine the kind of draw I'll get by combining a hunk like you with one of those sweet puppies in the same shot."

She took Micah by the hand and dragged him toward the photo station.

Micah craned his neck to look at Remedy. "Are you coming, too?"

As much fun as that sounded, she waved him off. "I can't. Too much to do, but you two have fun."

"I'll find you later," he called.

"Not if I find you first."

That turned out to be easier said than done. The ball was a smashing success, not that Remedy had a single spare moment to enjoy it. Though everything was going smoothly, with no noteworthy problems beyond the usual hiccups, she and her assistants never stopped moving, directing the replenishment of the bars, rotating the serving staff and bartenders, directing the food service, and keeping the live band happy and hydrated, among a thousand other duties.

It weighed heavily on her that she and Micah had snapped at each other before the ball. She wanted badly to make things right with him and apologize, but every time she spotted him in the crowd he was busy mingling, dancing, eating, or being led around by Granny June and the leashed Dalmatian that she'd somehow convinced its trainer to let her walk around with for the rest of the night. The dog was being a good sport and the other Dalmatian was loving all the extra attention by being the only dog at the photo station, so Remedy couldn't find it in her heart to ruin Granny's, or Micah's, fun.

It was infinitely easier to be the person in the shadows, watching the revelry and making sure everyone else had a good time. Remedy's comfort zone, as it had always been. Around the time that the beef tenderloin was served, she found herself hovering at the edge of the room next to Emily. She hadn't forgotten Emily's discomfort at the idea of being a guest at Albert and Tabby's wedding. Though Emily and Remedy clashed at every turn, they did have that in common.

"Sometimes I feel like an alien, if you know what I mean," Remedy ventured.

Emily blinked at her in her typical deadpan style. "Absolutely. I feel like you're an alien all the time. That explains a lot, actually."

Remedy smacked her arm. "Shut up."

Emily's wry gaze cracked into a smile. "We did good tonight."

"We did better than good."

"We're about twenty minutes from the Baked Alaska presentation. Do you still want to help light one of them?"

"I can't wait. Thank you." Remedy wasn't sure what the bigger shock was—that Emily was following through with that long-ago promise or that she was sharing her moment of glory. She still wasn't sure if she and Emily were friends, but perhaps, more important, they were allies now.

Emily nodded toward the crowd. "Your lover boy's on his way. That's my cue to scram. I'll text you when it's showtime."

"Hey, you," Micah said.

"Hey, yourself. Having fun?"

He lifted a shoulder in a shrug. "Some. I would've rather had you by my side instead of stealing glances at you while you're flitting this way and that, running the show."

"I would've rather been with you, too."

He nodded toward the photo station. "Got time to snap a picture with me while everyone's busy eating?"

Remedy surveyed the room. The bartenders looked re-laxed, the band was on break, and the servers didn't seem to be having any issues. Could it be that she had a spare moment to take a breath and be with her man? "You have perfect timing. I'd love to."

Hand in hand, they walked to the photo station in the back of the room. From the boxes of dress-up clothes Micah found her a parasol, bonnet, and dusty-smelling crocheted shawl that he wrapped around her shoulders. "There. You look like a virgin librarian from days of yore."

He swapped his cowboy hat out for a firefighter helmet, then peeled a fake mustache from the sheet of them displayed on an adjacent table, a fun touch that had been Tabby's idea. "What do you think? Am I ready to rescue you?"

"Ready, but just a sec. I'm curious about something." Rocking up to her tiptoes, she angled her lips over his. She'd never kissed a man with a mustache before. It tickled her upper lip and nose, but it was kind of fun—right up until her mother's voice popped into her head asking Remedy if Micah was anything like Tom Selleck. *Gross.*

"You want me to grow a firefighter mustache?" he asked, waggling his eyebrows.

"Nope. Your perpetual five o'clock shadow is perfect. No mustache necessary. Let's take this picture before I have to get back to work."

Standing in front of the firehouse facade, Micah lifted her into his arms for the pose. She stretched out her parasol and tried to look the part of the damsel in distress. When the photographer gave them a thumbs-up, Micah set her down.

"Hey, before you get called away again, there's something I didn't get a chance to ask you earlier," he said.

"Good or bad?"

"Good, I hope." He took her parasol and twirled it. "My dad's birthday is coming up next week. He's having some people over for a barbecue to celebrate on Sunday. It's not going to reach the lofty heights of a Remedy Lane event, but my dad smokes a mean brisket. I'd like you to be there to meet everyone, and I'd like them to get to meet the woman I've been telling them all about."

That was quite the magic trick he'd mastered, making her feel cherished and torn all at the same time. He wanted to take their relationship to the next level. He'd told her that morning that he would fight for her and that was exactly what he was doing. A little push out of her comfort zone, done in a loving way. She couldn't imagine turning him down.

She hooked her fingers behind his belt and pulled him snug against her. "I'd love to meet your family."

"Good. That's good." He hooked his arm around her neck and kissed her, that silly mustache tickling her nose again.

Remedy's phone vibrated.

It's time, read Emily's text.

"I've got to go," she told Micah. "It's time for the Baked Alaska. You should find a seat. This is going to be quite the presentation."

Micah cringed. "I'd forgotten I'd agreed to that."

She gave the corner of his mustache a tug. "It'll be safe. I swear. Just go find a seat and enjoy yourself."

"You're not lighting any of the Baked Alaskas on fire or serving them, are you?"

She gave him a gentle nudge toward the tables with the parasol. "Don't you worry your pretty little head about it." Then she hurried off, knowing that Emily wasn't going to wait around for her to arrive.

"God help us all!" he called behind her, pushing her smile even broader as she hotfooted it through the staff-only, S-shaped hall to the kitchen's staging space, where an army of servers had gathered, each stationed next to a rolling cart carrying a large silver platter of a delectable Baked Alaska.

Standing before them and looking every bit the part of

a fierce and proud commander was Emily, who'd changed into a crisp, freshly laundered chef's jacket and a black skullcap. She waved Remedy to her side, then made a show of entrusting her with a lighter and a measuring cup of liquid that smelled like orange liqueur.

Remedy set down the parasol she'd forgotten she'd been carrying and took the lighter and measuring cup in hand.

"As promised," Emily told her. "You can do the honors of lighting the dessert, and then you and I can serve the Briscoe family table together."

"Thank you again. I just want you to know that it's an honor to work with you. You're an amazing chef." Perhaps that was a bit too gushy, but Remedy was feeling the love tonight.

"Yes, I am."

Remedy laughed out loud at that, it was so *Emily* a response.

Emily faced her troops. "This is the moment of truth. The grand finale. We've practiced, and we've prepared until each and every one of you convinced me that you could do this blindfolded. You're ready. Tonight, you've not only represented this resort, but you've been the face of this kitchen. You've done me proud and you've earned this moment of glory."

A smattering of applause broke out.

Sharp metal poked Remedy in the ribs. She whirled on Emily, who was brandishing her lighter. "Ow! What the—"

"What is that thing doing in here?" Emily muttered out of the corner of her mouth, nodding to the hall that led to the ballroom. A single white homing pigeon bobbed its head and blinked.

Crap. Those damn pigeons were out of control. Micah was right; this meant war. But first she needed to get this one out of sight before any of the guests noticed the interloper.

"No idea, but I'll take care of it. Carry on without me." It sucked that she'd miss out on lighting the dessert on fire, but those were the breaks in show business.

She crept around the side of the room.

Behind her, Emily said to the staff, "On the count of three, pour the Grand Marnier. Three, two, one . . ."

The room filled with the bracingly strong scent of sugary alcohol and oranges.

Remedy flattened against the wall, attempting a surprise ambush on the bird. She wasn't keen on touching it, much less grabbing it and carrying it all the way outside, but she didn't have a choice. She hoped it wouldn't squawk and draw attention to their tussle or retaliate and peck her hand off. A flash of inspiration struck and she ripped off the shawl she'd been wearing and held it like a net.

"And now the flame," Emily said. "In three, two . . ."

Remedy pounced, tossing the shawl, but the pigeon was ready for her and lit off the ground in a fluttering hop that ended inside the ballroom that had been darkened to add to the dramatic impact of the Baked Alaska presentation.

Remedy couldn't afford to miss her mark on her second try. Grabbing the shawl, she harnessed her adrenaline and tightened into a crouch. She sprung forward, arms outstretched and shawl at the ready as twenty-four servers pushing carts of flaming silver trays plowed her way. It was all she could do to dodge the stampede. The room of ball guests erupted into loud applause.

The pigeon soared over the fray in the direction of the paper trees.

Over the din of the applause, Remedy heard a dog's frantic barking. In the firelight, Granny June came into view, being tugged through the tables by one of the Dalmatians.

"Don't let go of that leash!" Remedy called to her.

But the leash fast became the least of Remedy's worries as Granny and a tall, burly server collided. Unfazed, the Dalmatian jumped through the middle of the cart and continued its pursuit, but the tables surrounding the wreck collectively gasped. Micah and another firefighter seated nearby dove for the floor beneath Granny as she fell, and managed to slip beneath her in time to provide a cushion for her fall.

Behind the collision, the Dalmatian pushed toward the paper tree in which the pigeon had landed, though its speed was compromised by the cart its leash had tangled in and that was now dragging behind it, the Baked Alaska still on fire.

"Get that dog!" Remedy hollered.

But it was too late. While the dog made a frenzied attempt to climb the tree after the pigeon, a string of paper butterflies went up in flames, then another. Before Remedy's gasp of horror had left her throat, the tree was engulfed in fire.

The only sound Remedy heard besides the beating of her own heart was the friction of hundreds of chairs scraping backward against the hardwood floor as every firefighter in the room sprung into action.

Chapter Sixteen

Remedy sat on the lowered tailgate of Micah's truck in the Chapel Hill parking lot, wearing the dress-up bonnet like a badge of shame and swilling champagne straight from the bottle. A pan of half-eaten Baked Alaska sat melting on her lap. Yes, she knew how pathetic she looked, but it couldn't possibly compare to how pathetic and embarrassed she felt. Her first signature event at the resort—and she'd nearly set the whole building on fire.

Some career reboot she'd orchestrated. More like career demolition.

She'd chosen Micah's truck to self-implode at because she figured, in a worst-case scenario, he'd eventually finish cleaning up the mess after the fire and find her passed out with her face in the melted ice cream, which might make him more likely to take pity on her.

She didn't notice that she had company until a shadow fell over her. "Tailgate party for one, huh?"

Emily hopped up on the tailgate and sat next to her.

"Do they need me back there?" Remedy said. "After I helped clear the guests out of the building and returned the Dalmatians to their handlers I started to feel like I was in the way, so it seemed like a good opportunity to sneak away and wallow in self-pity."

Emily took the champagne bottle and glugged a long drink. "You throw a hell of a party."

Remedy swirled her fork through the melted ice cream. "And you make a hell of a Baked Alaska."

"I caught sight of Micah a few times," Emily said. "He was safe. I don't think anyone got hurt, actually, but several years ago I briefly had a boyfriend who was a deputy sheriff and I hated worrying about his safety when he was on the job, so I thought you might want to know that he's okay."

Of all Emily's personality quirks, her penchant to ramble when she was nervous or uncomfortable was the one Remedy found most endearing. Remedy had also seen glimpses of Micah coming and going among the fire engines and emergency response vehicles, so she'd already figured he was fine, but Emily's gesture was still sweet.

"Thanks. I've never had to worry about a boyfriend's actual physical safety before," Remedy said. Then, in the spirit of her and Emily's budding friendship, she added, "In high school, I surrendered my V card to a bad-boy stuntman on the set of my mom's movie. For the few weeks we were an item I'd hated watching the stunt scenes he filmed, because it was disconcerting to watch my boyfriend get set on fire take after take, but having an actual firefighter boyfriend is so much scarier."

Emily polished off the last of the champagne. "This fire was my fault. I shouldn't have pushed so hard for the Baked Alaska." She picked at the corner of the bottle's label. "It sucks, because even though no one was hurt, the ballroom's a soggy, sooty mess and, even worse, I lost any kind of leverage with Micah, Alex, and you. You went out on a limb for me and I blew it."

"We both blew it."

Remedy's words hung in the air while the two sat in silence. They noticed Micah at the same time. He broke away from the crowd of firefighters he'd been talking to and stalked up the hill toward Remedy and Emily with jolting, stiff steps, a murderous scowl on his face.

"Crap," Emily said.

Remedy shoveled a massive forkful of ice cream and cake in her mouth. "You can go. I've got this."

"He looks pissed." Emily took the fork from her and sliced off a huge bite for herself. "Think I'll stick around. No one will accuse me of being a coward."

Remedy didn't have the energy to rise and meet Micah eye-to-eye. What she really wanted was a second bottle of champagne to ease her anxiety at the sight of the simmering rage in Micah's eyes.

He stood before them, breathing hard through flared nostrils, his hands on his hips.

Remedy drew a tremulous breath. "Micah, I—"

"My crew had confronted me that I was giving you special favors because you were my girlfriend and I told them they were full of shit." Micah's voice was low and tight, as though he was barely clinging to his civility. "I swore to them that I could keep my personal life and my professional life completely separate. But tonight, I had to face my colleagues and my subordinates, and a boss or two, and own up to my error in judgment in allowing you two to serve that stupid Baked Alaska. My clout with Ty Briscoe, gone. My clout with my crew, gone. All the leverage I've busted my ass to cultivate all these years, all gone." He snapped his fingers. "Like that. A lot of people could have been hurt tonight and it's all on me. But that won't happen again."

Angry tears sprung to Remedy's eyes. She swiped them away before Micah or Emily noticed. She felt weak and pathetic enough as it was. "Micah, will you listen, please. Let me apologize for—"

"No, it's not all on you, Micah. You, either, Remedy," Emily said. "What happened tonight is my fault."

"Wrong again, Emily," Micah snapped. "The buck stops at the fire marshal. You might have tried to coerce me into agreeing to your ridiculous dessert plan, but I went along with it. I ignored my gut."

A loud sniff caught all their attention. They turned to find Ty Briscoe standing behind Micah. While Micah had seemed angry when he'd approached the tailgate, Ty's whole body quivered with a barely harnessed rage. "Leave us, Emily," he hissed.

Remedy's stomach lurched, the mix of champagne and ice-cream cake suddenly feeling toxic and volatile. Out of pure pride and self-preservation, she forced her shaky legs to stand along with Emily, who leveled a supportive and pitying look at Remedy before skulking off.

Ty waited until Emily was out of earshot to turn to Micah. "I just had a look at the ballroom. It's ruined, isn't it?"

Micah's eyes were dull. "Probably. With the water and smoke damage, you might need to remodel that whole wing of the building. It won't be ready for that celebrity wedding next month or any other weddings at the resort the rest of the summer. Maybe not even in time for the Christmas weddings."

Ty turned to Remedy. "This is your error."

"I know. We'll have to move the weddings to tents, but it's doable. I'll make sure the brides are happy and that each wedding is even more special than expected."

Ty's voice boomed off the chapel wall. "That's not the point. The point is forcing bridal parties and guests to walk from the resort to the tent in the summer heat and humidity. The point is disappointing guests who have paid us thousands of dollars to give them exactly what they want for the most important day of their lives."

"You're right," Remedy said, trying to infuse her voice with a confidence she was nowhere near close to feeling.

"But there's nothing we can do about that now except make sure every detail of every upcoming wedding is perfect."

"Damn right you will. Do whatever they want you to. Make everything bigger, splashier, than they could imagine. If Wynd Fisher's bride wants Redneck Chic, then you fly goddamn Jeff Foxworthy in to perform. Do you hear what I'm telling you?"

A hand closed on her shoulder and forced her to the side. "Watch your tone of voice with her," Micah said, cutting between her and Ty as though he were her shield.

"Tell me that I sound any different from the tone you were talking to her with when I got here."

Micah shut his mouth, his jaw going tight.

Now that Ty had brought it up, there was no difference, actually, and his insight got Remedy wondering what she was doing standing there taking so much crap from two posturing Alpha Bubbas. Yes, she was sorry for her role in the ballroom fire, but that didn't turn her into a punching bag.

Ty shifted to look at Remedy. "As I was saying, for the trouble we've created make sure we comp them their fireworks display."

"There's a burn ban in effect. No more fireworks." Micah's voice was calm this time, though Remedy could still hear the strain behind his even tone.

Ty's scalp was so beet red, and the veins popping so prominently, that he looked like he was about to give a new, literal meaning to the idea of blowing one's top. "I don't give a flying fuck about your burn ban, son."

Micah gave a bored shrug. "That's fine with me. Just know that if you violate the law, then I'll have you arrested. Don't think I won't go there."

"If you think my longtime friend and golfing buddy Sheriff Dennihoff will arrest me, then you have no idea how this county actually operates."

"You corrupt son of a bitch."

Remedy sidestepped away from the bickering men. She took another step and then another. Maybe what had happened here tonight didn't actually involve her. As she'd known from the start, she was in the unenviable position of being trapped between two warring parties in a battle that had started long before Remedy had arrived and would probably continue long after she left.

If she left.

She took another step back and gazed at Micah's silhouette, her heart breaking. It seemed inevitable now that the two of them were over. She'd known it wouldn't last, but she wasn't ready for their time together to end.

Ty gave a hard laugh and got in Micah's face. "Do not forget that little discussion that you and I had a few weeks ago. All I have to do is say the word and the county council will strip you of your fire marshal duties faster than you can say 'job demotion.'"

Micah had never told her Ty had threatened him like that. Why would he hold back such a critical piece of information from her? She shoved the question to the back of her mind and instead focused on the horrible realization that Remedy's uncanny ability to create disaster, along with her relationship with Micah in general, had played a pivotal role in Micah's job being compromised. It was unbearable.

She marched back to Ty and Micah and wedged her body between the two men, facing Ty. "Don't go to the county council yet. We'll find another way to smooth things over with Wynd and Cambelle, and all the other upcoming brides and grooms. We don't need fireworks that badly. I'll figure something else out. Something even better."

"Stay out of this, Remedy," Micah said.

"She will not stay out of it, because she's going to fix it," Ty said. He shifted his beady eyes to Remedy. "Do you not think I know your career is riding on this wedding?

Do you think I don't know what happened to you in Hollywood with that Zannity couple? Do you think if you are responsible for another celebrity wedding disaster that you'll ever find work again?"

No, she didn't. But it was a possibility she'd refused to dwell on.

"I own you, young lady, and you will make this right for all of us or I'll see that you never work in Texas or Los Angeles or anywhere else in the event-planning industry ever again."

"Don't threaten her again or you and I will be exchanging more than words," Micah said.

Ty sniffed, then turned his head and spit on the ground. "I've said my piece. And if Remedy and you do what you're obliged to, then I won't have to go threatening either of you again. This is all in your hands now. Your futures are up to you."

With that, he strode away.

Micah and Remedy watched him go in stunned silence, both of them fuming.

"Of all the goddamn jobs in the world, the woman I love is working for my oldest enemy, who's now using that fact to try to coerce us both," Micah said quietly.

The woman he loves? "We won't let him coerce us. He's not *that* powerful."

Micah gave her a grim smile. "Is that your trust fund cushion talking right now?"

Maybe it was. But Remedy refused to go down in flames in her chosen profession again, no matter how much money she had in the bank. "Micah . . ."

He held up his hands. "Wait, please. I don't think it's the right time for us to talk, we're both so pissed off and emotional."

She'd never been so relieved at a suggestion before. "You're right."

"Good, okay. You're not going to say anything more,

and I'm not going to say anything, either. And we're each going to walk away and get some air and calm down. Separately. And then we'll talk tomorrow." She could hear the leashed fury in his tone and could well imagine the effort it was taking him to keep his cool.

Another round of angry tears threatened. "Yes. Agreed."

"I'd better get back down there. It's going to be a long night of paperwork and cleanup." Then he was gone, walking back toward the resort the same way Ty had gone, disappearing into the smoky darkness.

Chapter Seventeen

Remedy never left the hotel that night after the fire. She'd tried to rest her head on the desk in her office for a while but gave up the effort as useless and instead passed the hours by scribbling ideas and notes for upcoming weddings on a notepad, but it was tough to feel creative given all that had transpired. In the end, she crumbled up the pages of notes she'd written and threw them away.

By sunrise, her mind was churning faster than ever but not getting anywhere productive. Restless and needing a change of scenery, she grabbed a coffee from the hotel kitchen, then wandered throughout the resort and grounds without knowing where she was headed. Her job, her reputation, her parents' reputation. Micah's job, the safety of Ravel County, her relationship with Micah, if he didn't break up with her over this—it was all so fragile, as though she were juggling eggshells.

It wasn't until she stopped in front of the fountain in the lobby that she knew her next move.

Brides by Carina, Carina Briscoe Decker's bridal boutique, opened into the lobby next to the men's formal-wear rental shop. A glass wall adjacent to the boutique's storefront offered resort visitors a view of Carina's workshop

and a taste of her process for creating exquisitely crafted
couture wedding gowns. Today, the glass wall revealed the
workshop to be empty of people, though several partially
constructed dresses adorned headless mannequins and a
piece of fabric rested beneath the needle of a sewing machine, as though she'd walked away in mid-stitch.

Carina wasn't on the boutique's storefront side, either,
but when Remedy approached the sales counter she caught
a glimpse of Carina tucked in a cluttered storage room,
perched on a stool while straddling a dress-clad man-
nequin.

Remedy knocked on the counter as though it were a
door. "Carina?"

Carina didn't seem to hear her but continued to embroider a flower with white thread onto the dress's bodice.
Maybe this wasn't the best time. Or the best idea. Maybe
Ty had already filled his daughter in on Remedy's wedding-
planning defects and Carina would pounce on the opportunity to defend her father's actions.

But that was silly. Carina had been nothing but kind to
Remedy, and if anyone could help Remedy figure out how
to appease all the warring parties tugging at her for alle-
giance it would be Carina. After all, one didn't achieve patron saint status by accident.

Remedy walked around the counter and knocked on the
wall next to the storage room door, harder this time. "Excuse me, Carina?"

Carina's fingers froze, a needle in one hand. She glanced
at Remedy. "Remedy? Hello. I hope you haven't been
standing there long. I get so absorbed when I embroider.
It's like a free stitch meditation."

Remedy would have to take her word for that. "Would
you mind if I came in?"

Carina moved a bin of threads off the stool to her right
and patted it. "I told you when we met that my door's
always open, and so it is. Come on in."

Remedy took a seat, her eyes on the gown that Carina had been working on. Delicate white-and-gold embroidery swirled through the bodice and skirt. "This dress is exquisite."

"Thank you. I'm definitely partial to it."

"What are you doing working back here and not in your workshop?"

Carina offered a disarming smile. "Yeah, about that. I thought my mom's idea of building a window into my workshop was genius, like free advertising. I honestly didn't think I'd notice or care about random resort guests watching me work because I get so focused on my projects, as you saw just a moment ago."

"I take it that turned out not to be the case?"

"Uh, no. When I go in that workshop, it's like there's a force field around it keeping my muse from entering with me. I can't accomplish a single creative thing when I'm in there. Even when no one's got their faces pressed up against the glass, I still feel like a zoo animal."

Made sense to Remedy. "I think I'd be the same way." She doubted she'd be nearly as effective at her job if the resort added a window through which guests could watch her. "We're event planners. We prefer to work behind the scenes. We don't want to be the scenes."

"Amen to that."

And there was Remedy's opening. "Speaking of event planning, I could use some advice on dealing with your father."

Carina's chuckle was filled with affection and warmth. "He's not the easiest person to work for, is he?"

"No, he's not."

"He gets into this zone I call bulldozer mode where he plows over everything and everyone in his path," Carina said.

That was the perfect description of the man.

Carina cringed. "I can tell by your expression that

you've experienced bulldozer mode for yourself. I'm so sorry. You did the right thing coming to me. Tell me what's going on and we'll see what we can do to fix it."

Carina's eagerness to help and her deprecating humor about her father had already helped set Remedy's mind at ease. Drawing a fortifying breath, she plunged into a retelling of the WestWynd situation and the stalemate between Ty and Micah, with Remedy caught in the middle.

Carina listened without interrupting, then said, "I always felt that Micah and my dad didn't get along because they were too much alike."

Yeah, no. "You think so?"

"I do. They're turf defenders. It's as if they each had this big cosmic stick that they each drew a circle with, then put everything and everyone they care about inside it. And now they pace around the outside of the circle like a guard, ready and willing to fight to the death to defend it all. It's sweet, really."

"You're right. They're a lot alike. But it's only sweet when the rest of us aren't caught in the middle," Remedy said. "How do I appease both of them, as well as the bride and groom? And in four weeks. It's feeling impossible right now."

"I've been there, and am I going to share with you what I learned the hard way as a wedding planner. You have something that neither my father nor Micah nor the bride and groom have. Artistry. You're not a project manager or a vender coordinator; you're the artist, the mastermind. Don't give them what they think they want. Distill that down to what they're really trying to tell you. In this case, my father and the wedding party both want spectacle and grandeur and Micah wants safety. That's totally doable."

At Carina's words, a lightbulb went off in Remedy's head. "Oh my God, you're right. I could explain how their idea is pedestrian. Fireworks at a wedding happen all the time. They're nothing special."

"Exactly," Carina said. "Open their eyes to artistic possibilities that are beyond what any of them could imagine in their nonartist minds. Give them something beyond their wildest imagination. Being a wedding planner can so often feel like you're powerless, that you're nothing but a well-paid servant. But neither my father nor the bride and groom hired you because you're good at doing others' bidding. They're paying you to take control. So take control."

Remedy was too restless to be contained in her stuffy cottage. Though hundreds of disparate ideas and Carina's advice rambled through her mind, none of those work thoughts compared to the dread and anxiety she felt about making things right with Micah. So much so that she found herself slipping into her shoes and heading down the stairs from her back deck into the woods, headed to the place where it all began for them.

She walked along the same shady path she'd taken the day Chet and Dusty had crashed through the creek after their runaway cooler, then followed the winding trail upstream, zigzagging close to the road, then down to the water's edge, all the way to where the creek met the river. After slipping off her shoes, she stood where Micah's chair had been planted in the sand that first day they'd met, where he'd sat on his throne looking like he was the redneck king of Texas.

She kicked the water, then again, splashing her frustration out. When she'd flown into Texas as a bright-eyed city girl, she'd had a plan. She'd known exactly what she wanted with her career and her life. She'd known what she didn't want—to get stuck in Texas. So then, when had getting stuck in Texas started to sound so right? How had everything gotten so complicated?

The most worthwhile things in life are complicated.

Carina had told Remedy not to give her clients what

they thought they wanted but something beyond their imaginations. But the joke was on Remedy, because that was exactly what had happened to her in her life. What she and Micah had together was beyond anything in Remedy's wildest dreams, and the affection she felt for the sweet, quirky town of Dulcet and its citizens was something she could have never predicted, not in a million years. Instead of excitement that a little slice of home was coming to visit her, her instincts were shouting at her to protect this rural haven from Hollywood's toxicity.

Closing her eyes, suddenly weary, she lowered herself into the water and sat, relishing the bite of cold that seeped through her dry-clean-only skirt suit. She stretched her legs out and watched the mottled pattern of shade and sun through the water on her skin.

A sound of wings against air had her peeling her eyes open again. A dozen or more of Skeeter's homing pigeons had landed a few feet away. All eyes were on her.

"Hey, guys. What's your deal, huh? Why are you stalking me like this? I'm sure Skeeter misses you."

One of the birds got brave and skittered closer to her hand. Remedy held perfectly still and held her breath. The bird climbed onto the back of her hand. "So we're buddies now?" she said under her breath.

The bird cocked his head and blinked.

Buddies, then. Though these wild friends had very little in common with her wild friends back in Los Angeles.

She maintained her frozen state until the bird thought better about being so close to her and skittered off to rejoin his pigeon pals. Content, Remedy sank into her arms, tipped her head up, closed her eyes, and let the tinkling sound of the water, the rustle of leaves above her, soothe her frayed nerves. As her peace expanded, she started to notice other, less obvious sensory delights, the tickle of the water between her toes, the musty smell of forest dampness, the sound of insects, and the cooing of the pigeons.

She might be in Texas, but the Frio River felt exotic and tropical. She let the details soak into her imagination. Maybe someday she could use this place as inspiration for a tropical wedding. The southeast end of the resort's golf course was bordered by a lake that included mangroves, which made Remedy think of the Amazon River and damp, dense jungles. She could hang LED lanterns in the trees and string lights overhead. On the golf course there would be plenty of room for a tent and a band and a—

"Cambelle's wedding."

Remedy's laughter echoed off the trees. Just like that, she knew how to fix the wedding from hell. Carina had been right. This was what they paid Remedy the big bucks for. This was going to be a wedding for the ages. She lay back again and got to work dreaming up the details of her plan.

She wasn't entirely sure how long she'd been lying on the riverbank when she heard footfalls crunching over sand. She boosted herself up on her elbow and cocked her head toward the tree line. Micah.

He seemed leery of approaching her, so she smiled, a peace offering. "Hi."

"Hi. I didn't know this was where I was going until I ended up here," he said.

She swirled her foot through the water. "Story of my life. One blind turn after another, living by feel. Which is how I ended up sitting in the river with all my clothes on."

His long shadow stretched across the sand to her as he walked her way. "I figured you'd fallen in."

"One might think that, given my track record."

"Mind if I join you?"

"I was hoping you would," she said.

He kicked his boots off, then shoved his jeans to the ground and stepped out of them. His shirt was next. Dressed in his boxer briefs, he walked to her and stood in the water.

At the sudden shock of cold water, goose bumps sprouted on his legs. She couldn't resist smoothing her hand over his thigh, tracing the muscles below his hairy, tanned skin. He sat next to her, inhaling sharply when his hips sank into the water.

He didn't seem to be in a hurry to talk about what had happened that afternoon and neither was she, but she couldn't go a moment longer without knowing where they stood as a couple.

She flexed her fingers, then reached her hand across the inches that separated their bodies. Had she ever felt so vulnerable as she was right now, reaching for the man she cared about, wanting him to care enough about her that he was willing to keep trying? As the backs of her fingers brushed the side of his hand and he flinched, she closed her eyes. *Please, Micah.*

Then his hand covered hers and held it tight. He threaded their fingers, locking their hands together.

"Micah, I'm sorry I—"

"You can stop right there." Releasing her hand, he roped an arm around her shoulders and pulled her close. "How am I going to be the noble one who apologizes first if you beat me to it?"

Relief washed through her. Everything was going to be all right. "That is a conundrum."

She wiggled closer, until her cheek rested on his shoulder. He planted a lingering kiss to her hair. She closed her eyes and concentrated on just being, still and peaceful next to her man on a quiet riverbank. The very spot at which they'd first met.

"Loving you is turning out to be a wild ride, California."

A confusing, overwhelming ache intensified within her. They were the sweetest words she'd ever heard, but she had no idea what to do with them. Could this really be love? Was she seriously considering giving up on her dream of returning to California because of a gun-carrying, toothpick-chewing, Alpha Bubba good ol' boy? If only Micah were as simple as he'd appeared from the outset, her answer would be easy. But Micah was so much more. He was smart, funny, generous, and kind. And he was so good to her, good for her.

Rather than try to pick the right words from the storm of them whirling through her head, she cupped his cheek and showered his stubbled jaw with kisses. There was nothing saying she had to return to Los Angeles anytime soon. She could wait until she was good and ready, and the longer she waited the more time her reputation in the industry would have to recover.

"Does this mean your offer for me to meet your family this weekend still stands?"

"Of course it does. And speaking of family, I got to thinking on my way here about a lot of things," he said. "About you, and your parents, and about your family friends who are getting married that Ty Briscoe is salivating over."

She had no idea where he was going with this, but unease slid up her spine. "Okay."

"I'm not sure how polite this question is, but I think you and I are past politeness now."

"Agreed," she said.

"Okay, here's the question. Exactly how loaded are you?"

Remedy's breath stuttered out of her on a laugh, the question was so random. "What?"

"Money. How much money do you have at your disposal? Because despite every indication that you have enough to buy the whole town of Dulcet and turn it into your own personal amusement park, you haven't bothered installing an air-conditioning unit that works worth a damn and you're working a crappy job that basically forces you into servitude for a bunch of entitled rich jerks, and with an asshole boss. It doesn't add up."

Ah. They were back to the same old question again. "You're still wondering what I'm doing in Texas."

"I am."

"You've been asking me that same question off and on since the day we met."

"I haven't gotten an answer that makes sense yet," he said. "Most people have jobs because they have to. Until you mentioned a trust fund, I figured you worked because you need the money, just like the rest of us. But now, after hearing the way Ty talked down to you and the way that idiot bride and her mother talked down to you, I wonder why you take that crap. You have a trust fund. So I'm back to square one, asking that same question. What are you doing here, with this job?"

She heard the unspoken follow-up question in his words plain enough. *How long are you planning to stay?* That's what he was getting at, and damn it all if she didn't have an answer for him.

"My parents set up a trust fund for me when I was born, to be bequeathed to me when I was twenty-five."

"And you're twenty-nine now. So how much money are we talking about?"

Disclosing money specifics was an uncomfortable conversation for her that invariably called into question her motives for talking about what she was worth, as well as the motives of the person asking. But Micah loved her and, just as surely, she was falling in love with him. He didn't care about her wealth and so she shouldn't mind sharing this other part—this constant beating heart of the family she'd been born into—with him.

"Twenty-five," she said. "One for every year of my life."

"Thousand or million?"

She raised her eyebrows. That he'd asked only highlighted what different worlds they lived in.

Shock rippled across his face before he schooled his features. "Twenty-five million dollars? Sweet Jesus."

"The money's either gone or accounted for," she rushed to add before biting her lip to keep herself from explaining herself away or apologizing for who she was.

He made a strangling sound.

"What does that noise mean?" she said.

"Nothing. I . . . The money's gone? What did you do to blow twenty-five million dollars in four years? You're not the type of person to waste a fortune like that on material goods, so that makes no sense."

"You're right, I'm not that person." Had anyone ever seen her so clearly as Micah? She sincerely doubted it. "When my parents released the money in the trust fund to me, they said, 'Don't let this make you lazy.' I knew it wouldn't because I grew up with my parents as role models and they're two of the hardest-working people I know. They worked constantly, long hours and often overseas, and all while keeping their marriage healthy and raising me. I work because that's the kind of person I want to be. Someone who values an honest day's work."

He rolled to his side and propped his upper body up on an elbow. His free hand splayed over her belly. "So then, where did all your money go?"

She rested her hand over his and let her fingers explore the bones of his wrist. "A lot of places. I created five funds with a million in each, one each for any future children I might have."

He blinked down at her. "You want five kids? Xavier has two and that seems daunting enough."

"I like the idea of two kids, but you never know. I remember thinking when I set the funds up, what if the person I marry already has kids from another marriage and then with our two we have five. Stuff like that happens all the time."

He curved down and angled his lips over hers in a sweet, closed-mouth kiss. "Well, I don't have any kids from a previous marriage, and I think five kids might be three too many, for the record."

His earnest response melted her heart. She looped an arm around his neck and pulled him to her for another kiss, this one deeper. His tongue teased the edge of her lower lip until she gave herself over to him and opened her mouth. He pressed her body back until her head rested against the sand.

"Back to your money and where it all went. We've now accounted for five million. Twenty more to go."

His prompt evoked a smile. Her discomfort about sharing her financial specifics all but vanquished by his disarming earnestness. "I used one million in the first year or so, give or take, for fun and administrative expenses, a new car, a personal assistant, and so forth. And I donated fifteen million to various charities."

There was that strangling sound again. "That's a lot of money."

"Not really. There are a lot of people in this world who need help. Fifteen million doesn't make a dent, but it's a start. And the last four million I invested. I use the interest from the investments to live on. And then every year I cut the investment amount back down to four million and split the rest among my favorite charities. I like having that cushion of money, the four million. My fallback fund. Having a safety net has helped me take more risks in my career. It's one of the reasons I think I've been so successful as an event planner."

"I can't wrap my mind around that kind of cushion. Money was always elusive for my family. There was never enough, and my dad worked himself to the bone for thirty-five years as a welder. After we lost everything in the fire, the settlement from the insurance was barely enough to cover the cost of rebuilding and new furniture. There was never anything left over. I worked to pay my own way through college and struggled to pay off student loans until I was thirty."

"Money would have solved a lot of your family's problems, I know. But please believe me when I say it brings with it a whole new set of problems."

He stroked her cheek. "I would've never believed that before I met you, but I can see now how it would. Here's the thing, though. When the Zannity scandal happened, why didn't you give the finger to the wedding-planning industry and move to some tropical beach?"

"I did take a big break from the industry when that all went down. I rented a yacht and traveled the Virgin Islands with my friends. After a month, I was bored silly. It was time to get back to work."

"But why here?" he pushed.

Tamping down her annoyance that their every personal conversation circled around to that same question, she rubbed her temple. "We're back to that again."

"Yes, we are, because it doesn't make any sense why you would want a job with so much drama, working for that asshole Ty Briscoe. You have a multimillion-dollar nest egg. You don't need to put up with all this."

"You're right. I don't." Especially if working at Briscoe Ranch started to harm her reputation even more, as some of Ty's veiled threats had insinuated. "But I told you why I'm here. I want to fix my reputation. This was always supposed to be temporary." God, she hated the way that sounded, even if it was the truth.

He settled on his back again and gave a frustrated shake of his head. "You've been up-front with me about you being a short-timer here in Texas from the get-go. I thought I'd be content just to have you to myself for a little while, before you moved on. That some time with you was better than no time. I don't feel that way anymore and it scares the piss out of me that this situation with Ty is going to drive you away even faster."

He was so honest and he deserved an honest answer in reply. "I don't know what I'm going to do. I keep thinking this feud with Ty will blow over. My plan was to stay here long enough to make a name for myself in the industry. I thought I had years, not weeks. I don't want to leave yet. You and I are still unfinished business."

He turned his head and looked into her eyes for a long time; then he pulled her into his arms. "On paper, we're all wrong for each other. We should have never happened in the first place."

He was right. "We don't make sense, except that we do."

"I'm asking you not to quit your job yet. I'm asking you not to leave. Will you give me a chance to make this right for both of us with Ty?"

"Micah, you're the one whose job is on the line. I can't stand by and watch your career fail. Love doesn't work like that."

Love? She bit her lip.

He wrapped his arms more tightly around her. "No, it doesn't. Which is why I'm asking you to let me take the lead on this one. Let me see what I can do before you think too hard about quitting before you're ready."

She peppered kisses on his chest. *Such an alpha.* "My friends back home warned me about falling for the charms of a cowboy."

"I'm no cowboy, but merely a humble public servant."

She brushed her thumb over the five o'clock shadow on his cheek. "Lose the word *humble* and you'll be on the road toward the truth."

"You think your parents are going to approve of your public servant boyfriend? I'll get to meet them in a few weeks at this celebrity wedding you're putting on, I do believe."

The ache inside her from the thought of leaving Micah and Texas behind morphed into a rock in her stomach. "That's true. I can't even imagine it, you and them in the same room. Heck, I can't imagine the two of them in the same room together, for that matter. They're the embodiment of everything you despise. Forget about them approving of you. I don't see how you could approve of them."

"I'd like to think I've evolved a bit this summer, thanks to you."

She hugged him tight. "This summer has changed me, too."

"Tell me more about your folks. Are they better drivers than you?"

Remedy had always fancied herself a darn good driver, but it would have been impossible to defend her skills without coming across like Rain Man. "My dad's better at driving golf carts, which is probably because he gets a lot of practice, playing golf as often as he does. But my mom's worse than me, with golf carts and cars. At least, that's my memory from when I was a kid. She hasn't driven in years. That's how much she hates it."

"Really? How does she get around?"

"She has a driver."

He groaned. "You're right. I might not have evolved as much as I'd thought. Tell me some normal things about your parents; set my mind at ease."

Her mom having a driver and her dad's obsession with golf were her world's normal. She wanted Micah to like her parents, but they were who they were and there was no changing them. "My dad likes to grill. He fancies himself an amateur chef. My mom . . ." There wasn't very much down-to-earth about her mother. She'd worked hard in the film industry since she was a kid and had earned her eccentricities. "My mom loves her dogs. Like, so much. They're her life." *Dogs* might be a stretch to describe the yapping balls of fluff she carried everywhere in a customized purse, but Remedy wasn't about to confess as much to Micah.

"My dad's that way, too, with grilling and with dogs," Micah said. "He's got three German shepherd mixes now. Sometimes I think he loves them as much as his grandkids."

Talking about Remedy's parents and Micah's dad made Remedy starkly aware of who they hadn't yet discussed. "I hope someday you'll feel like you can talk to me about your mom."

Micah propped his hand behind his head and tipped his chin up to watch the treetops. "A while ago I decided she wasn't worth my time or energy thinking about anymore."

This from the man who'd insisted to Remedy over and over that where a person was from and what their family background was held infinite importance in their life. She decided to risk one more question. "When did she die?"

"She's alive. I'm not sure where. We haven't spoken in years." He huffed. "So many years. By her choice. And it's the choice I'm most comfortable with, too."

She kissed his shoulder. Remedy's world would capsize if she and her mom were to sever ties. She couldn't even imagine it, but it was a truth Micah lived with every day.

"How old were you when she . . ."

"Twelve. And that's all I'd like to say about it for now."

Remedy nodded, even as she drew lines in her memory with other stories he'd told her about his youth. He was eleven when the fire struck. He and his family had spent nearly a year at his grandparents' house while their home was rebuilt. And his mother left in the middle of all that upheaval, when her children needed her most? Unfathomable. Absolutely despicable. No wonder he didn't want to talk about her.

Time for a subject change to break the grim mood. "You mentioned your dad having grandkids, so that means you're an uncle, right?"

"Oh, yeah. Thanks to my older brother and two younger sisters. I earned my Favorite Uncle status one water gunfight and trip to the ice-cream store at a time. My brother has two girls and my sisters both have boys. You'll meet the whole crew on Sunday."

"I can't wait. Just . . . they're not going to serve any of those weird Jell-O and mayonnaise salads like we had at Albert and Tabby's wedding, are they?"

He chuckled, his grief seemingly forgotten. "It's always possible. In fact, I might volunteer to bring one. Just for you. Maybe I'll sprinkle some raisins on top as decoration."

She poked him in the ribs. "Is that your idea of sweet-talking me?"

"No. And neither is this." In a flash he'd rolled to his side, his hands out, tickling her. She squirmed and lurched all over, splashing water and squealing and laughing until the tickling got too much and she pleaded with him to have mercy.

"I told you I'd file that ticklish information away for another time."

She slid her leg across his body, then pushed herself up to straddle his waist. "So you did."

Then she threaded their fingers together and pinned his hands into the sand near his ears.

Sand and water sprinkled over his taut chest and muscled shoulders, and a few grains of sand had found their way into his long, dark eyelashes. He was so beautiful. He was hers.

"You're bringing me home to meet your parents." The wonder of it. Of them together. The Hollywood event planner destined to leave and the small-town fire chief with roots planted so deep that he could never leave without giving up the very essence of the man she was falling hard for.

His eyes glowed with affection. He brushed her hair away from her face and tucked it behind her ear. "Just do me one favor, would you, darlin'?" he drawled.

She loved the way his twang got more pronounced when his voice turned husky and low like it was now. "Anything."

A boyish grin broke out on his face. "Try not to burn my dad's house down while you're there."

"Micah!"

"Or break any windows. Or crash your car through the porch steps. Or sic your pet pigeons on the dinner spread."

His belly laugh vibrated through her thighs and shook her body. She released his hands so she could tickle his ribs, but before she knew what had happened she was flat on her back, Micah on top of her. No more laughter in his eyes. All she saw was heat and need and love as he caged her head between his arms.

She searched his gaze. "When I saw you here, I thought you and I might be through. For a fleeting second, I wondered if you were here to break up with me."

"Not even close."

"I'm responsible for the fire at the ball," she said.

"Not you. It was my error in judgment. I'm pretty pissed off at myself. I should've never let Emily sucker me into agreeing to something I knew was dangerous."

"I don't know if you've noticed, but I have a way of conjuring disaster." The threat of tears stung her eyes. Copping to that flaw wasn't supposed to feel so vulnerable, but she needed Micah to see her for everything she was, the good and the bad—and she needed him to choose her anyway.

Affection bloomed in his eyes. "I did notice that, actually. And I'm not sure if you've noticed, but Xavier tells me I have a compulsive need to swoop in and save the day."

"I think Xavier's on to something."

He stroked a tendril of hair from her cheek. "So I'm working on a theory involving your disaster-conjuring gene and my hero syndrome being perfectly suited to each other."

In other words, they didn't make sense except that they did. She lifted her head and kissed him. "I think you might be on to something."

He fingered her shirt collar. "Speaking of saving people, I think I need to do something about these wet clothes you're in."

"Could be dangerous."

He popped the top button open. "I can't allow that."

While he unbuttoned her shirt, a splash of white color caught Remedy's eye. The pigeons, inching ever nearer to Remedy and Micah. "We're being watched."

Micah craned his neck to follow her gaze. "I'll be damned. You were right; those birds are stalking you."

"They love me."

He splayed her shirt open. "Never thought I'd have something in common with a bunch of pigeons." He tugged her bra cup down and drew her nipple into his mouth with a hard suck that pulled a whimper from her throat.

She combed her fingers through her hair, reveling in the dual elation of his mouth on her flesh and her learning that he loved her. "Take me here, now. Just like this."

She registered the desperation in her voice, the urgent need to connect after so much strife and uncertainty between them. With her on the pill and both of them recently tested, they'd abandoned condoms the night they became an exclusive couple. There was nothing stopping them from joining together in the very spot in which they'd first laid eyes on each other.

There was that lazy, lopsided smile that melted her heart. "It's kind of our thing, isn't it? Making love by the riverbank like a proper redneck couple."

With her hands, she memorized the planes and curves of his shoulders and back. Her palms followed the contour of his spine to the dip of his lower back and the flare of his taut backside before it disappeared into the waistband of his briefs. "I would have never imagined this for myself before you." *And now I'm having trouble imagining my life any other way.*

His caressing hands dipped lower. He bunched her skirt at her hips, then peeled her wet underwear off and tossed it on top of his pile of clothes. "I'm gonna add this pair to the collection I started in my truck, to go with that first pair you left hanging on my rearview mirror the first time we slept together."

"I forgot about those." That night seemed like a lifetime ago, when she'd thought of Micah as an adversary, rather than a force of change and happiness in her world.

Their bodies joined together in an exquisite sharp bolt of pleasure. Her fingers slid over her belly to her clit, working it in time with his hips. Their mouths searched each other out and locked together in a never-ending kiss as they rocked in a slow and steady grind that seemed to stretch each second out with each dragging thrust of friction and flesh. As if they could stay in this moment together forever. As if there weren't a thousand forces trying to wedge them apart.

Remedy's buildup was swift. "Micah, I'm already there. Oh, damn."

She allowed herself only quiet whimpers in such a public place. Thrusting her hips, she brought herself all the way home with her fingers on her clit and his cock pounding inside her. Tears crowded her eyes and slipped down her cheeks as her release welled up from a deep, dark corner of her being. A swirling, raw stew of bliss and heartache and need.

Micah's thrusts turned erratic, his breathing uneven. On a grunt, he pulled out of her and knelt, his hand rubbing himself in compact circles until he raised his face to the sky with a grimace and spent himself into the water.

"Not in me?" she croaked, empty now that the act had been so brief.

He collapsed next to her on the sand and pulled her into his arms. "I'm not done with you yet, not by a long shot." He kissed her temple. "Let me take you to your place so I can get you naked and love on your body in a proper way. I'm in the mood to hear you scream my name."

She scratched the hair at the base of his softening cock. "Only if I get to love on your body, too."

"Darlin', I'll take whatever you give me. That's always been the case."

A note of anguish touched those last words. As though she held all the power, his heart in her hand. She took hold of his head and arched up to kiss him full on the mouth. "Then I guess we'd better get going, because I plan on giving you everything you want."

Touching and kissing, they hurried along the trail to her house, her in her wet suit, minus her underwear, and him going commando in his jeans, with his wet briefs and shirt stuffed into the waistband of his pants. When they arrived at the steps up to her back deck, he pressed her against one of the deck's wooden support pillars and took her mouth in a demanding kiss that left her dizzy and needy all over again.

A car drove by, breaking the spell. "Let's get upstairs," he said. "You first so I can admire your ass."

Remedy realized halfway up that the door to her back deck was open. "I didn't leave that door open. I'm sure of it."

Micah swept past her, all business. "There's a white SUV parked in front and a big bruiser of a guy guarding it," he whispered. "I don't know what's going on, but let's get back to my truck and call the cops."

"Surprise!" came a booming voice from above.

Remedy nearly leaped out of her skin. Judging by the looks of it, Micah had experienced the same reaction. Hanging over the deck railing was none other than Remedy's mother.

It took a moment for Remedy to recover her wits before she could answer. "Mom? What are you doing here?"

Micah looked from Remedy to her mother in a stupefied silence, his eyebrows raised. Then, silently, he donned his T-shirt. Remedy sent him a silent apology. At the sight of pink fabric in his pocket, she got his attention and gestured for him to stuff her panties deeper inside.

"We heard on the news about the fire at the resort."

"We?" Remedy said as her father stepped out of the back sliding door and stood shoulder to shoulder with Mom.

Remedy shifted her gaze between the two, stunned silent. It took a nudge from Micah for her to find her voice again. "You're both here. Together. Why? I mean, what a nice surprise. No. I take that back. I mean, why? Seriously."

Her dad's smile crinkled the skin at the corners of his eyes. He set a hand on her mom's shoulder, as though that was the most natural thing in the world to do. "We wanted to make sure you were all right."

Remedy tore her gaze from his hand and let her focus shift between her parents. "Why didn't you call? I could've told you I was all right over the phone."

Her mom waved off the suggestion. "Surprises are a lot more fun. Plus Cambelle, Wynd, and Helen heard about the fire, too, and they wanted to come find out if it was going to affect their wedding. So I called your father up and we decided, What the heck? Let's join them."

A tingling started in Remedy's throat. "Cambelle, Wynd, and Helen are here? Where?"

"At Briscoe Ranch. They were golfing, last I heard," her dad said.

Oh boy.

"Why don't you two come on up and we'll have some champagne," Mom said. "I can't wait for you to introduce us properly to your strapping firefighter man"—she cupped a hand on the side of her mouth as though telling a secret—"who doesn't look a thing like Tom Selleck, just like you told me he didn't."

Micah raised an eyebrow in question, but Remedy shook her head. "You don't want to know."

He took her hand. "Something tells me I'm about to find out anyway."

Chapter Eighteen

"Two words: *Vintage Safari.*"

Remedy couldn't decide if Helen's blank expression was due to abject horror at the idea or because of a recent Botox treatment.

"You're kidding, right?" Wynd Fisher's gaze shifted from one end of the golf course to the other, whipping his salt-and-pepper ponytail this way and that.

The night before, after an awkward cocktail hour in the heat of her un-air-conditioned house in which her parents sat weirdly close to each other on her sofa and peppered Micah with all manners of crazy questions that he indulged like a champ, Remedy had suggested they relocate to the resort. Micah begged off joining them because he had to go to work. *Lucky duck.*

At the resort, Remedy's parents had disappeared up the elevator, off to their respective rooms with the promise of meeting Remedy again for dinner. Remedy's next stop had been her office, which was where she learned that Ty's secretary had scheduled a Sunday morning meeting with Cambelle, Helen, and Wynd.

Which was how she found herself on Sunday morning leading a caravan of golf carts onto the twelfth green, completely ignoring the fact that the midday temperature was pushing ninety-eight degrees. Perhaps if she didn't acknowledge the extreme weather the bridal party wouldn't, either.

"Vintage Safari Chic is no joke. It's a trend waiting to happen." Remedy tipped her head toward the bank of the river where the mangroves with their gnarled roots turned the setting exotic and cool, and where she'd commissioned a crew of maintenance workers to arrange a sitting area for them, complete with a chilled bottle of champagne resting in an ice bucket. "Walk with me."

She led them into the shade. "Picture the glamour and romance of traveling to far-off lands in bygone days. It answers the question what if the *Titanic* had gone south instead for a vacation plucked from the film *Out of Africa*? This will be the ultimate in destination weddings because your guests won't have to leave the country to be swept away to another time and other land."

"You have a month," Helen said, wrinkling her nose and smoothing a bead of perspiration off her temple. "Can't you make that wedding barn larger to accommodate five hundred guests? I don't want to have a reception in a tent. That's so low-class. We're not hobos."

"I see you're not familiar with the caliber of tents that are available for luxury weddings these days," she said with just a hint of condescension. "Tent weddings are the peak of glamour, but only for those who can afford the right kinds of tents. Air-conditioned, crisp linens, vaulted ceilings. I don't expect you to be in the know about the latest technology for weddings. That's my job."

Cambelle balked. "I'm not sure about this. We agreed on a Farm Chic theme."

Time to put Carina's advice in action. Remedy gestured to the artfully arranged chairs and tables she'd had the resort crew set up in the shade of the mangroves in advance of their arrival; then she poured each of them a glass of the resort's most expensive champagne. "I'm not sure how to put this delicately, but we're all friends here, so I think we're beyond politeness, yes?"

Wynd puffed out his barrel chest. "I'd like to think so. What's on your mind?"

Remedy painted a condescending smile on her face. "Here's the problem. You told me you're looking to make a statement. You want to show the world, your friends and your fans, something they've never seen before. This wedding will not only be launching your lives together but launches your careers into a different stratosphere altogether. Cambelle, you're going to be a household name like you've always dreamed of becoming—if we do this right." Time to pour on the pity for these poor, uninformed clients. "But I've been giving a lot of thought to your wedding ideas, and"—she faked a cringe—"I have to be honest with you. I feel that we're in danger of falling short of that goal."

Helen gasped. "What are you trying to say? My Cambelle's wedding ideas were brilliant."

Remedy went Method acting and tried to channel the look on her dad's face that one time he was trying to pass a kidney stone. "I always try to honor the bride's vision for her special day, but I feel like you have the right to know that this year alone at Briscoe Ranch Resort we've hosted twenty-four Farm Chic weddings. And even though I'd make sure yours surpassed all of those, there's no getting around the truth that Farm Chic is passé. It's been done before. A lot."

Remedy placed a hand over her heart. "As I said, it's against my policy to bring that up. But you hired me because I have the skills and the vision to give you something new, something fresh. I understand the demands of Hollywood and the trends of the wedding industry better than anyone else in either business alone. Let me show you how to give the world a wedding they've never seen before. Let me make you a star, Cambelle."

Cambelle's expression turned giddy. She hugged

Wynd's arm. "That's what I want, baby. Don't you want your little girl to be a star?"

Remedy squelched a shudder of horror at that sentiment because she had them hooked real good now. She spun away, her arms outstretched to frame the shot for them. "Picture the customized, luxury tents over here, the tent walls completely open and airy, but with canopy tops so the media helicopters can't get a clear shot of you or your guests. That way you'll be able to control your own spin and sell your own, tasteful, perfectly rendered photos to the media outlet of your choosing."

"That's a great point," Helen said. "You really have thought of everything."

Indeed. "Over here, we'd stage a Polaroid photograph station, complete with live animals to pose with. For a touch of whimsy, your guests can dress up in vintage clothing and accessories for their pictures." They didn't need to know that Remedy had just utilized that very idea for the firefighter ball.

Cambelle made jazz hands in the air. "What kind of animals? Because Jade Iovine had a panther at her wedding in this huge metal cage, just like Beyoncé used in that video. I've got to top that."

"And so we will. I've already reserved six luscious parrots for your wedding at your request. I was thinking of adding peacocks, a zebra, and—this is short notice, but I have a personal connection with a company who rents out elephants." God help her if the elephant handlers sent Gwyneth again, but that was a risk she had to take. So much for that elusive *no live animals* policy she dreamed of enacting. But she had a feeling that might be the tipping point for Cambelle.

Helen said, "I like this new theme, but we'll have to reorder invitations."

"That is something the resort would be delighted to comp you on."

"Not necessary," Wynd said. "When I told these two girls of mine that I'd spare no expense for this wedding, I meant it."

"You're a generous man," Remedy cooed, smiling. "For the invitations, I'm thinking we'll overlay the font over vintage, sepia-toned maps of Africa. You and your guests will be attending the ultimate exotic destination wedding. We'll bring the savanna to Texas. Instead of golf carts, we'll bring in safari Jeeps to transport your guests. As Wynd said, no expense will be spared, no detail left unrealized."

"I have one question left. How many safari-themed weddings have you planned this year?" Helen asked.

Remedy offered Helen her most radiant smile. "This would be the first, not only for me but for the resort. Perhaps for all of the United States. I certainly haven't heard of one this grand, with the inclusion of live animals and safari Jeeps. You really can't do that anywhere else but Texas due to laws and a lack of availability of exotic animals in most states, so consider yourself lucky that you're holding it here."

"What about fireworks?" Wynd asked. "My darling wanted fireworks to celebrate our marriage. Will they allow those on the golf course?"

Remedy was ready for that question. "The exotic animal handlers won't contract for a wedding that includes fireworks. It stresses out their animals too much. But I guarantee you won't miss the fireworks at all."

"Oh, Cambelle, you can do without those," Helen said. "This is what you want. A true one-of-a-kind event."

Carina had been right. All Remedy had needed to do was take control.

From the back of the limousine that Wynd had rented for the weekend, Remedy checked the time on her phone as discreetly as possible. Four hours until Micah was picking her and her parents up for his family barbecue. Four hours that she should have devoted to the flood of details of Cambelle and Wynd's wedding that demanded her attention now that they'd settled on a new theme and venue.

But Helen had insisted Remedy and her parents all enjoy a lunch together in celebration of the new wedding plan, and Cambelle had latched on to Remedy as her long and distant friend, insisting that they catch up with the details of each other's lives. There had been a time that Remedy had thought of Cambelle as one of her closest friends, and so in the name of nostalgia, and because Remedy's parents would also be joining them, she'd agreed to accompany the group to San Antonio for lunch.

They'd only made it as far as Dulcet's Main Street when Wynd had a change of heart.

"Remedy's our local girl," he said. "How about a tour of town first? Maybe there's somewhere you can take us to eat around here."

Remedy's mother smiled brightly at her. "What a great idea! Remedy, tell the driver where to go. Where does your young man live? That would be a fun place to start."

Remedy might have spent the past eight weeks in Dulcet, but she doubted that the places she frequented would hold any interest. Maybe Petey's, since it was filled with old-time TV paraphernalia, but that was about it. "Well, okay. I don't go out much because my job keeps me so busy, but um, let's see what we've got. Turn onto Main Street," she said to the driver.

She pointed out the two bridal boutiques, the grocery store, the bars, and the church where Albert and Tabby's wedding had been held.

"This place is so quaint," her mother said, not sounding entirely enthusiastic in her assessment.

Quaint was one of those words that Remedy had used a lot when she'd arrived in Dulcet, but she'd since figured out, with Micah's help, how patronizing the term was to the proud residents of the town. "I don't think *quaint* is the term you're looking for," Remedy prompted gently. "Maybe *charming* or *small*?"

"No," her mother decided after a moment's pause. "I mean 'quaint' and 'run-down.' Look at the crumbling paint on all the walls of that row of storefronts. It's as if these business owners don't care about their town's appearance at all."

While the town was wearing a bit at the edges, it had a comforting appeal that had grown on Remedy. None of the business owners were well-to-do, but they all worked their asses off and did the best they could. More important, they looked out for one another and they cared deeply about their hometown.

"They do, Mom. Trust me. You remember what it was like growing up in Tulsa, the way Grandpa's shop sometimes got run-down when money was tight."

Her mom hmphed, as in denial of her humble roots as she ever was.

"I'm with you, Virgie," Remedy's dad said, touching her mom's knee.

Virgie? Since when did her dad call her mom that? Not since they'd been married. But Remedy was the only one in the car who seemed to notice the uncharacteristic display of affection.

"It's hard to believe a world-class resort is drawing in elite clientele from all over the world and only a few miles away the townspeople can't be bothered to clean up after themselves," her mom said. "You'd think they'd be grateful for the business the resort brings in."

Yikes. Had Remedy really sounded like that only a couple months ago? She cleared her throat. "And that's Micah's house, next to the fire station."

Cambelle's face screwed up. "That's where your boyfriend lives?"

"Yep."

Cambelle pressed her hand to the window. "Like, that tiny brown . . . thing?"

Remedy chewed her lower lip, her irritation mounting. "It's a house. And a perfectly nice one at that."

"You didn't tell me you were dating down. What happened to *suits, not boots*?" Cambelle said.

Dating down was a term that had been passed to them by their mothers' generation and it was never thrown around in a positive way. Dating down was the opposite of what Cambelle was doing with Wynd, and it meant the woman either was suffering a nervous breakdown or had turned delusional about the importance of wealth and status in the world. No woman in her right mind would subject herself to a lifetime of washing her own dishes or making do with less than four thousand square feet of property. Remedy had never consciously subscribed to that way of thinking, but she must have, given the disdainful way she'd viewed Micah and his crew that first time she'd met them. Guilt settled in her chest like a stone.

"Don't give her a hard time," Remedy's mom said. "She's happy. What more could a mother want?"

Remedy's dad made an odd choking sound, a not-so-subtle protest. Clearly, he was siding with Cambelle.

"No, it's okay, Mom. I've got this. Cambelle, I'm not dating down. I found a man I liked—a lot, by the way—who happens to wear boots and work hard for a living."

"I work hard for a living," Wynd said, "but I'd never even subject my maid to living in a house like that. What kind of life will he give you?"

"Exactly," Remedy's father said.

"That Micah fellow seemed nice enough when we met him yesterday," Remedy's mom mused. "But Wynd has a point."

Remedy's hand curled over the limo door handle. She would give anything, *anything,* to get out of that vehicle and away from this conversation before she was forced to confront her parents over a prejudice she'd never realized they had. How could the two people who'd hung the moon for her for so long—her heroes, her family—think such ugly things about Micah and the town she'd come to love? Especially since both her parents had grown up in small midwestern towns. Had fame stolen their memories of what it meant to be members of working-class America?

What if Remedy's lifelong feeling of not belonging anywhere had come from her parents? They were out of touch with reality in some really significant ways that had surely impacted Remedy's view of the world. They didn't want to belong. They didn't want humble roots; they weren't choosing to relate with compassion to people whose lives and circumstances were different from their own. Were all those military charities her dad supported just for show?

Rather than flee the situation, she turned her focus to her parents and looked at them with fresh eyes. "I thought you just wanted me to be happy."

Her mom shifted and took her father's hand. "We do, dear. But . . . happiness is such a complicated beast."

"Okay, time-out," Remedy said. "Since when are you two so chummy? Why are you holding hands? I feel like a broken record lately, but seriously. You two hate each other."

Her parents exchanged glances, their expressions trouble. "We don't. I know it seemed like that for a long time, but when you were going through the whole Zannity mess my heart was breaking for you, so I reached out to the only other person who'd know exactly what I was going through."

"And now you're . . . you're . . ." Remedy gestured to

their joined hands. It was going to take Remedy a long, long time to process this turn of events.

"We're family," her dad said. "That's what we realized. We're your family and we're each other's family. And we're worried about you all over again."

"Give me a break! Worried about what? If I wanted a bigger house, I'd buy a bigger house for myself. But I don't want that. You have nothing to worry about anymore." She loved Micah's place. She loved her quirky cottage with Luke the temperamental air-conditioning unit. And the only thing she wanted from Micah was his love.

Helen tsked. "What a waste."

Remedy stared blankly at Helen and Cambelle. How had this weekend gone so sideways? Helen, Cambelle, and Wynd were her clients, and she refused to be drawn into an argument with them. So she decided to fall back on her professional playbook and not let them see her sweat. She forced herself to go numb. "Across the street from Micah's house and the fire station is Petey's Diner, which is named after the dog in *The Little Rascals* TV show. Dad, I know you loved that show when you were younger because I distinctly remember you trying to get me to watch it with you."

It took a moment for her dad to process what Remedy had said. "You're right. That was a great show. I got all the VHS tapes through one of those infomercials, but you refused. I think that Alfalfa character scared you."

Remedy thought back but couldn't remember having a feeling about Alfalfa one way or another.

"We should stop in at the diner," Wynd said. "Let's see what this town's got."

"I don't think that's such a good idea," Remedy said.

"Nonsense." Helen knocked on the partition, getting the driver's attention. "Circle back around the block and stop in front of that diner we passed back there."

The driver was already pulling around before Helen had

finished issuing the request. When the limo pulled to a stop, the whole lot of them piled out and then into Petey's, much to the bewilderment of Barbara, Petey, and the rest of the diner patrons, who'd been enjoying their lunch.

As it usually did, it took the diner staff and patrons a few minutes to realize who Remedy's parents were. They were perusing the myriad of framed photographs and magazine articles when the first patron approached, looking for an autograph from Remedy's dad. In no time they were swarmed by dozens, who'd abandoned their meals in favor of waiting for autographs.

After so many years of being in the spotlight, Remedy's parents were gracious and accommodating, which she had come to expect. As was her typical routine when such a swarm happened, she hung back and tried to avoid any kind of recognition, because most people, when they figured out that Remedy wasn't a famous actor, lost complete interest in her at all and were usually pretty rude about it. She'd decided a long time ago that it was best to leave the celebrity status to her parents.

Cambelle, Helen, and Wynd, as it turned out, did not share Remedy's disinterest in the spotlight. They swiped menus from a table and cackled loudly at the "disgusting" menu choices. They made a big deal about how sticky the menu was and marveled at the A grade the diner had gotten from the county health inspector, going on about how they expected to find roaches in the kitchen.

Remedy endured it for five whole minutes before she couldn't take it anymore. She had no idea how Petey and Barbara could keep themselves so composed, standing behind the bar listening to the filth coming out of Cambelle's and Helen's mouths especially.

Hands shaking in anger, Remedy corralled them and Wynd toward the door. "It's time for you three to wait in the limo. You've done enough."

"Don't be such a killjoy," Cambelle said, pouting.

"Don't be such a bully," Remedy countered.

Wynd hung a cigarette from his lips and lit it. "I have high standards. That doesn't make me a bully."

Remedy yanked the cigarette away and stubbed it out on the floor. "You don't see how you're hurting the people who work here? Actual people with actual feelings?"

Wynd sneered. "Look at you, Remedy. I remember when you were yay high, when your dad would bring you out during parties to charm his guests. You wanted to be a princess, but here you are, slumming with these inbred, backwoods Texans."

Remedy had never been so livid. "Leave. Now."

"Come here, baby," Cambelle said. She hooked an arm around Wynd's neck, then snapped a selfie of the two of them standing in front of the pie counter. "We'll post that on Instagram and your place will be famous," she said to Petey. "You should be thanking us."

Remedy held her breath until they'd disappeared into the limo. Cambelle certainly wasn't the first bride to sneer down her nose at Remedy and the hardworking people around her, nor would she be the last, but at least at Briscoe Ranch the brides left after the wedding. At least there were good-hearted people for Remedy to spend time with and a man who adored her. If she moved back to L.A., she'd be surrounded by the Helens, Cambelles, and Wynds of the world all day, every day.

The crowd was thinning around her parents, but they couldn't be done fast enough for Remedy's way of thinking. "I'll take two cherry pies," she said to Petey, sliding a handful of twenties across the counter. "Keep the change. I'm so sorry those idiots were so rude to you."

Petey plucked a pie from the refrigerated case. "You're Micah's girl, right?"

She loved that description all the more now. "Yes, I am."

"Why are you hanging around with those no-good people, then? Even if they are famous."

"Good question."

With her boxed pies in hand she lingered outside the door for her parents to emerge, and when they did Remedy's parents asked Helen to give them a moment of privacy with their daughter.

Remedy's mom took her hand. "Honey, I know what you're thinking."

"Do you, Mom?"

"You're upset with us."

"Uh, ya think?" Remedy said. "I don't think I ever realized what a bitch Cambelle is. Her and her mom. Wynd, too."

"Remedy, please. They're our dear friends and no one's perfect."

"They might be your friends, but they're not mine. Not anymore."

Her mom looked distraught. She squeezed Remedy's hand harder. "They're not so bad. They just didn't like the diner. They've got expensive taste. We all do. You're my champagne and caviar girl, remember?"

Remedy pulled her hand away. "Can you hear yourself right now?"

"Your mother's point is that you shouldn't let a little dis-agreement with Cambelle change your mind about mov-ing home. It's not about Cambelle or Helen or Wynd. It's about our family being together again." Remedy's father slid an arm across her mom's shoulders. "After all these years apart, don't you think it's time?"

Remedy was nowhere near ready to deal with her parents' out-of-left-field romance today, but she was ready—beyond ready, she realized—to stand up for herself. "Whether you two are together or apart, we'll always be a family. But I'm ready to make my own life, my own family. And I think I might want to do that here in Texas."

Her mom's face blanched.

Her father said, "Wynd was right, honey." He pointed

across the street to Micah's house. "That man will not give you the life you deserve."

The disdain in his voice set Remedy's teeth on edge. "I give myself the life I deserve. Not a man. Not you two. Me. And I'm doing just fine, thank you very much."

"So this is it?" her mom said. "You want to live in a poor town and you want to spend the rest of your life working to the bone for women who should have been your peers?"

That was one way of putting it. Though it broke her heart, Remedy knew what she had to do. "You know what? I'll drive back to the resort in the limo with you, and I'll even put on a good face for the rest of the afternoon around you and your friends, my clients, but I'm uninviting you from Micah's family party tonight. I wouldn't want any ignorant, low-class people like you two spoiling all the fun we're going to have."

Chapter Nineteen

Micah pulled his truck around the circular drive of Briscoe Ranch Resort, ignoring the valet drivers. Radio blaring, he was feeling good about introducing Remedy to his family. Never mind that her parents were gonna be there, too. That was bound to be strange and probably a little awkward, but he'd prepped his family about the celebrities who would be in their midst and all had assured him they'd be on their best behavior. No fan gushing, no autographs, no problems.

Her parents weren't driving over with Micah and Remedy, though. They planned to be fashionably late. Or, as Remedy told him last night in bed, what they really had planned was staging a grand entrance for maximum effect, as they were wont to do.

According to Remedy's text message, she was waiting for him on the second-level veranda having cocktails with the bride, Cambelle, her mom, and the groom. Wynd, she'd called him, whatever the hell kind of crazy Hollywood name that was. Sure enough, there they were, on the vine-and-lattice-covered patio above the hotel's west wing. The tiny table they were grouped around was loaded down with martini glasses full of pink drinks and everyone looked fresh from a tennis match in crisp white, sporty attire save for Remedy, who was so dolled up and pretty, Micah gave a low whistle under his breath at the sight of her as he parked his truck right below where she sat.

She looked sophisticated up there on the patio with a martini and that fancy dress and heels that probably cost as much as Micah's entire wardrobe combined. She and Cambelle were laughing and talking. Remedy was so far out of his league it was hard to believe she'd had a good time at a sawdust-covered roadhouse like Hog Heaven that first night they got together.

"Your cowboy's here to whisk you away in his big old truck," he heard one of the women say.

Damn right he was. He poured out of his truck and donned his favorite black Stetson, then tipped the brim to the ladies in greeting, which got them twittering, right on cue.

Remedy leaned over the white wrought-iron railing. It wasn't until that moment that he sensed something was off in her eyes and in the faltering curve of her smile.

His protective instincts kicked up. Something was wrong. Something had happened to her, and, whatever it was, someone was going to have hell to pay if they hurt her.

"Stay there and I'll escort you down those stairs," he asked.

"Not necessary."

Maybe not necessary, but with those skinny little heels she had on and her penchant for disaster he wasn't taking any chances.

At the top of the stairs, he pecked Remedy's cheek, then took the time to look every person at her table in the eye in search of a clue about what had happened to rattle Remedy and let them know without words that she was not to be messed with. His attention snagged on Wynd. Malice simmered below the surface of his smirking smile and sharp eyes.

"Everything go all right today?" Micah asked him with a nod.

"More than all right. Our girl Remedy has a lot of brains in that pretty little head of hers."

What a dick. "More than you, I'm guessing."

"Let's go, Micah," Remedy urged, picking up a stack of pie boxes from the table.

Wynd leaned back in his chair and rubbed his mustache like a rich miser in an old-time movie. "Not so fast, now. Before you got here we were debating something, but Remedy refused to weigh in. Maybe you can help us."

"Wynd, no," Remedy said. Her tone was strained and quiet.

Micah draped a fortifying arm around her. No wonder he'd read distress on her face. She'd spent the day fielding a bunch of ignorant comments and questions from this asshole. "All right. Go ahead, Wynd. What's the debate?"

Wynd saluted Micah with his pink martini. "Texas isn't like the rest of the South, right? No cousins marrying cousins and all that *Deliverance* nastiness? Your ma isn't also your aunt, is she?" he added with an artificial twang that reminded him of the act Remedy used to pull when they'd first met.

"An inbreeding question. Original. Is that kind of like how Cambelle isn't really your daughter you're marrying, although she's just about that right age? Is that the sort of nastiness you're talking about?"

Laughing like Micah had told him a hilarious joke, Wynd stood and puffed his chest out. He really had that old-time miser act down pat. "Remedy, why don't you stay here with us tonight? I'm sure whatever the resort serves in their restaurant won't be as tasty as roadkill stew or whatever's on the menu over at Micah's redneck palace, but I'm sure we'll manage."

Micah itched with the need to defend his home turf and his family, but he could feel Remedy leaning away from the conflict and see her casting longing looks at the parking lot as though she'd already gone to a happy place in her head and distanced herself from the conversation at hand. She's already pleaded with Micah to leave, so getting her away from such a disgusting display of ignorance trumped everything else.

Micah eased the pie boxes from Remedy's hands so she could hold on to him while traversing the stairs. "We're leaving now, Remedy. Got your purse?"

It took her a moment to register that he was talking to her. "Yes."

"Then let's get out of here."

The drive to his dad's house was quiet and tense.

"I'm sorry you had to hear all that from Wynd. He's a jerk," Remedy said when they turned onto Micah's dad's block.

Wynd was a lot worse than a jerk, but that didn't need mentioning. Micah set a hand on her knee. "I was thinking about how sorry I was for you for the same reason. It's hard to believe those are your friends." He gnashed his teeth together, regretting the inflammatory comment immediately.

"It is, isn't it? I thought that today, more than once."

It was tempting to ask her why she'd want to return to Hollywood if those were the type of people she'd be going home to, but her plan to leave was already a sore subject between them and Remedy had suffered enough distress for one day. "What kind of pies are those we're bringing?"

"Cherry. From Petey's."

"My family's favorite. They're gonna love you just for that, guaranteed." He set a hand on her knee and gave it a squeeze, but her expression remained distant, so he dropped it.

Minutes later, they stood before his dad's two-story brick and pale blue siding house set close to the street in the heart of a sleepy residential neighborhood. As opposed to their neighbors on either side, their home boasted no trees in the yard, nor any visible in the backyard. Just grass and a cracked concrete driveway and a rusty off-road Jeep, Dad's one tribute to redneck country living that drove his kids up the wall.

"This is where you grew up?" Remedy said.

"Yes and no. My folks didn't change the layout of the house's interior when they rebuilt after the fire, but the garage is new, as is a fair amount of the dirt under that lawn. But this is the spot."

"It's hard to imagine everything you lost in the fire. You don't have any baby pictures, for example?"

"Only the ones my parents sent to my grandparents and other family."

He sensed the pull of sorrow tugging at her, the same feeling he'd gotten after picking her up at the resort. He wiggled their joined arms. "Don't get sad. We escaped that fire with everything that mattered." *Even if it had cost him his mother, a few months later.*

"The Jeep is a nice touch."

He chuckled. "Don't say that around my sisters. They're always harping on Dad to get it fixed or they'll have it towed. And then he tells them if they'd stop sending the grandkids over for him to babysit, then he'd have time to work on it. But he loves those grandkids, so I think it's more about them all liking to snip at each other when the mood strikes them."

"Kind of like you and me."

He released her hand so he could hug her tight against his side. "Maybe that's where I get it from. Who knew I was subconsciously looking for a woman to bicker with, just like I'm used to with my own family?"

She nuzzled his shoulder with her face. He loved the way she rubbed up against him every chance she got, all curves and sweetness. "Don't forget the making up after the bickering," she said. "That's my favorite part."

"I would never forget that. It's my favorite part, too." He glanced around to make sure no neighbors were watching too closely, then let his hand stray to her backside. "Doesn't look like your parents are here yet."

Her head fell to his shoulder, not playfully like she'd nuzzled him, but as though she needed him to support the weight of her burden. "They're not coming. Something happened today that I'm not ready to talk about, and I asked them not to come."

He kissed her hair. "Maybe later you'll feel like talking?"

She nodded, then settled her gaze on the Jeep. "I might be asking to borrow that Jeep for Cambelle and Wynd's wedding. It looks kind of safari-like, and it wouldn't be a favor to them; it'd be a favor to me."

Micah wondered if they'd still want the wedding there, given the ballroom fire and their obvious dislike of Texas, but he wasn't about to voice that curiosity to Remedy, nor how wonderful he thought it'd be if they canceled and took themselves out of his and Remedy's lives for good. "All right, then. You know I can't say no to you, and you're soon to learn that my dad's as big a pushover as I am. Sounds like everyone's around back. Let's go."

Micah's dad's backyard was crowded with people of every age, and it took a few beats for them to realize Micah and Remedy had arrived, because they were intently watching two kids dangle peanuts from fishing poles trying to lure squirrels into two clear plastic barrels that seemed to have held cheese puffs, according to the labels.

"Watch this," Micah whispered. "Savannah and Duncan are having a squirrel-fishing race. Whoever gets a squirrel in the barrel and gets the lid on first is the winner."

Joining in with Micah's family to watch children racing to see who could trap a squirrel first was the perfect antidote to the day she'd had with Cambelle's group and her parents. "What does the winner get?"

"Don't know. Probably just bragging rights, but that's a pretty big deal for the Garrity clan."

Savannah seemed to be the sure bet. She had a patient touch while reeling the peanut toward her barrel, where more peanuts waited inside to entice the hungry squirrel. With each inch the squirrel chased the peanut, Remedy found herself leaning in with bated breath like the rest of the audience.

A tall, handsome black man stepped next to Remedy and nudged her with his elbow, a knowing smile on his lips. Remedy recognized him immediately.

"You must be Remedy," he whispered.

"You must be Xavier." She stuck her hand out, but Xavier enveloped her in a jovial hug. When he released her, Micah draped a casual arm around her shoulders and nodded his hello to Xavier.

"Where are your twins? I've been dying to meet them," Remedy said.

"Alex has them inside. They're too young to understand the rules of squirrel fishing and aren't very good at staying quiet on command."

"That's what Micah and Alex have both told me. Are they still teething?"

Xavier rolled his eyes, nodding.

"I love those kids," Micah said in a whisper, "but this teething phase is getting real old, real fast."

"Tell me about it," Xavier said.

A kid standing in front of Remedy whirled around and shushed them. Xavier and Remedy devolved into chuckles. No wonder Micah loved Xavier so much. He was fast becoming one of Remedy's favorite people, too. She couldn't quite visualize how he and Alex worked as a couple, because Alex was so cool and distant while Xavier was all warmth and genuine kindness, but maybe by the end of the party their connection would make more sense to her.

The next moment, the crowd erupted in cheers. Duncan jogged a victory lap with his barrelful of squirrel, then released the poor thing near the downslope at the end of the maintained lawn.

"I really thought Savannah had that," Remedy said to no one in particular.

Micah stuck his fingers in his mouth and let loose with a loud whistle of cheer. "You'll get it next time, Savannah. You can't let your cousin win all the time!" He smiled at Remedy. "She's a smart cookie. Reminds me a lot of you. Bossy as all get-out."

"Hey!"

"But also as sweet as sugar," he added.

She kissed his cheek. "Nice try."

"You must be Micah's girl!" a booming male voice called out over the crowd.

The crowd hushed again; then Micah and Remedy were rushed by at least a dozen adults, and almost as many kids, all introducing themselves and pulling Remedy in for bear hugs. There were too many names for her to remember, but she tried to do her best to memorize which people were married to each other and who their children were.

They were all disappointed that Remedy's parents had to cancel, but she made up an excuse about an unexpected phone interview with an Australian radio talk show that her dad's publicist had neglected to add to his calendar. Micah would know that was a lie, though his family seemed to buy it hook, line, and sinker.

The booming voice belonged to Micah's dad, who was an inch or two shorter than Micah and with a stomach that was a few inches wider but otherwise was an older, perfect mirror to him. Bubba Senior, as the family was teasingly referring to him today, with an emphasis on the *Senior* since they were celebrating his birthday, it was explained to her.

After a hug and a kiss on her cheek, Bubba cracked

open a can of beer and stuck it in her hand. "Let's toast to you putting up with our Micah here. God love him."

"Gee, thanks, Pops." Micah tried to extricate the beer can from her grip. "She's more of a champagne type of lady, though."

Remedy held fast to the can. "You don't know that I don't like beer. Heck, you bought me a beer on our first date."

"That was before I knew about . . ." He let his voice trail off with a flip of his hand.

"About what?" She wanted to hear him say it out loud, how many assumptions he made about her based on her upbringing. About some things he was almost as bad as Wynd or Cambelle.

He wrinkled his nose at her, smiling patiently. "About how much you love champagne. It's all you keep around your house."

Nice save.

Alex was the next familiar face she saw. He walked her way with a friendly smile while holding the hands of two toddling brown-haired cuties. "Fancy seeing you here," Alex said.

Remedy knelt down. "I'm so happy to finally meet these little sweethearts. Hi, Isaac. Hi, Ivy," she said with an exaggerated wave.

Isaac only had eyes for Micah. He raised his hands and gave a grunting whimper until Micah scooped him up in his arms and whisked him away for some tickles and kisses. Ivy wiggled a few fingers at Remedy before turning bashful. With a drooly smile, she hid behind her daddy's leg.

Remedy stood again. "I see why you're in such a hurry to get home every night. You have a beautiful family."

"Thank you. I do."

Xavier appeared at Alex's side, an arm loosely around his waist. "And now that you're planning the weddings at

Briscoe Ranch, Remedy, he's starting to remember what his beautiful family looks like again."

"Oh, spare me," Alex said, though his eyes glowed with affection.

"I think they're about to serve dinner, so how about you come sit with us? We'll save a seat for those two," Xavier said, nodding to Micah and Isaac.

There wasn't a single table large enough to accommodate such a big crowd, so after everyone filled their plates from the mouthwatering spread on the kitchen table everyone gathered in clusters of chairs around a loose, uneven circle, with Bubba holding court at the head of the circle in a wide wicker chair that resembled a throne.

The brisket was to die for. She might have made some orgasmic sounds similar to those that had snuck out the first time Micah had taken her to Hog Heaven.

"Hey, Remedy," said a woman sitting across the circle, who Remedy was fairly sure was married to Micah's brother. "Micah made us swear not to ask you about any celebrity stuff, but I can't help it."

"Aw, geez, Connie. Really?" Micah said.

"You shut your piehole. This is between me and Remedy," Connie said. "Now, I've got some questions about Zannity."

There was a term Remedy could've lived her life without hearing again. She washed her bite of brisket down with a swig of beer. "What would you like to know?"

"Was Serenity really as bitchy as she came across on TMZ?"

"My lawyer advised me to never speak of those two again. So I plead no comment." Then she cupped her hands around her mouth and whispered, "She was worse, actually. A lot worse."

Xavier leaned closer. "What about Zander? Nod your head if he was really that big of a spoiled, rich twit as they made him out to be. Nod twice if he's even worse than Justin Bieber—which he is, if you ask me."

Oh, he was. He definitely was. "No comment," she said, nodding twice.

Xavier flashed her a thumbs-up.

"Okay, new topic," Connie said. "Your father has made nine films with Spielberg. Did you ever go to the Spielberg house for dinner? I heard Steven mans the grill when they have guests."

"Sure we did. My parents and the Spielbergs are still close."

"Does he really grill? He doesn't have a personal chef do that?" Alex asked.

"He does it. Definitely. He and my dad are both pretty proud of their grilling skills."

Xavier pressed a hand to his chest. "Preston Lane can cook? That silver fox just gets better with age."

"Ew, that's my dad," Remedy said in her best mock-offended voice.

Micah sent warning eyes to Xavier and cleared his throat. "Moving on."

The family asked her a few more questions about her parents and other celebrities, but soon enough the topic petered out in favor of a rousing discussion of Texas A&M's chance of winning a bowl title the next season.

After dinner, as everyone basked in their contented fullness, Micah pulled Remedy to the side of the yard under the shade of the deck cover and gave her a cuddle. "Thought I'd check in with you. Are you having fun?"

She nipped his lower lip with kisses. "Your family is so wonderful. I love them. Xavier too. This is the best night." To her mortification, her throat constricted and her eyes filled with unshed tears.

He cuddled her closer. "Those tears have anything to do with whatever happened today?"

She dropped her chin to his chest. "I wish I had a family like yours."

"That can be arranged." He said it so quietly, she wasn't sure at first that she'd heard him correctly. She was saved from articulating a reply by Micah's sister Maisy, who appeared in the sliding glass doorway holding a huge birthday cake covered in lit candles.

Micah held Remedy's hand and led her to the edge of the group where they joined in with the singing of "Happy Birthday," then found new seats and settled in to enjoy the cake and ice cream. When Micah finished his dessert, he lifted Ivy from Alex's arms so he could eat in peace. Remedy followed his lead and did the same with Isaac and Xavier, but it wasn't long before Micah disappeared in the house with Ivy to change her diaper, leaving Remedy, with Isaac bouncing on her knee, alone with Alex and Xavier.

"Tell me about you and Micah when you were kids," she asked Xavier.

Xavier grinned. "That's a big topic."

"Start at the beginning. How did you two get so close?"

"Back in the day, I used to love provoking bullies. Bring it on and all that shit. I was so stubborn, so angry at the world. I wanted the fight, to show them I was bigger and tougher than they'd ever be. I wanted them to get beat up by a gay kid in front of all their bigot friends. But I could only ever get a few licks in before Micah came charging in the middle of every fight while it was brewing, his fists out, trying to break it up, to keep me from getting in trouble from the school or my parents. He knew they'd whup me good if I was caught fighting, because he'd seen it happen, being that we were next-door neighbors.

"I used to get so spittin' mad at him for breaking up my fights. He's always been the peacemaker, the one avoiding trouble, while I was the one running headlong into it. He doesn't get many opportunities to try and save me from myself anymore now that I'm a boring stay-at-home dad. He still tries."

"And now his job is to run straight into trouble," Remedy said.

Xavier wagged his finger at her. "Good point. I never thought about it that way." He tipped his head to the side, studying her. "You're a rule breaker, too, or so I've heard."

Remedy nearly choked on her cake at that assessment. "Not really. I love rules and order. It's just that trouble has a way of following me around."

Alex and Xavier both let out belly laughs. "So Alex has mentioned," Xavier said. "You're shaking Micah up the way I always did when we were kids, challenging all those careful rules he makes for himself. I like that about you. Don't let him fool you. He likes it, too."

Micah appeared behind her, a freshly changed Ivy in his arms. "Likes what? Who we talkin' about?"

She tipped her chin up. "You like me."

"That's true." He bent down and gave her a kiss.

"Xavier was telling me about how you two became friends."

Micah groaned. "He only survived his teenage years because I was there to keep him from doing crazy shit."

"Doing crazy shit is what being a teenager is all about, except you because you were born with the soul of a sixty-year-old," Xavier said.

"That is not true."

She nudged his ribs. "It's kinda true."

"And now it's time for the real fun!" a different male voice bellowed. Remedy turned toward the voice, which turned out to belong to a red-faced Junior, who stood in front of a closed garage door.

"Uh-oh," Alex said. "Looks like Junior's been hitting the Shiner Bock too hard again."

Junior's outstretched arms lowered. He pointed at Remedy. "We've got a special guest with us tonight, and I bet my pansy-ass brother hasn't even told her what our family does for fun round here."

"Not the family!" Micah called. "What you do for fun. Leave the rest of us out of this."

Still seated on his wicker throne, Micah's dad raised his beer can in Remedy's direction. "My Junior here is a state champion off-road racer. He's been featured on ESPN."

Remedy's eyes glittered. "Oh my goodness. That's really something. What kind of off-road racing?"

At least five people collectively groaned.

Junior rubbed his hands together. "I'm glad you asked."

With a practiced flare, he yanked the garage door up, revealing four Power Wheel toy cars and Jeeps, complete with pink plastic bodies trimmed in purple, purple plastic seats, purple roll bars, purple wheels, and the Barbie logo splashed on the sides of the doors.

"Power Wheels," Junior said. "Barbie Power Wheels, to be specific. It's a new sport, only been round for the past five years or so, but it's no passing fad. It's here to stay."

"I had a Barbie Corvette when I was a kid," Remedy said. She used to ride along her house's circular driveway pretending to be a race car driver at the Indy 500, but she'd barely fit in hers by the time she was eight years old, so she didn't see how Junior could possibly wedge his husky body in one.

"So did my sisters. People in my sport—"

"It's not a sport," Micah muttered into his beer can.

"People in my sport have started branching out from Barbie. There's all kinds of licensed character vehicles on the market these days. Call me a traditionalist, but I'm all about the Barbie Jeep."

"How do you fit in them?" Remedy asked.

"Like a hog wearin' panty hose," Micah's dad said with a laugh.

Remedy wrinkled her nose at the visual that conjured. "Don't they only go, what, five miles per hour?"

Junior looked at her with sympathy, as though she'd spent her life under a rock. "We trick 'em out with go-cart and lawn mower engines."

"I would've killed for one of those when I was a kid. I've always loved speed." Speed just didn't always love her back.

Nodding toward the garage, Junior winked at Remedy. "Wanna try 'em out?"

"No, she does not," Micah said, at the same time Remedy answered, "Sure."

Junior clapped and let out a hoot. "We're gonna have us some fun tonight!"

Micah whipped his face around to glare at her. "Uh, no."

"Uh, you're not the boss of me."

"Clearly. But you should trust me on this. I've seen the way you handle golf carts," Micah said.

"I second that," Alex chimed in.

Remedy stood and handed Isaac to Xavier. "I don't have to listen to this."

"Good for you," Xavier said. "Don't let him boss you around."

Micah followed her to the garage. "I've seen enough of these ridiculous Power Wheels races to see every kind of injury imaginable. If you've got a hankering to go off-roading, then I'll make it happen, but not in these Frankensteined kids' toys."

"We've got an off-road course in the field out there. It's for beginners," Junior said with as much seriousness as a drunk man could muster. "Only a mild downhill. She'll be as safe as pie."

Remedy wasn't sure what pie and safety had to do with each other, but she was certain that this was something she wanted to do. "I'm learning to embrace a new motto in my life: What would Granny June do?"

"This is all kinds of bad," Alex muttered.

Micah tugged on her elbow. "Remedy, you can't be serious. This isn't you."

"Who am I, exactly, Micah? A California princess, like you call me? A sophisticated heiress to a Hollywood dynasty, as the media's been calling me since I was born? Or is it like my parents keep labeling me, as their homesick, spoiled daughter who needed them to rescue her? Or is it like Cambelle and Wynd told me in so many words today, that I'm their bitch, bought and paid, their servant when I should have been their peer? Maybe I just want to be the quirky, awkward girl who's not afraid of anything and who made a choice a long time ago to forge her own destiny—no matter who tries to stand in her way."

That shut them all up, Micah included. He studied her with a pensive look.

Into the gaping silence, she stuck out her hand to Junior. "I'm going to need a helmet."

Junior glanced at Micah again.

"Aw, let her do it," Micah's father said. "What's the harm?"

"The harm?" Micah spluttered. "Dad, are you kidding me?"

Xavier handed his son to Micah's dad. "I'll take a helmet, too. Count me in on the race."

Alex stood by Micah. "Honey, you can't be serious."

"I'm dead serious," Xavier said.

"Okay, well, you're about to be just dead. Period," Alex said. "Who's going to watch the kids if you break both your arms?"

"That's all I am now? The child-care provider?"

Even Remedy cringed at that assessment.

"Xavier . . . ," Alex said before giving Micah a pointed look. "Tell him to stop being snippy and melodramatic."

"Only if you'll tell Remedy she's gonna get herself killed if she pulls this stunt."

"Look at those two sticks-in-the-mud," Xavier said to

Remedy, gesturing to Alex and Micah. "At least I finally figured out how to help you two bond. You're both think you're the boss of me. I'll tell you what, while I'm kicking Junior's ass in a Barbie Jeep you two can commiserate about how impossible I am."

Micah pulled Remedy aside. With Ivy tugging on his ear, he bent close to Remedy. "You don't have anything to prove to my family. Or to your family, either. Or to yourself, for that matter. I love you just the way you are, California princess and all that other stuff."

She gave him a tender kiss. How could she tell him how much his love meant to her but how desperately she needed to let loose tonight and get a little crazy? "Life's too short to play by the rules."

"A trust fund safety net won't save you from a concussion or broken arm."

That was over the line. "You keep bringing up my trust fund like it means something significant. I confided that to you, so you're not allowed to throw it back in my face. And you're not allowed to try to save me, either, Mister Hero. But you can cheer me on."

"I'll do you one better. I'll take you to the hospital after you crash and hurt yourself, and then I'll try to keep my *I told you so*'s to a minimum."

"You're such a good boyfriend."

She leaned in for another kiss. Giggling sweetly, Ivy slapped Remedy's cheek, then latched on to her hoop earring. After she extricated her earring from Ivy's shockingly strong grip, she joined Junior, Xavier, and Micah's brother-in-law Davey in the garage.

Up close, she got a great view of a line of Barbie dolls mounted on the backs of the Jeeps, frozen in obscene positions, legs spread, some of them fondling each other or locked in embrace. "Nice touch."

"I thought so. The wife's not impressed though."

Actually, Junior's wife, Connie, seemed to be a very tolerant woman, all things considered. The X-rated Barbies must have been the last straw for her.

Being a gentleman, as Junior pointed out that he was, he let Remedy pick her vehicle first. She chose the classic Barbie Jeep with a Barbie-on-Barbie-on-Ken three-way happening on the hood.

She putted to the start of the trail. At Bubba's wave of a flag, they were off. The drive was bumpier than Remedy expected. She had to grit her teeth to keep from biting her tongue accidentally, which was inconvenient, because she couldn't stop laughing. Steering in the Jeep was nigh impossible, too. The darned thing just seemed to go where it wanted to.

After the first turn, one in which Remedy turned too wide and scraped up a bunch of bushes, Xavier, his lanky body wedged in a purple glitter Cadillac Escalade, pulled alongside her. He gave her a thumbs-up, but when she tried to return the gesture she lost control of her Jeep. Xavier swerved in her direction and reached for her, trying to help her regain her balance.

Unfortunately, that sent his SUV careening off the path. She thought she saw him launch out of the Escalade with a yelp, but she was already too far down the trail to look back. In no time, she was neck and neck with Junior for the lead. She pressed the gas pedal. The engine lurched faster, revving menacingly as it thumped and bumped over rocks and around corners. She knew the finish line was in sight because Connie was there, waving a maroon-colored A&M flag. Remedy gunned the Jeep again. She thought she might win when Junior swerved into her, bumping her not to help, as Xavier had, but to try to knock her off course.

Remedy fought back. She cranked the wheel and knocked her Jeep's bumper into Junior's Jeep's door. His Jeep tipped onto two wheels, but hey, those were the breaks. There could be only one victor and she was determined to take that crown. She cranked the wheel again and slammed into Junior's vehicle as the trail narrowed and grew steeper.

The whole front axis of Junior's Jeep popped off. In seemingly slow motion, the Jeep nose-planted into the dirt. Junior went toppling over the hood of Remedy's Jeep, taking it out with him. Remedy tumbled onto the dusty trail and knocked her helmet against a bush.

When she looked up, she discovered she was less than two feet from the finish line, a chalk line drawn into the dirt. Remedy stretched her foot over the line without moving the rest of her body an inch.

Micah's whole family erupted in cheers. Remedy raised her hands in a victory salute. Micah's shadow fell over her. "You okay?"

"I think so. I won!"

"I saw that. Nice work. Terrifying in a lot ways, but impressive nonetheless."

A bloodcurdling scream rang out behind her. Remedy sat up and turned around. Junior was lying in the trail, Remedy's Jeep on top of him. His father tried to pull the Jeep off, but Junior's wails only grew louder. "Get it off me!" he yelped.

Micah scrambled to help his dad and the two of them pulled the Jeep off Junior's legs.

The sight of blood spreading over Junior's shorts sent nauseating tingles over Remedy's skin. One of the X-rated Barbie dolls was sticking out of his thigh. She was standing perfectly upright, all perky smiles and bouncy hair, except that one of her legs had disappeared into Junior's shorts and was surrounded by an expanding circle of red. From the looks of it, he'd been impaled by Barbie's leg up almost up to her knee.

"Oh my God, Junior, I'm so sorry," Remedy said, crawling over to where Junior lay. "Quick, Micah. We need to get him to a hospital."

Xavier fell to his knees next to Remedy as the spectators sprung into action, with Micah leading the charge. After a quick visual inspection of the wound, Micah whipped off his T-shirt and folded it into a compress as Xavier wrapped a hand around Barbie.

"On the count of three, I'll pull it out," Xavier said.

Junior squeezed his eyes closed. "Aw, shit," he said with a groan. "Just do it."

Already nauseated enough at the gruesome scene, Remedy averted her eyes.

To his credit, Junior made no other sounds but a solitary grunt followed by some quiet cussing as Micah declared the wound small enough not to need stitches. Abandoning the Barbie Jeeps on the trail, the whole party crowd moved as a unit toward the house, assisting Junior and recounting the details of his injury in hushed voices.

A half hour later, with guilt still gnawing at her, Remedy delivered a cold beer to Junior, who looked no worse for wear, with his thigh neatly bandaged by Micah.

"I'm really sorry, Junior," she said. "I know I already told you that, but I should've known not to race those Jeeps with you. I'm a klutz and a menace. I don't mean to be, but I can't seem to stop myself. I hate that you got hurt."

Remedy looked at Micah. "Go ahead with your *I told you so*'s. I deserve it. I'm a danger magnet."

He looked from his older brother back to Remedy; then a grin broke out on his face, followed by his first snort of laughter. Micah's dad was the next to burst out laughing, followed by Junior's wife. Pretty soon, the whole party of people were doubled over with glee, save for Remedy and Junior.

Micah's dad staggered over to Remedy and enveloped her in a bear hug. "You're one of us now, honey. Welcome to the family."

It struck her in that moment how badly she wanted to be a part of Micah's gregarious, hard-loving family. She wanted to be a part of Dulcet, Texas, in all its contradictions and crazy, disparate parts.

Micah's dad slapped Micah's back. "Son, you'd better get a ring on this girl before she comes to her senses."

Her parents chose that moment to text her. She shuffled down the rest of the trail past the finish line and fished her cell phone from her back pocket. The message was from her mom.

Remedy, we're so sorry about what happened. We only want you to be happy. You'll be coming home to Los Angeles soon. I can feel it.

For too long, Remedy had been conditioned to believe that she could only belong in the narrow bubble of her parents' world. Why did they insist that she choose them over everything else? Why did it have to be one lifestyle or the other? As Remedy looked over her shoulder at Micah, surrounded by his family, it became clear for the first time where her heart belonged—and where she belonged, once and for all time.

Chapter Twenty

THREE WEEKS LATER . . .
After a long night of multiple emergency calls followed by a morning of putting his team through their regular drills, Micah had stolen away to his house in the early afternoon for a cool shower and a hot cup of black coffee in an effort to perk up his energy levels. Maybe it was a by-product of nearing forty or maybe he could thank his late-night lovin' with Remedy, but the idea of crashing for a quick nap was starting to appeal to him, though it never had before. The only thing stopping him from indulging in one was Xavier's teasing remark about him having the soul of a sixty-year-old.

The shower helped, and the coffee even more so, but he was still a bit bleary-eyed when he opened his front door for the short walk to work.

He startled at the sight of a young woman approaching his front porch, a plain paper bag in her hand. "Emily Ford? You've got to be kidding me."

Eyes wide, she raised her hands in surrender, the paper bag dangling from her right hand. "Hey, this isn't what you think."

Micah took the bag from her. "What I think is that I've discovered the identity of my secret admirer." As absolutely unbelievable as that might be. Emily? Really? Because there was no way the two of them were in any way a match. Not to mention that she was Remedy's coworker, so she knew the two of them were a couple.

She had the audacity to scoff. "Secret admirer? You wish."

"I figured it was Mrs. Mayfield because I saved her cat from a tree last year." Plus she lived behind him, so it'd be easy for her to sneak over with the baked goods without anyone noticing.

"Cats really can get stuck in trees, like, for real? I thought that was a myth."

He didn't know what else to do but shrug. Yeah, it was a myth, except for the occasional overly concerned cat owner who doubted their kitty's climbing or jumping skills. With Mrs. Mayfield, he was pretty sure she'd called the fire department because she'd been lonely since Mr. Mayfield passed.

"Honest to God, Micah, I'm not some moony, lovestruck admirer."

"You say that, but tell me this. . . ." He shook the bag. "Am I going to find in this bag the same cinnamon rolls you make at the resort? Or is it muffins this time?"

Her mouth screwed up like she'd sucked on a lemon. "Blueberry muffins."

Score. Those were his favorite, by far. Even better than cinnamon rolls. It made sense that they were so delicious, seeing as how the best chef in the county had baked them. Baked them with love, apparently. "Am I that obtuse? Because I never once noticed any flirting or signals from you that indicated that I was . . . that you were . . . I'm with Remedy, you know, and—"

"Garrity, stop. Oh my God. I will never understand the male ego. I'm not into you. At all."

"Your muffins say different." Dang, that sounded dumb. And vaguely sexual. "That came out wrong."

"Will you listen, please?"

Clearly, that was the better plan. He clamped his lips shut with a nod.

She rolled her shoulders, growing taller. "I'm only doing this because I'm helping a friend. A superstitious friend. Who may or may not have a tiny little crush on you. But that's beside the point."

There was only one resident in Dulcet synonymous with the word *superstitious*. And she was old as Moses and an even worse golf cart driver than Remedy. And, yes, the odds were good that she had a tiny little crush on him. But even with that hunch, Micah wasn't connecting the dots. "I don't get it. How does sneakin' me baked goods help this superstitious friend of yours?"

"She first asked me to send some cinnamon rolls your way earlier this year because she thought you were cranky—"

"I'm never cranky."

She rolled her eyes. "Fine. She thought maybe the stick you've got stuck up your ass during the fire marshal inspections was because you didn't have a good woman cooking for you. Her words, not mine. She wanted to butter you up before you had to make some key decisions about an event that was coming up on the resort." She cringed. "And I think I just gave too much away."

"You can cut the crap. We both know who we're talking about. And I'm guessing the event in question was the rodeo for the grand opening of Briscoe Ranch's new equestrian complex this past April, complete with a fireworks spectacular and an old-fashioned hoedown."

"Exactly."

"I approved all the elements of that rodeo, yet you're still being enlisted to bring me sweets all these months later?"

"You've been in a better mood and you've been giving

your stamp of approval to just about every event at the ranch. She didn't want to jinx it by stopping."

"You can tell her that she won't jinx it if she stops, because I have a good woman in my life now, like she wanted for me all these years." And didn't that feel damn good to say?

Emily leveled a pointed glare at Micah. "Don't ever let Remedy near a kitchen appliance. That woman is a walking disaster."

"Noted. But that still doesn't explain why you've been going along with Granny's—I mean, this woman's—superstitious notions all these months, taking time out of your hellish workday and all."

Emily threw her hands up. "I know. It's crazy. But she was the one who convinced that asshole, sexist son of hers to hire me even though he was of the mind that"—she affected a heavy twang—"everybody knows girls can't cut it as professional chefs. It's just the laws of nature." She shrugged. "I owe her, plain and simple."

There was no arguing with that. "For the record, I would have accepted 'because she's Granny June' as a perfectly acceptable explanation for anything she asks you to do."

"Noted. Enjoy the muffins."

"I always do."

After Emily had gone, he looked at his watch. Perhaps a well-timed visit to the resort was in order that evening. Right as the sunset and a certain superstitious friend was taking her evening cocktail on the chapel bench. And while he was there, he'd find Remedy and make things right with her. It was time to get some more love advice . . . and maybe some ring advice while he was at it.

Sure enough, he found Granny June exactly where he expected to see her.

"I had a visitor at my house today," Micah said after sprawling on the bench next to her.

"Was it Remedy's pigeons? I swear they're getting more

and more domesticated now that they're wild. It's the darnedest thing."

"They've been around a lot, too, especially when Remedy is visiting me, but I was referring to Emily Ford. She brought me two blueberry lemon muffins."

Granny avoided his gaze. "That was right nice of her."

"I thought I'd finally discovered the identity of my secret pastry supplier, but it turns out Emily was just the delivery person."

"She sounds like a blabbermouth, too," Granny grouched.

Micah bit back a smile. He lifted Granny's delicate, chilly hand and cradled it in his. "Thank you for taking such good care of me."

She patted his hands with her free one. "Somebody had to. You got crankier and crankier about the rules until you and Ty were going at it like two dogs chained in a yard. And so I said, 'June, you know just how to fix this.' And so I did."

Micah beamed at her. "So you did."

"I'm going to keep sending sweets your way, give you something to feed that woman of yours. She's a keeper. I knew that you two were meant to be the first time I laid eyes on the two of you together."

"On a subconscious level, I think I knew it then, too." All he had to do now was figure out how to convince Remedy that she belonged by his side, forever.

"You want me to stop bringing over sweets so Remedy can be the only woman taking care of you?"

"Actually, if you're up for it, then I'd love you to keep on with it. Remedy likes the cinnamon rolls for breakfast when she sleeps over. I think she gets a kick out of eating food left for me by an admirer."

Granny June gave a hoot of laughter. "What woman wouldn't?"

"Your identity can stay our little secret."

"I do love a nice, juicy secret."

He bent over and planted a kiss on her cheek. She held him in place, patting his cheek.

"Micah, before you take off tonight, I have something I've been meaning to tell you, that I've been thinking a lot about since the ballroom caught fire. I don't know how much longer I've got in this world before I go to be with my Tyson, so I've got to talk to you before it's too late."

Whatever it was, he sensed distress in her tone and in the agitated trembling of her fingers. Micah stroked her hand with his thumb and waited patiently for her to collect her thoughts and continue.

"The fire happened on my watch, when I was still running the resort alongside my son. I've played that day over and over in my mind and there's no getting around what happened, but I finally had to make my peace with the truth that there wasn't anything I would have done differently that day or with that wedding.

"If we hadn't provided the wedding guests with sparklers, who's to say those two young men wouldn't have started that fire with a cigarette or a lighter from the joints they were smoking? Only the Lord knows the reason that fire had to happen, but I wanted to tell you that I'm sorry. Even though our lawyers strongly advised us not to apologize, I want you to know that I'm sorry for the role our resort played in the fire and that your family and so many others were devastated like they were. It is a guilt that will go with me to my grave."

Whatever Micah had thought Granny June wanted to tell him, it wasn't that. All these years, he'd carried around a bitterness about the resort's role in the fire and the Briscoe family's refusal to claim any degree of responsibility, but he didn't want Granny June to live with a gnawing guilt any more than he wanted to keep carrying around his grief about all he lost in the fire like a heavy yoke. Maybe it was time for them both to make peace with their linked past.

"I can't express how much it means to hear you say that,

Granny. I lost a lot in that fire, not as much as some, but more than others, and it haunts me every day." His throat constricted. How could something that happened more than twenty years ago still have the power to wound him? "But I think you're right that the Lord had a plan, and I'd like to think part of that plan was me becoming a fire-fighter. I owe a lot of my life today, most of it, really, to that fire. I love my job and my life, and most of all, I love the people in my life, so that's a hard truth to reconcile."

She nodded. "We'll never know how many people's lives you've saved with your efforts."

Just like they'd never know if providing the guests with sparklers or not that fateful night would've mattered or if God's will would've found a way to get a fire started regardless. "No, we won't, and thank you for saying that."

"And if you hadn't been inspired by that fire to become a firefighter, you might not have ever met Remedy. And wouldn't that have been a shame."

The greatest shame of his life. "I'm in love with her."

"I know that, child. Like I also know you're worried that this Hollywood wedding she's putting on will inspire her to move back to California."

That was exactly what he was afraid of. "How'd you guess?"

She tapped her temple. "I've got a God-given sixth sense when it comes to couples who are meant to be. So believe me when I tell you that she's here for good, as long as we play our cards right."

We?

Before he could ask for clarification, Granny June whipped out her cell phone. "Now get in here close for a picture. And how about this time you—"

"I know, chin up to help with the neck wrinkles."

"Forget about that today. Pucker up and give this old lady a little sugar on my cheek for our selfie. Wait until my Facebook friends see that."

It came as no surprise to him that she made him do four takes of the cheek kiss before she got the shot she wanted. When she was satisfied, he nodded to the heliport near the Briscoes' private compound where a sleek-looking helicopter that looked like it seated at least eight people sat at the ready.

"Which bigwig guest is staying here tonight?"

"That's Wynd Fisher's helicopter. Or at least that's what brought him here from the airport, him and that tart little fiancée of his. I didn't see 'em touch down, but I heard talk from some of the workers."

"Remedy didn't mention that to me."

"I'm sure she didn't want to worry you about a meeting for last-minute wedding details, which is what I'm sure they're meeting about."

Granny June was probably right, but something didn't feel right with Micah, especially after Remedy came clean to him about what had gone down at Petey's with Wynd, Cambelle, and her parents. Maybe he'd just drop her a text and make sure Remedy didn't need any moral support.

Remedy sat behind her desk across from her parents, Wynd Fisher, and Helen and Cambelle West. At a week until the wedding or, rather, six days until the rehearsal dinner, it wasn't unusual for a bride to schedule a visit to shore up last-minute details, but Remedy couldn't imagine the reason for this unexpected ambush a week before the wedding—by all of them, her parents included. In fact, the thick tension in the room and the "five against one" tone they'd fostered by grouping together across the table from her smacked of a bad episode of television's *Intervention*.

"Tell me what we're all doing here," Remedy said. "I don't have time right now for unscheduled appointments." Yes, she sounded like a bitch, but she no longer cared. She didn't owe any of them a single thing. Though her parents had left her several tearful apologies over voice mail, Remedy hadn't been ready to forgive them for their unfair judgments of her life. To be honest, she still wasn't.

Wynd cleared his throat. "We're here because we all care about you, Remedy."

Oh boy.

A familiar face popped into view through Remedy's office window. Micah. When he registered who her guests were, his eyebrows crinkled.

You okay? he mouthed.

Remedy gave a small shake of her head in reply. No, she most certainly wasn't okay. And a moment in the hall with Micah so she could catch her breath and get her bearings was exactly what she needed.

"Excuse the interruption," she said, standing. "I'll be right back."

All eyes turned to her office window.

"Ah, Micah," Wynd called. He leapt up and opened the door. "Come on in. You right on time to hear the good news."

This meeting was getting more bizarre by the second.

Micah met Remedy's eyes, gauging. "Good news?"

Remedy gave an almost-imperceptible shrug. She couldn't shake the feeling that whatever her parents and their friends were about to announce would be the exact opposite of good. She let her wide-eyed gaze rove over her unexpected guests in a silent attempt to tell him that all of this was completely unexpected.

Micah's jaw stiffened, as though he got her message loud and clear that she might need his support. He stepped fully into the room, his hand extended to Remedy's mom first, then the other women, her father, and, finally, Wynd. "Saw your helicopter outside. Sweet ride. Did y'all just come into town today?"

Wynd lounged back in his chair and strummed his fingers on his belly. "We did. Because I've got an exciting

proposition for Remedy. The chance of a lifetime for someone like her."

Someone like her? What the heck did that mean?

Micah sidestepped behind Remedy's desk, kissed the
top of her head, then set a supportive hand on her shoulder.

"Remedy," Wynd started again. "I've been doing a lot
of thinking since our last visit with you, and I've been talking with your parents a lot about you and your particular
skills as an event planner. The critics and the media got it
all wrong when they skewered you over the Zannity fiasco.
It's common knowledge among my circles that you got
screwed in that whole business, which is how I know that
nobody in that town will begrudge you another change.
After all, Hollywood is the town of second chances."

Micah's hand stiffened.

"I did get screwed, and I'm glad the scandal has blown
over," Remedy said, choosing her words carefully. She had
a sinking feeling about what was coming next out of
Wynd's mouth.

"It's what you've been waiting for," her mom said.
"Your path home is free and clear now."

Her path home. *Maybe once upon a time, but* . . . "That's
not my home anymore."

Wynd dismissed her quiet declaration with a wave.
"Nonsense. Let's cut to the chase. I'm here to offer you a
job as my production company's event planner, beginning
with our pre-party for the upcoming Grammy Awards,
with a few album launch parties mixed in. This is it. Your
chance to play in the big leagues."

Remedy's jaw fell open. With Wynd endorsing her,
she'd be set for life as an event planner in Los Angeles.
This was her dream opportunity—or, rather, what used to
be her dream opportunity. Not so much anymore. "That's
a really generous offer."

Micah shifted next to her. His face was blank, his body
as stiff as stone. He released her shoulder.

Wynd clasped his hands behind his head. "I know it is, which is why I know you're going to take it."

Next to Wynd, Remedy's father was clearly trying to get Remedy's attention. She looked instead at her mother, who had her phone pressed to her ear. "We're going to need at least four bottles of champagne brought to Remedy Lane's office. Whatever the hotel's sommelier recommends, no matter the price." She ended the call and beamed a bright smile at the room. "Tonight we're celebrating the news of Remedy's homecoming!"

Micah cleared his throat. "Congratulations, Remedy. This is what you've been waiting for."

Really? He was jumping to conclusions like that, as if he didn't know her at all? "I haven't agreed to anything."

"Yet," he whispered.

Panic tickled her throat. This meeting needed to slow the hell down so Remedy could process the offer, as well as Micah's and her mother's assumptions.

"But you will agree," Wynd said jubilantly.

Remedy's mother clapped. "Bravo, Wynd! We're so grateful to you for helping bring our Remedy back to us."

Cambelle and Helen joined in the clapping.

Micah's phone buzzed. He pulled it from his pocket and gazed blankly at the screen.

Remedy took hold of his arm. "Don't get that. Let's step out for a minute and talk."

"I'm getting a Code Two notification from work. I've got to go."

He couldn't just leave like this, thinking she'd made her choice already. "Please, can it wait until we talk?"

He planted a wooden kiss on the top of her head, then twisted his arm out of her grip. "Code Twos don't wait. I'll be in touch."

Stunned by the distance in his tone and expression, she rose from her chair and followed him to the door, determined to reassure him that she wasn't leaving. Or was she?

Wynd's offer was exactly the door she'd wanted opened for so long.

Cambelle skittered between Remedy and Micah, a pout on her lips and her arms braced on the frame, blocking Remedy from passing. "You can't go after him. Our party's just getting started. Your mom ordered champagne. And I need you here, so we can talk about the wedding next week. We're paying you to be here."

Ty's words echoed in Remedy's head, except this time in Cambelle's shrill voice. *I own you.* If Remedy took the job as Wynd's event planner, they'd believe they owned her indefinitely. Remedy had worked too hard for too long to stay hidden in anyone else's shadow—not her parents; and not Wynd Fisher's.

Micah glanced over his shoulder once. The hurt in his eyes stopped Remedy's heart. Then he disappeared from view down the hall.

"Please move your arms so I can pass," Remedy said, nice and civil this one last time.

Cambelle's pout intensified. "But Remy—"

"I've done my job and you're going to have the wedding of your dreams next week, so unless you plan on compromising that, I suggest you move before I make you."

Wynd stood. "Make her how?"

Remedy's dad attempted to wedge himself between her and Cambelle. "Oh, shut up, Wynd. This is my daughter you're speaking to like that. And Cambelle, you heard my girl. Step aside."

Wynd put his arm across Cambelle's shoulders in a show of solidarity. Cambelle's pout turned to a sneer. "What happened to you, Remedy? I used to idolize you when we were kids. You had everything I wanted for my life, but now look at you. It's this place. It's messed with your head."

"Yes, it has. It's messed with my head. It's messed with

my heart. And it's changed me in irrevocable ways. I'm grateful for every single bit of that change."

Not in a million years would she have imagined that she would've had to lose herself in Los Angeles so she could find herself again in a tiny Texas town. But somehow, miraculously, in the middle of the Texas wilds she'd found a place she belonged, where she could be herself and forge a new future in her career—and where a certain firefighter showed her that deep, abiding love wasn't a corporate motto but something she wanted. With him.

Yet he was running toward danger again tonight, risking his life, having no idea how deeply she'd fallen in love with him or how unimaginable the thought of leaving him and Dulcet had become. It was nearly enough to bring her to her knees. "I've got to go. Now."

She all but shoved her way past Cambelle and took off jogging down the hall, bursting through the employee exit doors into the balmy evening air. She'd gone a few yards toward the chapel parking lot where Micah usually parked when she heard her mom's voice. "Remedy!"

Remedy whirled around to see both of her parents. "Can't you two stop, for once? I love both of you so much. But can't you see that you're suffocating me?"

They took a tentative step toward her. "Remedy, honey. I have something to say," her dad said.

Remedy panted, shocked by how short of breath she was, how shaky and shrill her voice had sounded. "Then you'd better make it fast. I can't let Micah leave like that."

"Look, the thing is, we didn't handle you moving away from home very well," Dad said. His usually sparkling eyes had turned heavy with regret. "We honestly thought we were doing the right thing by you."

Her mom took her dad's hand. "With the Zannity scandal and you leaving so abruptly, we were distraught, and we took solace in each other. But as nice as it's been getting to know each other again, it became clear that something's missing from the equation. It wasn't long before we figured out that you're what's missing. We wanted you back home, with us."

Remedy bridged the distance between them. Her anger faded, replaced with compassion. What a crazy pickle they'd all gotten themselves into. "Maybe nostalgia isn't a good enough reason to be together. If you two still feel like something's missing when you're together, then maybe you're trying too hard to make it work. When I'm with Micah . . ." She swallowed hard. "When I'm with Micah, it's the most perfect feeling of belonging. Finally, for the first time in my life, I feel like I'm exactly where I'm supposed to be. He's my home."

Saying it aloud filled her with a kind of warmth and purpose she'd never known. What a miracle that just when she'd given up searching for a place to belong—just when she'd given up on love—somehow he'd made her believe again. *Like magic.*

A shiver tingled over her skin at the realization. She turned her chin up and let her gaze skim over the resort she'd come to love almost as dearly as Micah. The sun was dipping low in the western sky, casting a golden glow over the rolling hills of grass and gardens where resort guests strolled and sat together on benches, talking, laughing. And on the hill, looking down over all of them, was the chapel. Hallowed ground for couples in love for more than fifty years. A place that made love stories come true. Suddenly, more than anything, Remedy wanted to be part of the chapel's history of successful marriages. With Micah.

"Honey." Her mom took her hand. "I'm sorry I didn't support you about dating Micah. We got caught up in the idea that we knew what was best for you, that we couldn't see how happy you already were. It's so clear to me now that you love him. I can't stand in the way of your happiness any more than I can stand being estranged from you."

Fresh tears crowded Remedy's eyes. "Not talking to you has been hard for me, too. You're one of my best friends, Mom." She reached out and took her dad's hand. "Dad, you too. And you're right, Mom. I do love him. So much. If you and Dad don't feel that deeply about each other, then there's nothing I can do to save you both, even if I was home with you. I couldn't when I was twelve, though I tried, and I can't now. You both deserve a love that's profound and everlasting. You do. Just like I've found here."

"We want that, too," her mom said. "And, Preston, I want to try for that with you."

Dad's arm slid around Mom's back. "Maybe we can upgrade to the honeymoon suite tonight." He winked, the sparkle in his eyes returning in spades.

Remedy winced, squeezing her eyes closed. "Dad, please don't paint that picture for me. Ugh. Don't want to know."

"Sorry, sorry," her mom said, smiling.

The sound of Dad's laughter had Remedy peeling her eyes open again. "I love you both," she said. "And I forgive you."

They pulled her into a tight hug.

Her mom stroked Remedy's hair, then released her and stepped back. "Now, see? We're holding you back again with all this mushy stuff when you've got a firefighter to chase down. You can't let your future run off into the sunset without you."

Her future, her love, her everything. She gave her parents each a kiss, then took off running.

Chapter Twenty-One

Remedy ran through the resort and across the lawn to the Chapel Hill parking lot after Micah, but she was too late. Halfway there, she watched his truck drive away.

Granny June was having her evening cocktail on her favorite bench near the chapel. "You just missed him," she called.

Remedy trudged the rest of the way and dropped onto the bench. "Yeah. That sucks."

"He was angry, and I figured he'd clashed with you since that's where he'd been headed, or else I would've stalled him for you."

"It's okay. He's upset because Wynd Fisher just offered me a job in Los Angeles."

Granny took a sip of her drink. "Are you going to take it?"

Wasn't that the question of the hour? At least Granny June asked her and waited for an answer instead of jumping to conclusions. "No. It was everything I wanted once upon a time, but my life has changed. I've changed. I probably shouldn't tell you this, but originally I didn't expect to stick around here at the resort for long."

Granny patted her knee. "I suspected that might be the case. But then you met Micah."

"Yes. Then I met and fell in love with Micah, and I can't imagine leaving him or this place. Ever."

"Micah didn't get the memo on your change of heart?"

"No."

"Men can be such clueless lugheads sometimes. He was just here earlier trying to figure out how to win you over once and for all. I swear, there's nothing to be done but love our men through it until they come to their senses. My Tyson was the same way, as stubborn as a cat on a leash. Just like Ty, and just like your Micah. It's the Texas in their blood."

Remedy liked everything about the Texas in Micah's blood, even his stubbornness, so she'd have to forgive him for jumping to conclusions about her leaving Dulcet for California again. She wouldn't dream of compromising his focus on a Code Two injury situation by calling him now, but she fully planned to wait at his house for him to return so she could lay her heart bare for him.

"I should get back to my office. My clients are waiting." Though the idea of spending another minute with Cambelle, Wynd, and Helen—and, really, with her parents, too, if she was being honest—sounded as much fun as flying a red-eye in economy class from L.A. to New York while surrounded by crying babies. None of those components on their own were inherently odious, but combined they made for one hell of an unpleasant night.

Granny saw the pigeons first. "There they are. Oh, this time we've got the jump on 'em, because I'm a crack shot." She flipped Remedy her golf cart keys. "You drive; I'll shoot."

There was a time when Remedy would have relished the chance to wipe those flying rodents out, but no longer. Remedy wasn't sure how it'd happened, but somewhere

along the line she'd developed a soft spot for those darned
runaway-from-home pigeons, as though she'd imprinted on
them as surely as they'd imprinted on her. Luckily, she'd
seen Granny's aim in action and knew she didn't have a
prayer of hitting a moving target—especially if Remedy
ensured that she didn't with a bit of strategically erratic
driving.

What better excuse to delay her return to the meeting
from hell?

Remedy stood, keys in hand. "Let's get 'em!"

Moving with a spry step that defied her age, Granny
shrugged out of the peach blazer she'd been wearing, re-
trieved a shotgun from inside the golf cart's rear bench
seat, and scrambled into the passenger seat.

"Couldn't we use a net to trap them?" Remedy asked.

"And then what?"

"I don't know, call Skeeter to come get them?"

Granny loaded cartridges into her gun. "Not when I've
got a hankering for dove stew."

"Just don't invite me over to eat it with you."

"Fire in the hole!" Granny shouted.

Remedy timed a tug on the steering wheel with Granny's shot. She nicked the edge of the bench and it tipped
forward, overturning.

Remedy slammed on the brakes, so annoyed with herself she could spit. Would she ever get the hang of driving
these ridiculous things? How complicated could it be?

"Keep going!" Granny said, gesturing with her shotgun
as though they were headed into battle. "We're losing them."

The birds sought refuge in the trees beyond the edge
of the resort grounds, tucking themselves out of sight
in the thick brush. Remedy floored the golf cart and
sped in the direction she and Granny June had last spotted
them, skirting the edge of the wilderness.

Granny got another wide shot off. Remedy swerved,
pointing them in the direction of the chapel.

Remedy was the first one to spot the smoke. "Granny, look. The chapel."

Against the fading light in the sky, she saw the unmistakable glow of a bright orange flame. The trees surrounding the chapel's east wall were burning.

Remedy drove them to the resort at top speed while Granny hollered for help to any resort workers within earshot. With Remedy's heart racing, she dialing Micah's number. He didn't answer by the fourth ring, so she ended the call and dialed 911.

By the time she got through, the chapel roof had caught fire.

"The chapel at Briscoe Ranch Resort is on fire," she told the dispatchers. "It's on the northwest side of the resort, on a hill and—"

She crashed the golf cart into a low brick fence. Granny fell from her seat to the ground. In horror, Remedy flew out of the cart and dropped to her knees next to Granny, but she pushed Remedy away and stood. "I have to get to him. My Tyson."

Granny's forearm and right hand were bloody, the skin ripped like tissue paper. Still, she evaded Remedy's efforts to take hold of her and lurched up Chapel Hill at a fast clip.

Remedy raced to catch up, calling, "Granny, no. It's not safe!"

Workers from the hotel swarmed around Remedy shouting directions and asking Remedy what had happened. "I already called 9-1-1," she told them. "But let's hook up garden hoses to use until Micah's team gets here."

She turned back to Granny in time to see her racing up the chapel's front steps, shouting Tyson's name. Remedy gave chase, only to watch Granny disappear into the burning building.

Remedy followed her in through the main doors, calling her name. Smoke had filled the air inside the church, reducing visibility to a few feet off the floor. Remedy crouched, looking for Granny's legs amid the worsening visibility. If she were Granny June, she'd try to save their wedding album first. Remedy ran to that side of the vestibule. The wedding album was gone.

She ran to the other side, where the family Bible was kept. But the glass was broken and the Bible gone. In its place was a wooden cross.

Choking on the dense smoke that now licked at her knees, Remedy dropped onto all fours. Calling Granny's name, she crawled through the main aisle of the sanctuary, trying to decide where Granny would go next. The altar that Tyson made? The cross hanging behind it? None of that made sense.

Remedy's lungs burned. Her eyes watered, stinging so badly that she had to force herself not to close them. It was hard to tell given the darkness and smoke, but she thought she saw the flicker of a flame against the wall. The fire was spreading, but she still hadn't found Granny June. She crawled on her belly to the altar, but Granny June was nowhere in sight.

"Granny!" she called before devolving into a coughing fit.

The light in the room grew dim as only a couple feet of breathable air remained. Maybe Granny had gotten the wedding album and Bible and left again through another exit. She snaked her way around the corner, to the small room behind the organ.

Granny's legs were visible, though she lay facedown, clutching her precious treasures in her bruised and bloodied arms.

"Granny! Oh my God. Please be alive. Please, please, please."

She rolled her over. Granny coughed and her eyes fluttered open.

"I'm going to get you out of here!" she called above the roar of the fire and snapping wood and breaking glass.

"Door won't open," Granny said weakly. "I need to get to my Tyson out behind the church."

But Tyson's grave was too close to the building to be safe for Granny June. "I've got to get you out of here first." Remedy threw her shoulder against the side door. The wood was hot. Reaching up through the smoke, she searched blindly for the doorknob only to burn her hand on it. "The other side of the door's on fire. I think we need to break a glass window to get out."

"You go," Granny said. "I need to get to my Tyson, but you need to get to your man, too."

Every last remnant of Remedy's cynicism about weddings had been vanquished. This church, and the weddings it had held within its walls, meant something deep and holy, something beyond the superficial displays that Remedy had thought they were. She wanted to marry Micah in this building. If she got out of there alive, she'd tell him how she felt; she'd make him understand that she didn't want to live without him ever again. She wanted what Granny June and Tyson had, a love that lasted forever.

"I'm not leaving you," Remedy said. "You and I are going to rebuild this chapel, Granny. I can't do it without you. You have so many more weddings to bless here with your presence. Hopefully even mine someday soon."

Granny clutched her wedding album and Bible, burrowed her face in the carpet, and wept.

"Let's get out of here, Granny."

Granny tried to pull herself forward, but she was weak. "You go ahead. I'm right behind you."

Remedy put her arm around Granny's back. "No. Crawl with me."

"I can't, child."

Over the roar of flame and the crackling of wood, a man's voice called Remedy's name, or at least she wanted to believe it was real.

Remedy twisted, putting her back to Granny. "Hug me;

don't let go. I'm getting us out of here together. I'm not
leaving without you, Granny, so if you want to save me,
then hold on tight."

The clear air in the room was limited to only inches of
space above the floor. Remedy flattened, securing Granny
on her back. She pushed with her feet, pulled with her elbows, and army crawled back into the sanctuary toward
the voice she'd heard.

They were not going to die like this. Not now, not when
they both had so much more living to do. Micah's image
in her mind spurred her on. Was he the one calling her
name? Was he searching for her? If he was, then he was
in danger, too. The sooner she got to him, the sooner they
could all get to safety.

Though her eyes stung bitterly and her lungs were closing, she did not stop. She did not think of the pain or the
weight of Granny on her back, pressing into her ribs and
lungs, making the labor of breathing nearly impossible.
She reached her arm out, dug her nails into a wooden floor
beam, and pulled them toward the voice calling for her.

Micah didn't remember the drive to Briscoe Ranch Resort
from the Code Two garage fire he'd been overseeing. He
didn't remember coordinating with his crew or pulling to
a stop in the Chapel Hill parking lot. The only thing in his
head was the call he'd gotten from Ty Briscoe only seconds before that workers had told him that his mother and
Remedy had run into the burning church.

Resort workers had three garden hoses trained on the
blaze, but their efforts were in vain in a fire raging this
much out of control, with so much old, dry lumber as fuel.

Muffled voices spoke all around him as he buttoned his
flame-resistant uniform jacket and donned his hat and
mask, suiting up to face the blaze.

A hand grabbed his jacket by the scruff. Chet, getting
in his face, slamming him against the side of the fire

engine. "You're not leading this operation. You're too close, emotionally."

"Screw you, Chet. I'm tired of you dogging me with your jealous bullshit."

"I'll sock you if I have to, man. You're not in charge this time. Turn it over to me. It's the only way. Look at you." He flipped Micah's radio, which was dangling at his waist, though it should have been affixed to his chest. "You're not thinking straight."

"You want to run this?" Micah said. "Fine. Makes no difference to me. I'm going in after her." He'd rather die with them in that building than stand outside and watch a fire murder the love of his life and the woman who was like a grandmother to him.

"Not alone, you're not."

"Damn right, I'm not. Send the whole crew in. Every man. We've got to get her and Granny June out of there before a flash point hits."

"Roger that. I'll get the crew together. You wait for my call after we get water on those flames."

Sure he would. He'd get right on that. Micah fixed his radio, shrugged into his breathing apparatus, and strode to the front door of the chapel, the only spot on the building not engulfed in flames. That building's wood had been baking under the Texas sun for a half century. There would be a flash point as soon as the interior temperature crested and the chapel's whole interior would incinerate as though a nuclear bomb had exploded, no actual flame necessary.

He paused by Granny June's bench, which had been reduced to smoldering shards of wood and carbon. Surrounding the bench, tire marks dug into the earth below the singed lawn as though the bench had been hit by a car. Or a golf cart. Micah had been so upset with Remedy when he'd left the resort that he hadn't stopped to say hello to Granny June while she took her usual cocktail hour on the bench with her glasses of bourbon and a candle. Flame and accelerant. *My God* . . .

He had to get them out of there. The alternative was too overwhelming to consider. He was angry with Remedy and Granny for going into such a deadly situation and angry at God for screwing him over like this. After all the sacrifices he'd made, the devotion with which he'd undertaken the burden of protecting what he loved from fire, this was what he got in return. Two of the people he loved the most in this world trapped in mortal danger by a fire.

Dusty and three other men fell into step behind him.

"We've got your back," Dusty said. "Let's go get 'em."

Ty Briscoe was his next obstacle. He met Micah near the chapel steps, a frantic, desperate look in his eye. "I'm going with you."

Micah shoved him out of his path. "You're not trained and you don't have the right gear. I do. My men do. Do not get in our way and make our jobs any harder. Do not make this about you."

"I can't just stand here and wait."

Micah leveled his fiercest glare at him. "You'd better. That's the only way you can help right now."

James Decker appeared behind Ty, restraining him the best he could.

Micah shut out the sight and pounded his chest, forcing the air from his lungs, draining the fight from his blood. This rescue had to be accomplished with nothing but cold, calculated skill or it wasn't going to work. He shut it all down. His fear, his love. Everything except his job. The only emotion coursing through his veins was resolve. He was not coming out of that chapel alone.

"You bring me my mother and you can have anything you want!" Ty bellowed to him. "My money, the resort, power like you've never known. I'll give you anything; just bring her out alive, goddamn it."

Chapter Twenty-Two

Micah dropped to his knees at the chapel entrance and proceeded forward, crawling, into the building. There was still a good six inches of visibility beneath the smoke, which filled him with hope that smoke inhalation hadn't killed both women yet.

On their hands and knees, the firefighters fanned out in the vestibule, each taking a side to methodically search, not only for Remedy and June but for any other unknown victims. Micah took the center, crawling through the open doors to the sanctuary and down the center aisle, his head on a swivel. Visibility was declining rapidly, and he strained to scan down each row of pews.

Every few feet he called Remedy's name, but he was nearing the front of the sanctuary and had yet to find any sign of them. The altar and stage behind it were completely engulfed in smoke. He couldn't even tell where the flames were and which walls were on fire, the smoke was so dense. He was running out of time. A flash point was coming and it would kill them all when it did.

Then, through the darkness, a woman's hand reached out on the wood flooring.

Micah rushed forward. "I've got two women, alive but

injured, in the center aisle of the sanctuary," Micah said into his radio. "Need backup in here."

He crushed any emotions he felt back into a safe, locked box in his heart and reclaimed his cold, calculated skill. "I'm going to get you both out of here, but we need to hurry."

Dusty scrambled through the encroaching darkness and reached Micah's side in no time. More firefighters swarmed around them. "We're getting you both out of here. Right now."

Micah lifted Remedy's semiconscious body into his arms. Dusty did the same with Granny June. The men didn't think, they didn't take their time—they headed for the doors at a sprint. They'd barely cleared the base of the hill when the flash point struck. Windows exploded. A piece of the roof splintered, then caved in. Angry orange flames licked at the sky as the building started to collapse.

Micah and Dusty and the rest of their team kept running toward the waiting EMTs, past the additional fire trucks that had arrived on scene and had their fire hoses trained on the building. In the distance, Micah could see that another couple fire crews were maintaining the firebreak line between the chapel and the wilderness beyond the resort.

Micah and Dusty gently laid the injured women on two stretchers, then stepped back so the EMTs could get to work. From under Granny June's shirt slid a bound volume. It fell to the ground and opened, its pages flapping in the wind. Ty and his children and wife crowded closer.

"My mother's wedding album," Ty said, his voice cracking. "That's why she went in there. To save her album."

"We need space to work. I need everyone to back up," an EMT said.

Micah turned his attention to Remedy. Chet hovered over her, affixing an oxygen mask to her face while another EMT started an IV drip.

"Tell me she has a pulse," Micah said.

"She has a pulse and it's strong. As soon as I put the oxygen mask on her, she opened her eyes," Chet said.

Praise God.

Micah leaned in nearer. Remedy's eyes shifted to look at him.

He tamped down the relief and fear and lingering anger, all the emotions that would undo him if he let them. He'd fall apart later, when no one was counting on him. Meanwhile, he had a family to update.

Standing behind the taped-off barricades along with the rest of the curious hotel guests, he found Remedy's parents. The only way he could think to describe the looks on their face was *stricken*. It was ironic how these two larger-than-life celebrities had sunk so low in his mind, the more he'd learned about them. But they were Remedy's flesh and blood, and they deserved to know what was going on with their daughter.

"She's awake again and lucid," he told them. "Not sure about smoke inhalation damage yet, but she's alive."

Remedy's mother bowed her head and wept uncontrollably.

"Let's go," he heard an EMT behind him say. "She's ready for transport."

He turned in time to watch the ambulance doors close with Granny June inside. Ty Briscoe was putting up a fight again, though Decker was doing his best to restrain him. Stripped of his cockiness, Ty was just a worried son, like any of the hundreds Micah had seen throughout his career.

"Let me ride with her. I'm her son," Ty said.

"I can't let you do that, but she's in good hands, I can guarantee you," Micah said. "My men are taking her to the Tri-City Memorial Hospital. Close by. You can meet her there."

"I'll drive you and the rest of the family," Decker said. "Let's get moving so we can follow them directly."

Decker, Carina, her sister, Haylie, and Ty's wife lit off

across the lawn, but Ty lingered. "Is she going to be all right?" he asked in that same scared voice Micah had heard from so many loved ones over his years working as a first responder.

"Hard to say, given her age, but if anyone can pull out of this, it's June. You're lucky that the fire roads held so the fire didn't spread to the resort or the woods. This could've been a whole lot worse."

"And the hydrants you insisted we get—" Ty said.

The mention of hydrants brought Micah right back to how pissed off he'd been during the grand battle between the two of them over their installation. "You mean the ones you fought me on every step of the way? Doesn't seem like such a waste of money anymore, does it?"

Ty's face was stripped of any ego, any pride. "No. It doesn't."

Micah knew his adrenaline was responsible for the way his anger was whipping up as potently as a firestorm, but he couldn't find it in himself to hold back any longer. "And it's not only me you've been jerking around. You've been fighting the whole fire department for years trying to tie our hands and limit our power. Don't you see? This time we saved your mother, but when someone's trapped in a fire it's always someone's mother. It's always someone's loved one."

Ty screwed his face up in anguish. "You win."

Micah just about cracked wide open like a volcano with that asinine pronouncement. "It wasn't about that. It's *never* about that for me or my crew. You're the only one who thinks all this is a game."

"I don't want to be your enemy!" Ty shouted. "No more fighting your burn bans or regulations. I have too much to lose."

Micah's attention shifted to Remedy, who was sitting up, looking stronger by the minute, while Chet held a stethoscope to her lungs. "We all do."

"Thank you for saving my mother."

Micah shook the hand Ty extended. "It was my honor."

Ty turned away.

"Hey!" Micah called after him. "She's going to be okay. She's too strong not to be."

Ty gave a terse nod, then jogged after the rest of his family.

The lawn and parking lots were jammed with firefighter vehicles from all over Central Texas. The fire looked close to containment. Micah would let the other crews handle that. There was only one thing on his mind. Remedy.

Standing apart from the crowd, he allowed a small storm of feelings to swell up inside him. She'd nearly died. He would never forget the way she looked on the chapel floor, crawling to safety, Granny June on her back. The conviction in her eyes, the strength. His own profound relief at finding them, of not being too late.

He shed his jacket and wiped his sweaty, soot-covered face on his sleeve, getting a grip again. When he reached her, all those feelings came exploding up to the surface again. He braced tight fists on either side of her hips so she wouldn't see how his limbs shook. He locked his watery gaze to hers.

She took down her oxygen mask and stroked her hands through his hair. He jerked his head away.

"Could you give us a minute?" he told Chet.

"Only a minute, though. We're gonna get her to the hospital for a more thorough exam."

When Chet and the other EMTs had cleared out, Micah forgot everything he'd been prepared to say. It was all too much. The hurt, the fury, the fear that nothing he did would ever be enough to keep everyone he loved safe. "What happened? The fire looks like it may have started at Granny's bench. Was that it? Was it her candle for Tyson that did it?"

"I was driving the golf cart. Granny wanted to chase

the homing pigeons and we were having so much fun. I crashed the golf cart into her bench. The candle knocked over. Her drink and the second drink she had sitting there both knocked over. And the rest happened so fast." She closed her eyes. "So damn fast."

"You should have waited for a fire crew to arrive."

"When Granny June ran in the chapel I knew I couldn't wait for someone else to go in after her. And then, with the smoke and the heat in there, I couldn't get Granny to leave and I was tired. I wanted to give up, but I put you in my mind. I had to get back to you, Micah, because I love you. There was no other choice but to see you again."

"And here we are," he bit out. "Granny June unconscious and you in the back of an ambulance and a lot of lives risked." Her shoulders sagged, but he couldn't dwell on that. "You almost left me today." His tone came out sounding harsher than he'd meant, and maybe she could have mistaken it for anger if not for the roughness charged in each word.

"I had to save Granny June."

"You should have waited for me and the other firefighters to go get her. That was reckless and irresponsible, and just like you to pull that crazy shit without thinking it through to the consequences."

Her face screwed up, angry and hurt. "I know."

"Lay off her or get away from my ambulance," Chet said. "She's been through enough."

A small voice in Micah's mind told him Chet was right, but the rest of him was tired of holding back, tired of the constant trouble she caused for him. "The worst part is that it's my fault, really. I never said anything to Granny June about those candles she burned. I was too busy getting her advice about romancing you. Same as the ballroom fire. That's on me, too. I told you the first time we slept together that I wasn't going to let you interfere with my job, but that was exactly what I went and did. I let you get into my head and cloud my reasoning. The ballroom fire, the choices I made to authorize that damned dessert and those flammable trees and those dogs—all that nonsense—put hundreds of lives at risk. And for what?"

"I cosigned every authorization that night, too, man," Chet said.

The hurt tasted thick and bitter as mud in Micah's throat. "How dare you sashay into town with your trust fund safety net in place and wreck my life and the lives of so many others? Wynd offered you a job in Hollywood and I think you need to take it."

The devastation on her face nearly brought him to his knees. He girded himself and held steady.

She looked at Micah, then past him, to her parents, who'd crossed over the barricades and were fast approaching the ambulance.

"Chet, am I clear to go? Can Micah or my parents drive me to the hospital?"

Chet shook his head. "I'm not comfortable with that. I want to keep you on oxygen and an IV."

"Let her go if she wants to go. That's what I've had to learn the hard way," Micah bit out.

Tears dripped down her eyes. "I love you with all my heart," she said.

He couldn't listen to that anymore. He couldn't listen to anything else except his instinct, and right now his instinct was telling him to let her go and leave good enough alone. "I've got to get out of here."

"Hey!" Chet called to him. Micah turned around. "You're a fucking idiot," Chet said.

He blinked at Chet, trying to think of something biting to say, something that would wound, but his brain had gone numb. Turning on his boot heel, he stalked to his truck.

Time to make his way to the hospital to check on June, instead of brooding about a relationship that was doomed from the get-go.

A hand pulled on his shoulder. Micah whirled, his fist up, ready to strike. "Not in the mood, Chet."

It wasn't Chet but Xavier who faced him, his fists at the ready. "You can hit me if it makes you feel better, but you know I'd hit you back."

All the steam leached out of Micah. Of all the people who could've shown up in that moment, Xavier was the only one with the power to talk him down off the ledge. He let Xavier pull him into a tight hug. "How'd you know to come here?"

"Alex called," Xavier said, backing up to clasp both of Micah's shoulders. "In his first call he nearly gave me a heart attack when he told me you'd run into a burning building that hadn't been contained yet. I was already on my way when he called again to tell me that not only were you safe, but you'd saved Remedy and June."

Micah huffed. "Then I'm guessing you watched that fight. She's leaving, you know. She got a job offer in L.A. It was the offer she'd been waiting for. She's outta here."

"Sounded to me like you practically guaranteed that."

Micah rolled his neck. "I don't need you to rag on me right now."

"She's the best thing that ever happened to you."

Like hell she was. "She brings out the worst in me."

"Are you sure about that?"

Yes, he was sure. "She drives me to distraction; she compromises my professional integrity. Because of her, Ty threatened my job, my crew hates me, and I'm responsible for two major fires at the resort in the past month. Not a bunch of rich, entitled punks, but me, Xavier. It's like everything I worked for all these years was a lie. I thought if I could control it, if I could just get the resort to comply with the law, that I could keep everyone safe. And God's trying to tell me over and over again that it's not true. That he didn't give me that gift after all. It was only foolish pride."

Xavier shook Micah's shoulders and drilled him with a piercing stare. "I want you to listen to me, man. And listen good. Your mom would've left your family anyway."

"What the hell are you talking about her for? This has nothing to do with her."

But Xavier didn't seem to hear him. He shook Micah's shoulders again. "Shut up and listen. She would've left your family and she would've left your father with or without the fire happening. Maybe not as soon as she did because of the fire, but leaving was in her bones. It was never your fault. It wasn't the fire's fault or your dad's fault. Some people are just the leaving kind."

Exactly. Some people had it in their blood to leave.

In a flash of memory, he was twelve, waking up in the morning and finding that note on the kitchen table. She'd had to know Micah would be the one who found it. She'd had to. He was always the first person up in the morning. He'd taken that as a sign that it was his job to go bring her home, maybe even before anyone else in the family realized she'd left, to spare everyone else the heartache that he felt.

He would never forget the panic of not being able to get his dad's truck started. It took him nearly ten minutes to figure out he had to put the clutch in for the engine to turn over. He would never forget the hair-raising grind of gears with every awkward gearshift. He would never forget his determination to save his family from this new horror. Even back then, he'd fancied himself a hero.

Tears pricked his eyes. It had all been a lie, all that hope and optimism. What a waste. He'd driven that truck in circles around the town, then the county. He'd driven until he'd run out of gas and been forced to trudge to the nearest gas station to beg a quarter for a phone call.

He tore away from Xavier's hold and smacked his palms against his eyes to rid them of the unwanted tears. "You know who else is the leaving kind? Remedy."

Her name crushed his heart, splintering it into a million shards that would never be put back together again. He turned his back to Xavier and braced his hands on his truck while he fought to neutralize his expression.

Behind him, Xavier gave a hard laugh. "So in that big, stupid, redneck brain of yours you figured you'd push her away before she could leave you?"

She was leaving regardless of anything he did or said. So he'd beat her to the punch, big deal. Didn't change the facts. "Stop drawing connections where there aren't any. This is about Remedy not belonging in Texas. It's about her not belonging with me."

"No. This is about you being afraid to take a chance on losing another person that you love from your life."

"I said stop it with the psychobabble bullshit."

But Xavier persisted. "The chapel fire is only going to take Remedy away if you use it to push her away. Not like the fire that took your mom away, and that took me and my family away from you."

Micah had a protest on the tip of his tongue, then stopped, considering Xavier's point. He'd never thought about the Knolls Canyon Fire from that angle. That single event had stripped so many fundamental parts of his life away from him. His home, his mother, his best friend. "But we're still friends; the fire didn't take you from me."

"It took me far enough away that you and I were never the same," Xavier answered in a quieter voice. "We had to reinvent what it meant to be friends and that took a long time. It took until we were adults to really figure it out."

"But we did."

"Yes, because that's what people who love each other do. They figure out a way."

Micah dropped his chin to his chest. *That's what people who love each other do.* Why did that statement hurt so much? After all these years, how did his mother's lack of love still carry with it such a crippling bite? If she'd loved him, if she'd loved her family, she would have found a way to stay.

"You are not the leaving kind, Micah. But right now, the way it stands with Remedy, that's exactly what you're doing. You're the one leaving her. Where's the man who sacrifices everything—even at the risk of his own heartache—to be there for the people he loves? Where's my friend?"

Well, shit. Xavier was right. Micah wasn't the leaving kind. He was the go-for-broke idiot with the hero complex who gave his everything to the people he loved. Why would he change who he was now, after everything?

He whirled around. "I screwed things up with Remedy."

"Yeah."

Panic rattled through him like an earthquake. "How do I make this right? What do I say to her?"

"You don't need anybody to tell you that because nobody else knows her like you do."

True enough.

He tried to pour into his hug to Xavier everything he didn't know how to say, how relieved he was that the two of them had found their way back to their friendship after the fire, how much it meant to him to be the godfather of Xavier's children, how much he couldn't bear to live without him. "I really do love you, man."

Xavier clasped Micah's shoulders and shook him. "You're telling the wrong person that tonight. Go get her before she's gone. You don't want to have to chase her all the way out to California."

That he did not.

Chet was standing at the rear of an empty ambulance.

"Where is she?" Micah said.

"She pulled her IV out and took off when I wasn't looking. The sheriff's department and her parents are out looking for her now."

"Shit."

"Yeah. I'm waiting for their call to come get her again so she can get the treatment she needs."

Micah tore through the streets of Dulcet in a blur, his siren and lights on, fielding phone call after phone call from worried townsfolk as he drove, every last one of those calls telling him exactly where Remedy had fled to.

When he got to Petey's Diner, he saw Remedy through the window right away, alone at a table in the far corner of the room. Barbara was behind the counter, absentmindedly wiping a glass and watching Remedy eat a burger with downcast eyes.

Micah had seen enough. He pulled the door open and went to her.

At the sight of him, she set down the partially eaten burger on her plate and swallowed hard. Her eyes were filled with pain and he hated himself in that moment, knowing he was the cause.

"You were right," she said, her voice cracking. "This is a terrible cheeseburger. No offense to Petey."

His relief was a living, breathing force that swept through him faster than a wildfire. He pulled out a chair. "Now you know for sure that Hog Heaven's burgers are the best in Texas."

Her gaze slid into the distance. "How did you know where to find me?"

She rubbed her arms. It was all he could do not to wrench her hands away and hold them in his own.

"Dusty saw you and called me. And then Delinda, and Tabby, and then Petey himself."

"Like I've said. Everybody is in everybody's business in this town," Remedy said.

"And thank goodness for that, because then I knew where to find you so I could say what I have to say."

She rolled her focus to him. Those red-rimmed eyes killed him. He would never, ever forget the hurt he'd caused her. "You already said it," she said.

No, he most certainly did not. "I was wrong. About what I said to you earlier, and about a lot of things. It turns out that being afraid of having people taken from you because of forces beyond your control is something that sticks with you, even when you don't know that it has."

He swallowed hard. "My mother . . ." How could he explain it to her? "It's a funny thing about loss; you think it teaches you what's really important. That's what they tell you. You're supposed to learn that a house isn't a home; family's your home. Or that material possessions are meaningless, and all that talk, but you know what? That house was my home. And I lost it, forever. And Xavier was my next-door neighbor and my blood brother, but I lost him for a long time, too. My mother was my family, and I lost her.

"None of that was my fault—and I know that now— and I think I even knew that then, but I guess it didn't register all the way into my DNA, because it didn't stop me from growing up to believe I had the power to stop more loss, more fires. That if I just tried hard enough and fought tirelessly I would never again have to worry—no, *to fear*— losing what mattered to me. Stupid, right?"

She took his hand in hers. "Not stupid."

"A little stupid. Because the maddening thing about fire and about loss is that there's no way to control it one hundred percent. There's no way to guarantee it won't happen."

Her eyes turned pained again. "No."

"As Xavier helped me see tonight, the only thing I can control is my fear. And that's a stubborn son of a bitch."

"I've found that to be true, too, with my life and my fears."

He brought her hand up to his lips to kiss. "You saved Granny June."

Her exhalation was almost a quiet chuckle. "You and I have been over that already. You saved her, not me. I'm the one who nearly got her killed. I'm the one responsible for the fires at the resort. The reason I don't fit in anywhere is because I create destruction everywhere I go. The ballroom, your brother's injury, now this. I am chaos incarnate."

The description evoked from him a sad smile. "I know you are."

Tears slid down her cheeks. "There is no place for me in this world. I keep waiting for all the pieces of my life to click into place, but nothing ever clicks."

"You and I clicked. Instantly."

"Why? Because I set the fires and you put them out? Is that our yin and yang?" Her voice was bitter and weary, so far away from the Remedy he knew and loved.

"You once said to me, 'What's a town hero without a little trouble to keep him in business?' "

"And you told me that I wrecked your life."

Goddamn, it destroyed him to watch her hurt sweep over her face. "I was wrong. And I was scared."

"You're right to be scared of me, because I'm a mess."

"No. I meant I was scared of losing you, scared that you would leave me." Such foreign words. They lurched out of his mouth and sounded distant to his ears. Him, the bad-ass firefighter, the kid who beat up bullies and could kill and skin a buck by the time he was twelve, was frightened beyond measure of being left by someone he loved.

A breathtaking, ancient sadness welled up from the depth of his soul, one he hadn't known he'd been dragging around, as heavy as a weight. He'd forgiven his mother years ago, so how could it be? But it was. He rotated his jaw and decided that he might be weak and he might be afraid, but he'd never stopped being brave—and tonight he needed to be brave enough to let Remedy see his true heart, brave enough to risk her leaving and know that he would survive it. She was worth this leap of faith. *They* were worth it together.

He let it all wash through him. He let it take hold of him and rock him where he sat. The better to get the worst of it out of his system before he begged Remedy to give him another chance.

When he could finally speak, he chose his words with care. "You said before that there's no place for you in this world, but you were wrong. You belong here with me. By my side." He took her hand. "Where I need you to be for the rest of our lives."

Her lower lip trembled. "How can you mean that? How can you want to sign up for a lifetime of disaster and chaos?"

How could he explain to her all she'd done for him, how she'd changed him and his life irrevocably? His chair legs scraped the linoleum as he scooted around to her side of the table. He took her hand, then kissed her temple, reverently, lingering there to breathe in her hair.

"I have no interest in returning to the humdrum gray world that my life was before you were in it. No interest at all," he whispered against her skin.

She drew a tremulous breath and wiggled her hand out of his. "I burned down the chapel."

He took her hand again. "An accident."

She withdrew and wrenched her face away. "I burned down the main ballroom."

He set a finger on her chin and turned her to look at him. "Technically that was the fault of the dog and the Baked Alaska."

"You blamed me, and you're not the only one who did."

"I blamed you because I was scared of losing all that control I'd convinced myself I had over the resort and nature and dogs and Baked Alaska. I know better now, and I only hope you can forgive me."

She studied him as though testing his conviction.

"I learned a lot tonight about the man I thought I was and about the man I want to be. I figured out that I'm not some indestructible town hero who has all the answers. Because I don't, clearly. What I am is this town's caretaker—one of many. It takes all of us to keep the land and the people here safe and happy. Ty wants to separate the fire marshal and fire chief jobs, and I think he's on to something. It's time for me to trust that everything's gonna be okay even when I'm not in control of every little detail."

"You figured all that out tonight?"

He shrugged. "It's been a long time coming. Sometimes it takes a fire to shine a light on a situation."

"It was the same for me tonight. My life came into focus when I was in there. I know what I want for myself."

"And that is?"

She raised her chin a notch. She touched his cheek. The pain was gone from her eyes, replaced by the fiery spark of life and adventure he'd grown accustomed to seeing there. Then she angled her head and pressed her lips to his. Nothing in his life had ever felt so exactly right as the two of them kissing and touching and trembling together.

She pulled back and fluttered her eyes open. "I want to rebuild the chapel with my trust fund," she said. "I want to make it happen for Granny June and for this town. Our town. Our home."

Did that mean . . . could he possibly hope? "I'm pretty sure Ty Briscoe won't have a problem with you donating the funds, if that's what you've got your heart set on."

"I do. And then I want to be the first to get married in that chapel, the same way Granny and Tyson were the first to get married in the chapel they built."

His chest ached with the burgeoning hope. "What happened to you wanting to get married by a justice of the peace, with no wedding at all?"

"I changed my mind. I want to be part of an epic love match, like Granny June and Tyson."

His body thrumming with joy and relief, he brushed another kiss across her lips. "I think you already are, California. And I think I am, too."

The faint sound of applause caught their attention and they broke apart to look out the diner windows. A crowd had gathered, including Litzy, Tabby, Dusty, Alex, and Xavier and many other townsfolk.

Right there in front of hell and creation, to the cheers of the crowd, Micah pulled Remedy into his arms and kissed her, long and slow and loaded with the promise of forever. He was going to marry this woman and it was going to be the craziest, most exhilarating ride of his life. He couldn't wait to get started.

Chapter Twenty-Three

Micah parked his truck in his usual spot near the blackened, soggy grass on Chapel Hill surrounding the charred shell of the building and eyed the circling helicopters. Remedy had warned him about those, as well as the hordes of obnoxious paparazzi who'd set up camp at the resort's entrances.

Despite the fire, the WestWynd wedding had gone ahead on schedule, though the wedding ceremony had been moved to a massive gazebo near the resort's winter wonderland garden. Micah was running late enough that he'd missed the ceremony itself, but he'd had trouble pulling himself away from Granny June's hospital bed. Though she'd suffered from minor damage to her lungs and throat due to smoke inhalation, she was awake and holding court from her bed for a rapt audience of family, nurses, and other hospital staff. And, of course, she was already on her smartphone, chronicling her hospital stay for her Facebook page, all the while with her wedding album tucked in the corner of her bed near her pillow.

When Micah rounded the corner of the chapel, he stopped short at the sight of Ty Briscoe sitting on a new bench near the same spot as the one that had gone up in flames. Micah slogged through the wet grass to the bench, as he'd done so many times before to share a few quiet minutes with Granny June.

When Ty noticed him, he tipped his chin in Micah's direction and greeted him with an expression that didn't give anything away. Micah nodded back, sensing the shift inside him at the sight of his nemesis. His hate was gone, vanished. What a difference a day made. They might be two men on different sides of a battle, but it'd become clear to Micah since last night's fire that Ty cared as deeply about his family and his land as Micah did about his. As Granny June had told Micah more than once, he and Ty were cut from the same cloth.

Today, on the bench next to Ty sat a bottle of bourbon and a lowball glass filled with two fingers of the liquor, just as Granny June had always done. Ty had brought a candle with him, too, but unlike the ones Granny had used, this one was a fake, with a faint glow of a harmless LED light flickering against the dark stain of the bench's wood. Maybe old dogs could learn new tricks after all.

Micah took a seat on the bench and sprawled back, then followed Ty's gaze to the now-empty gazebo where workers were busy taking down the décor.

"Fifty-two years of weddings here on the ranch and this is the first one my mother has missed," Ty said. His gaze holding steady on the ceremony, he lifted the glass of bourbon in a toast.

That was one impressive statistic. "She's a remarkable woman. One of my favorite people on the planet."

Ty took a sip of the bourbon. "She's the best person I've ever known. Crazy as a bat in her old age, but the best this world has to offer. Always was. My father was one of the few men in this world who was worthy of her. It's been a blessing and a curse having to follow in his footsteps with this place."

In all the years of hearing about Tyson Briscoe, Micah

had never once stopped to ponder the idea that Tyson's shadow loomed large over the ranch. He hadn't considered the pressure Ty must have felt inheriting the mantle of responsibility for the ranch's prosperity. And now, with his two daughters raised and busy with their own lives, the future of the resort hung in the balance once again. That had to be a heavy burden for Ty.

"It's a good thing you're such a tough old bastard, then," Micah said.

Ty chuckled. "There is that."

"What are you going to do with this place? How are you going to keep it in the family now that Carina decided she's not interested in running it?"

He made slow work of setting the glass on the bench, his expression turning sly. "I've got a few more tricks up my sleeve, if that's what you're gettin' at. How about you worry about your job and I'll worry about mine?"

"Fair enough," Micah said. "As long as part of my job is still giving you hell every now and then."

Ty nodded to the wedding gazebo. "Remedy tells me she's gonna rebuild the chapel, then get married in it. I have a mother, wife, and two daughters, so I'm used to getting bossed around by a bunch of women; they're just usually not my employees."

Micah supposed that meant Remedy hadn't been fired, contrary to her worry about that. "Did you green-light Remedy's plan?"

"Damn right I did. I've always fancied myself a smart man. If she's gonna foot the bill, then she can do what she wants—as long as she gets it done by wedding season in December so we're not compromising the legend of the Mistletoe Effect. Our resort has a reputation to uphold."

Ah, yes, the Mistletoe Effect. "A Christmas wedding sounds like a darn good idea to me." And he had a feeling his soon-to-be fiancée would agree.

Ty shifted and eyed Micah curiously. "A word of advice—"

But whatever Ty's advice was, Micah never got to hear it because a yelp of surprise caught their attention. They followed the direction of the sound in time to watch a female hotel guest flatten against a wall as an elephant appeared around the corner of the hotel. Micah blinked and shook his head in utter disbelief at what he was seeing.

The elephant was outfitted with a saddle strapped to her back and wearing an elaborate purple headdress as she galloped along the side of the hotel, headed toward the golf course. Her trunk swung gleefully and her ears flapped in a way that reminded him of a dog set loose from its leash, running for freedom.

Micah stood, agog. "Why is there an elephant on your property?"

Ty rose to his feet, muttering, "What in the holy hell is going on?"

Both men startled again at the sight of a golf cart rounding the hotel's corner at top speed in the same direction as the elephant. Remedy was behind the wheel, dressed in full virgin librarian mode with a short-sleeved shirtdress the color of coffee and her hair swept up into a tidy ponytail. Then again, she'd said something about a safari theme for the wedding, so maybe the look she was going for instead was that of a fresh-faced safari guide.

She did a double take on spotting Micah and Ty, then veered off-course, toward them. She screeched to a halt farther down the hill and called out, "Have you ever tried to stop a rampaging elephant before?"

No, Micah most certainly had not.

"Do you think she's talking to you or me?" Ty said.

Micah shrugged. "Even odds." To Remedy, he added, "Something tells me I'm about to experience it for the first time."

"Is that thing gonna hurt my guests?" Ty asked. "We

can't afford any bad publicity with all the media that's buzzing around today."

Remedy waved off Ty's concern. "That's just Gwyneth. She's harmless, but she's got a salty vocabulary and a thing for the seventh hole. Don't worry; the bananas are on their way."

Ty leaned in to Micah. "Did you understand a single word of that?"

"Not one bit." Micah started down the hill toward her, a grin spreading on his lips. "But I'm guessing I'm about to figure it out."

"Better you than me," Ty called. "Y'all are as crazy as my mother!"

Now *that* was a compliment.

Micah climbed into the passenger seat.

Remedy beamed at him. "This is going to be fun. You'll see."

Micah had no doubt about that, but, just to be on the safe side, he reached across her lap and buckled her in. Then he held on tight for yet another adventure in what had become a wild and remarkable ride of a lifetime, together with her.

Read on for an excerpt from
Melissa Cutler's next book

ONE MORE TASTE

Coming soon from St. Martin's Paperbacks

Chapter One

Not everyone was lucky enough to drive a haunted truck. Then again, *lucky* wasn't a word Knox Briscoe would use to describe his current predicament. On a prayer, he turned the key in the ignition, but the Chevy offered him nothing but a dull click in response.

"I don't believe in ghosts," he said, although if anyone had actually heard his declaration, it'd have to be ghosts, or perhaps some unseen wildlife, because there was nothing or nobody in this stretch of backcountry other than him and his truck, a roadside sign proclaiming Briscoe Ranch Resort straight ahead in three miles, and a wide, calm lake nestled in the Texas hills.

He tried the key again. Nothing but that maddening click.

He tapped a finger against the steering wheel, denying himself any more grandiose a reaction because Knox was nothing if not a man in command of his emotions. It had been the rule his dad had drilled into Knox's and his siblings' heads since they were little: *Never lose control.*

Knox popped the truck door open to the crisp October day. His freshly buffed black dress shoes hit the gravel with a crunch. Given the statement he'd planned to make on this, his first day as a part-owner of Briscoe Ranch, it wouldn't do to soil his suit with engine grease, and so he shrugged out of his sports coat, hung it on a hanger he kept in the backseat for just such a purpose, tucked the ends of his blue silk tie into his shirt, and then rolled his shirt-sleeves to the elbows.

He pulled the hood up and ran through his usual inspection. He'd never considered himself much of a car guy until he'd inherited this one through his dad's will two years earlier. It'd taken a lot of YouTube video viewing and conversations with his mechanic for him to get up to speed on maintaining the thirty-year-old truck, but it'd been worth every hour and dollar spent.

None of that new knowledge was going to help him today, though. Nothing obvious was broken or out of place and the engine had plenty of oil and other fluids.

Knox patted the truck's side. "Okay, Dad. Message received. You don't want your truck on Briscoe Ranch property. I get it. But would you at least let me get to the entrance of the resort before stalling the truck again?"

God, he felt like a moron, talking to his dead father like that. No way was Knox a believer in hocus-pocus, but even if his dad weren't haunting the '85 Chevy Half Ton, then at the very least he was up in heaven pulling some strings. Even in death, it seemed, his dad had decided to stubbornly hold his ground against the father and brother who'd excommunicated him from the family before Knox's birth—Knox's grandfather Tyson and his uncle Ty. Even in death, his dad refused to let his prized truck lay one speck of rubber down on Ty's property.

Soon to be Knox's property, if he could get his damn truck to start back up.

Behind the wheel again, he gripped the key in the ignition and closed his eyes. *Please work. Please.*

Click. Click. Click.

"Okay. But this sucks. I didn't want to show up in a

town car with a driver like a mobster goon who's there to shake them all down. I wanted you—"

A wisp of grief swirled like smoke around his heart, threatening his composure far more than his frustration had. He shook his head. Foolish heart. He'd wanted his dad there with him to watch Knox take control of the very business his dad had been robbed of. Poetic justice. Vengeance. The cost of doing business. Whatever the history books would end up labeling this not-so-friendly takeover.

He grabbed his messenger bag—his sister, Shayla, refused to allow him to carry anything as stodgy as a briefcase—and stepped out of the truck, rummaging around the copies of the Briscoe Ranch shareholder contract his lawyers had prepared until he found his cell phone.

He was pacing behind the truck as the phone rang with his office in Dallas when he spotted a *for sale* sign ahead of him, demarcating a gated driveway a few yards from the lake. He walked along the road to it, the phone to his ear. Was there a house at the end of that twisty, tree-lined driveway? Did the property border the resort? Perhaps he'd buy it and expand the resort even more than he'd originally planned.

Max, his private equity firm's office manager, picked up on the fourth ring. "Don't tell me Ty Briscoe's giving you shit already. I told you that you should've brought Yamaguchi and Crawford with you."

Maybe another boss would've bristled at such insubordination, but Knox had developed a deep mistrust of kiss-asses over his years as an entrepreneur. Linda Yamaguchi and Diane Crawford were his firm's lawyers, and Max was right. Knox probably should have brought them along as he usually did for acquisitions. But he wanted to close this deal on his own, eye to eye with the uncle he'd never met—the uncle he was going to ruin, just as Ty had ruined Knox's family. Not that he confessed as much to his equity firm team.

"You can tell me 'I told you so' later, but that's not why I called. My truck broke down three miles from Briscoe Ranch. I need a driver, and I need him to get here in—" He lifted the flap of a clear plastic box affixed to the *for sale* sign and pulled out a flyer.

The photograph gracing the center of the flyer caught his eye. A grand, modern house sitting on a hill overlooking the lake. It was exactly the kind of dwelling Knox was hoping to move into somewhere in the vicinity of Briscoe Ranch since he couldn't very well run the show from his home base of Dallas, five hours away.

"In what, Mr. Briscoe?"

"Sorry. Something caught my eye. If you could have the driver here in less than an hour, that would be great. Can you find me someone?" His meeting with Ty Briscoe wasn't for another two hours, but he wanted to take one last walk around the resort without any of the employees knowing who he was or why he was there.

"I can't imagine that being a problem." He heard the fast click-clack of keyboard typing. "And . . . let's see . . . Nope, no problem. Your car will be there within the half hour."

As the call ended, a crackle of tires on gravel snagged Knox's attention. He pivoted around, expecting to see a good Samaritan pulling to the shoulder to see if Knox needed help, but his truck was the only vehicle in sight—and it was rolling backward, straight toward the lake.

Dropping the flyer, his messenger bag, and his phone, he took off at a sprint. "No! No, no, no. Shit."

Surely he'd engaged the emergency brakes—hadn't he?

With every passing second, the truck was picking up speed. Knox lunged toward the door handle. He was dragged along a few feet before finding his footing again. He dug his heels into the ground and yanked. The door swung open. He staggered and hit his back against the side of the hood, but managed to rebound in time to throw himself in the cab as it lumbered perilously near the water.

He stomped on the parking brake. It activated with a groan, but the truck wouldn't stop. He pumped the manual brake. Nothing happened. The truck bounced over rocks hard enough to make Knox's teeth rattle. He turned the key. Again, nothing. Nothing except a splash as the back of the truck hit the water.

"Jesus, Dad! Help me out, here!" he shouted.

The truck slammed violently to a stop, pitching Knox forward. He bit his tongue hard. The burst of pain and taste of blood was nothing compared to his relief that the truck, with him in it, hadn't submerged any deeper in the water. Through the pounding of his pulse in his ears, he could hear his labored breaths.

"Thank you," he whispered, his throat tightening. "I can't lose your truck in some stupid lake."

With a hard swallow, he thumped a fist against his chest, jolting himself back into composure. All this talking to ghosts was getting out of hand. Today of all days, he could not afford to devolve into blubbering sentimentality. He fixed his Stetson more firmly on his head and gave himself a stern mental lecture on calming the fuck down.

All business again, he assessed the situation. Not knowing what had caused the truck to stop or if any sudden movements would jostle it back into motion, he rolled the driver-side window down and peered over the edge to stare at the brown-green water, thick with silt and mud that roiled through the liquid like thunderstorm clouds. The water lapped at the bottom of the door, not too deep, but the back tire and back bumper were fully engulfed. If the truck had rolled only a few more feet into the lake, Knox would've been in real trouble.

As things stood now, though, Knox's main problem now was that there was no way for him to avoid getting wet on his walk back to shore. Carefully, so as not to jar the truck back into motion, he unlatched his belt, then opened the zipper of his pants. Shoes off, socks off, then pants. If he got to his first day at Briscoe Ranch on time, in one piece and dry, it would be a miracle.

Clutching his pants, socks, and shoes to his chest, and dressed in only his shirt, a pair of boxers, and his black hat, he opened the door and stepped into the water, sinking knee-deep. Silt and muck oozed between his toes. The cold ripped up his bare legs, making his leg hairs stand on end on and his balls tighten painfully. Grunting through the discomfort, he shuffled away from the door until he could close it.

A series of exuberant splashes sounded from farther in the lake. It sounded like two fish were having a wrestling match right up on the water's surface. He turned, but only saw ripples. Setting his mind back on the task at hand, he pulled his foot off the lake bottom, muscles working to overcome the suction, and took a carefully placed step toward shore.

From seemingly out of nowhere, something blunt and slimy smashed into his calf. The surprise of the hit knocked Knox off-balance. With a yelp totally unbefitting a thirty-two year old Texan and former rodeo cowboy, he danced sideways, fighting for his footing and clutching the clothes in his arms even tighter.

He desperately scanned the water around him, but the swirling silt had reduced the visibility to almost nothing. He held still another moment, listening, watching.

"Holy shit, are you okay?"

The man's voice startled him. He looked up and saw a young guy of maybe twenty-two standing on the bank of the lake, dressed in a suit and with a panicked expression on his face. Behind him, a black sedan idled on the shoulder of the road.

"I'm fine. I think. Are you my driver?"

"Yeah, Ralph with the Cab'd driving service app. Max

at Briscoe Equity Group ordered a premium lift for Knox Briscoe. I'm guessing that's you since your truck's underwater."

And observant, too. "Yep. You see a cell phone and messenger bag somewhere up there, Ralph?"

"Hold up. Is that an '85 Chevy Silverado? That's a hell of a truck."

"It is." *Except when said truck was haunted and decided all on its own to take a swim despite its owner's better judgment.*

"You're lucky the tire got snagged on that rock."

Knox took a look at the front of the truck. Sure enough, the passenger side tire was stopped by a boulder, though he wasn't entirely sure luck had anything to do with it. "About that cell phone and messenger bag, Ralph. Would you mind?"

"Oh. Yeah. On it."

With Ralph in search of Knox's stuff, Knox chanced another step toward shore, keeping his head on a swivel looking for whatever the hell it was that had slammed into him. An attack beaver? Did hill country even have beavers?

Despite his vigilance, he still startled at the sight of a massive, charcoal gray-green fish swishing through the water, coming straight at him. It had to be longer than his arm. It turned on a dime and surged at him. Knox's curse echoed off the hills surrounding the lake.

Time to scram.

He made it two more steps before his foot snagged on a rock and pitched him forward. Desperate for balance, he reached out to grab onto his truck, but the fish had other ideas and head-butted his leg again. Knox splashed down, nearly dunking all the way underwater.

The bite of cold stole his breath all over again. He exploded back out of the water and onto his feet, spluttering and gasping.

"Fuck!" he shouted, loud enough that even if his father was in heaven and not haunting the truck, he would've heard him just fine. He held himself back from adding, *Thanks for nothing, Dad!*

Sloughing water from his face and breathing hard through flared nostrils, Knox shifted his attention to the water in search of the piranha on steroids that had put his ability to keep a cool head to the test. The fish was long gone. Though his pants floated around his knees like dark seaweed swishing in waves and his shoes bobbed like little black boats only a few feet away, his hat had drifted into deeper water. *Terrific. Just terrific.*

He was sopping wet from hair to feet and standing next to his equally waterlogged truck on the most important day of his life.

"What was that thing?" Ralph asked.

"I was hoping you'd gotten a clear view of it."

"Naw, but I did find your cell phone and bag."

Well, that was something, at least. Knox fished his soggy pants from the water, removed his wallet and set it on the roof of the truck, then tossed the pants in the truck bed. Next he grabbed his shoes and tossed them onto the shore. Maybe they wouldn't squish too loudly when he walked.

With that taken care of, it was time to get the inevitable over with. He loosened his tie, then unbuttoned his shirt and peeled it off.

"Uh, sir? Are you stripping? I mean, uh, why don't you get out of the water first."

"Going after my hat." It wasn't until he'd spoken that he realized his teeth were chattering. The sooner he was out of the water, the better. He added his shirt and tie to his pants in the truck bed, then drew a fortifying breath, and pushed into the water for a freestyle swim across the lake.

Technically, the hat was replaceable, but this particular hat had been the first he'd bought with his own money, back when he was fifteen and working his first real job outside of the local junior rodeo circuit. Over the years, it'd become a habit to wear it to new jobs or when he needed to be on his A game for a negotiation. He believed in good luck charms like he believed in ghosts—which meant surreptitiously and despite his better judgment—but there was no denying the slight edge that the black Stetson with the cattleman's crease and the rodeo brim provided him.

He was a solid fifty yards into the water when he reached the hat. Grabbing onto it tight, he ignored the fact that his legs were going numb and made short work of returning to shore. He shook the water off the hat and placed it firmly on his head again, then took his phone from Ralph and dialed his office again.

Max answered on the first ring this time. "Hey, Knox. If you're calling about a tow truck, one's already on its way."

Ladies and gentlemen, introducing Max McCaffery, World's Best Office Assistant. "Thanks for that."

"Figured you'd need one for that ridiculous truck you insist on driving. Most unreliable truck ever. Like, *ever.*"

Knox glanced again at the Chevy. It might be a pain in the ass, but some of the best memories of his life involved that truck. "It has its moments."

"Is the Cab'd driver there yet?" Max said. "Should be, any minute."

"He's here. Just one more thing. I need you to email me with some information on a property." He rattled off the address of the lakefront home from memory and thanked Max again. When the call ended, he turned to Ralph and sized him up. The two of them were roughly the same height and build. "You're, what, six-one? Two hundred?"

Ralph gave him the side eye, apparently on to Knox's plan. "Six even and one-ninety," he said hesitantly.

Close enough. Knox took out three, soggy one-hundred dollar bills from his wallet. "I'm going to need to buy your suit."

It wasn't the first time Emily Ford had spied on a VIP guest at Briscoe Ranch Resort. In fact, she considered it a mandatory part of her research as the resort's Executive Special Event Chef. Wowing elite guests with personalized, gastronomic marvels was her specialty. As long as the guests never checked her Internet search history or spotted her peering at them through binoculars, she was golden.

She didn't usually involve her best friend for life, Carina Briscoe, in her covert ops, but today was an exception. Because today's resort VIP was Knox Briscoe—a cousin of Carina's whom Emily had never met and Carina had only seen a handful of times, though they'd grown up only a couple hundred miles from each other, and who was about to sign on with Carina's dad as the heir apparent of the resort, making him Carina's future landlord and Emily's newest boss.

Since Carina was eight months along in a pregnancy that had supersized her whole body from her ankles to her face, stealthiness in this covert ops mission was not easily achieved. So, once Emily had gotten the call from the security guard manning the resort's cameras that Knox had arrived—two hours earlier than expected—Emily and Carina had settled for spying on him from a window in the bridal gown shop Carina operated in the resort's lobby.

A shiny, black sedan matching the description the security guard had given Emily came into view on the long road through the property leading to the circular driveway in front of the resort's main building.

Carina nudged Emily in the ribs. "This is exciting. I'm glad he's here. I'm glad my dad asked him to work for him."

"Why are you so happy about that? It could ruin everything." Including the dream that Emily had been working toward for a decade. Ty had finally, *finally* agreed to bankroll the building of her dream restaurant at the resort—and she had no idea how much Knox's entry into the family business would delay her grand idea from materializing.

"Don't be such a pessimist," Carina said. "He's family, and I'm proud of my dad for putting the rift behind us. It's ancient history." She wrapped an arm around her belly. "With a new generation of Briscoes coming, it's time for the family to forgive and move on."

The rift was the term Carina and all the Briscoes used to refer to the catastrophic falling out that had happened more than thirty years earlier between Carina's grandfather, Tyson Briscoe, and his two sons, Ty and Clint, that had resulted in Clint Briscoe being excommunicated from the family and their business. Whatever the three men had fought over that night, however, had remained shrouded in silence and speculation. To the best of Emily's knowledge, no one but Tyson, Ty, and Clint knew the reason—and Clint and Tyson had already taken that secret to their graves. Unless either Clint or Tyson had confessed it to his wife before their deaths, that is.

"I get it that he's family," Emily said. "But the man's amassed a net worth of nearly a billion dollars by buying and flipping failing businesses. So, then, why is he bothering with buying into Briscoe Ranch? How can we trust him not to sell us all out?"

"I was skeptical when my dad first told me his plan, but I trust my dad. And I trust his lawyers. They're too business savvy to make it possible for anyone to sell the resort away from the family."

When the car rounded the driveway and came to a stop, Carina and Emily crowded together, ducking their heads low in case either Knox or his driver looked their way.

Emily already knew what he looked like from photographs accompanying write-ups and interviews in business magazine and blogs, as well as the occasional photograph of him attending a charity ball or museum opening posted on a Texas society blog. By all accounts, Knox was loaded with money, charm, and ambition. An impeccable business reputation. A scandal-free personal life. By every account, he'd made his fortune the most ruthless way possible—fair and square.

None of that research, however, prepared her for the sight of him.

Knox Briscoe stepped out of the backseat of the sedan one long leg at a time. He fastened his black suit jacket and surveyed his surroundings, looking far more intimidating in person than the confident intellectual spirit that his photographs conveyed. He was younger. Larger. His features were darker and more brooding. His leather shoes were as shiny black as the paint job on the limo, as slick as his black hair and cowboy hat and suit.

"Oh wow," Carina said on a breath. "I forgot how much he looks like my dad."

Emily had been too wrapped up in ogling him to notice, but now that Carina mentioned it, he did look a lot like a young Ty Briscoe back before he'd decided to go bald. "The Briscoe gene is a strong one, there's no doubt."

"What are you feeding him and my dad at their meeting?" Carina asked.

Emily flushed with a sudden, rare case of insecurity as she considered the lunch menu she'd created for the menu. How could she possibly feed Knox Briscoe pheasant? He looked like he dined on nothing but porterhouse steaks and the tears of his enemies. "Brine-roasted pheasant with an heirloom sweet potato puree and a wild mushroom reduction."

"Sounds tasty."

"Everything looks tasty to you these days. You're an

eating machine, but look at Knox. I can't pair him with that menu."

Carina snickered. "He's not a wine."

Definitely not as decadent and sweet as a wine. He had the muscular grace of one of those hard-core CrossFit athletes who bench-pressed semitruck tires in his spare time and had a single digit BMI number. He probably didn't even drink wine. He definitely didn't eat sweet potato purees or mushroom reductions. Though he should. It would probably do him a world of good to indulge his senses like that.

Just like that, inspiration struck. "That man needs peaches."

Specifically, the late-season peaches she'd gotten that morning from her orchard supplier in Fredericksburg.

"Come again?" Carina said.

"Sugar. Butter. Fat." Inspiration jolted Emily like a zap of electricity. She slid down the wall to the floor, closing her eyes to visualize her new masterpiece. "Charred peaches with a balsamic vinegar reduc—no, not vinegar—a pinch of cayenne lacing a brown sugar brûlée crust. Oh my god, that'll piss him off." She rubbed her hands together like the evil genius she was. "All that butter and sugar. He'll hate that. Right up until he takes a bite. Then he'll understand."

Carina poked her with her shoe. "You're doing that weird fantasy food rambling thing again."

Emily barely heard Carina's teasing. She was too busy perfecting the recipe in her mind. "Huh?"

"I love you. But you're crazy."

Carina was right; Emily was crazy. All great chefs were. She stood, hung the binoculars around her neck, and smoothed out her chef's jacket. "I've got to go. I have a lot of work to do."

"I thought the meal was ready."

"Not anymore. I'm going to share my peaches with Knox Briscoe."

Carina poked her tongue against her cheek as her forehead crinkled with delight. "Someday, one of my lessons about double entendres is going to sink in."

Emily wasn't daft or naive. She knew a double entrendre when she heard one—or, more accurately, inadvertently said one—but it wasn't her fault that the vast majority of people didn't understand that sex and food were incomparable. The perfect meal trumped sex every time, and anyone who claimed otherwise had obviously never experienced Emily's cooking. Knox Briscoe didn't know it yet, but his tongue was about to have the ride of its life.

With food, of course.

Two hours later, Emily pushed a loaded food cart behind the resort's main reception desk, then through the maze of cubicles and offices tucked away from the guests' view. She nodded to Ty Briscoe's secretary, then let herself into his corner office, where Ty and Knox were deep in discussion at his conference table.

Ty afforded Emily the briefest of glances, but Knox's focus remained unrelentingly on Ty and the business at hand. With those dark eyes and hard-set jaw, he exuded the same fierce focus that Emily prided herself on in the kitchen. Except with Knox, the fierceness heightened the energy in the room, beating like waves of power through the air. Emily froze near the door, stunned to find herself suddenly, uncharacteristically intimidated. The spying from Carina's dress shop hadn't prepared Emily for that.

"That idea has merit," Knox was saying to Ty in a deep, firm voice. "But my equity firm's vision extends beyond a cosmetic update. This resort has the potential to become a self-contained city, a beacon for travelers from all over the world."

Even from the door, Emily could see beads of sweat on Ty's bald head. His thick, bulldog neck had turned red, something that only happened when he was keeping his anger in check. Emily wasn't sure she'd ever seen the larger-than-life man, her father figure for all intents and purposes for the past decade, be cowed by another man before. But he was definitely not the alpha in the room today. "Yes, I know, but not—" Ty said.

Knox plowed ahead. "Yes, but nothing, Ty. The vision I have for the resort, the vision you agreed to, is the reason I was able to put together a team of investors so quickly. They're expecting me to make their money back plus at least a twenty percent profit in record time, and I intend to do just that. Your focus here has been on branding Briscoe Ranch as a one-of-a-kind destination, but it's time to convert all that potential into real change. So let's not pretend we're going to give the resort a simple face-lift."

Emily shook herself out of her eavesdropping trance and busied herself creating place settings on the table in front of each man. She could have brought along an assistant to do such menial labor, but she'd wanted to make a strong first impression. As it was, though, Knox had yet to acknowledge her at all.

"I hear what you're saying, but we already have a world-class stable of horses and hill country's premier golf course. What more do you plan to add?" Ty said.

Emily set servings of chilled peach soup in front of Knox, then Ty, with a flourish. She'd labored for nearly two hours on the soup, which was in the running for her best culinary creation ever, if she did say so herself.

Knox picked up his spoon and poked crisp brown sugar brûlée. "We'll need to double the number of guest rooms, for starters. From there we add a bar or two, expand the number of upscale shops in the lobby, and add a five-star luxury restaurant. No luxury resort is complete without its own award-winning chef."

On his next breath, Knox frowned down at the soup, then pushed it ever so slightly away.

Emily gave a quiet gasp. *The nerve* . . .

"Agreed," Ty said. "And we just so happen to have plans for a new restaurant in the works. It's one of the reasons I asked our special event catering chef, Emily Ford, to showcase her skills by preparing us lunch today." He gestured to Emily, who was still gaping at Knox's untouched soup. It wasn't until Knox's eyes roved over her in a dispassionate study that she realized she was wringing the bottom of her chef's jacket in her hands.

Ty continued, "She's been working with me to develop a dynamic proposal for a world-class restaurant here at the resort. All we've been waiting for is the right investor, and here you are."

Knox's mouth gave an almost imperceptible frown. "No offense to Ms. Ford, but my investors have shelled out millions of their own dollars to transform Briscoe Ranch into a world-class luxury resort, so we need to aim higher."

Aim higher? And here she'd thought Knox's whole claim to fame in the business world was *not* being a jackass. Her loyalty to the Briscoes meant nothing to this man. And very little to Ty, either, obviously, who was allowing his family's business to be yanked away from them. No, not *yanked.* Knox Briscoe had too much poise to do anything so passionate as yanking. Rather, this was chess. Or, perhaps, Monopoly. A slow, deliberate erosion of his opponent down to nothing.

Standing tableside, she touched the edge of the plate on which Knox's soup bowl sat. Oh, how satisfying it would be to flip it over onto his perfectly pressed slacks. Her masterpiece deserved a better fate, but the temptation rippled through her with wicked glee.

Knox's body tensed. He knew what she'd been contemplating, too. His hand twitched as though in preparation to grab her wrist and stop her before she could soil his clothing.

"Emily," Ty warned.

Was she so obvious? So predictably reckless that both Ty and Knox could read her thoughts so plainly?

Screw them. Sure, they held her career in their hands, but neither deserved to eat her cooking today. With outrage pounding through her veins, she pulled out the seat at the head of the table between the two men and dropped into it. She slid Knox's bowl in front of her, grabbed his spoon, and—as both men gaped at her—cracked through the brûlée and dipped into the bright orange soup.

The soup exploded in her mouth in a burst of complicated, unexpected flavor. Perfection. Better than sex. Better than just about anything else this heartless, cynical planet could offer.

She flattened her palm over the bound stack of papers in front of Knox. His grand plans for her home, her livelihood and the livelihood of so many of her friends and colleagues. He was going to ruin everything and there was nothing she could do to stop it, not if Ty was just going to roll over and let Knox walk all over him.

She pulled the dossier in front of her. Ty and Knox sat, stunned, watching her. Neither had yet to say a word about her brazen intrusion. She flipped open the document.

How the hell was she getting away with this?

Her anger was too blinding for her to focus on the words or make heads or tails of the legal jargon. But she'd heard all she needed to know. Knox and his investors were going to turn the resort into yet another cookie-cutter chain hotel. "Ty, this is a bad deal. He's going to sell out. He's a business flipper. That's what he does. He doesn't care about the Briscoes at all."

"I am a Briscoe," Knox said in a dull, even tone.

Emily was too pissed off to look him in the eye. She took another bite of soup to keep herself from telling him that he wasn't a Briscoe in any way but his name. Instead, to Ty, she said, "If you do this, you're going to lose everything your parents built, everything you've worked your whole life for."

"That's enough, Emily," Ty said, but there was no mistaking the tinge of regret in his eyes.

Knox rose slowly, buttoning his suit jacket as he loomed over Emily. "Are you asking to be fired, Ms. Ford? Because I was hoping the chef I hire for the new restaurant would see the value in keeping on some of the resort's restaurant workers as line cooks."

Emily stood to face him nose to nose while visualizing the way his suit would look covered in mushroom reduction, sweet potato puree, and bits of roasted pheasant.

"Emily, leave us," Ty said, standing. "We'll serve ourselves the rest of the meal."

Ty's tone left no room for argument.

Emily stalked away from the table, but lingered in front of the serving tray near the door. She glanced back at the table, where both men were resuming their seats. Not too late to make a childish protest using one of the plated lunches. In the end, she decided against it, out of respect for Ty more than any sense of dignity or self-preservation.

With a sniff, she left the room. As the door closed behind her, Knox's voice wafted through the air. "I wouldn't have expected that from you, Ty. Sleeping with the special event chef. Interesting. And against my business policy."

Emily tenuous self-control snapped. She pivoted on her heel, pushed the office door open, and grabbed one of the lidded lunch plates. In one sweeping motion, she pulled the silver lid off and lunged at Knox, overturning the food into the bastard's lap. She stood over him, seething and watching glorious glops of gravy and sweet potatoes ooze like lava into the creases of his slacks.

Ty Briscoe is like a father to me. The father I never had. He took a huge risk in giving me a job when I was a no-name chef school graduate. His family took me in when I had nothing and no one. When I was goddamn homeless, you son of a bitch. Of course, she didn't say any of that. She refused to splay open her chest and give Knox Briscoe one single glimpse of her heart. His careless response to her peaches was proof enough of his lack of a soul.

For his part, Knox didn't rise or curse at her—as Ty was doing, she noticed out of the corner of her eye—nor did he attempt to clean himself off. He kept his cucumber-cool gaze locked on hers, a slight smirk curved on his lips. "Did I hit too close to home on that observation, Ms. Ford?"

Emily braced her hands on the table and the back of his chair. "I may not know what your father did to get disowned by the Briscoes, but it's no wonder you're trying to deflect some of that shame you inherited from him onto the people of this resort. Even after all these years, it still stings, doesn't it? Whatever he did to get shunned? The shame of it all?"

A shadow crossed Knox's face. Good. She'd meant for that to hurt. She picked one of the pheasant halves off his lap by the drumstick and took a bite of the meaty breast. Delicious, briny, and with a flavor profile that any Michelin star chef would kill to have created. She tossed the pheasant bones back on his lap.

"It makes sense, now, this whole alpha power vibe you've got going on. You know what they say about men who seem like they're overcompensating for something."

The shadow vanished from Knox's eyes and the shark-like calculation returned. "That they have big feet? Or am I mixing my old wives' tales?"

A hand closed around Emily's arm and tugged her away. Ty pushed between her and Knox, scolding her, apologizing to Knox. When did the giant she'd long revered as a force of nature turn into a spineless, apologetic noodle? She would've never expected her idol to fall from grace in the blink of an eye.

"Emily, please. Leave us," Ty said. "You're embarrassing yourself and insulting me."

That pulled her up short. She was way beyond caring if she embarrassed herself, but she did care about insulting Ty. She might not trust Ty to know what he was doing, not after this crippling deal with the devil himself. But she still respected Ty enough to honor his plea. With a nod, she walked with stiff, proud steps to the door.

"Ms. Ford, the suspense is killing me. What do they say about men who seem like they're overcompensating?" Knox said, sounding amused.

Gritting her teeth, she paused with one foot out the door and tossed a look over her shoulder, startling all over again at Knox's aura of cool perfection. The cut of his jaw, the fullness of his lips, eyes that were as cruel as they were wise. How had she ever thought she could win over a man like that with peaches and pheasant? Whatever family shame Knox was overcompensating for, it wasn't going to save Emily or her beloved resort. Knox Briscoe was beyond redemption, her career was over before it had even gotten off the ground, and life was never going to be the same again.

"Haven't you heard?" she said. "The thing about men who seem like they're overcompensating for something is that they always are."